CARTOON HANGOVER

BRAVEST WARRIORS™

CREATED by PENDLETON WARD

VOLUME FOUR

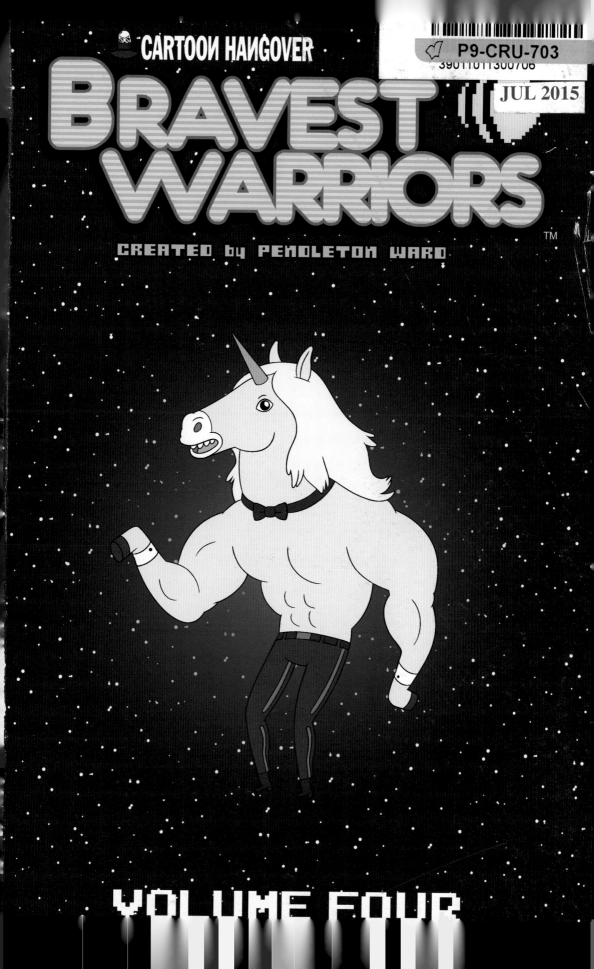

ROSS RICHIE CEO & Founder • MARK SMYLIE Founder of Archaia • MATT GAGNON Editor-in-Chief • FILIP SABLIK President of Publishing & Marketing • STEPHEN CHRISTY President of Development
LANCE KREITER VP of Licensing & Merchandising • PHIL BARBARO VP of Finance • BRYCE CARLSON Managing Editor • MEL CAYLO Marketing Manager • SCOTT NEWMAN Production Design Manager
IRENE BRADISH Operations Manager • CHRISTINE DINH Brand Communications Manager • DAFNA PLEBAN Editor • SHANNON WATTERS Editor • ERIC HARBURN Editor • REBECCA TAYLOR Editor
IAN BRILL Editor • CHRIS ROSA Assistant Editor • ALEX GALER Assistant Editor • WHITNEY LEOPARD Assistant Editor • JASMINE AMIRI Assistant Editor • CAMERON CHITTOCK Assistant Editor
KELSEY DIETERICH Production Designer • JILLIAN CRAB Production Designer • DEVIN FUNCHES E-Commerce & Inventory Coordinator • ANDY LIEGL Event Coordinator • BRIANNA HART Administrative Coordinator
AARON FERRARA Operations Assistant • JOSÉ MEZA Sales Assistant • MICHELLE ANKLEY Sales Assistant • ELIZABETH LOUGHRIDGE Accounting Assistant • STEPHANIE HOCUTT PR Assistant

BRAVEST WARRIORS Volume Four, January 2015. Published by KaBOOM!, a division of Boom Entertainment, Inc. Based on "Bravest Warriors" © 2015 Frederator Networks, Inc. Originally
published in single magazine form as BRAVEST WARRIORS No. 13-16. ™ & © 2013, 2014 Frederator Networks, Inc. All rights reserved. KaBOOM!™ and the KaBOOM! logo are trademarks of
Boom Entertainment, Inc., registered in various countries and categories. All characters, events, and institutions depicted herein are fictional. Any similarity between any of the names, characters,
persons, events, and/or institutions in this publication to actual names, characters, and persons, whether living or dead, events, and/or institutions is unintended

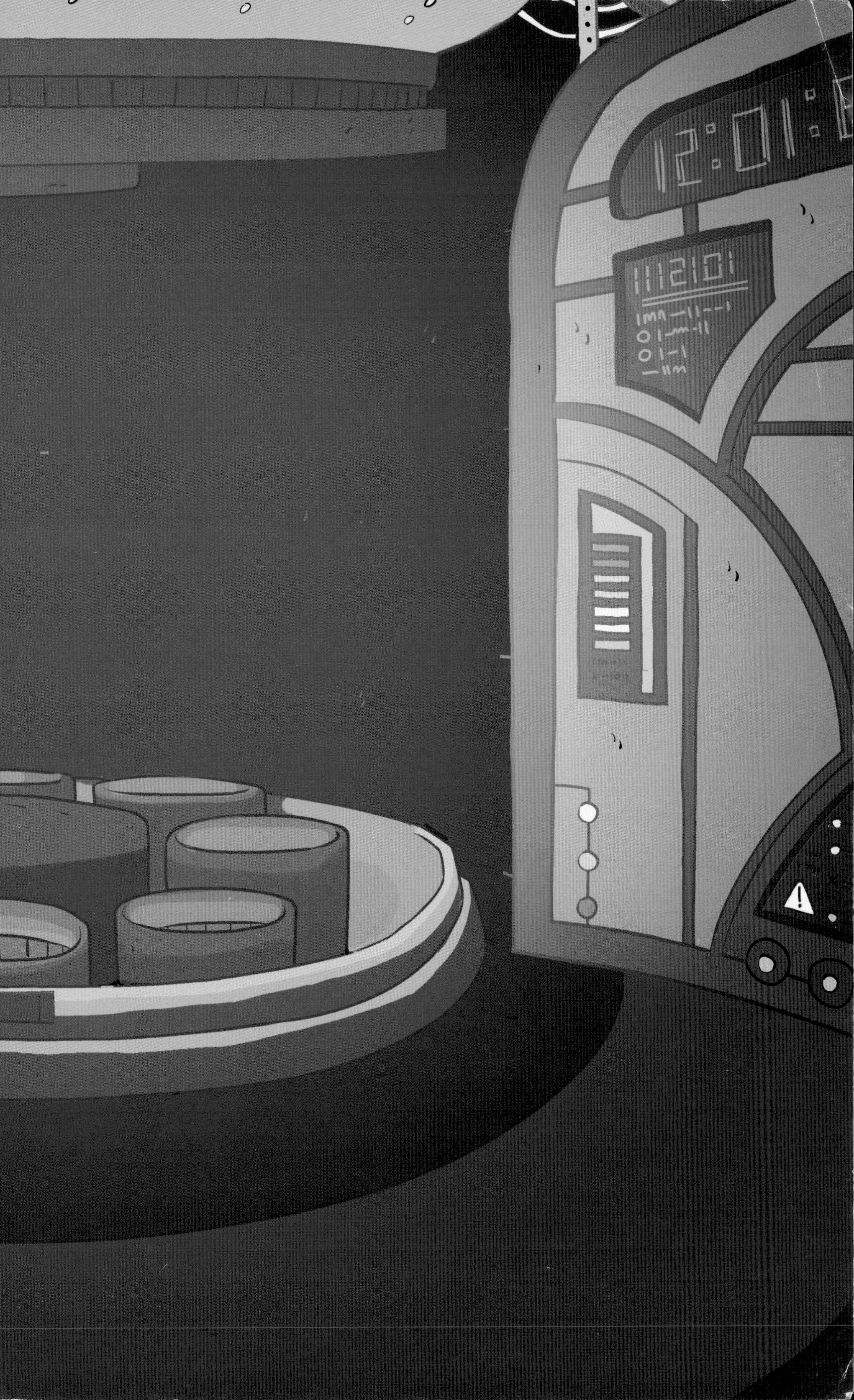

CREATED BY
PENDLETON WARD

CHAPTER THIRTEEN

WRITTEN BY
ERIC M. ESQUIVEL

ILLUSTRATED BY
MIKE HOLMES

COLORS BY
LISA MOORE

LETTERS BY
STEVE WANDS

CHAPTER FOURTEEN

WRITTEN BY
BREEHN BURNS & JASON JOHNSON

ILLUSTRATED BY
MIKE HOLMES

COLORS BY
LISA MOORE

LETTERS BY
STEVE WANDS

CHAPTER FIFTEEN

WRITTEN & ILLUSTRATED BY
RYAN PEQUIN

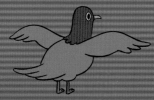

COLORS BY
WHITNEY COGAR

"DANNY DIVIDED"
WRITTEN & ILLUSTRATED BY
RYAN PEQUIN

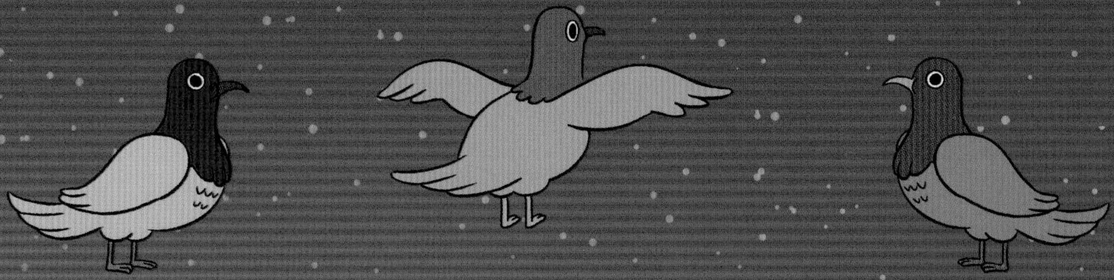

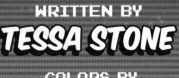

CHAPTER SIXTEEN

WRITTEN BY
TESSA STONE

ILLUSTRATED BY
MIKE HOLMES

COLORS BY
LISA MOORE

LETTERS BY
STEVE WANDS

SHORT MISSIONS

"A MOMENT WITH DANNY"
"YAY CAMPING"

WRITTEN & ILLUSTRATED BY
RYAN PEQUIN

COLORS BY
WHITNEY COGAR

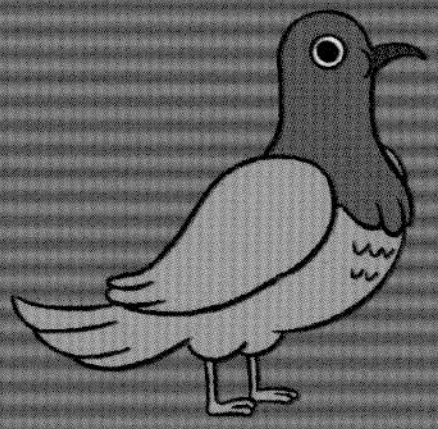

"FOOD COURT"

WRITTEN & ILLUSTRATED BY
COLEMAN ENGLE

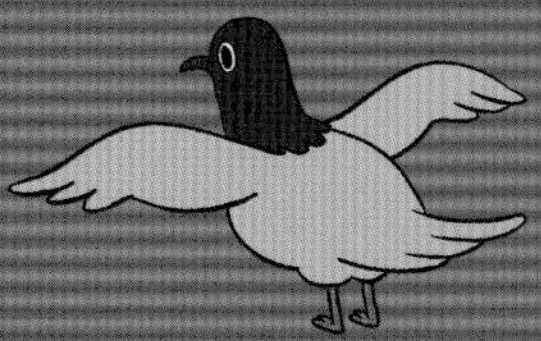

COVER BY
TYSON HESSE

DESIGN BY
JILLIAN CRAB

ASSISTANT EDITOR
CAMERON CHITTOCK

EDITOR
REBECCA TAYLOR

ORIGINAL SERIES EDITORS

ASSISTANT EDITOR
WHITNEY LEOPARD

EDITOR
SHANNON WATTERS

WITH SPECIAL THANKS TO BREEHN BURNS, ERIC HOMAN, FRED SEIBERT AND ALL OF THE CLASSY FOLKS AT FREDERATOR STUDIOS.

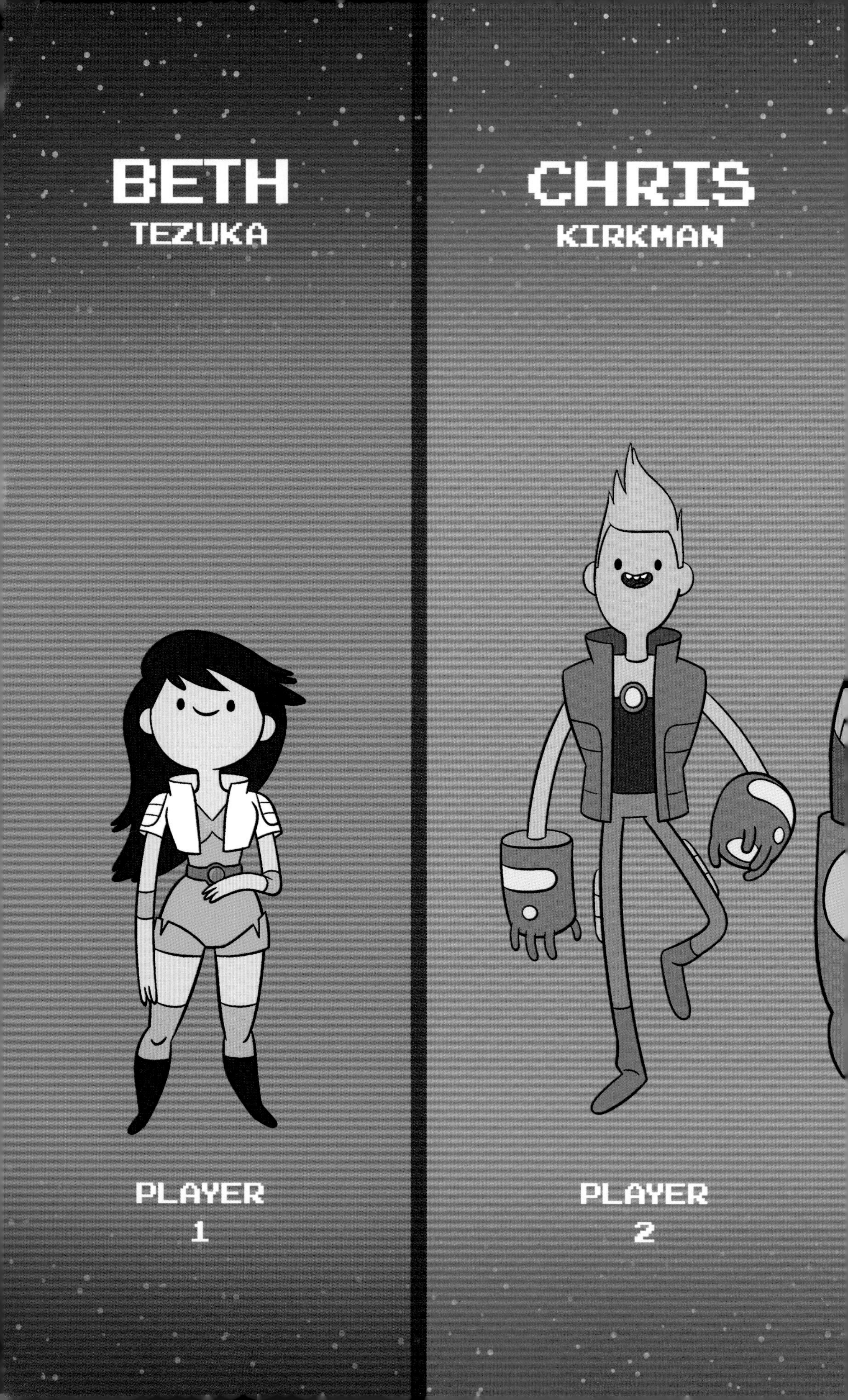
BETH
TEZUKA
PLAYER
1
CHRIS
KIRKMAN
PLAYER
2

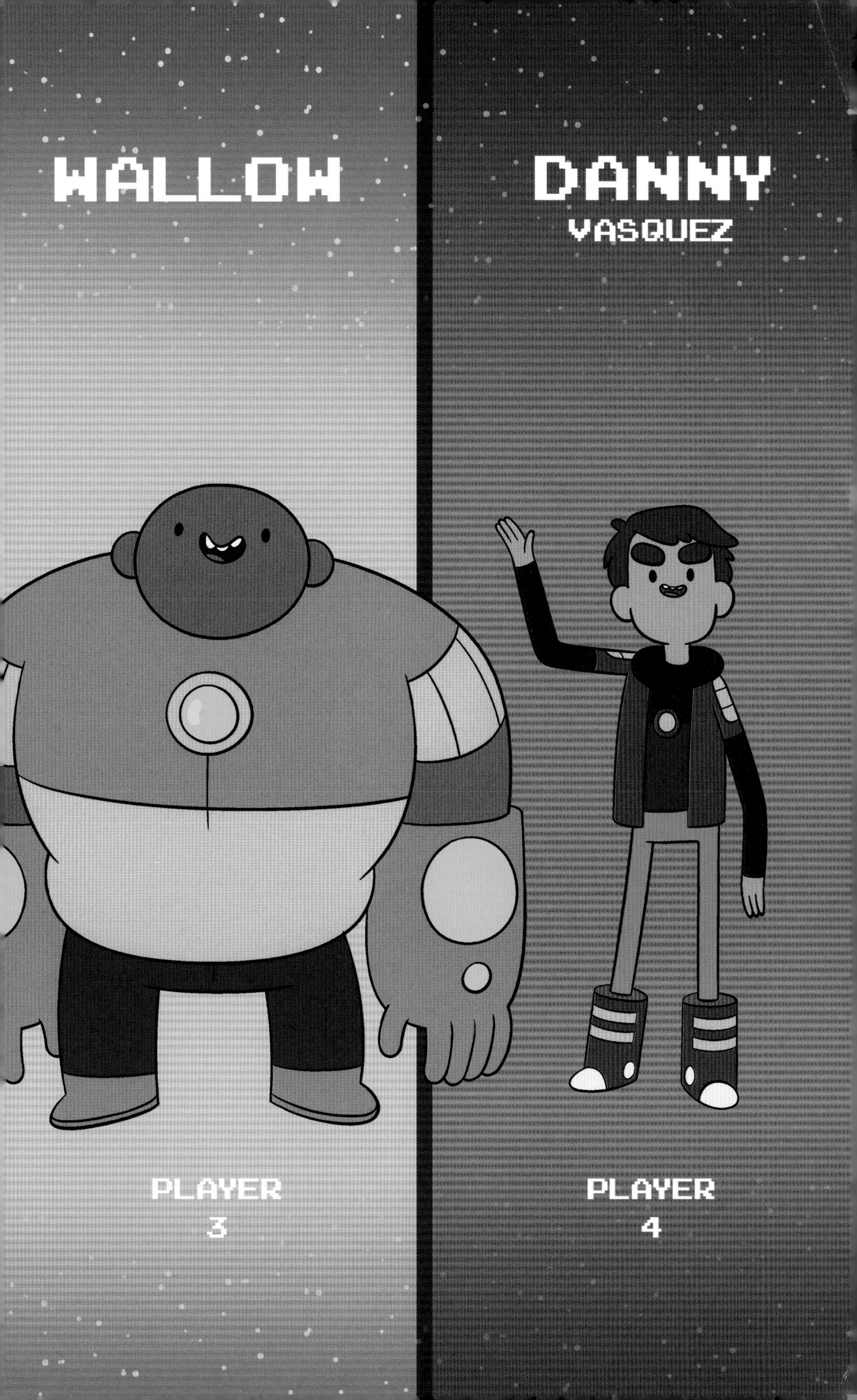
WALLOW
PLAYER
3
DANNY
VASQUEZ
PLAYER
4

CHAPTER THIRTEEN

UP, DOWN, LEFT, RIGHT
A, B, SELECT, START

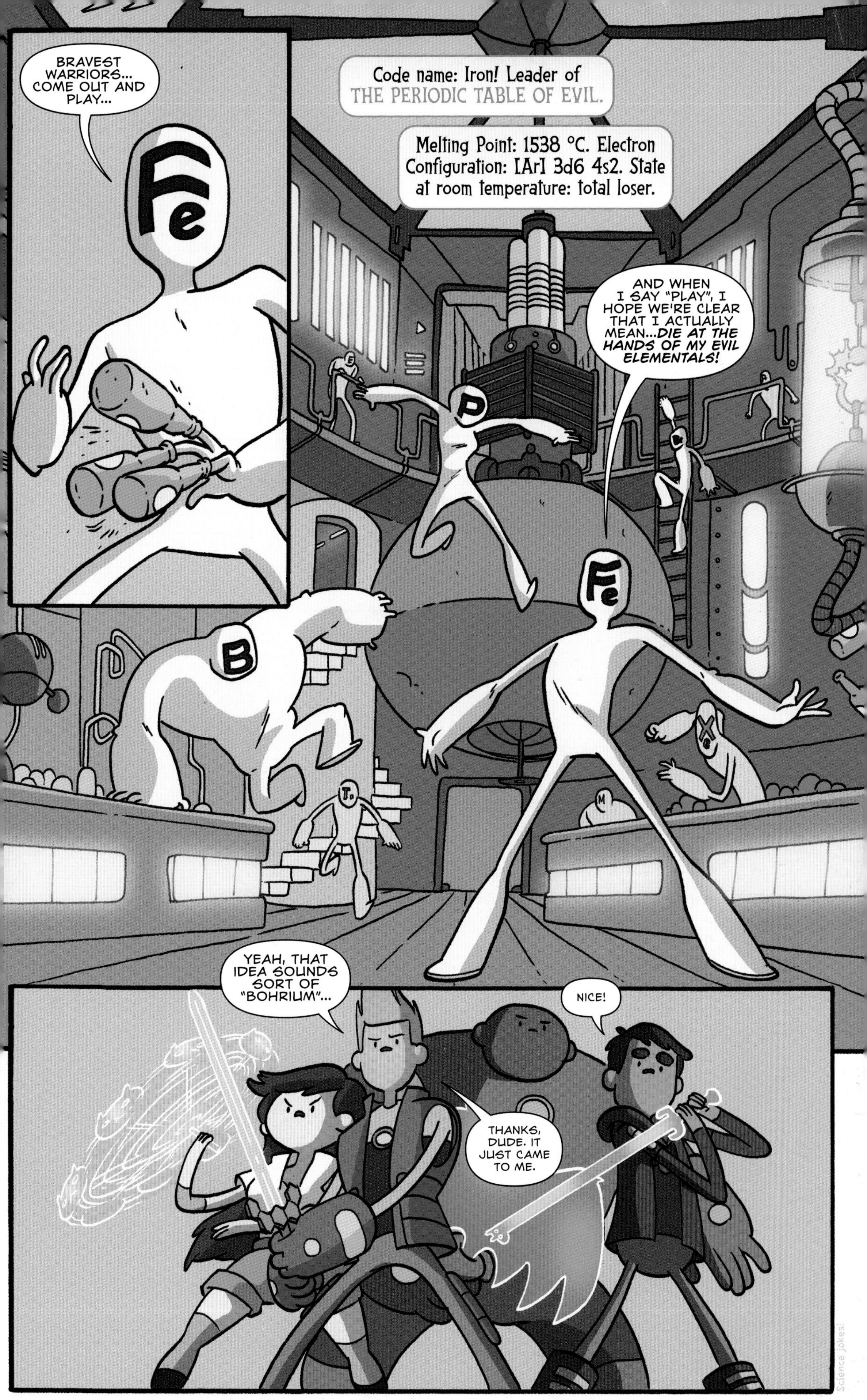
BRAVEST WARRIORS... COME OUT AND PLAY...
Code name: Iron! Leader of THE PERIODIC TABLE OF EVIL.
Melting Point: 1538 °C. Electron Configuration: [Ar] 3d6 4s2. State at room temperature: total loser.
AND WHEN I SAY "PLAY", I HOPE WE'RE CLEAR THAT I ACTUALLY MEAN...DIE AT THE HANDS OF MY EVIL ELEMENTALS!
YEAH, THAT IDEA SOUNDS SORT OF "BOHRIUM"...
NICE!
THANKS, DUDE. IT JUST CAME TO ME.
Science jokes!

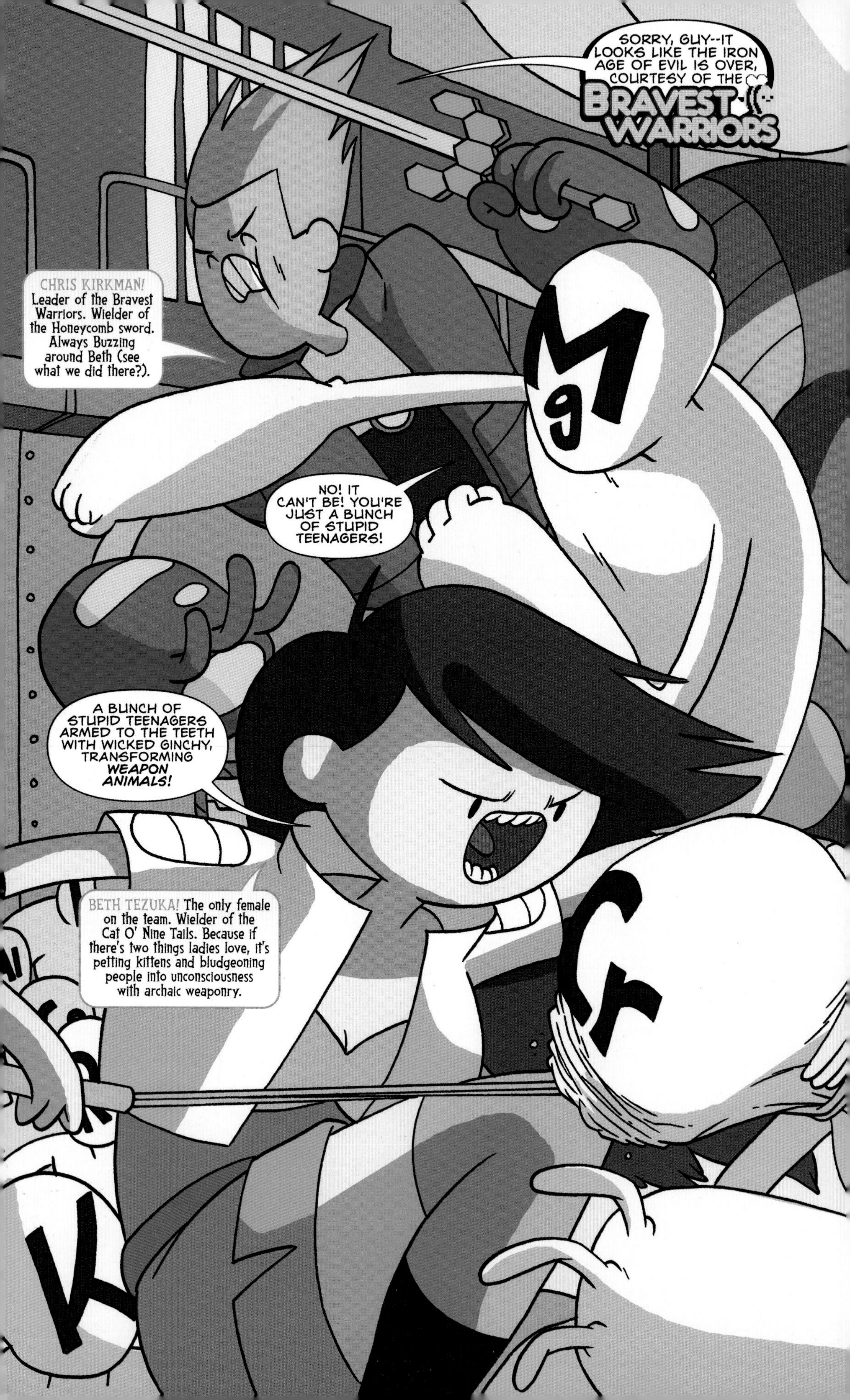
SORRY, GUY--IT LOOKS LIKE THE IRON AGE OF EVIL IS OVER, COURTESY OF THE BRAVEST WARRIORS
CHRIS KIRKMAN! Leader of the Bravest Warriors. Wielder of the Honeycomb sword. Always Buzzing around Beth (see what we did there?).
NO! IT CAN'T BE! YOU'RE JUST A BUNCH OF STUPID TEENAGERS!
A BUNCH OF STUPID TEENAGERS ARMED TO THE TEETH WITH WICKED GINCHY, TRANSFORMING WEAPON ANIMALS!
BETH TEZUKA! The only female on the team. Wielder of the Cat O' Nine Tails. Because if there's two things ladies love, it's petting kittens and bludgeoning people into unconsciousness with archaic weaponry.

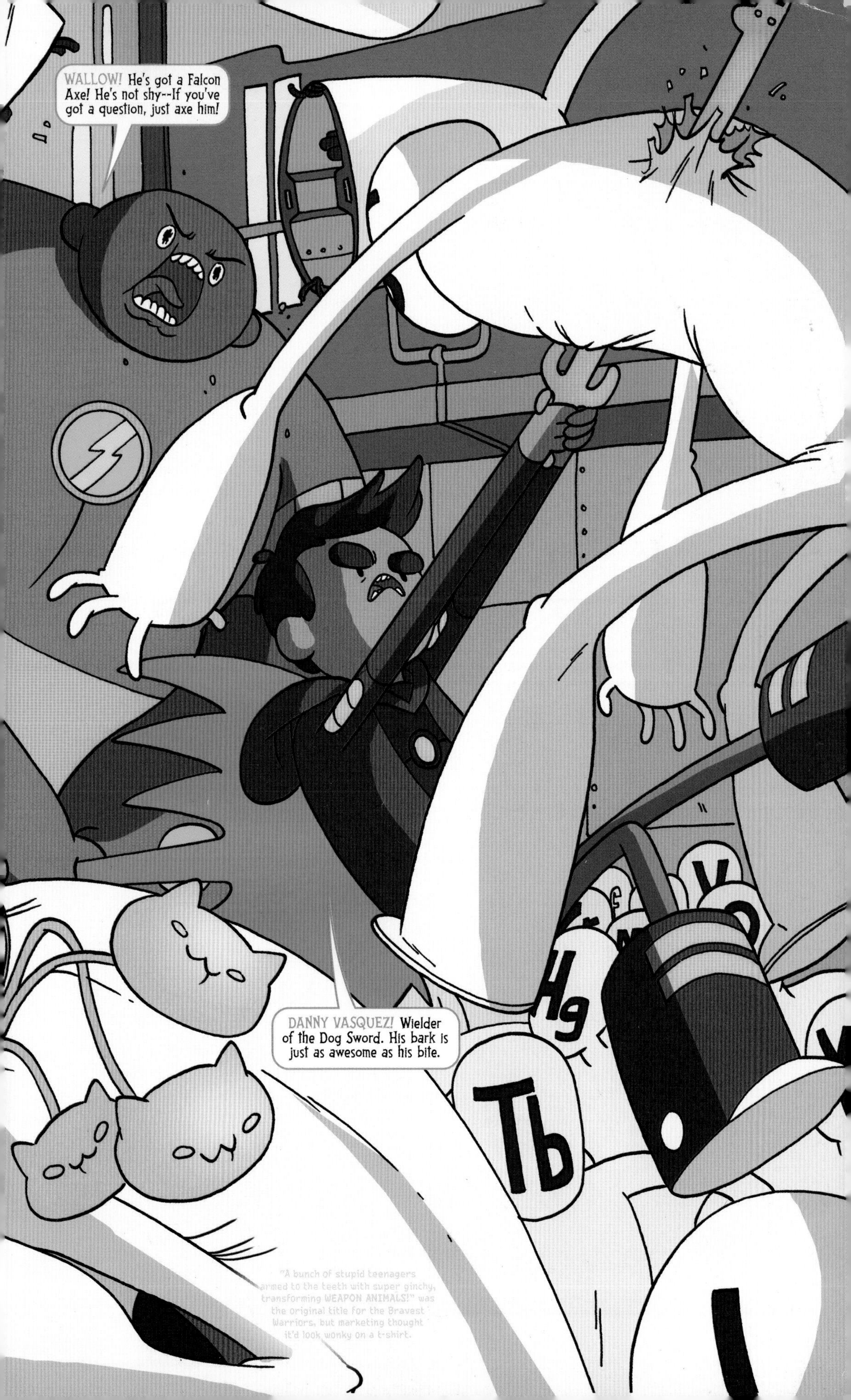
WALLOW! He's got a Falcon Axe! He's not shy--If you've got a question, just axe him!
DANNY VASQUEZ! Wielder of the Dog Sword. His bark is just as awesome as his bite.
Hg
Tb
"A bunch of stupid teenagers armed to the teeth with super ginchy, transforming WEAPON ANIMALS!" was the original title for the Bravest Warriors, but marketing thought it'd look wonky on a t-shirt.

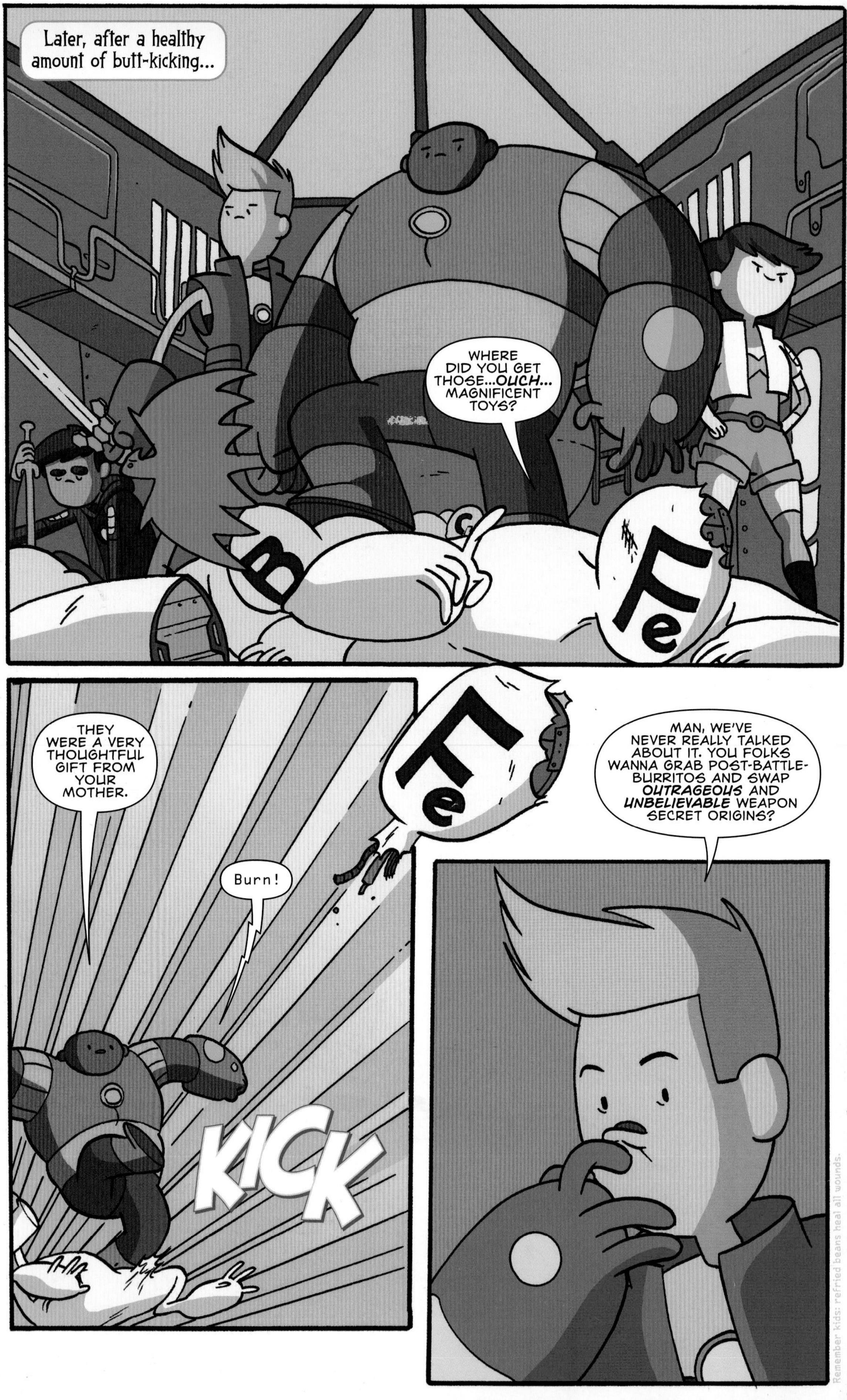
Later, after a healthy amount of butt-kicking...
WHERE DID YOU GET THOSE...OUCH... MAGNIFICENT TOYS?
THEY WERE A VERY THOUGHTFUL GIFT FROM YOUR MOTHER.
Burn!
KICK
MAN, WE'VE NEVER REALLY TALKED ABOUT IT. YOU FOLKS WANNA GRAB POST-BATTLE-BURRITOS AND SWAP OUTRAGEOUS AND UNBELIEVABLE WEAPON SECRET ORIGINS?
Remember kids: refried beans heal all wounds.

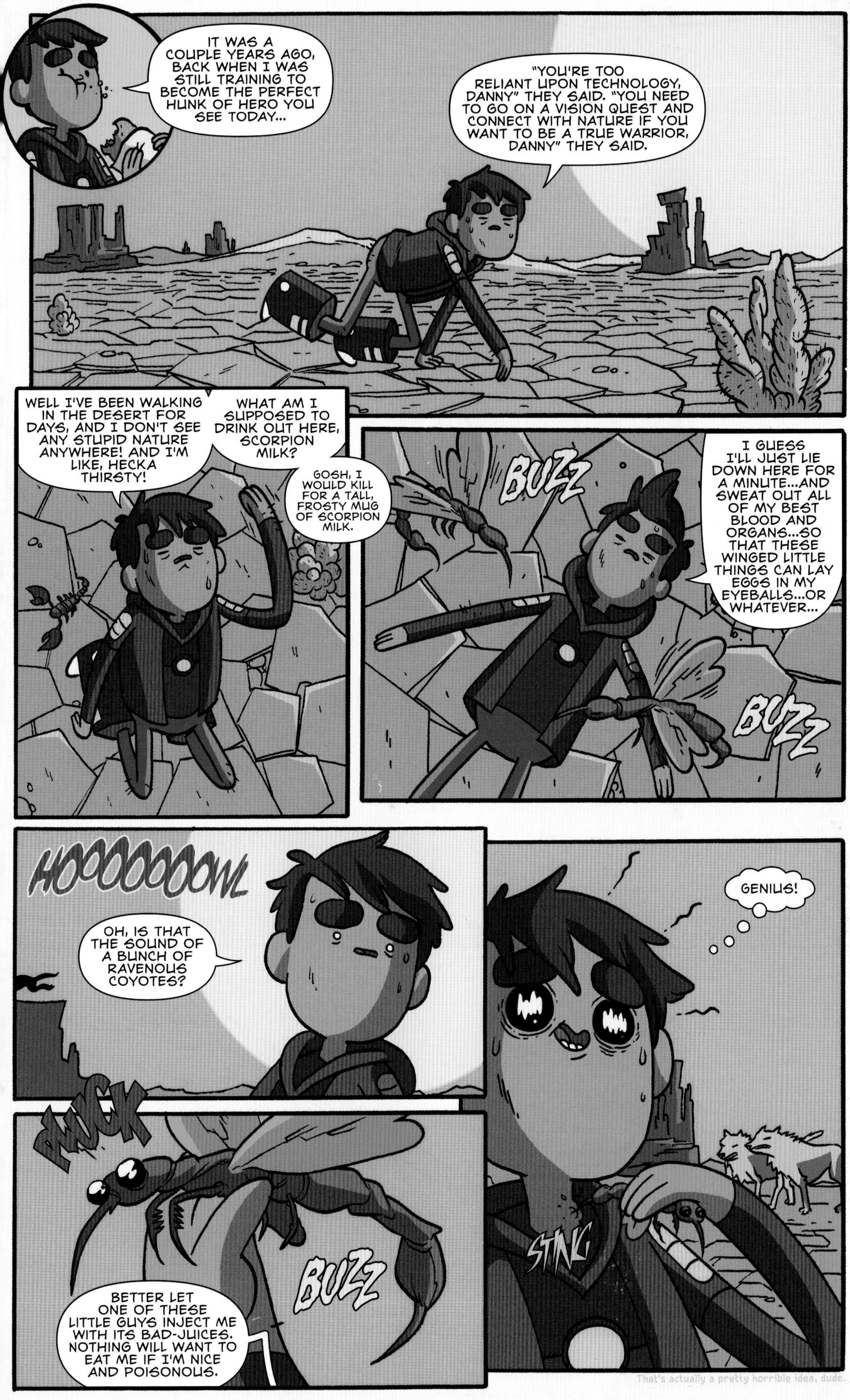
IT WAS A COUPLE YEARS AGO, BACK WHEN I WAS STILL TRAINING TO BECOME THE PERFECT HUNK OF HERO YOU SEE TODAY...
"YOU'RE TOO RELIANT UPON TECHNOLOGY, DANNY" THEY SAID. "YOU NEED TO GO ON A VISION QUEST AND CONNECT WITH NATURE IF YOU WANT TO BE A TRUE WARRIOR, DANNY" THEY SAID.
WELL I'VE BEEN WALKING IN THE DESERT FOR DAYS, AND I DON'T SEE ANY STUPID NATURE ANYWHERE! AND I'M LIKE, HECKA THIRSTY!
WHAT AM I SUPPOSED TO DRINK OUT HERE, SCORPION MILK?
GOSH, I WOULD KILL FOR A TALL, FROSTY MUG OF SCORPION MILK.
BUZZ
I GUESS I'LL JUST LIE DOWN HERE FOR A MINUTE...AND SWEAT OUT ALL OF MY BEST BLOOD AND ORGANS...SO THAT THESE WINGED LITTLE THINGS CAN LAY EGGS IN MY EYEBALLS...OR WHATEVER...
BUZZ
HOOOOOOOWL
OH, IS THAT THE SOUND OF A BUNCH OF RAVENOUS COYOTES?
GENIUS!
PLUCK
BUZZ
BETTER LET ONE OF THESE LITTLE GUYS INJECT ME WITH ITS BAD-JUICES. NOTHING WILL WANT TO EAT ME IF I'M NICE AND POISONOUS.
STING

That's actually a pretty horrible idea, dude.

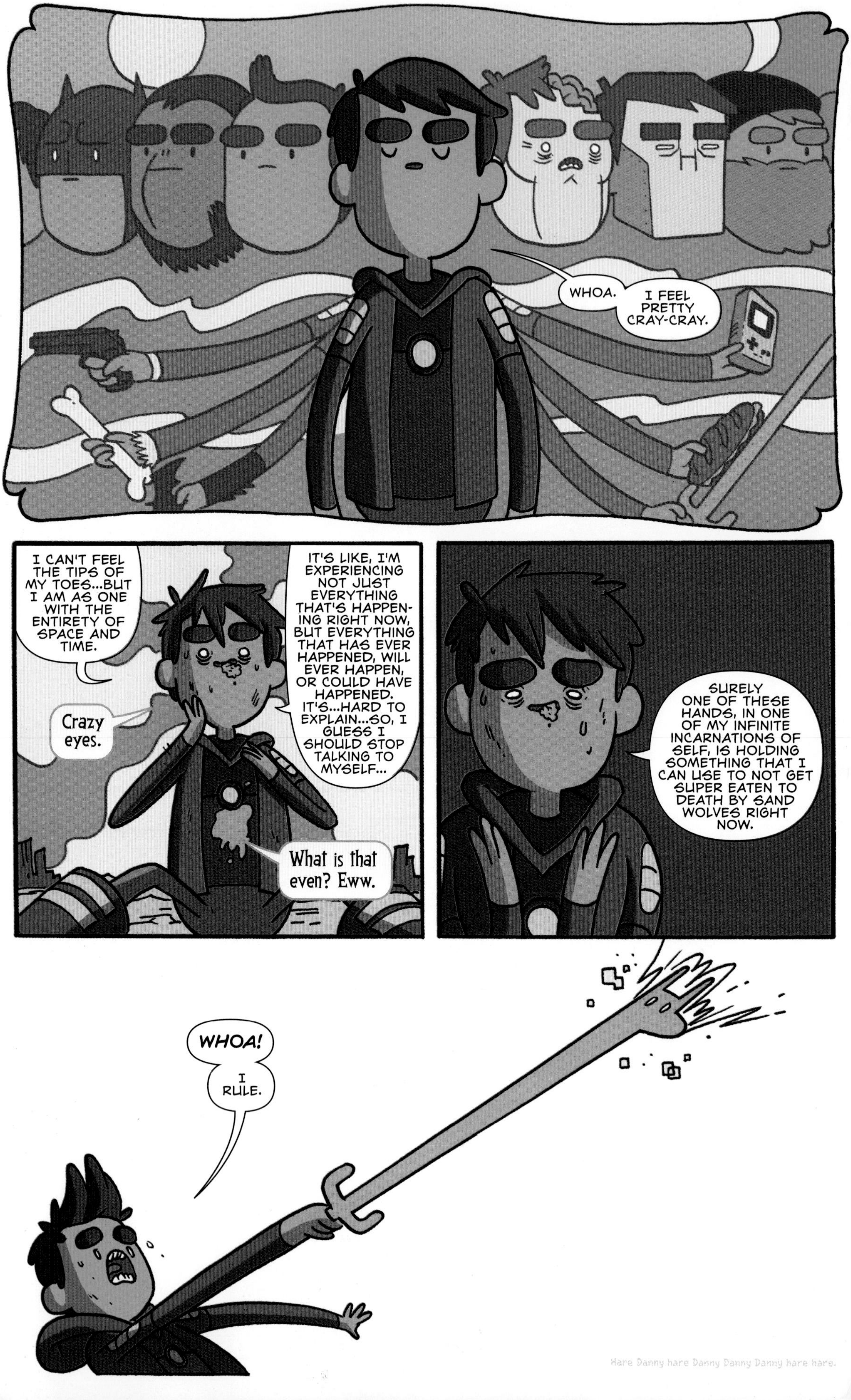
WHOA.
I FEEL PRETTY CRAY-CRAY.
I CAN'T FEEL THE TIPS OF MY TOES...BUT I AM AS ONE WITH THE ENTIRETY OF SPACE AND TIME.
IT'S LIKE, I'M EXPERIENCING NOT JUST EVERYTHING THAT'S HAPPENING RIGHT NOW, BUT EVERYTHING THAT HAS EVER HAPPENED, WILL EVER HAPPEN, OR COULD HAVE HAPPENED. IT'S...HARD TO EXPLAIN...SO, I GUESS I SHOULD STOP TALKING TO MYSELF...
Crazy eyes.
What is that even? Eww.
SURELY ONE OF THESE HANDS, IN ONE OF MY INFINITE INCARNATIONS OF SELF, IS HOLDING SOMETHING THAT I CAN USE TO NOT GET SUPER EATEN TO DEATH BY SAND WOLVES RIGHT NOW.
WHOA!
I RULE.
Hare Danny hare Danny Danny Danny hare hare.

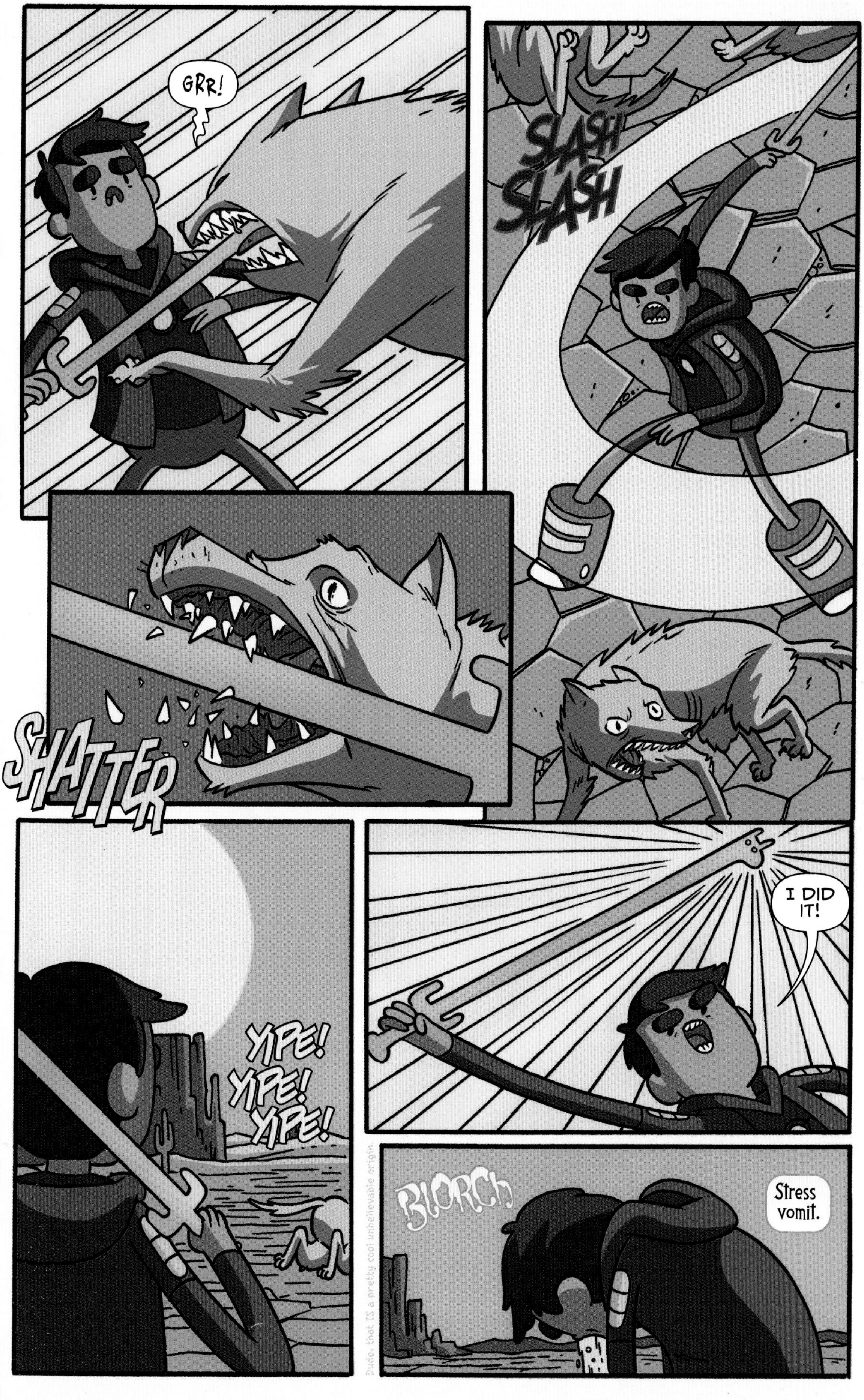
GRR!
SLASH
SLASH
SHATTER
YIPE!
YIPE!
YIPE!
I DID IT!
BLORCh
Stress vomit.
Dude, that IS a pretty cool unbelievable origin.

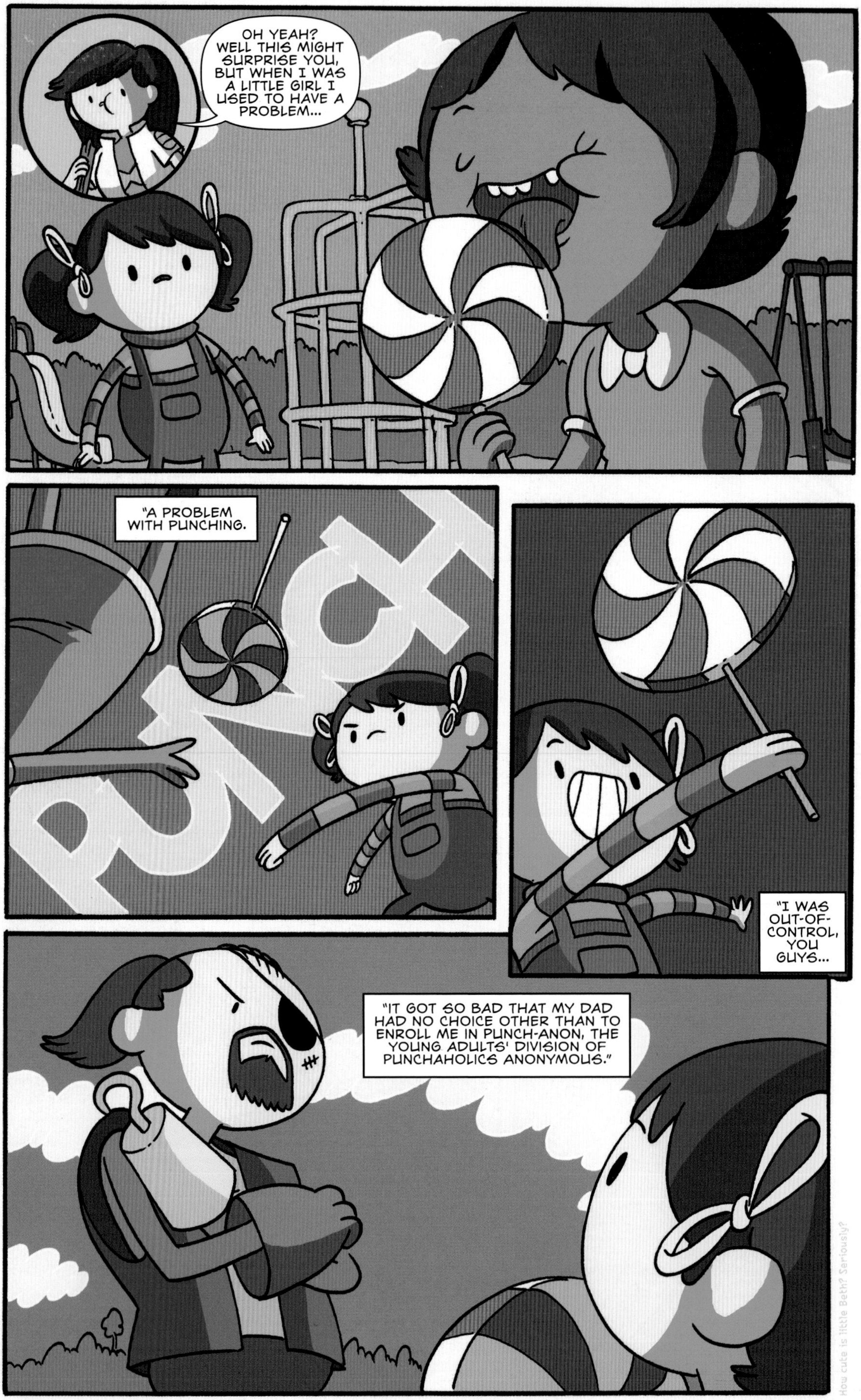
OH YEAH? WELL THIS MIGHT SURPRISE YOU, BUT WHEN I WAS A LITTLE GIRL I USED TO HAVE A PROBLEM...
"A PROBLEM WITH PUNCHING.
PUNCH
"I WAS OUT-OF-CONTROL, YOU GUYS...
"IT GOT SO BAD THAT MY DAD HAD NO CHOICE OTHER THAN TO ENROLL ME IN PUNCH-ANON, THE YOUNG ADULTS' DIVISION OF PUNCHAHOLICS ANONYMOUS."

How cute is little Beth? Seriously?

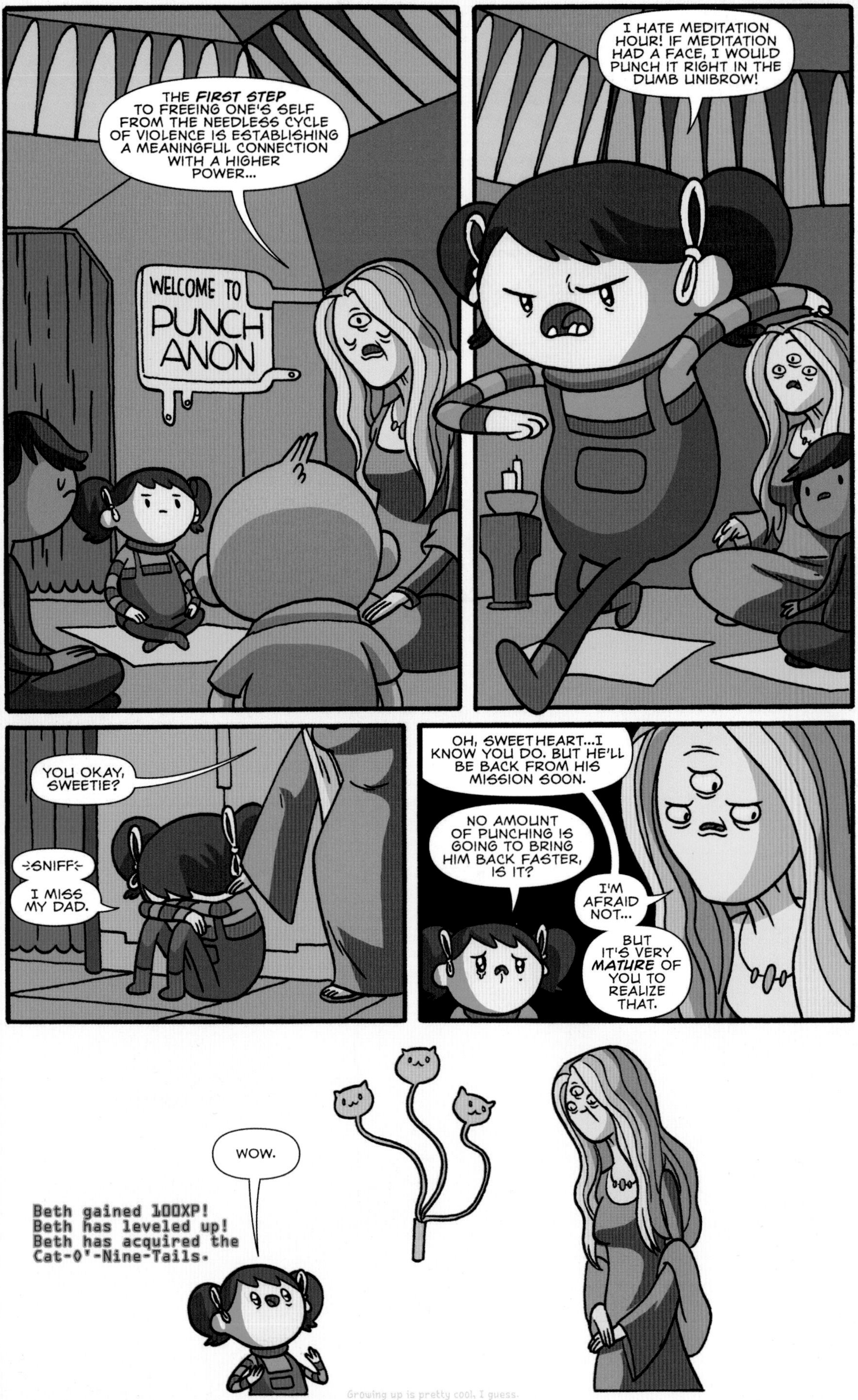
THE FIRST STEP TO FREEING ONE'S SELF FROM THE NEEDLESS CYCLE OF VIOLENCE IS ESTABLISHING A MEANINGFUL CONNECTION WITH A HIGHER POWER...
WELCOME TO PUNCH ANON
I HATE MEDITATION HOUR! IF MEDITATION HAD A FACE, I WOULD PUNCH IT RIGHT IN THE DUMB UNIBROW!
YOU OKAY, SWEETIE?
-SNIFF-
I MISS MY DAD.
OH, SWEETHEART...I KNOW YOU DO. BUT HE'LL BE BACK FROM HIS MISSION SOON.
NO AMOUNT OF PUNCHING IS GOING TO BRING HIM BACK FASTER, IS IT?
I'M AFRAID NOT...
BUT IT'S VERY MATURE OF YOU TO REALIZE THAT.
WOW.
Beth gained 100XP!
Beth has leveled up!
Beth has acquired the Cat-O'-Nine-Tails.

Growing up is pretty cool, I guess.

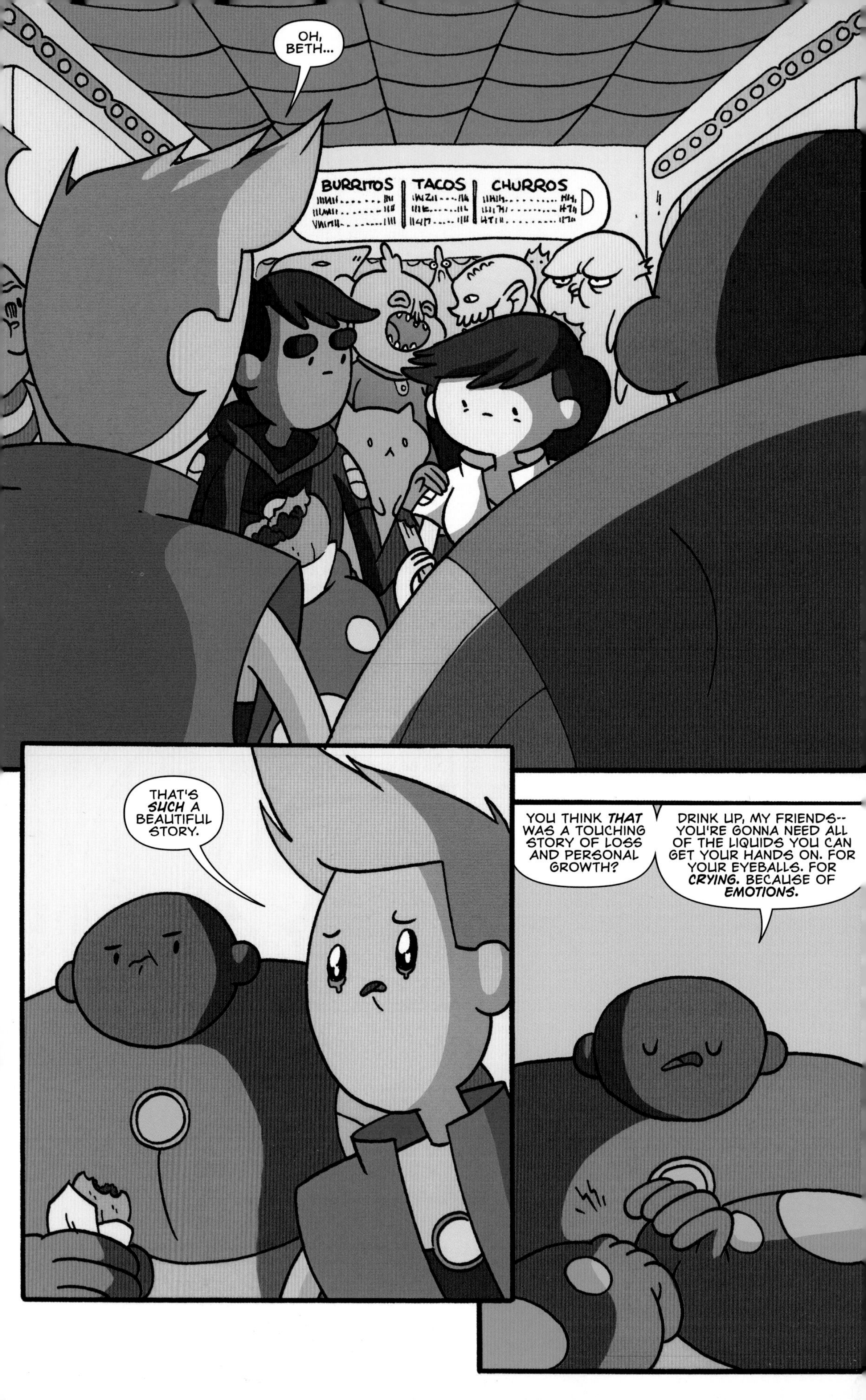
OH, BETH...
BURRITOS
TACOS
CHURROS
THAT'S *SUCH* A BEAUTIFUL STORY.
YOU THINK *THAT* WAS A TOUCHING STORY OF LOSS AND PERSONAL GROWTH?
DRINK UP, MY FRIENDS-- YOU'RE GONNA NEED ALL OF THE LIQUIDS YOU CAN GET YOUR HANDS ON. FOR YOUR EYEBALLS. FOR *CRYING*. BECAUSE OF *EMOTIONS*.

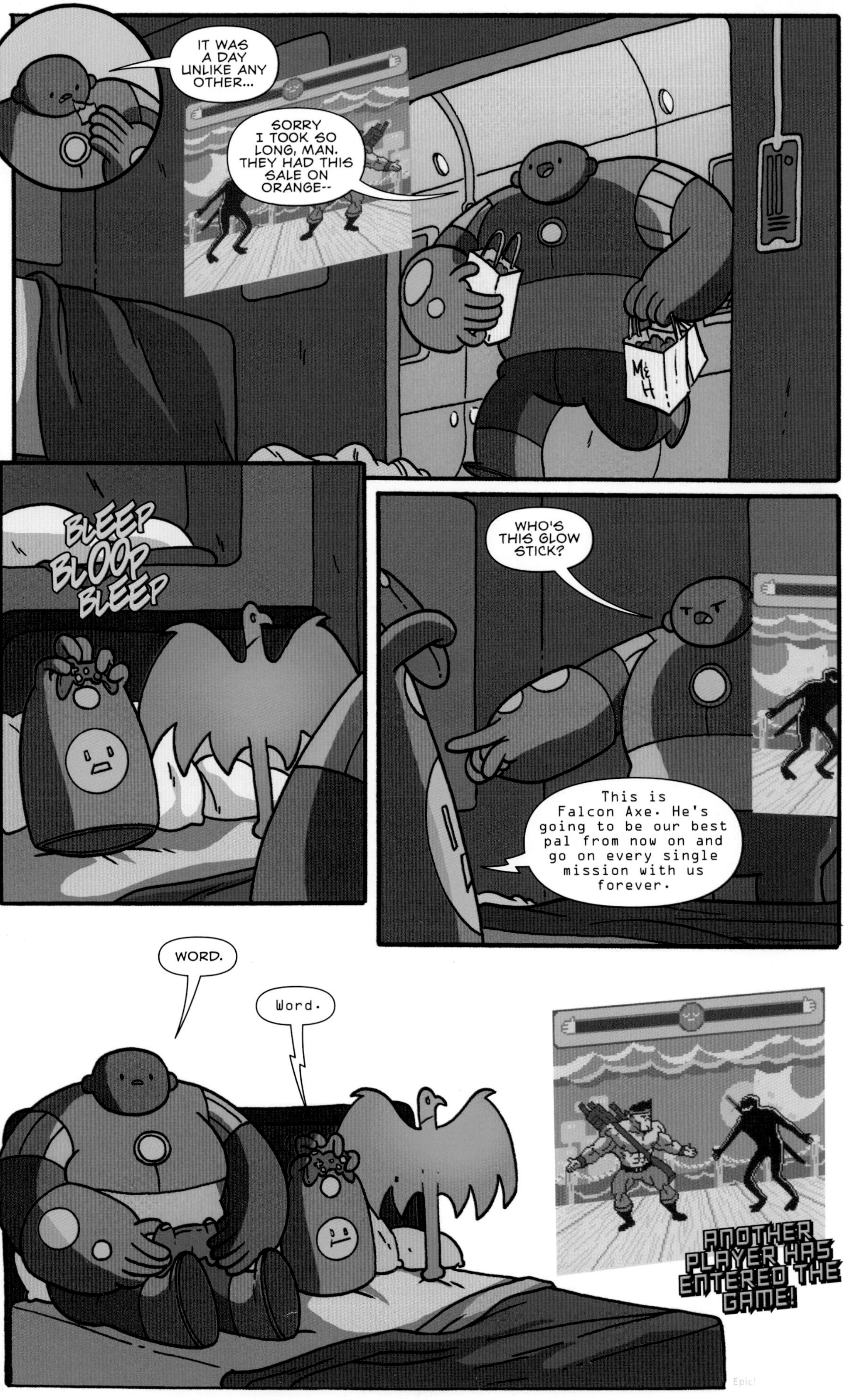
IT WAS A DAY UNLIKE ANY OTHER...
SORRY I TOOK SO LONG, MAN. THEY HAD THIS SALE ON ORANGE--
BLEEP BLOOP BLEEP
WHO'S THIS GLOW STICK?
This is Falcon Axe. He's going to be our best pal from now on and go on every single mission with us forever.
WORD.
Word.
ANOTHER PLAYER HAS ENTERED THE GAME!

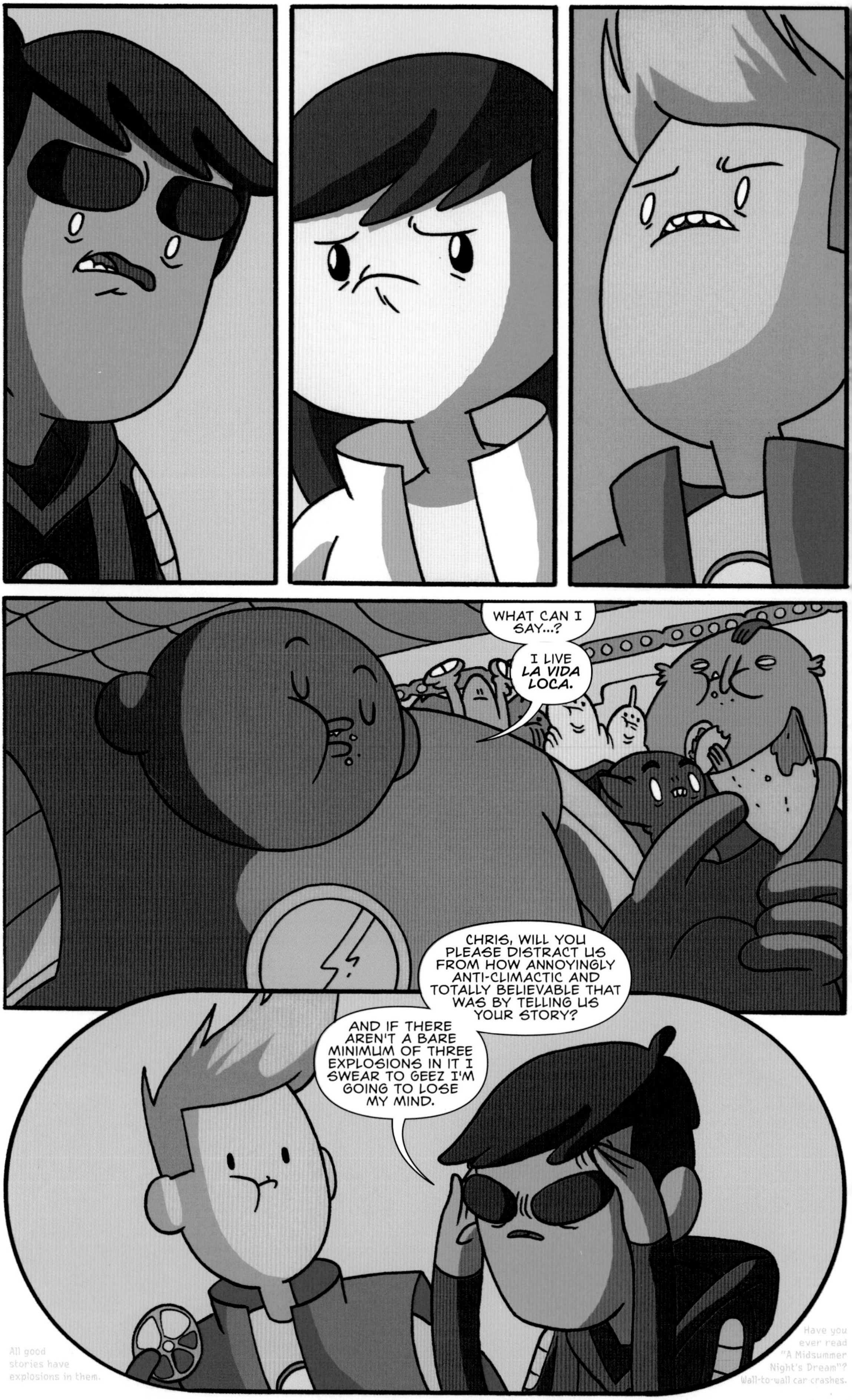
WHAT CAN I SAY...?
I LIVE *LA VIDA LOCA.*
CHRIS, WILL YOU PLEASE DISTRACT US FROM HOW ANNOYINGLY ANTI-CLIMACTIC AND TOTALLY BELIEVABLE THAT WAS BY TELLING US YOUR STORY?
AND IF THERE AREN'T A BARE MINIMUM OF THREE EXPLOSIONS IN IT I SWEAR TO GEEZ I'M GOING TO LOSE MY MIND.

All good stories have explosions in them.

Have you ever read "A Midsummer Night's Dream"? Wall-to-wall car crashes.

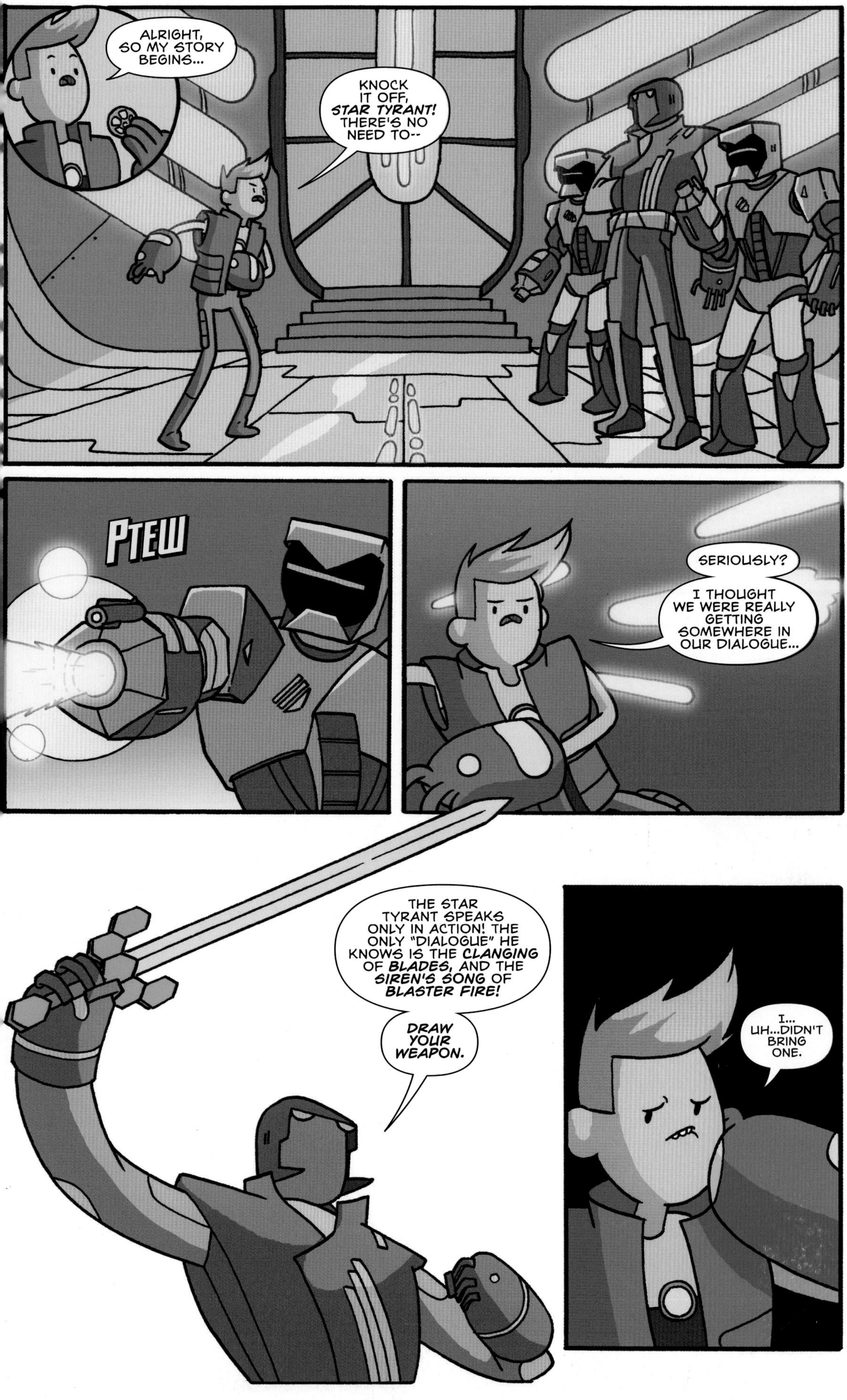
ALRIGHT, SO MY STORY BEGINS...
KNOCK IT OFF, STAR TYRANT! THERE'S NO NEED TO--
PTEW
SERIOUSLY?
I THOUGHT WE WERE REALLY GETTING SOMEWHERE IN OUR DIALOGUE...
THE STAR TYRANT SPEAKS ONLY IN ACTION! THE ONLY "DIALOGUE" HE KNOWS IS THE CLANGING OF BLADES, AND THE SIREN'S SONG OF BLASTER FIRE!
DRAW YOUR WEAPON.
I... UH...DIDN'T BRING ONE.

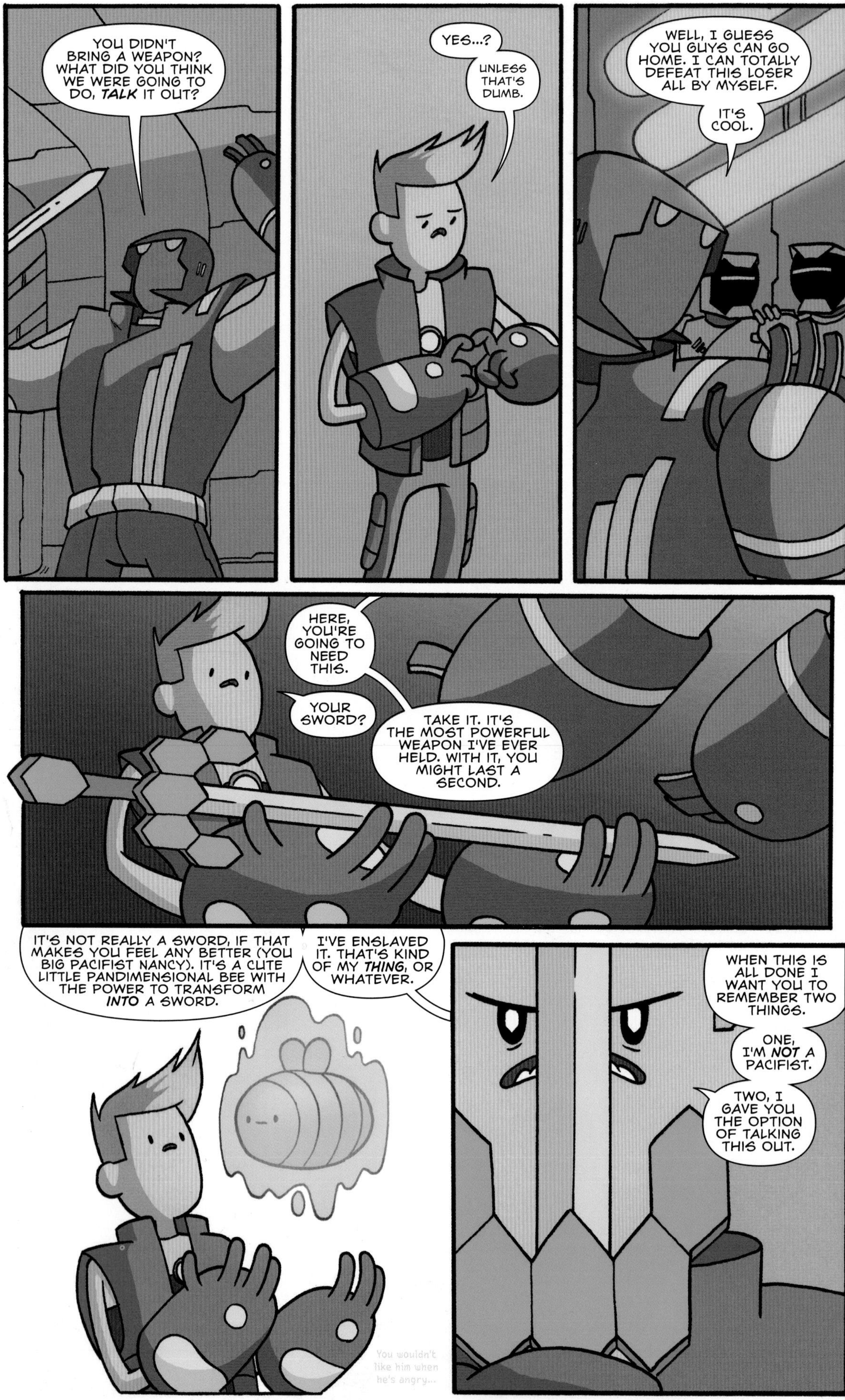
YOU DIDN'T BRING A WEAPON? WHAT DID YOU THINK WE WERE GOING TO DO, *TALK* IT OUT?
YES...?
UNLESS THAT'S DUMB.
WELL, I GUESS YOU GUYS CAN GO HOME. I CAN TOTALLY DEFEAT THIS LOSER ALL BY MYSELF.
IT'S COOL.
HERE, YOU'RE GOING TO NEED THIS.
YOUR SWORD?
TAKE IT. IT'S THE MOST POWERFUL WEAPON I'VE EVER HELD. WITH IT, YOU MIGHT LAST A SECOND.
IT'S NOT REALLY A SWORD, IF THAT MAKES YOU FEEL ANY BETTER (YOU BIG PACIFIST NANCY). IT'S A CUTE LITTLE PANDIMENSIONAL BEE WITH THE POWER TO TRANSFORM *INTO* A SWORD.
I'VE ENSLAVED IT. THAT'S KIND OF MY *THING*, OR WHATEVER.
WHEN THIS IS ALL DONE I WANT YOU TO REMEMBER TWO THINGS.
ONE, I'M *NOT* A PACIFIST.
TWO, I GAVE YOU THE OPTION OF TALKING THIS OUT.
You wouldn't like him when he's angry...

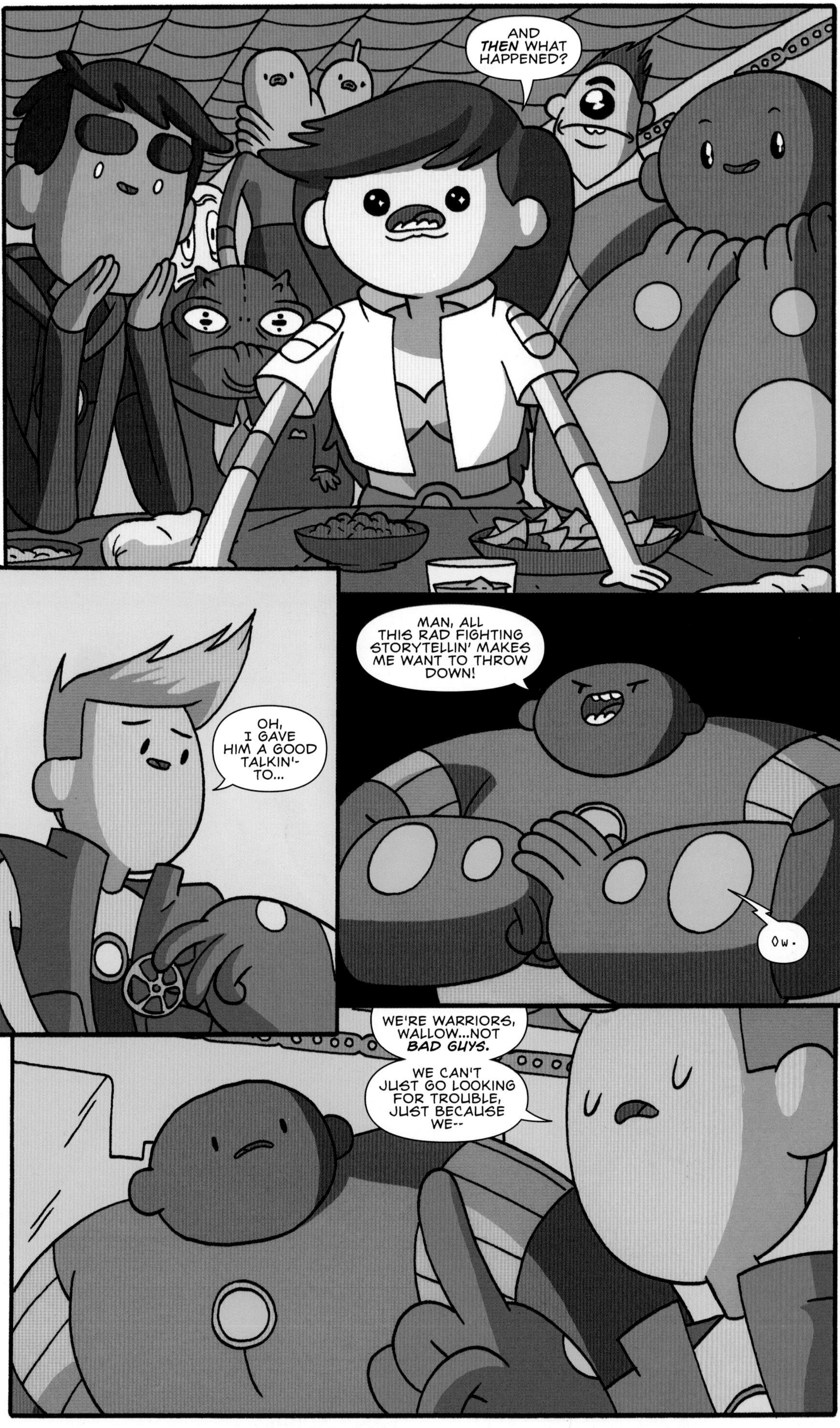
AND *THEN* WHAT HAPPENED?
OH, I GAVE HIM A GOOD TALKIN'-TO...
MAN, ALL THIS RAD FIGHTING STORYTELLIN' MAKES ME WANT TO THROW DOWN!
OW.
WE'RE WARRIORS, WALLOW...NOT *BAD GUYS.*
WE CAN'T JUST GO LOOKING FOR TROUBLE, JUST BECAUSE WE--

What? What was he going to say?

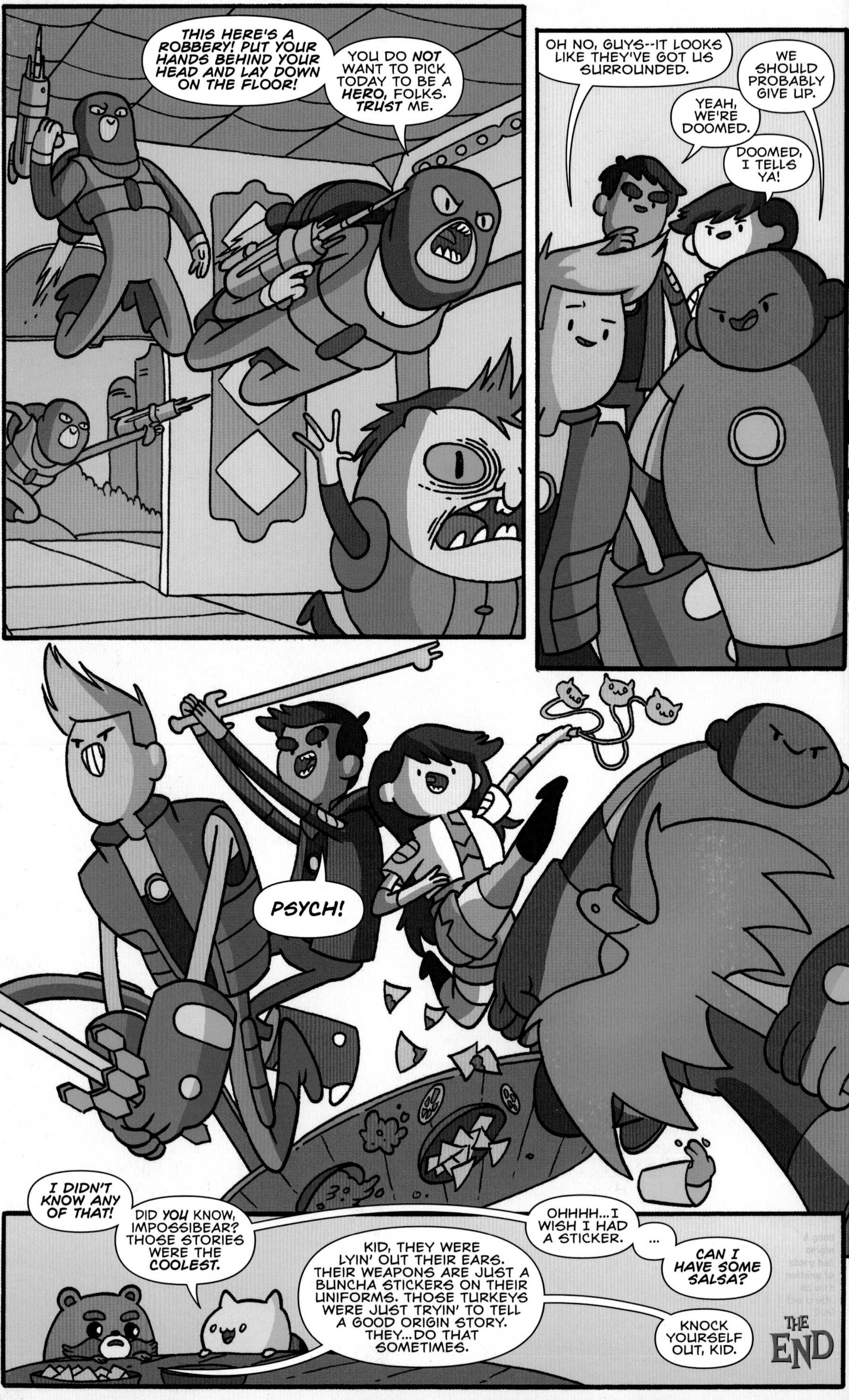

THIS HERE'S A ROBBERY! PUT YOUR HANDS BEHIND YOUR HEAD AND LAY DOWN ON THE FLOOR!
YOU DO NOT WANT TO PICK TODAY TO BE A HERO, FOLKS. TRUST ME.
OH NO, GUYS--IT LOOKS LIKE THEY'VE GOT US SURROUNDED.
WE SHOULD PROBABLY GIVE UP.
YEAH, WE'RE DOOMED.
DOOMED, I TELLS YA!
PSYCH!
I DIDN'T KNOW ANY OF THAT!
DID YOU KNOW, IMPOSSIBEAR? THOSE STORIES WERE THE COOLEST.
KID, THEY WERE LYIN' OUT THEIR EARS. THEIR WEAPONS ARE JUST A BUNCHA STICKERS ON THEIR UNIFORMS. THOSE TURKEYS WERE JUST TRYIN' TO TELL A GOOD ORIGIN STORY. THEY...DO THAT SOMETIMES.
OHHHH...I WISH I HAD A STICKER.
...
CAN I HAVE SOME SALSA?
KNOCK YOURSELF OUT, KID.
A good origin story has nothing to do with the truth.
THE END

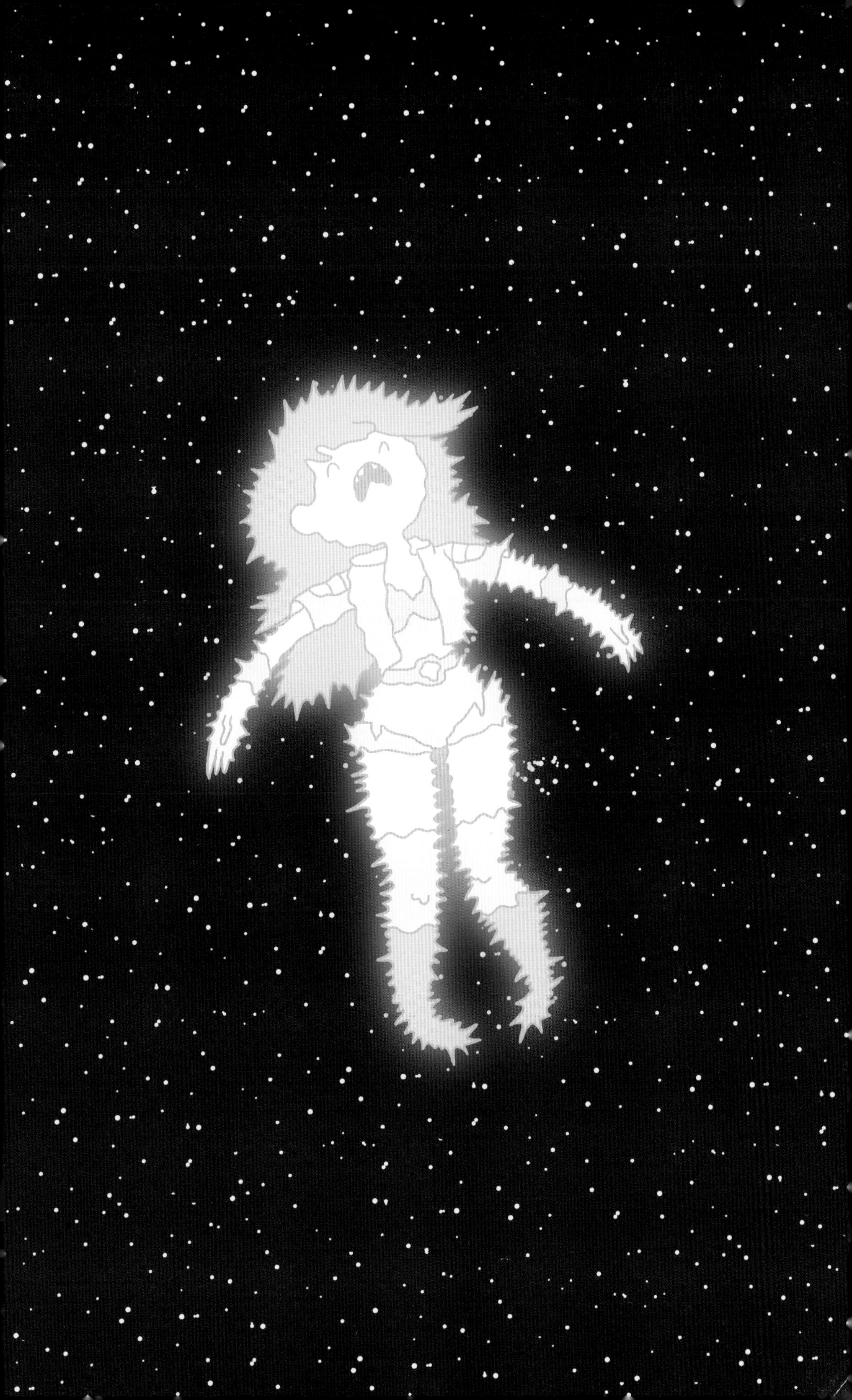

CHAPTER FOURTEEN

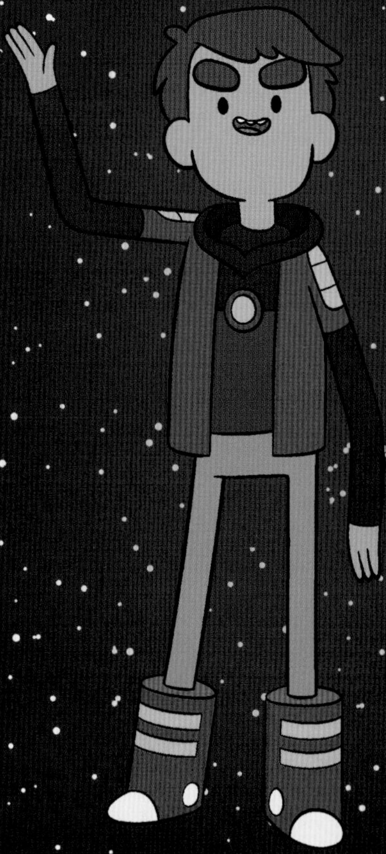

DOWN, DOWN, LEFT, RIGHT,
B, B, SELECT, START

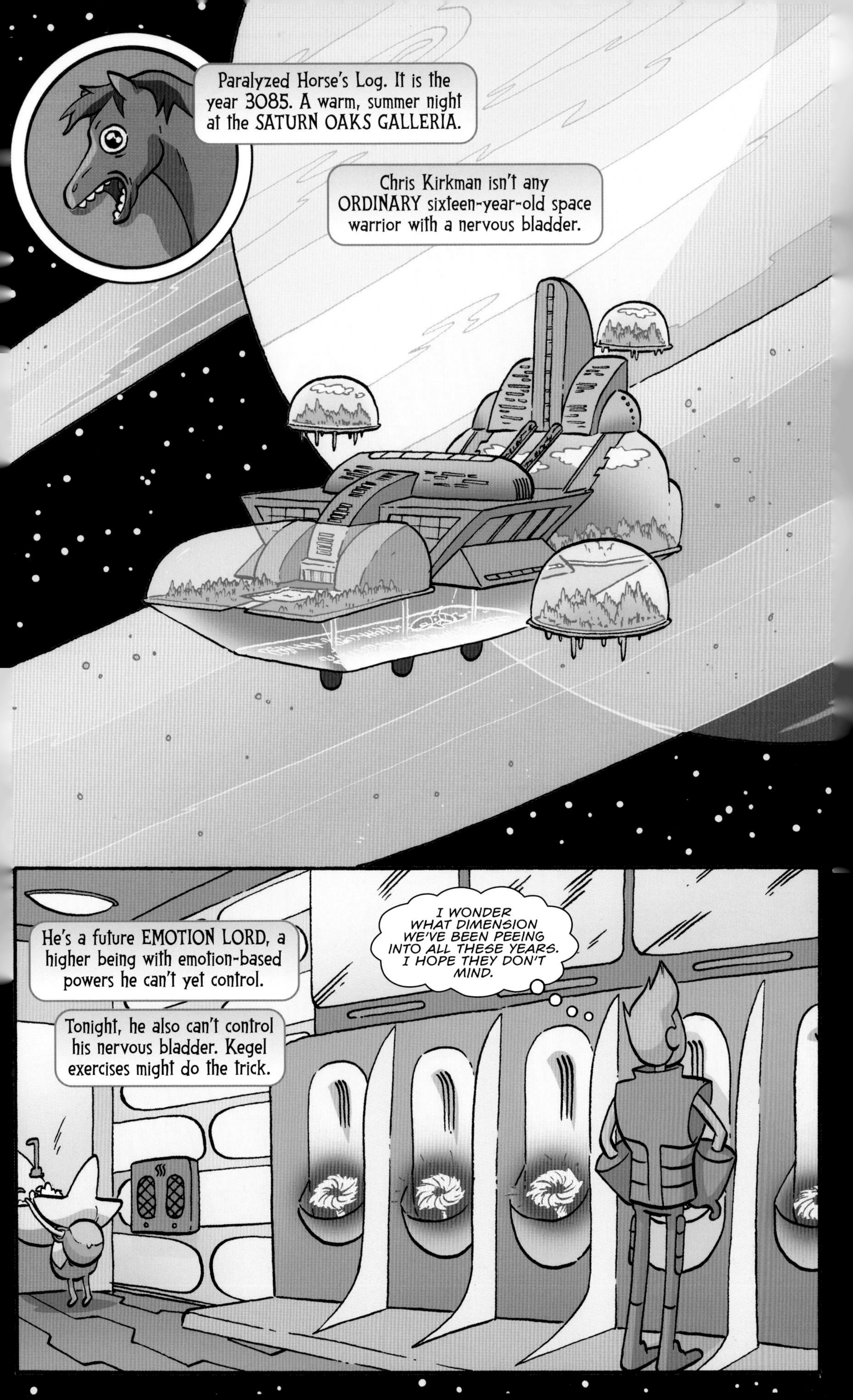

Paralyzed Horse's Log. It is the year 3085. A warm, summer night at the SATURN OAKS GALLERIA.
Chris Kirkman isn't any ORDINARY sixteen-year-old space warrior with a nervous bladder.
He's a future EMOTION LORD, a higher being with emotion-based powers he can't yet control.
Tonight, he also can't control his nervous bladder. Kegel exercises might do the trick.
I WONDER WHAT DIMENSION WE'VE BEEN PEEING INTO ALL THESE YEARS. I HOPE THEY DON'T MIND.

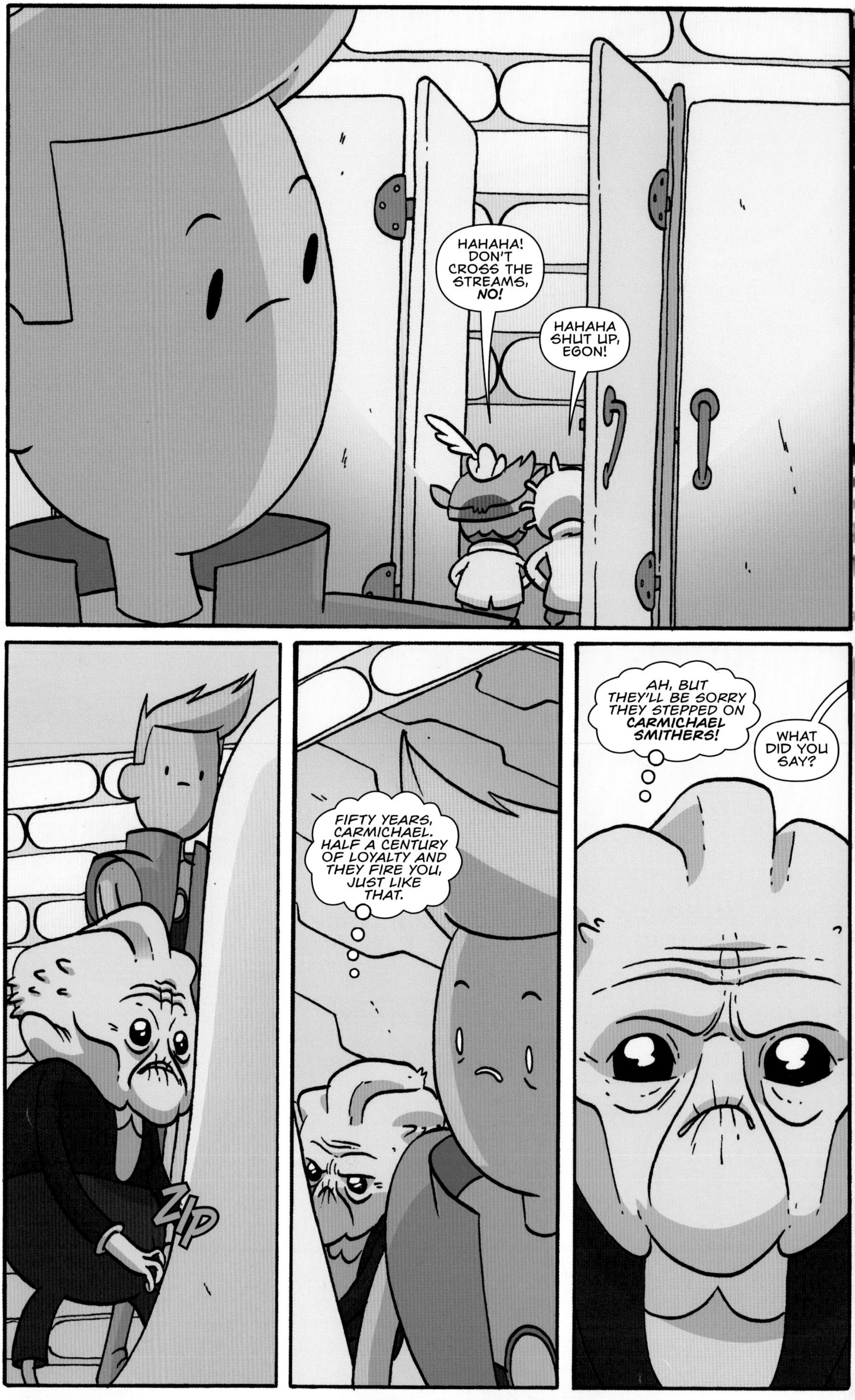
HAHAHA! DON'T CROSS THE STREAMS, NO!
HAHAHA SHUT UP, EGON!
ZIP
FIFTY YEARS, CARMICHAEL. HALF A CENTURY OF LOYALTY AND THEY FIRE YOU, JUST LIKE THAT.
AH, BUT THEY'LL BE SORRY THEY STEPPED ON CARMICHAEL SMITHERS!
WHAT DID YOU SAY?

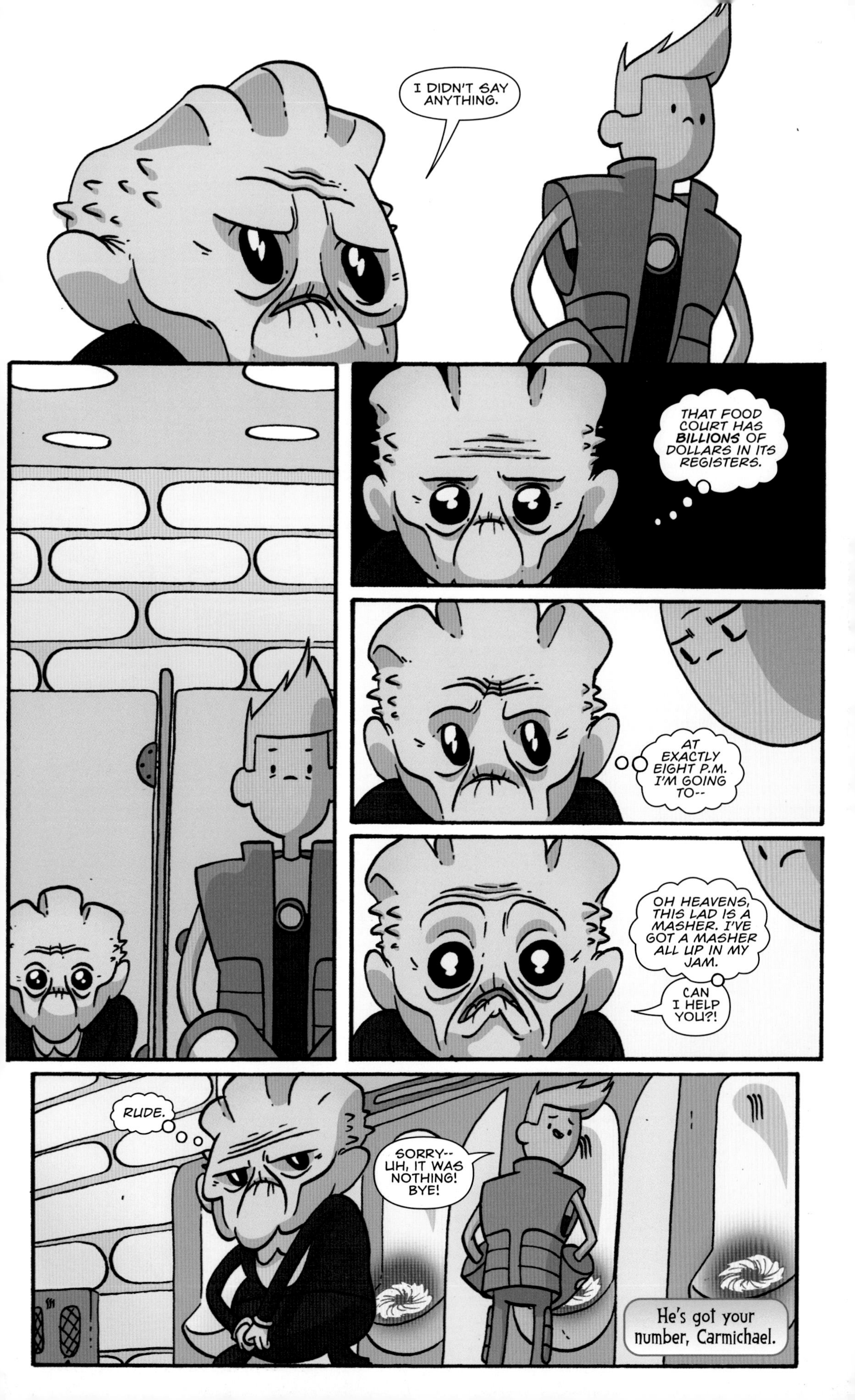
I DIDN'T SAY ANYTHING.
THAT FOOD COURT HAS **BILLIONS** OF DOLLARS IN ITS REGISTERS.
AT EXACTLY EIGHT P.M. I'M GOING TO--
OH HEAVENS, THIS LAD IS A MASHER. I'VE GOT A MASHER ALL UP IN MY JAM.
CAN I HELP YOU?!
RUDE.
SORRY-- UH, IT WAS NOTHING! BYE!
He's got your number, Carmichael.

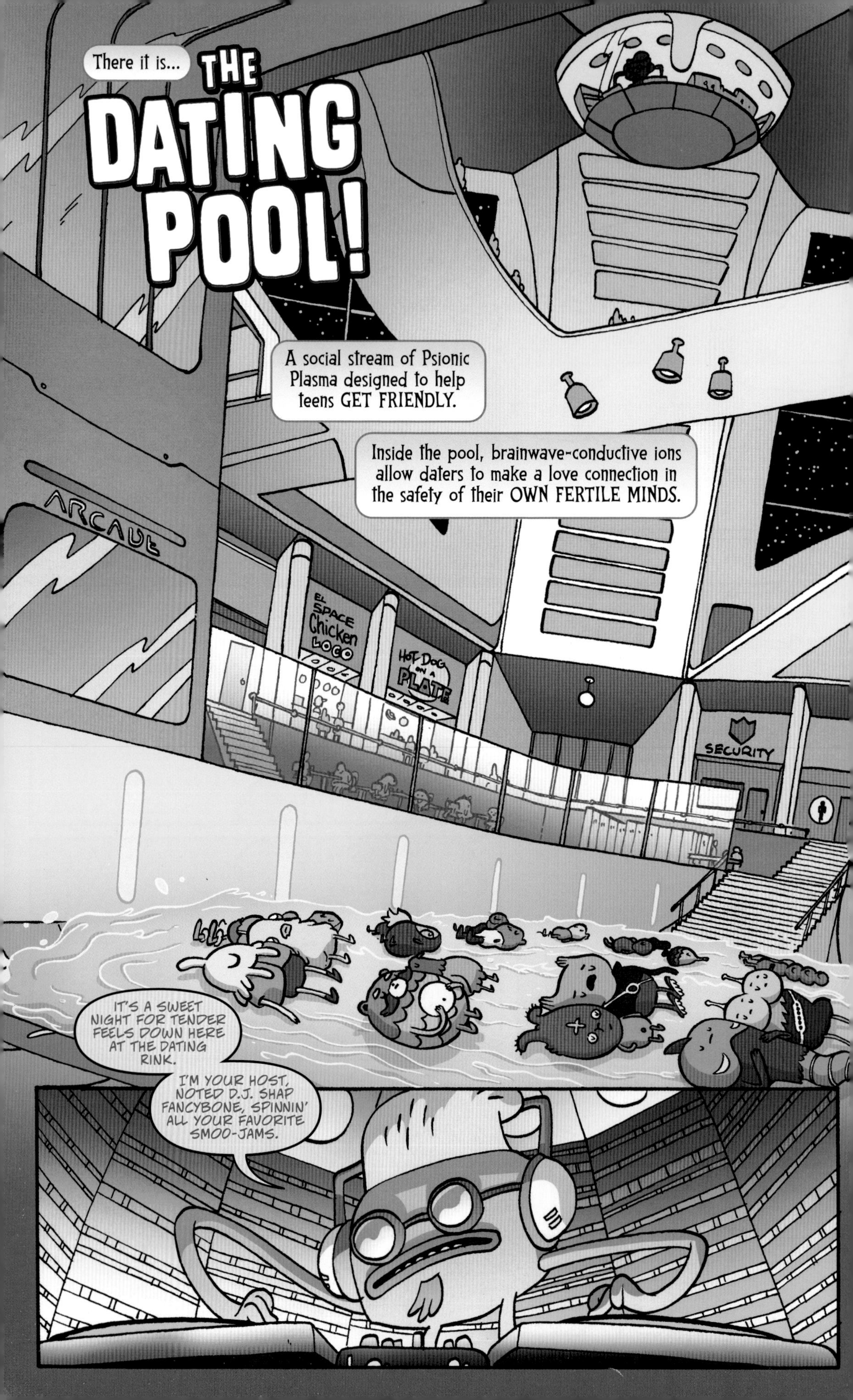
There it is... THE DATING POOL!
A social stream of Psionic Plasma designed to help teens GET FRIENDLY.
Inside the pool, brainwave-conductive ions allow daters to make a love connection in the safety of their OWN FERTILE MINDS.
ARCADE
EL SPACE Chicken LOCO
HOT DOG ON A PLATE
SECURITY
IT'S A SWEET NIGHT FOR TENDER FEELS DOWN HERE AT THE DATING RINK.
I'M YOUR HOST, NOTED D.J. SHAP FANCYBONE, SPINNIN' ALL YOUR FAVORITE SMOO-JAMS.

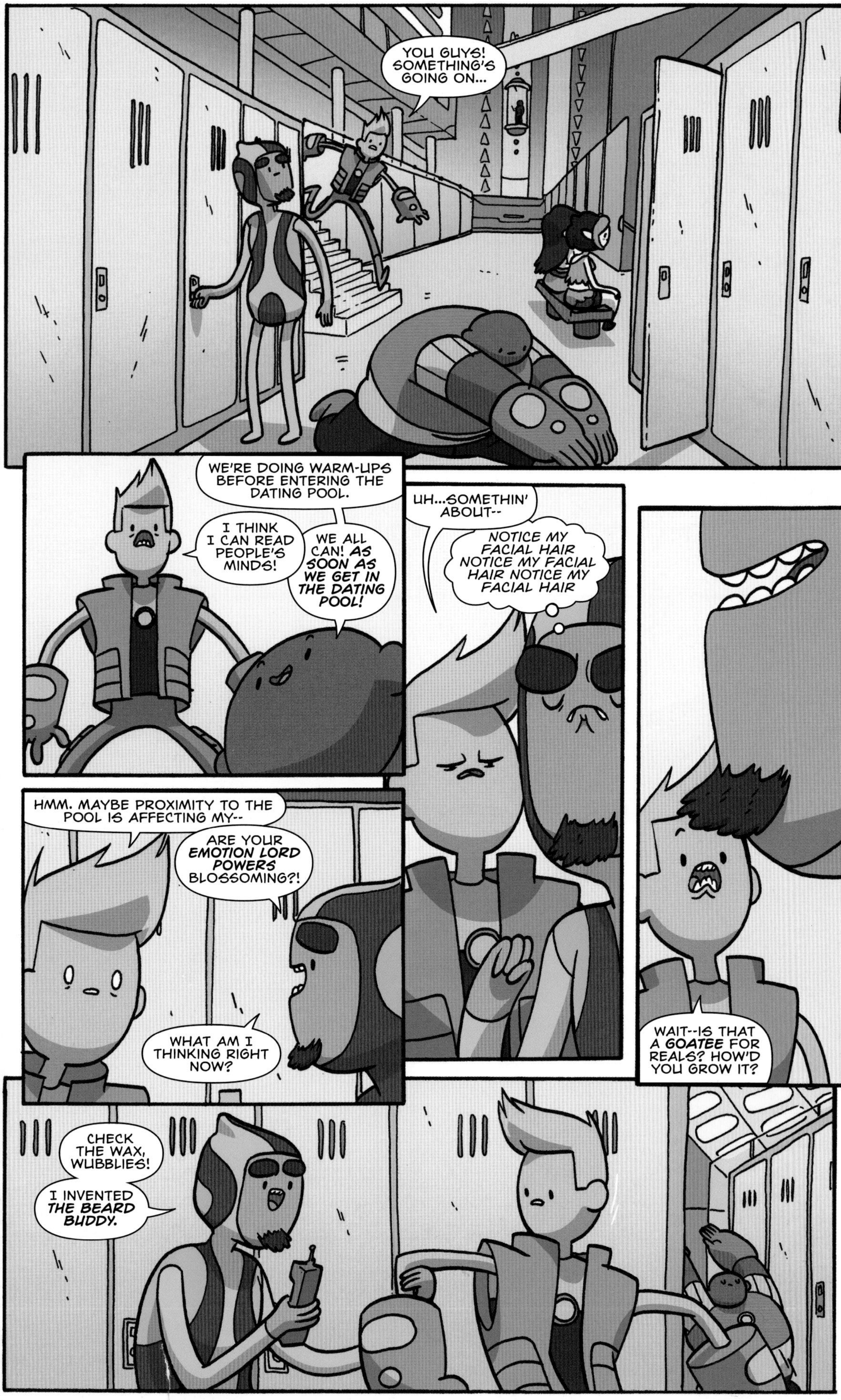

YOU GUYS! SOMETHING'S GOING ON...
WE'RE DOING WARM-UPS BEFORE ENTERING THE DATING POOL.
I THINK I CAN READ PEOPLE'S MINDS!
WE ALL CAN! AS SOON AS WE GET IN THE DATING POOL!
UH...SOMETHIN' ABOUT--
NOTICE MY FACIAL HAIR NOTICE MY FACIAL HAIR NOTICE MY FACIAL HAIR
WAIT--IS THAT A GOATEE FOR REALS? HOW'D YOU GROW IT?
HMM. MAYBE PROXIMITY TO THE POOL IS AFFECTING MY--
ARE YOUR EMOTION LORD POWERS BLOSSOMING?!
WHAT AM I THINKING RIGHT NOW?
CHECK THE WAX, WUBBLIES!
I INVENTED THE BEARD BUDDY.

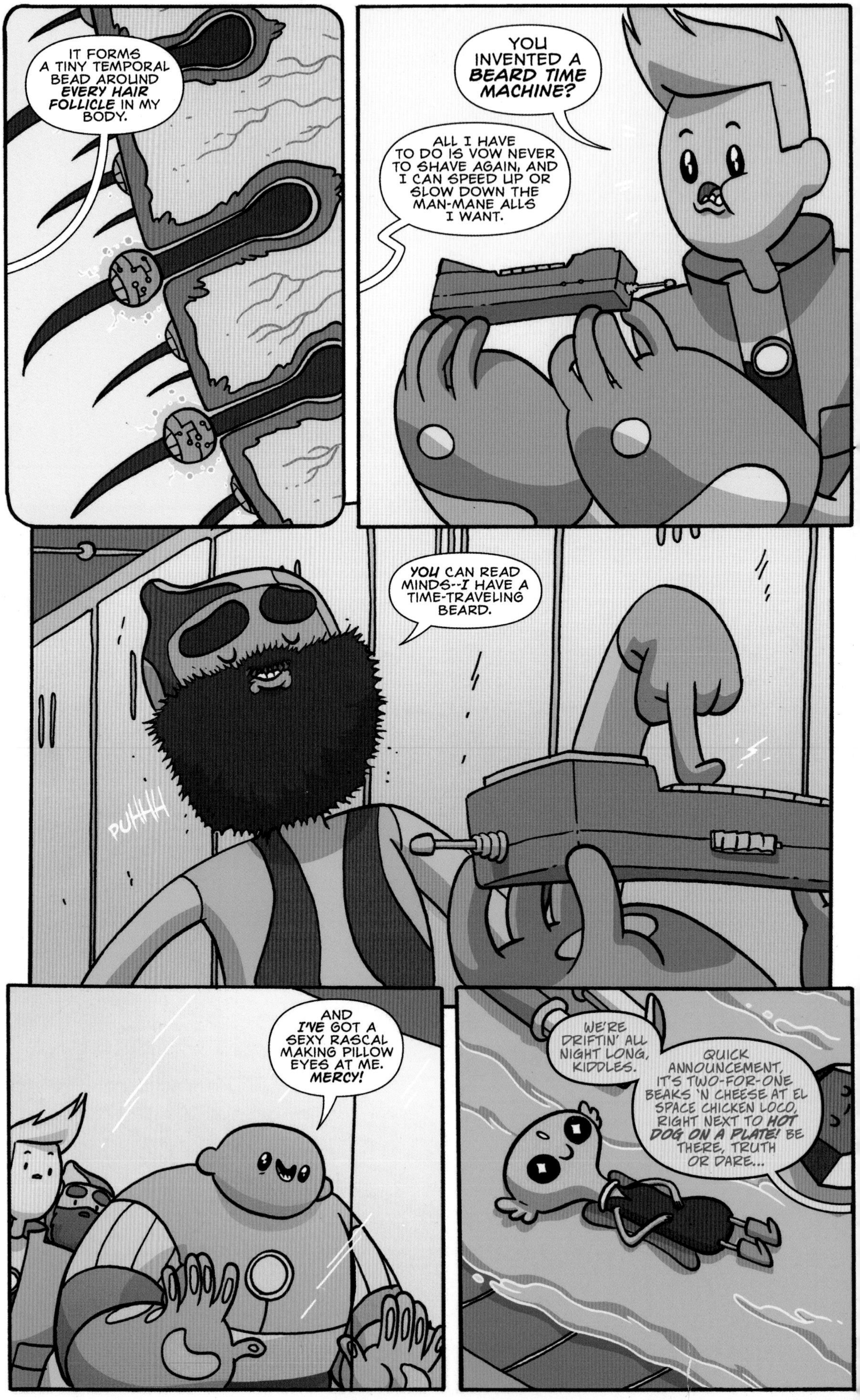
IT FORMS A TINY TEMPORAL BEAD AROUND EVERY HAIR FOLLICLE IN MY BODY.
YOU INVENTED A BEARD TIME MACHINE?
ALL I HAVE TO DO IS VOW NEVER TO SHAVE AGAIN, AND I CAN SPEED UP OR SLOW DOWN THE MAN-MANE ALLS I WANT.
YOU CAN READ MINDS--I HAVE A TIME-TRAVELING BEARD.
PUHHH
AND I'VE GOT A SEXY RASCAL MAKING PILLOW EYES AT ME. MERCY!
WE'RE DRIFTIN' ALL NIGHT LONG, KIDDLES.
QUICK ANNOUNCEMENT, IT'S TWO-FOR-ONE BEAKS 'N CHEESE AT EL SPACE CHICKEN LOCO, RIGHT NEXT TO HOT DOG ON A PLATE! BE THERE, TRUTH OR DARE...

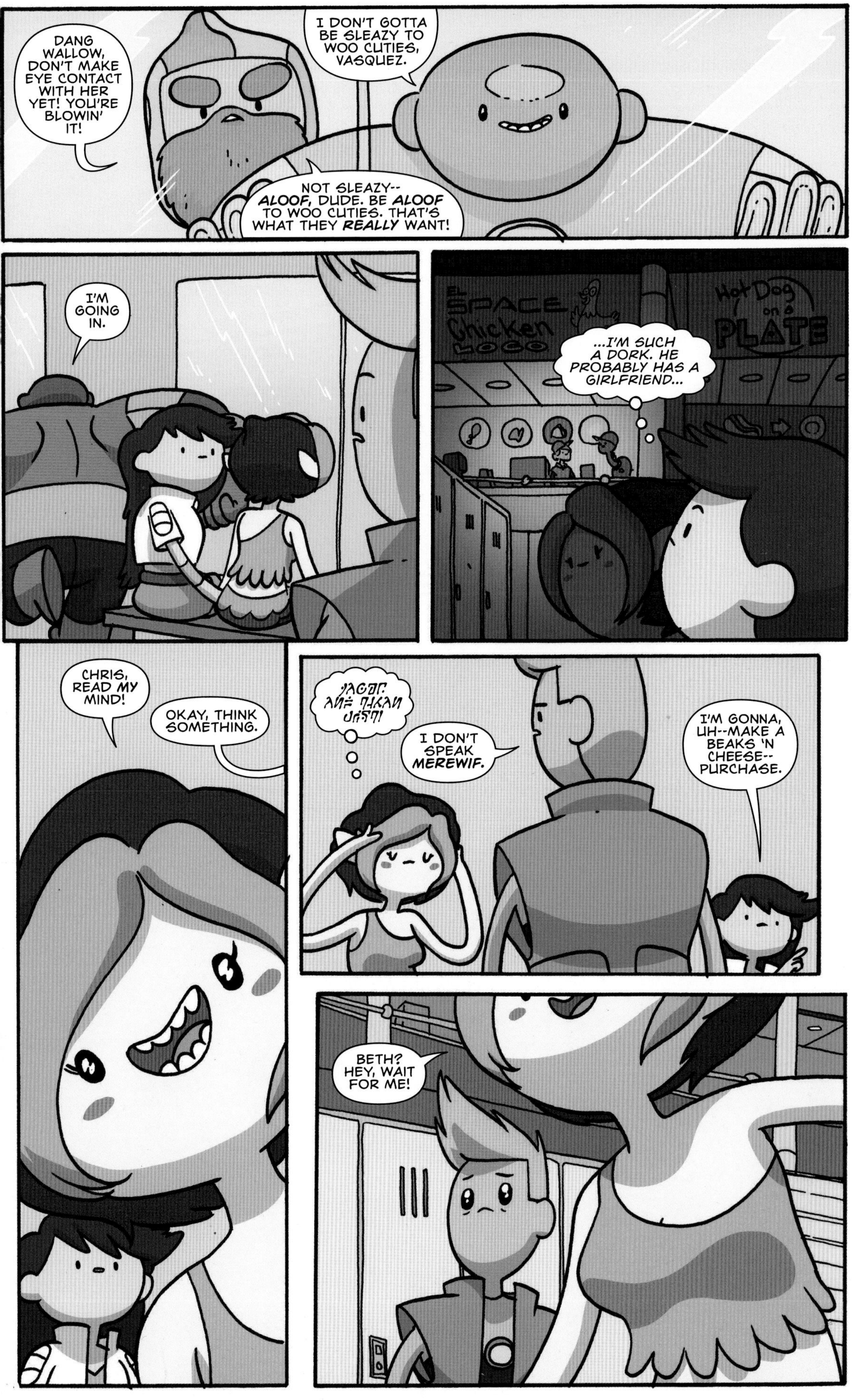
DANG WALLOW, DON'T MAKE EYE CONTACT WITH HER YET! YOU'RE BLOWIN' IT!
I DON'T GOTTA BE SLEAZY TO WOO CUTIES, VASQUEZ.
NOT SLEAZY-- ALOOF, DUDE. BE ALOOF TO WOO CUTIES. THAT'S WHAT THEY REALLY WANT!
I'M GOING IN.
EL SPACE Chicken LOCO
Hot Dog on a PLATE
...I'M SUCH A DORK. HE PROBABLY HAS A GIRLFRIEND...
CHRIS, READ MY MIND!
OKAY, THINK SOMETHING.
I DON'T SPEAK MEREWIF.
I'M GONNA, UH--MAKE A BEAKS 'N CHEESE-- PURCHASE.
BETH? HEY, WAIT FOR ME!

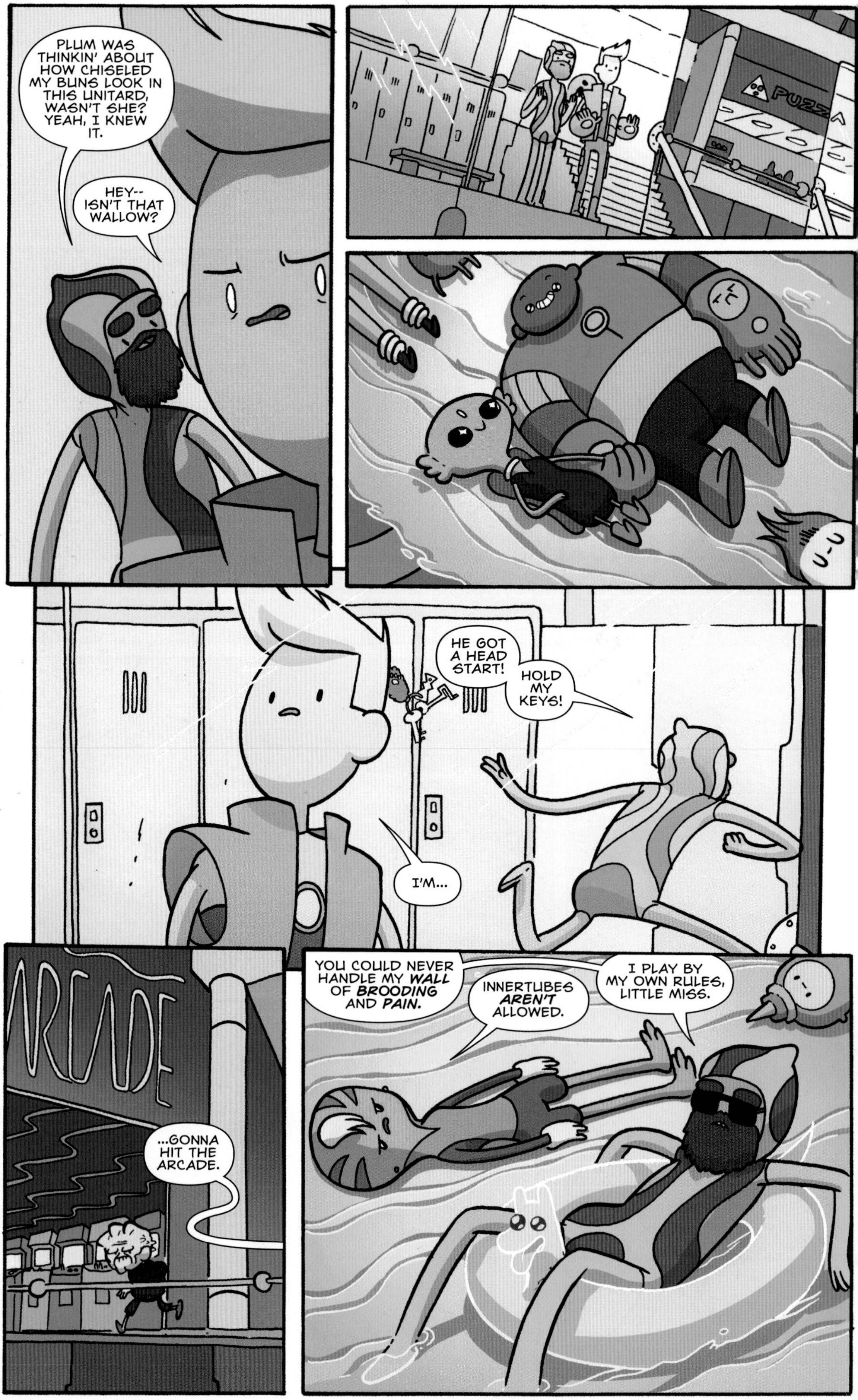
PLUM WAS THINKIN' ABOUT HOW CHISELED MY BUNS LOOK IN THIS UNITARD, WASN'T SHE? YEAH, I KNEW IT.
HEY-- ISN'T THAT WALLOW?
PUZZA
HE GOT A HEAD START!
HOLD MY KEYS!
I'M...
...GONNA HIT THE ARCADE.
ARCADE
YOU COULD NEVER HANDLE MY WALL OF BROODING AND PAIN.
INNERTUBES AREN'T ALLOWED.
I PLAY BY MY OWN RULES, LITTLE MISS.

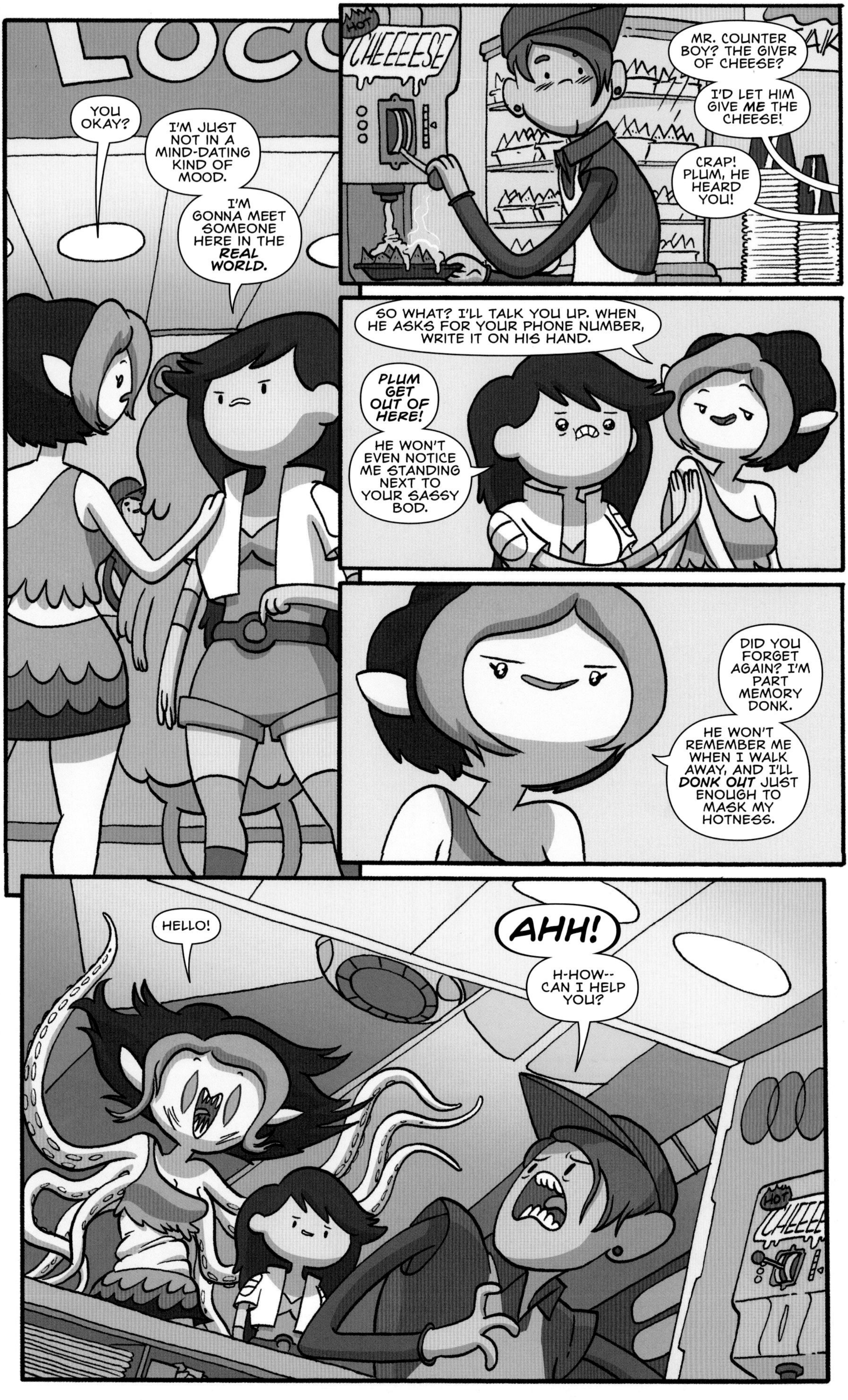
LOCO
YOU OKAY?
I'M JUST NOT IN A MIND-DATING KIND OF MOOD.
I'M GONNA MEET SOMEONE HERE IN THE REAL WORLD.
HOT CHEEEEESE
MR. COUNTER BOY? THE GIVER OF CHEESE?
I'D LET HIM GIVE ME THE CHEESE!
CRAP! PLUM, HE HEARD YOU!
SO WHAT? I'LL TALK YOU UP. WHEN HE ASKS FOR YOUR PHONE NUMBER, WRITE IT ON HIS HAND.
PLUM GET OUT OF HERE!
HE WON'T EVEN NOTICE ME STANDING NEXT TO YOUR SASSY BOD.
DID YOU FORGET AGAIN? I'M PART MEMORY DONK.
HE WON'T REMEMBER ME WHEN I WALK AWAY, AND I'LL DONK OUT JUST ENOUGH TO MASK MY HOTNESS.
HELLO!
AHH!
H-HOW-- CAN I HELP YOU?
HOT

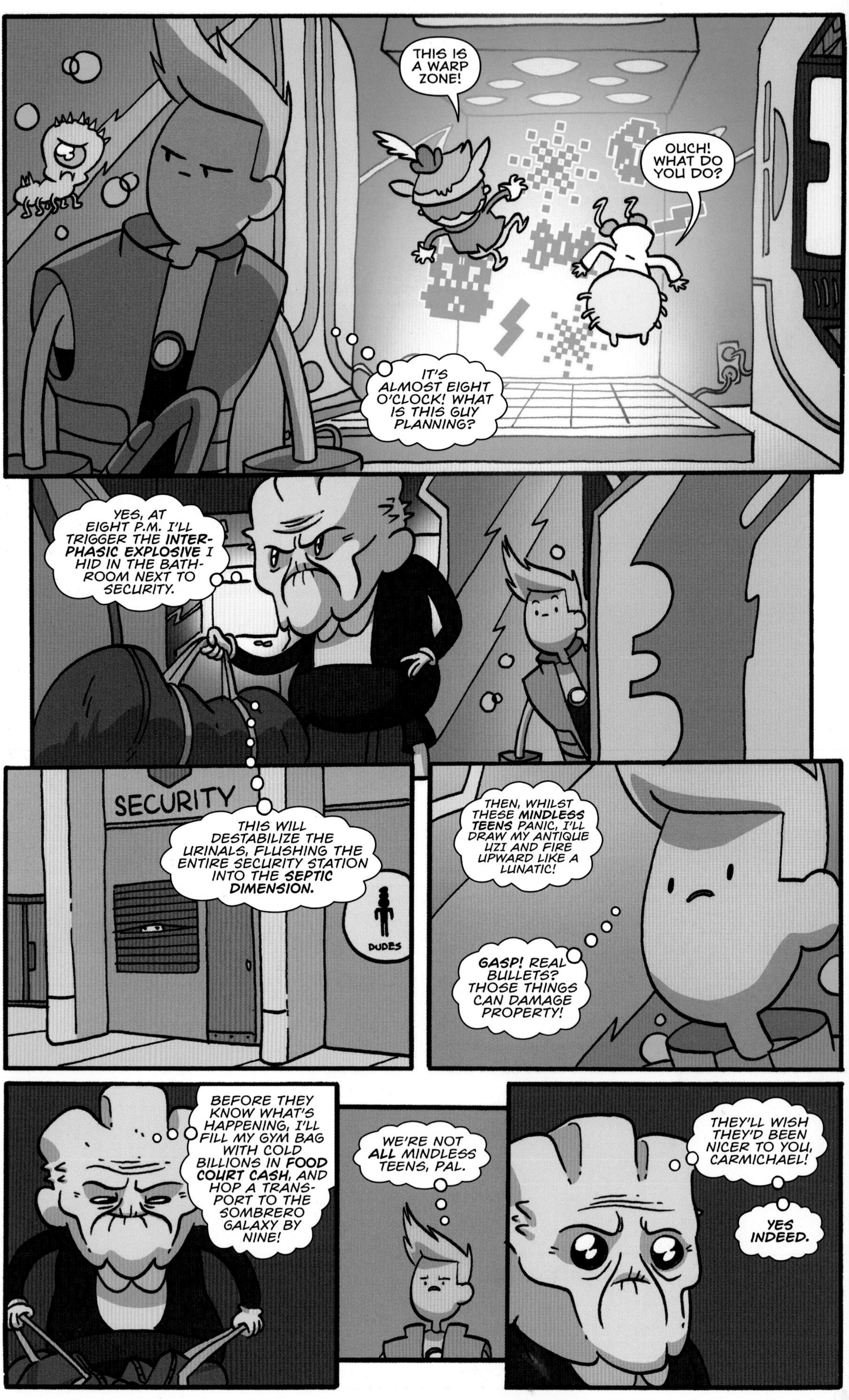
THIS IS A WARP ZONE!
OUCH! WHAT DO YOU DO?
IT'S ALMOST EIGHT O'CLOCK! WHAT IS THIS GUY PLANNING?
YES, AT EIGHT P.M. I'LL TRIGGER THE **INTER-PHASIC EXPLOSIVE** I HID IN THE BATH-ROOM NEXT TO SECURITY.
SECURITY
THIS WILL DESTABILIZE THE URINALS, FLUSHING THE ENTIRE SECURITY STATION INTO THE **SEPTIC DIMENSION.**
DUDES
THEN, WHILST THESE **MINDLESS TEENS** PANIC, I'LL DRAW MY ANTIQUE UZI AND FIRE UPWARD LIKE A LUNATIC!
GASP! REAL BULLETS? THOSE THINGS CAN DAMAGE PROPERTY!
BEFORE THEY KNOW WHAT'S HAPPENING, I'LL FILL MY GYM BAG WITH COLD BILLIONS IN **FOOD COURT CASH**, AND HOP A TRANS-PORT TO THE SOMBRERO GALAXY BY NINE!
WE'RE NOT **ALL** MINDLESS TEENS, PAL.
THEY'LL WISH THEY'D BEEN NICER TO YOU, CARMICHAEL!
YES INDEED.

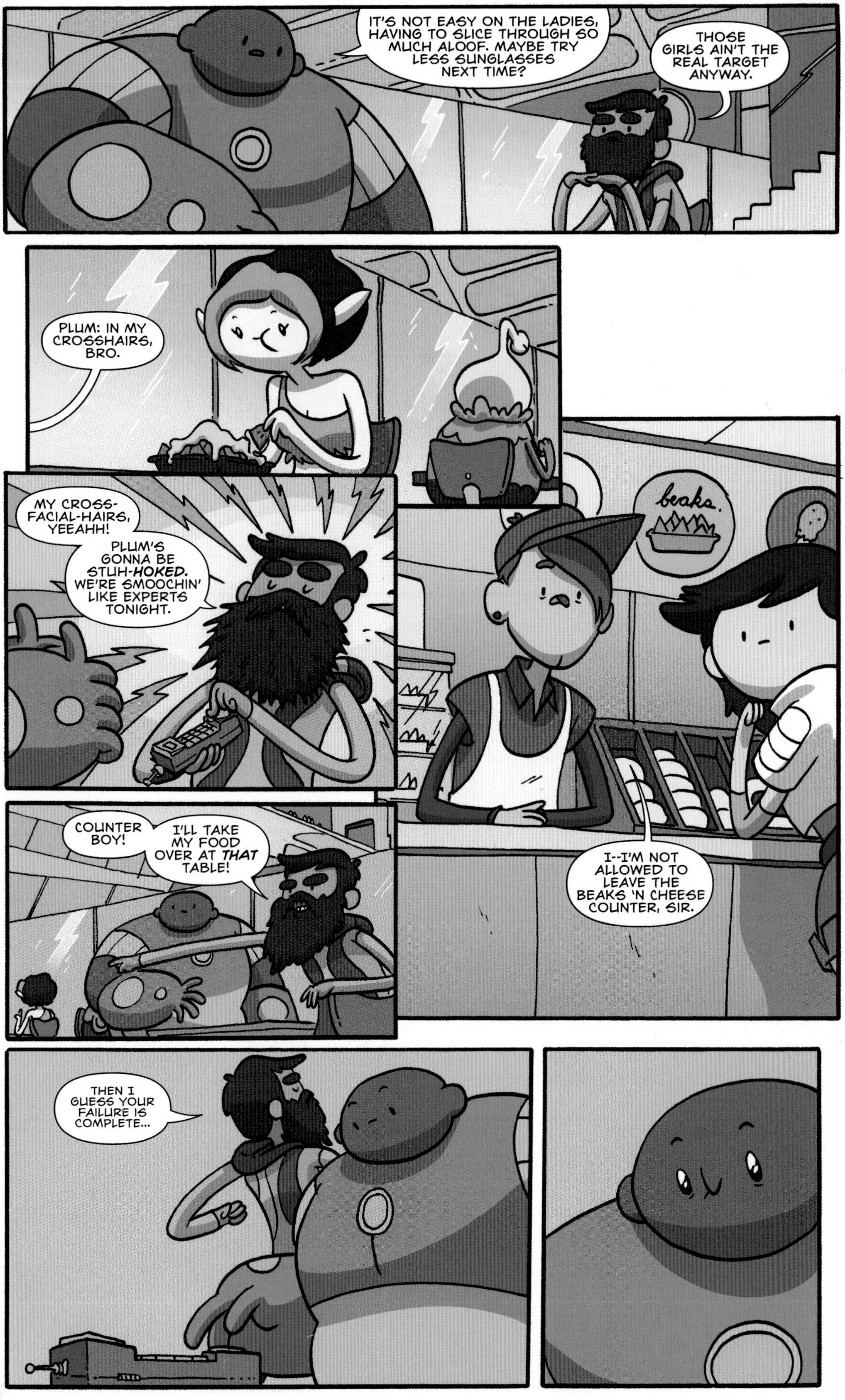
IT'S NOT EASY ON THE LADIES, HAVING TO SLICE THROUGH SO MUCH ALOOF. MAYBE TRY LESS SUNGLASSES NEXT TIME?
THOSE GIRLS AIN'T THE REAL TARGET ANYWAY.
PLUM: IN MY CROSSHAIRS, BRO.
MY CROSS-FACIAL-HAIRS, YEEAHH!
PLUM'S GONNA BE STUH-HOKED. WE'RE SMOOCHIN' LIKE EXPERTS TONIGHT.
beaks.
COUNTER BOY!
I'LL TAKE MY FOOD OVER AT THAT TABLE!
I--I'M NOT ALLOWED TO LEAVE THE BEAKS 'N CHEESE COUNTER, SIR.
THEN I GUESS YOUR FAILURE IS COMPLETE...

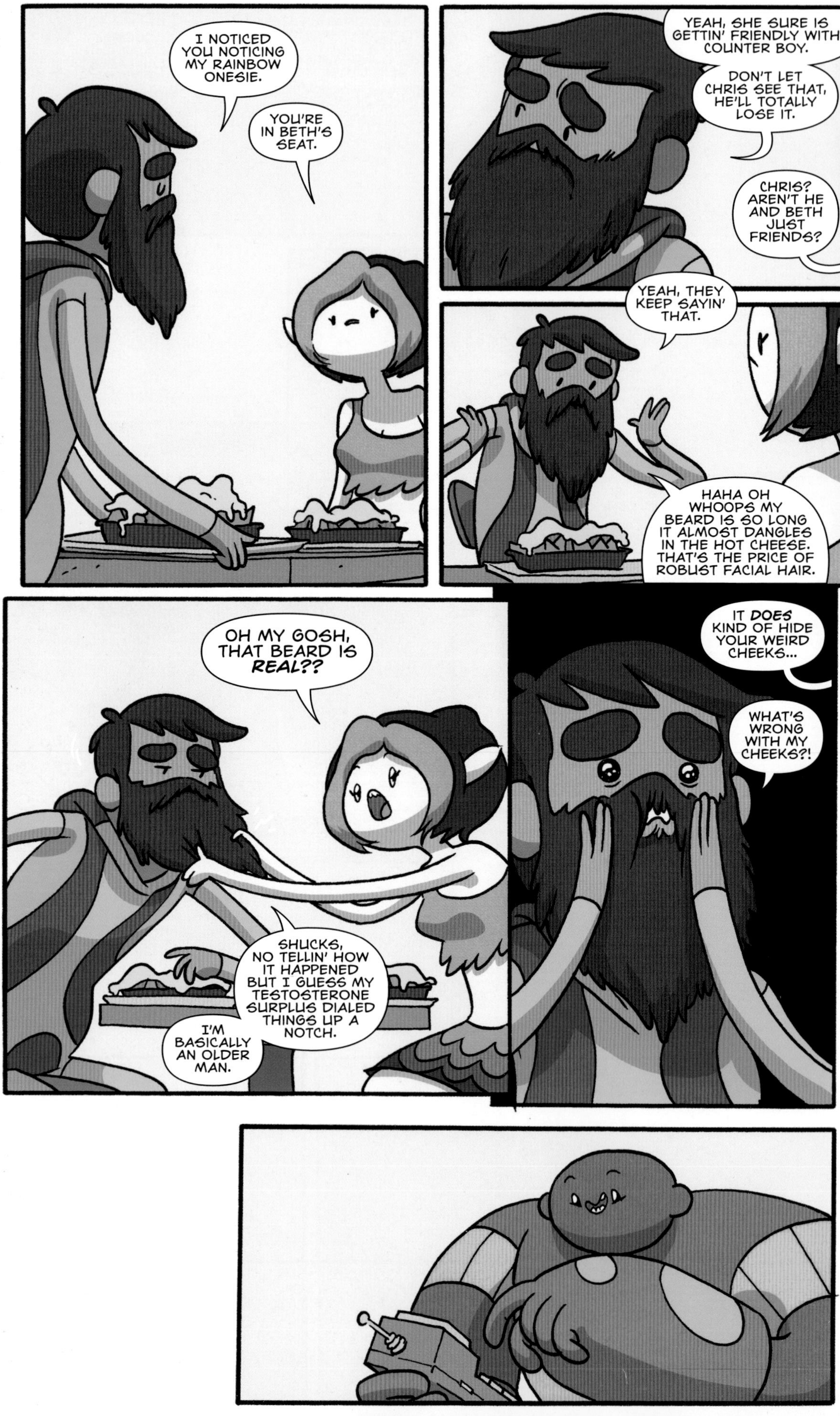
I NOTICED YOU NOTICING MY RAINBOW ONESIE.
YOU'RE IN BETH'S SEAT.
YEAH, SHE SURE IS GETTIN' FRIENDLY WITH COUNTER BOY.
DON'T LET CHRIS SEE THAT, HE'LL TOTALLY LOSE IT.
CHRIS? AREN'T HE AND BETH JUST FRIENDS?
YEAH, THEY KEEP SAYIN' THAT.
HAHA OH WHOOPS MY BEARD IS SO LONG IT ALMOST DANGLES IN THE HOT CHEESE. THAT'S THE PRICE OF ROBUST FACIAL HAIR.
OH MY GOSH, THAT BEARD IS *REAL??*
SHUCKS, NO TELLIN' HOW IT HAPPENED BUT I GUESS MY TESTOSTERONE SURPLUS DIALED THINGS UP A NOTCH.
I'M BASICALLY AN OLDER MAN.
IT ***DOES*** KIND OF HIDE YOUR WEIRD CHEEKS...
WHAT'S WRONG WITH MY CHEEKS?!

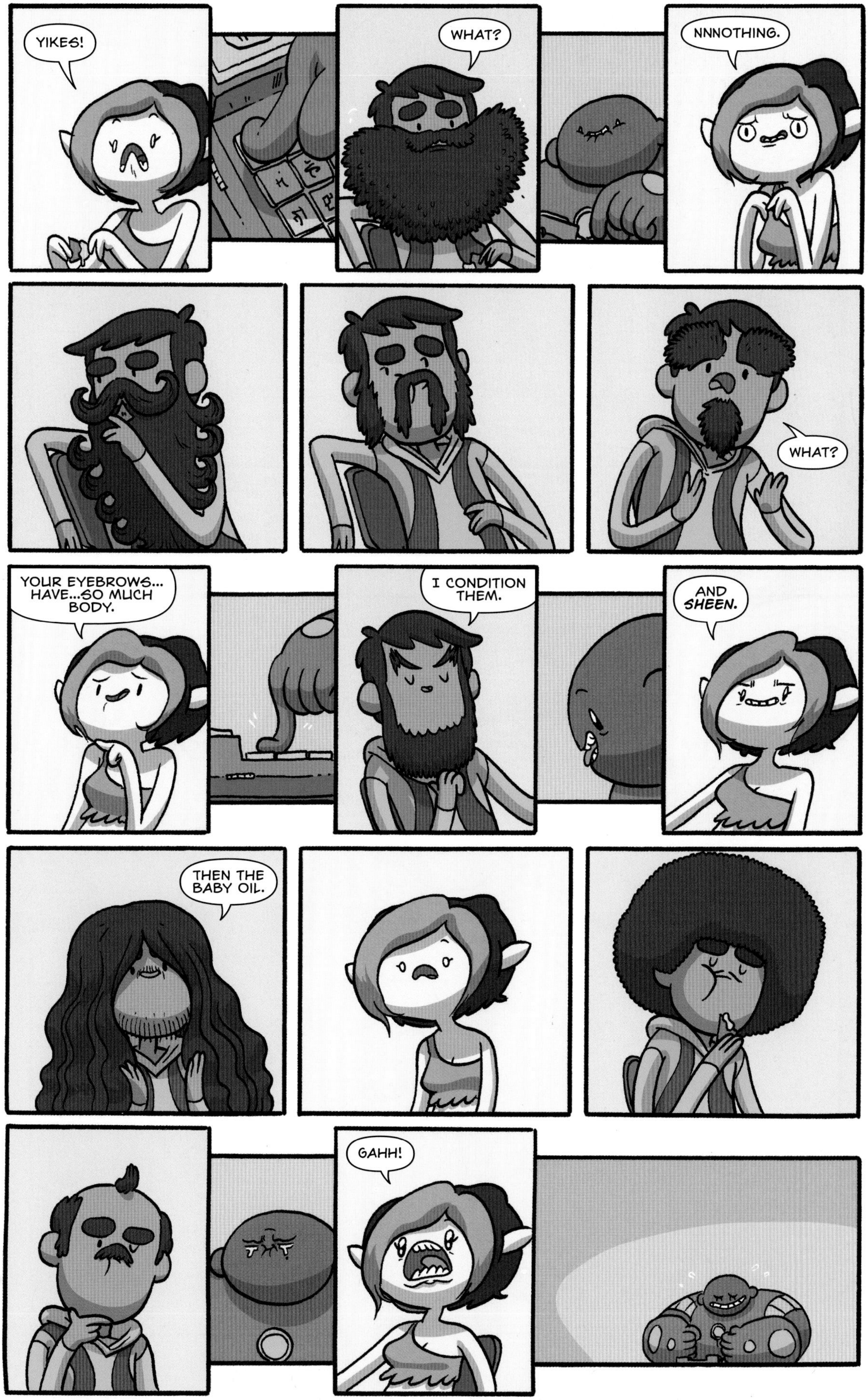
YIKES!
WHAT?
NNNOTHING.
WHAT?
YOUR EYEBROWS... HAVE...SO MUCH BODY.
I CONDITION THEM.
AND *SHEEN.*
THEN THE BABY OIL.
GAHH!

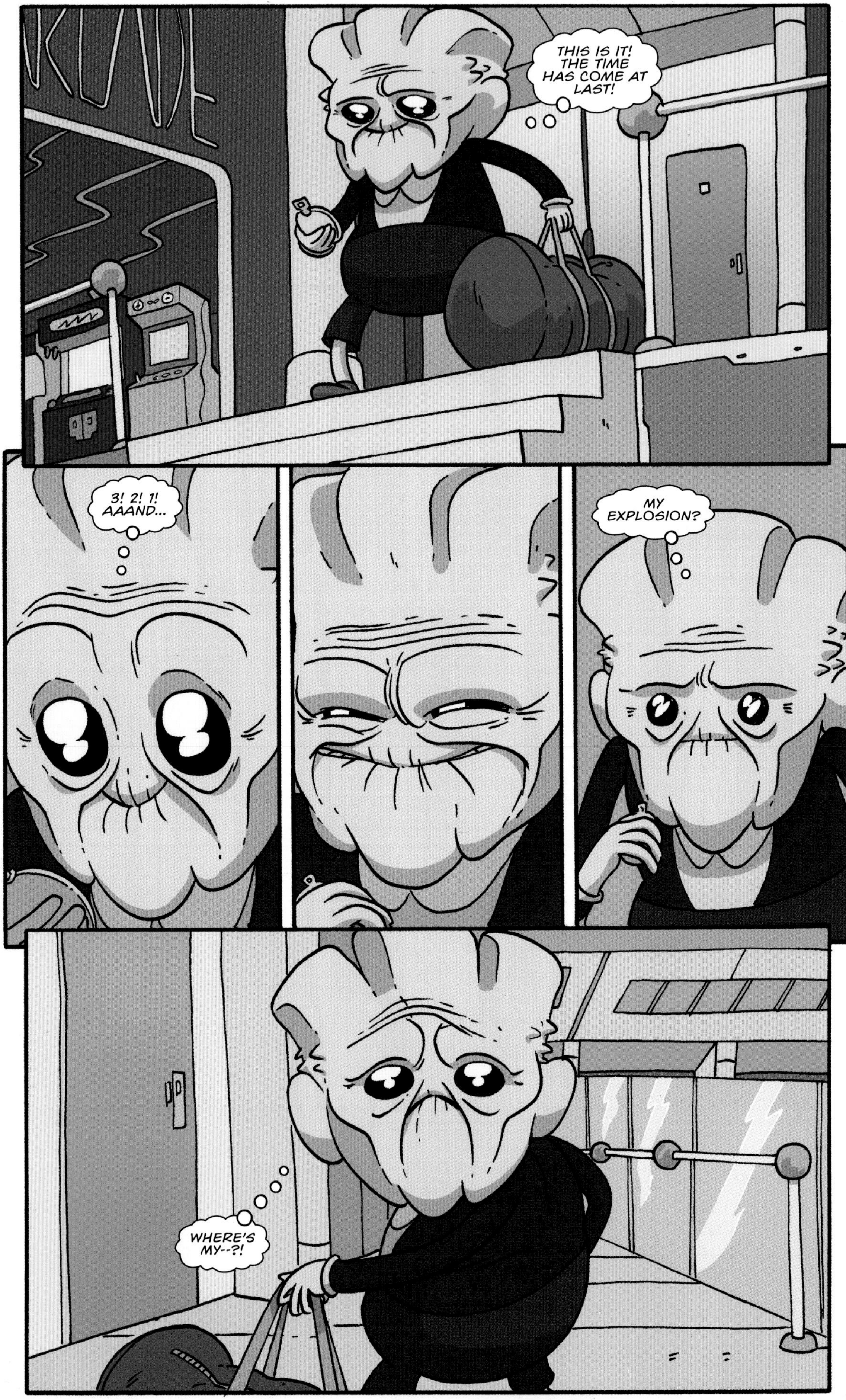
THIS IS IT! THE TIME HAS COME AT LAST!
3! 2! 1! AAAND...
MY EXPLOSION?
WHERE'S MY--?!

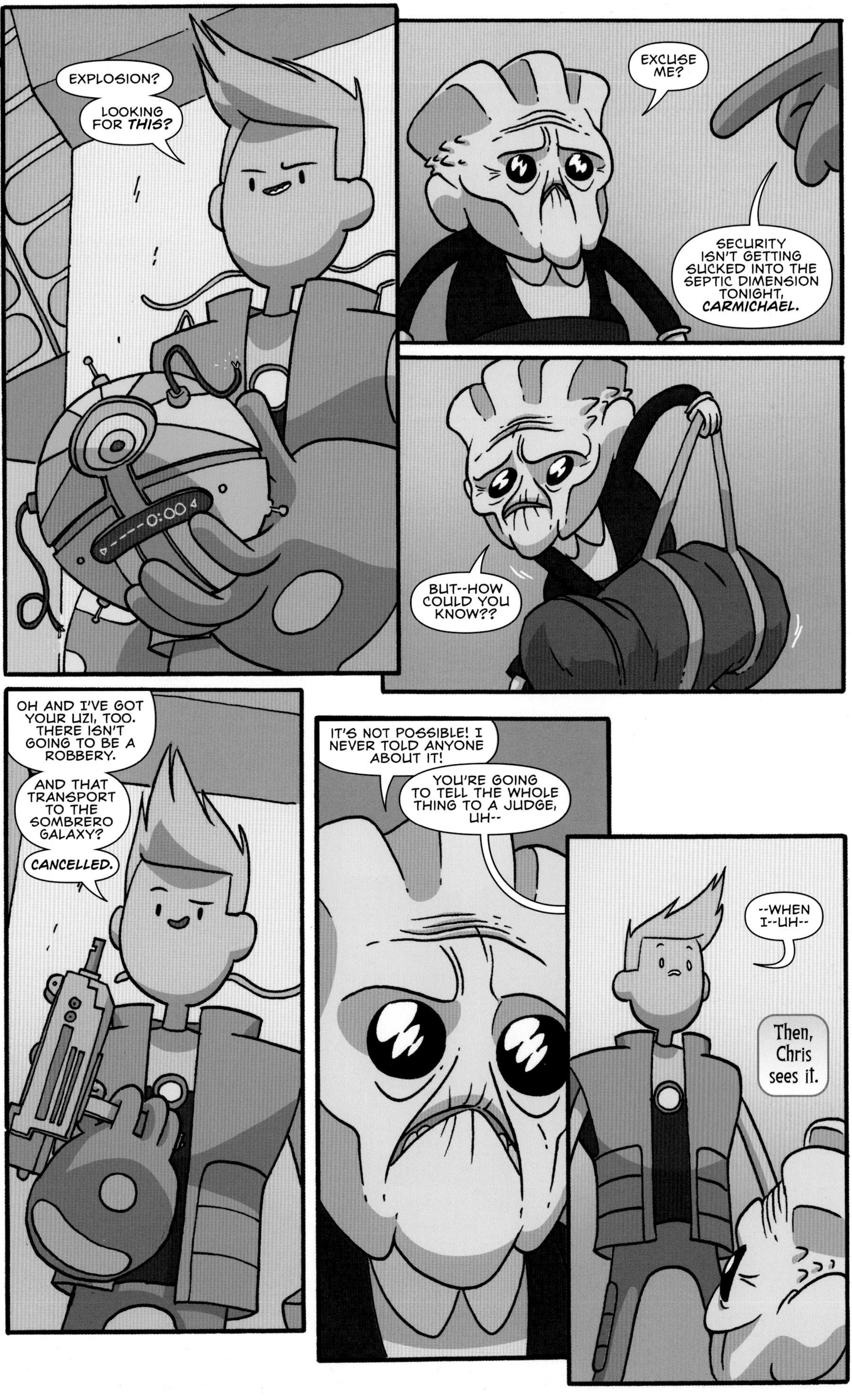
EXPLOSION?
LOOKING FOR *THIS?*
EXCUSE ME?
SECURITY ISN'T GETTING SUCKED INTO THE SEPTIC DIMENSION TONIGHT, *CARMICHAEL.*
BUT--HOW COULD YOU KNOW??
OH AND I'VE GOT YOUR UZI, TOO. THERE ISN'T GOING TO BE A ROBBERY.
AND THAT TRANSPORT TO THE SOMBRERO GALAXY?
CANCELLED.
IT'S NOT POSSIBLE! I NEVER TOLD ANYONE ABOUT IT!
YOU'RE GOING TO TELL THE WHOLE THING TO A JUDGE, UH--
--WHEN I--UH--
Then, Chris sees it.

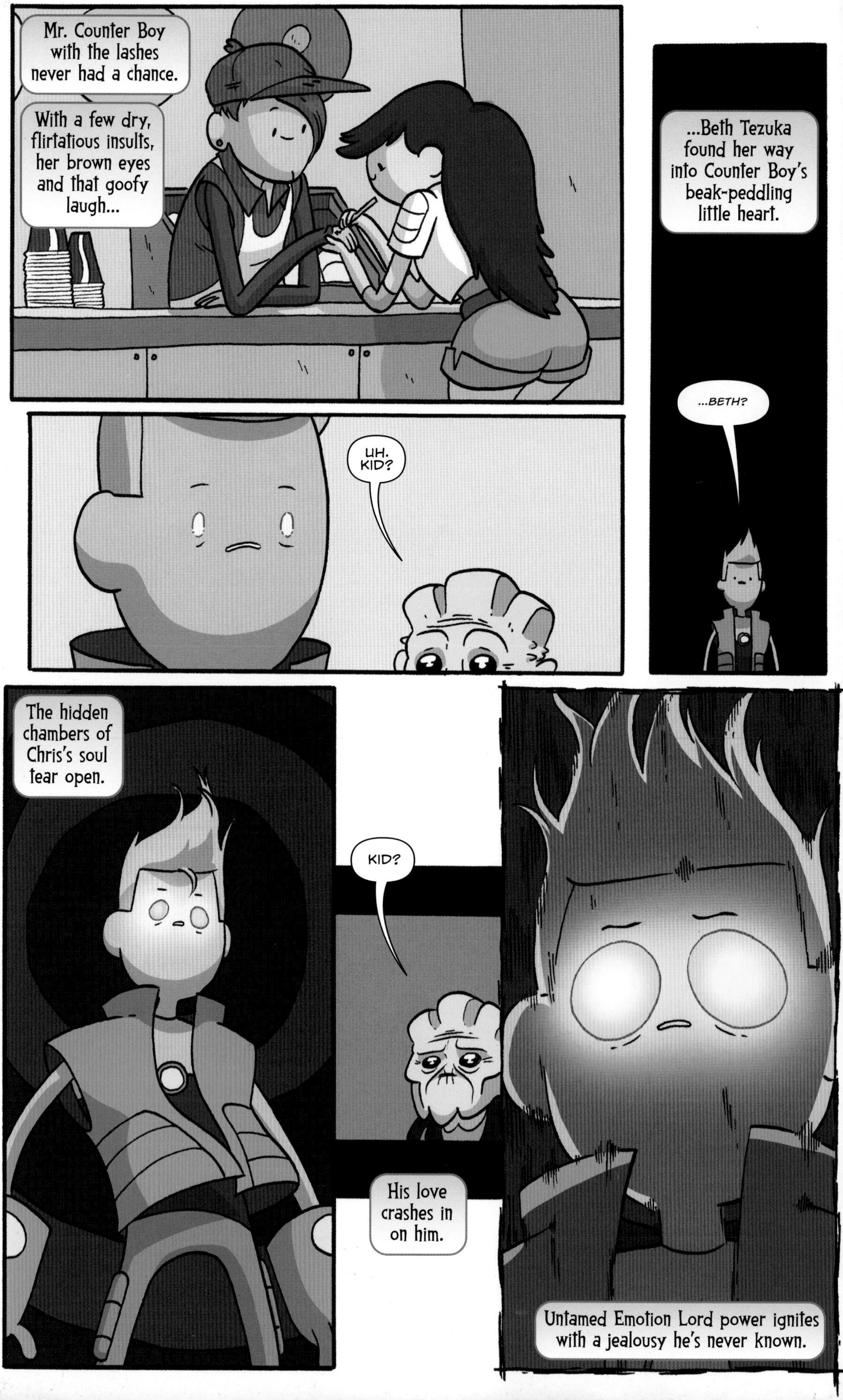

Mr. Counter Boy with the lashes never had a chance.
With a few dry, flirtatious insults, her brown eyes and that goofy laugh...
...Beth Tezuka found her way into Counter Boy's beak-peddling little heart.
UH. KID?
...BETH?
The hidden chambers of Chris's soul tear open.
KID?
His love crashes in on him.
Untamed Emotion Lord power ignites with a jealousy he's never known.

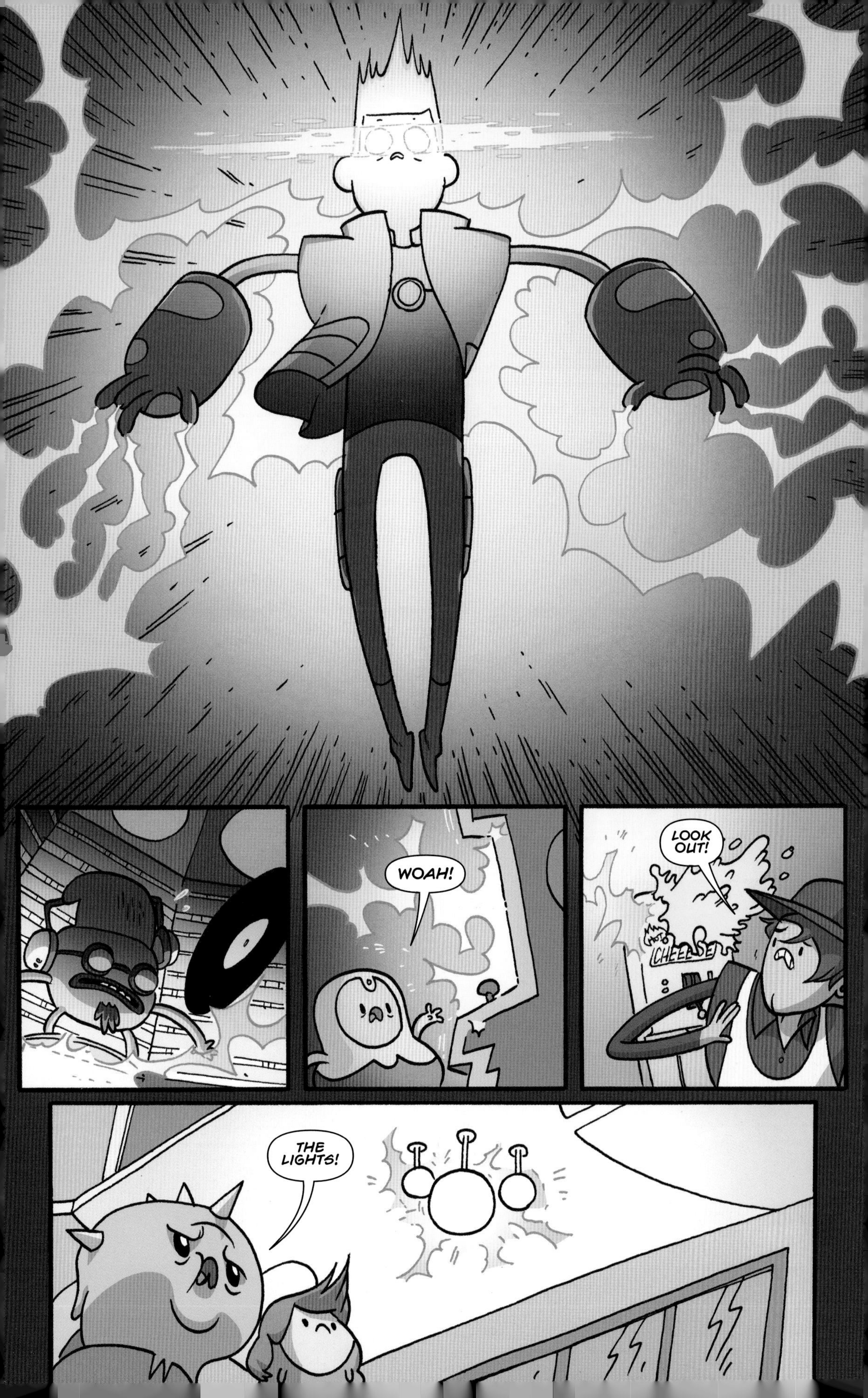
WOAH!
LOOK OUT!
THE LIGHTS!

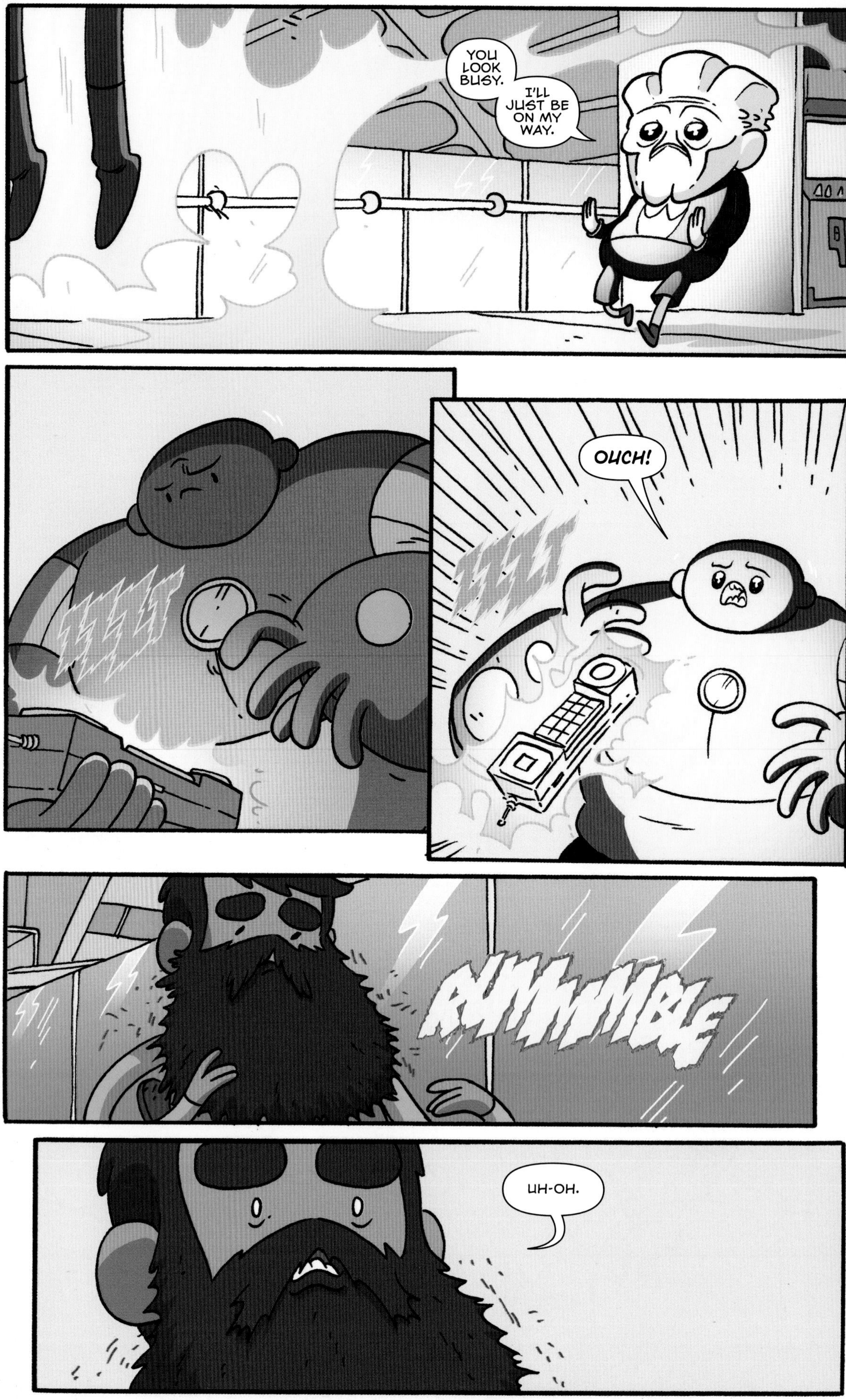
YOU LOOK BUSY.
I'LL JUST BE ON MY WAY.
OUCH!
RUMMMBLE
UH-OH.

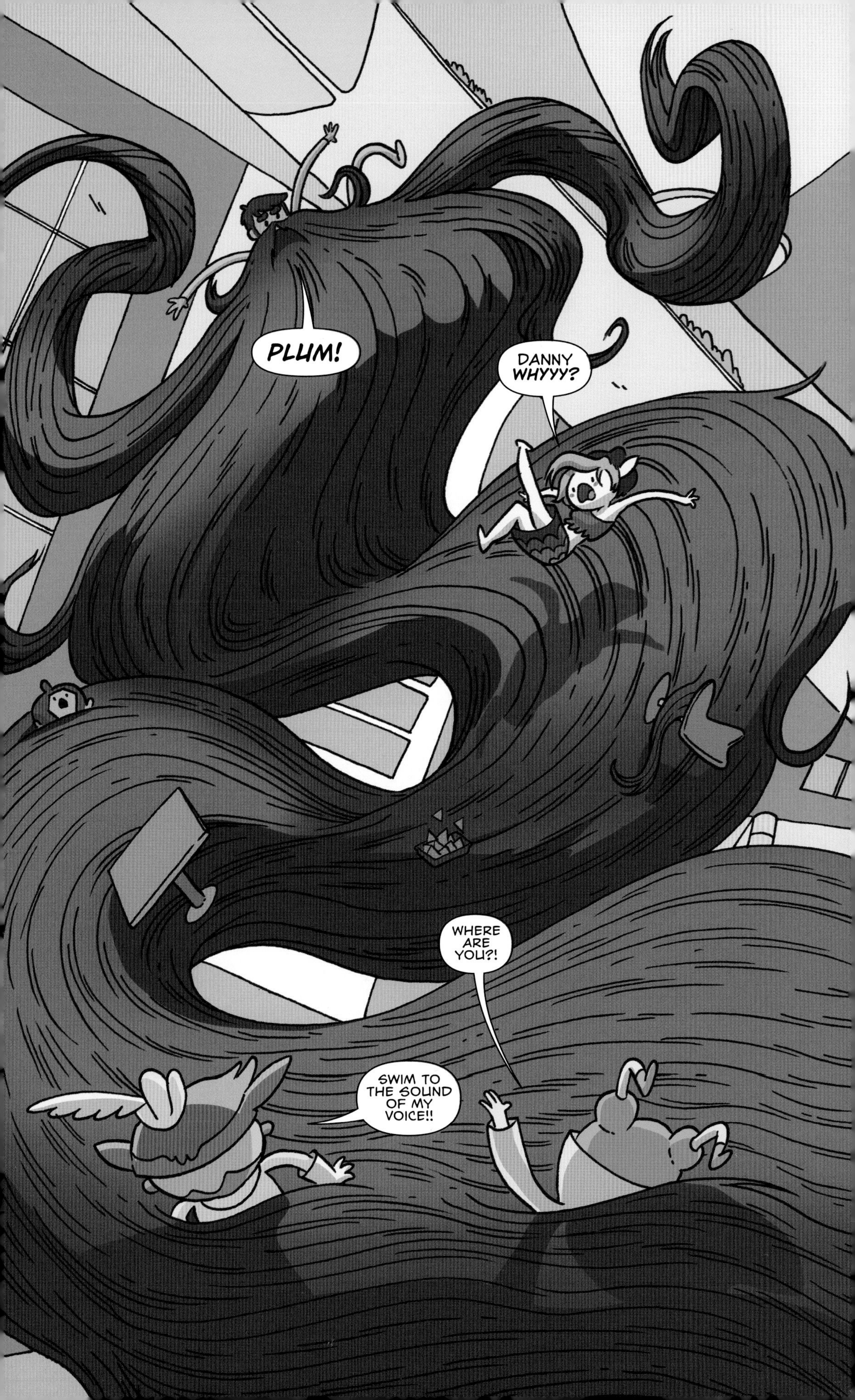
PLUM!
DANNY WHYYY?
WHERE ARE YOU?!
SWIM TO THE SOUND OF MY VOICE!!

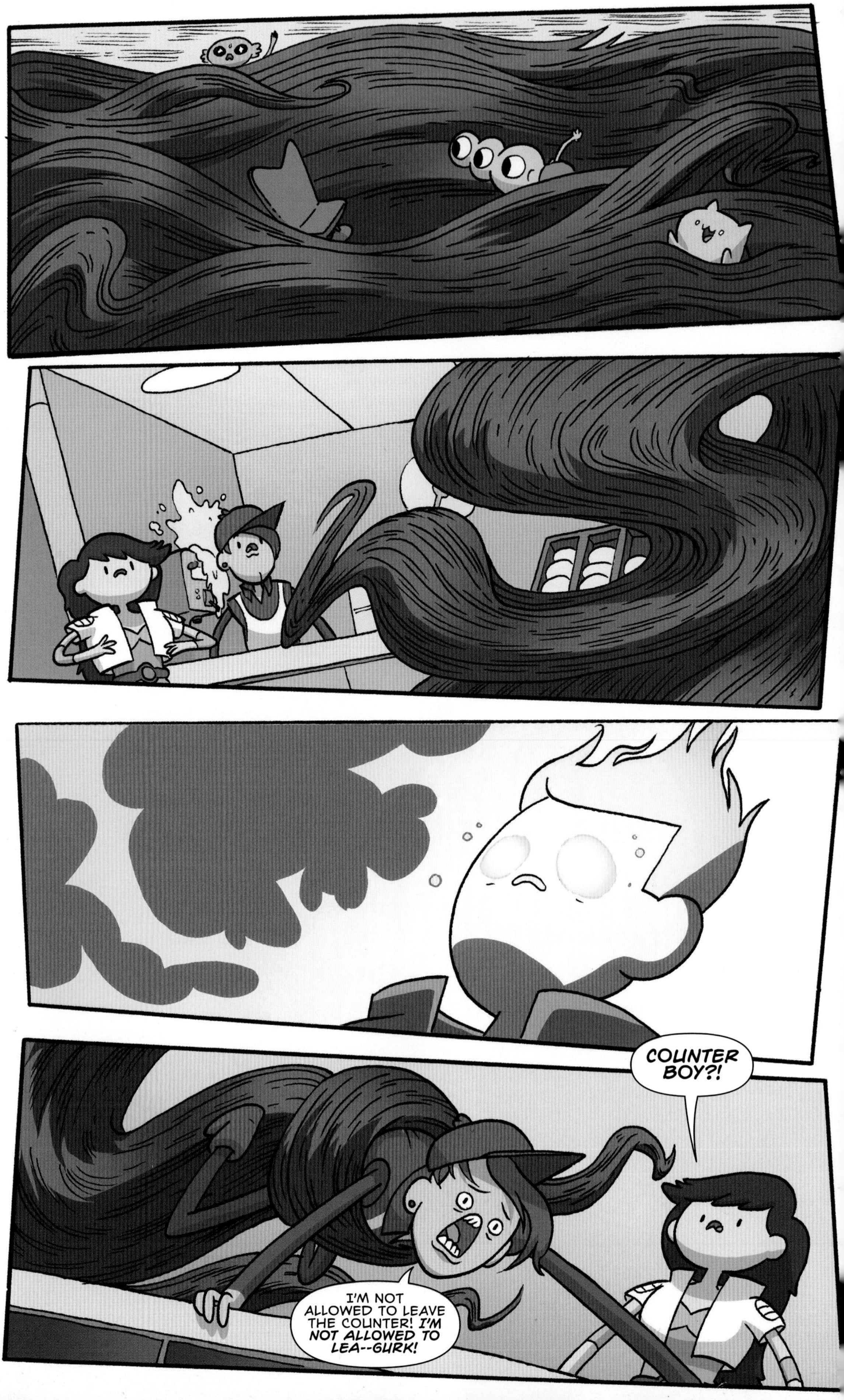
COUNTER BOY?!
I'M NOT ALLOWED TO LEAVE THE COUNTER! *I'M NOT ALLOWED TO LEA--GURK!*

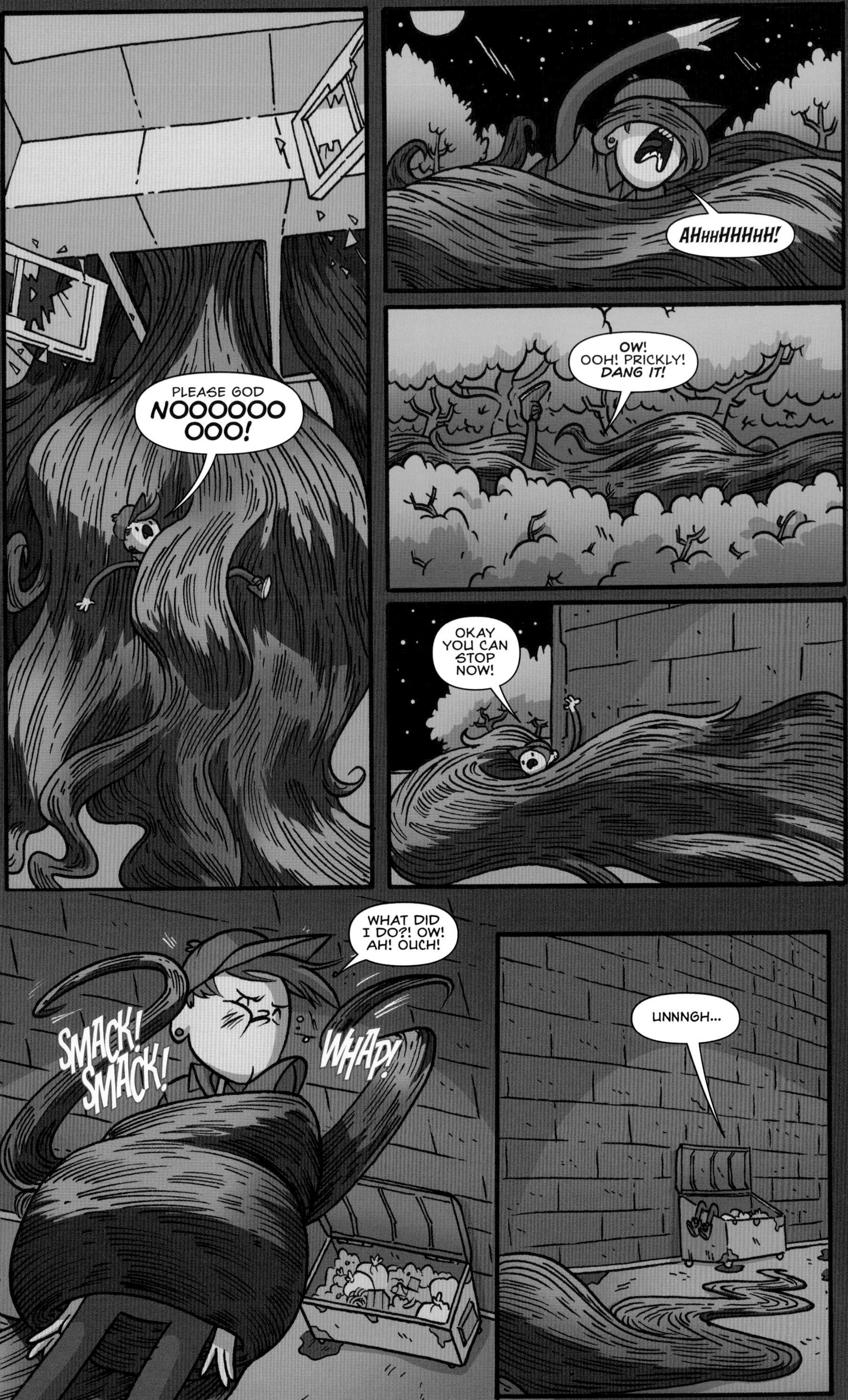
PLEASE GOD NOOOOOOOOO!
AHHHHHHHH!
OW! OOH! PRICKLY! DANG IT!
OKAY YOU CAN STOP NOW!
WHAT DID I DO?! OW! AH! OUCH!
SMACK! SMACK!
WHAP!
UNNNGH...

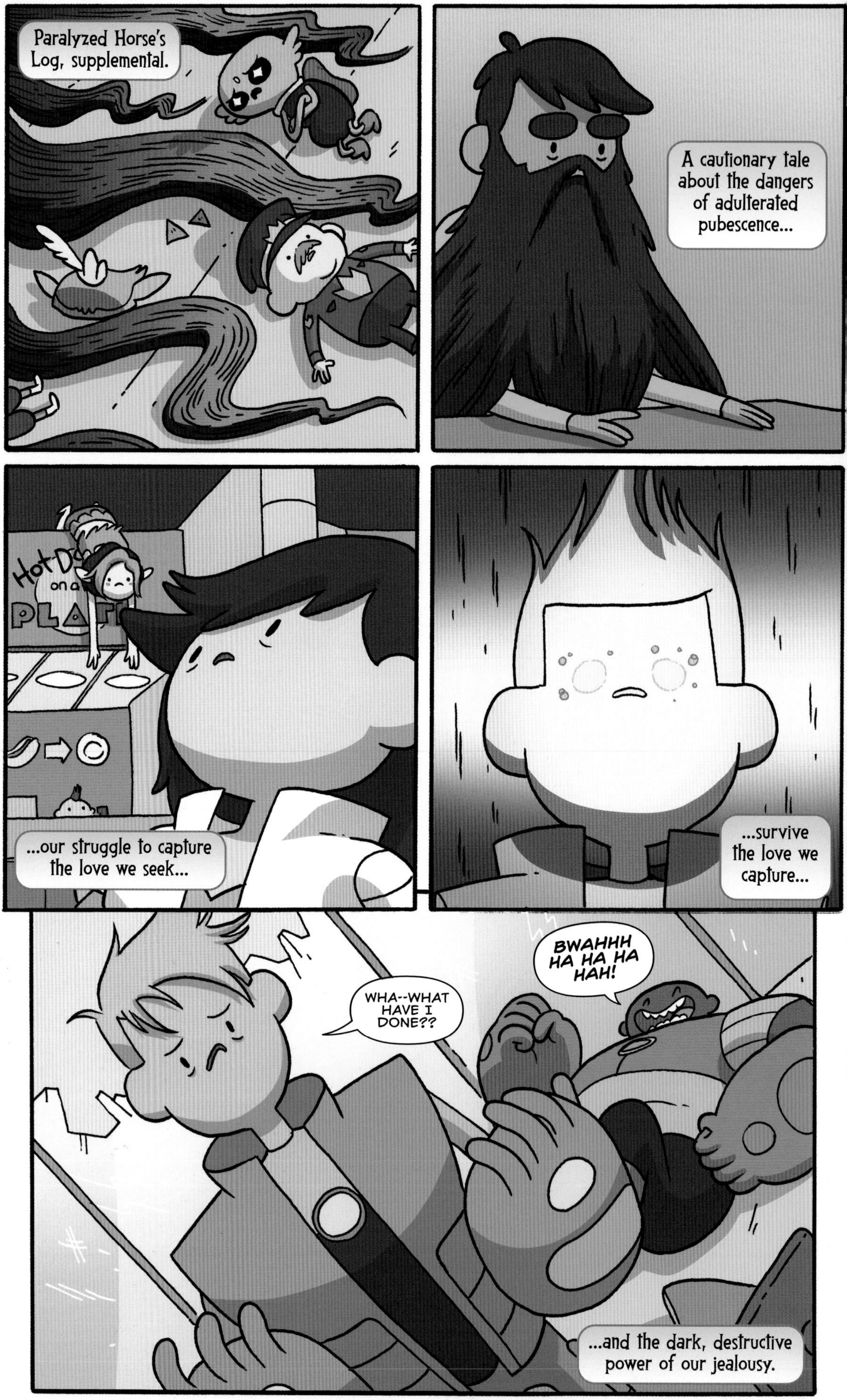
Paralyzed Horse's Log, supplemental.
A cautionary tale about the dangers of adulterated pubescence...
...our struggle to capture the love we seek...
...survive the love we capture...
WHA--WHAT HAVE I DONE??
BWAHHH HA HA HA HAH!
...and the dark, destructive power of our jealousy.

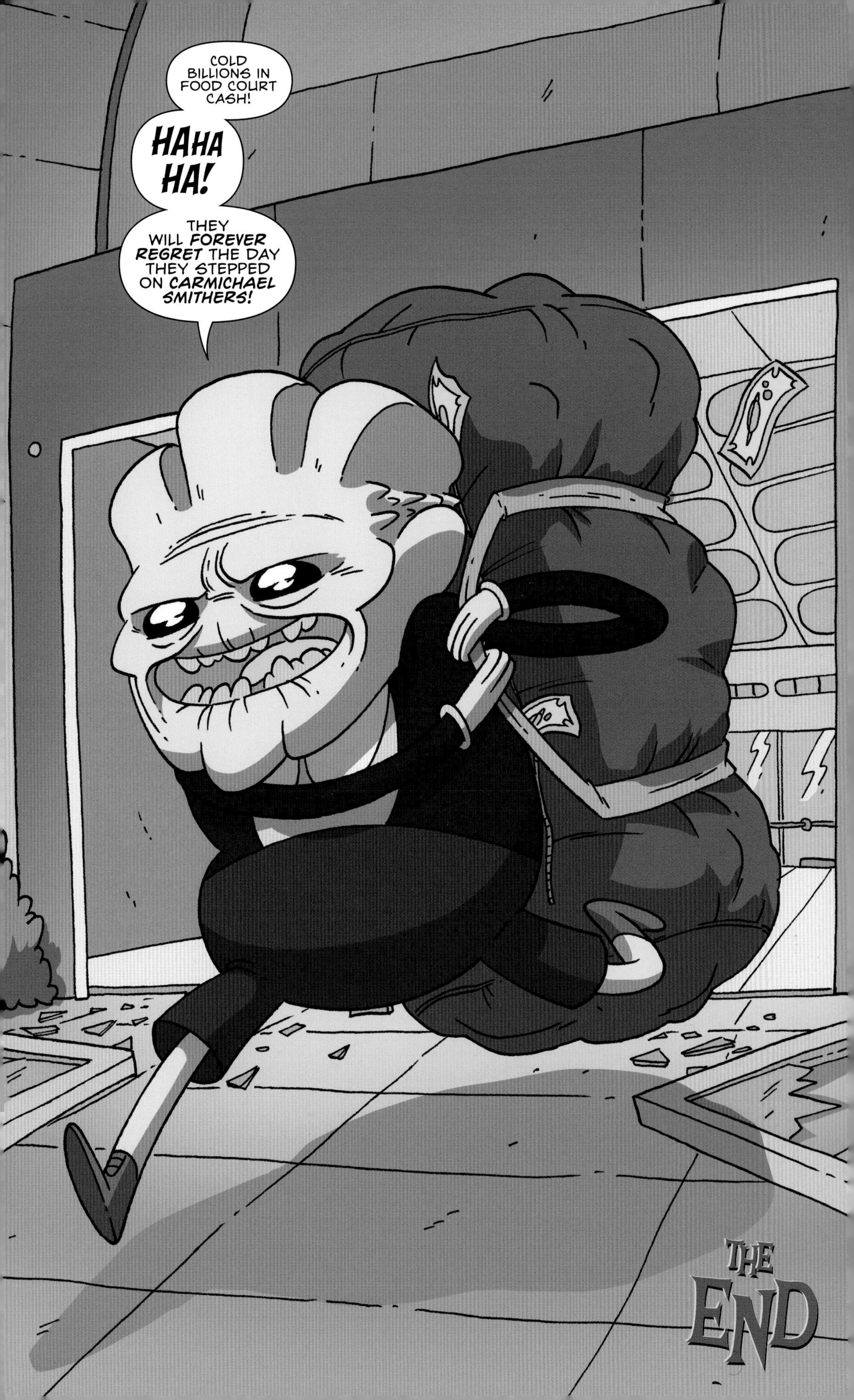
COLD BILLIONS IN FOOD COURT CASH!
HAHA HA!
THEY WILL FOREVER REGRET THE DAY THEY STEPPED ON CARMICHAEL SMITHERS!
THE END

CHAPTER FIFTEEN

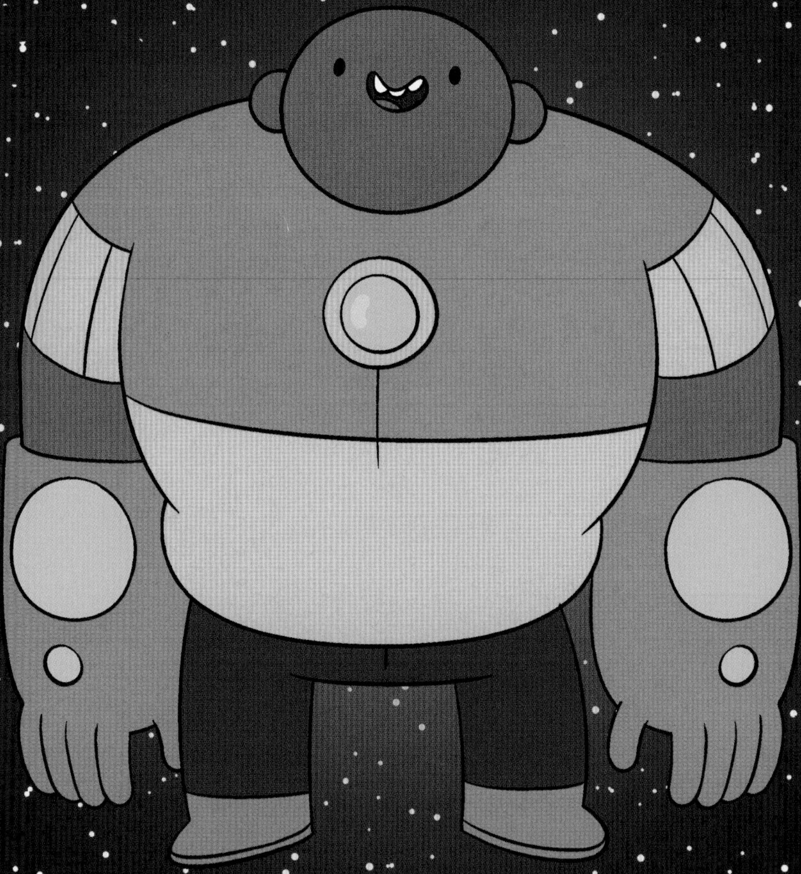

UP, DOWN, RIGHT, RIGHT,
A, B, SELECT, START

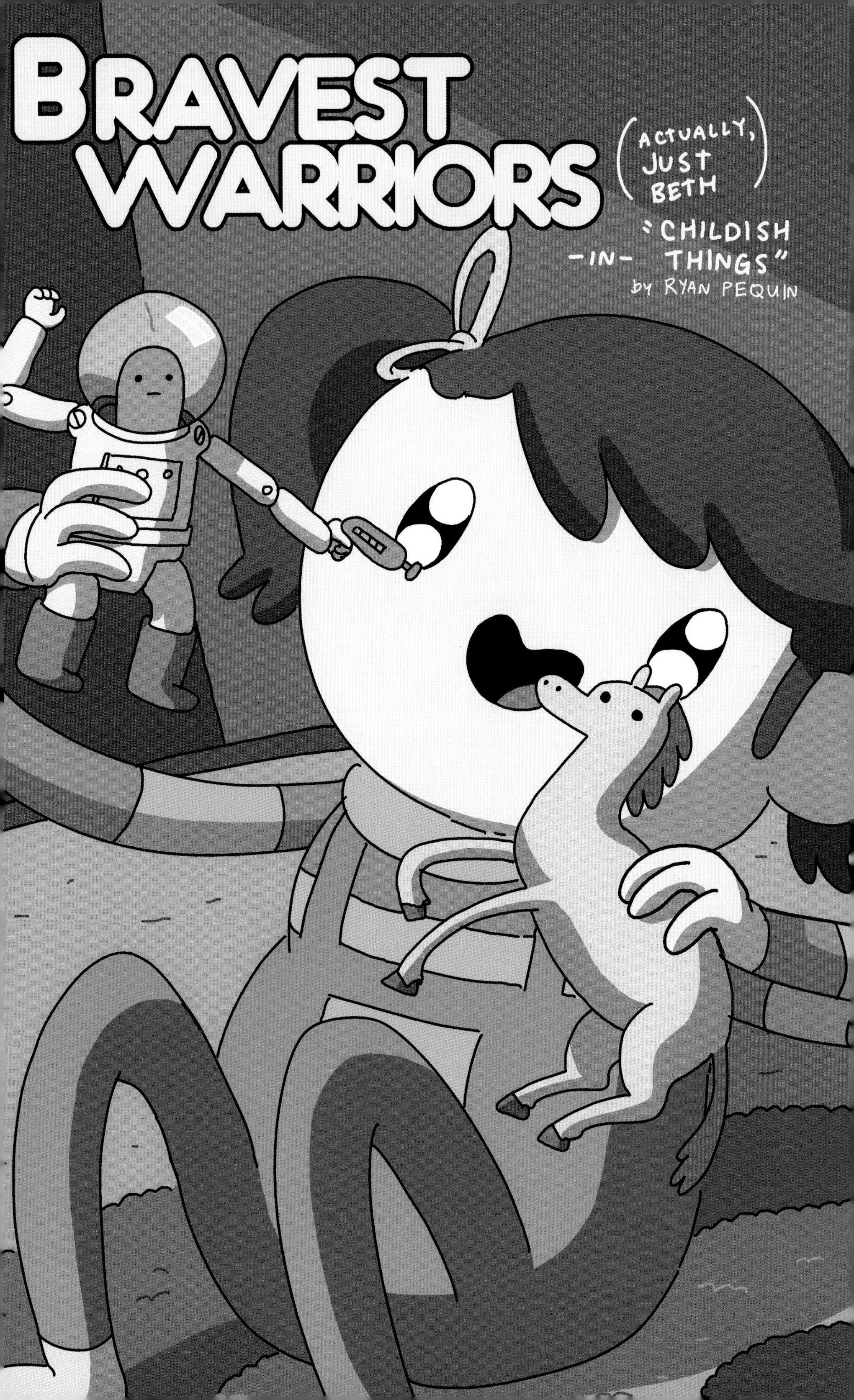
BRAVEST WARRIORS
(ACTUALLY, JUST BETH
-IN-
"CHILDISH THINGS"
by RYAN PEQUIN

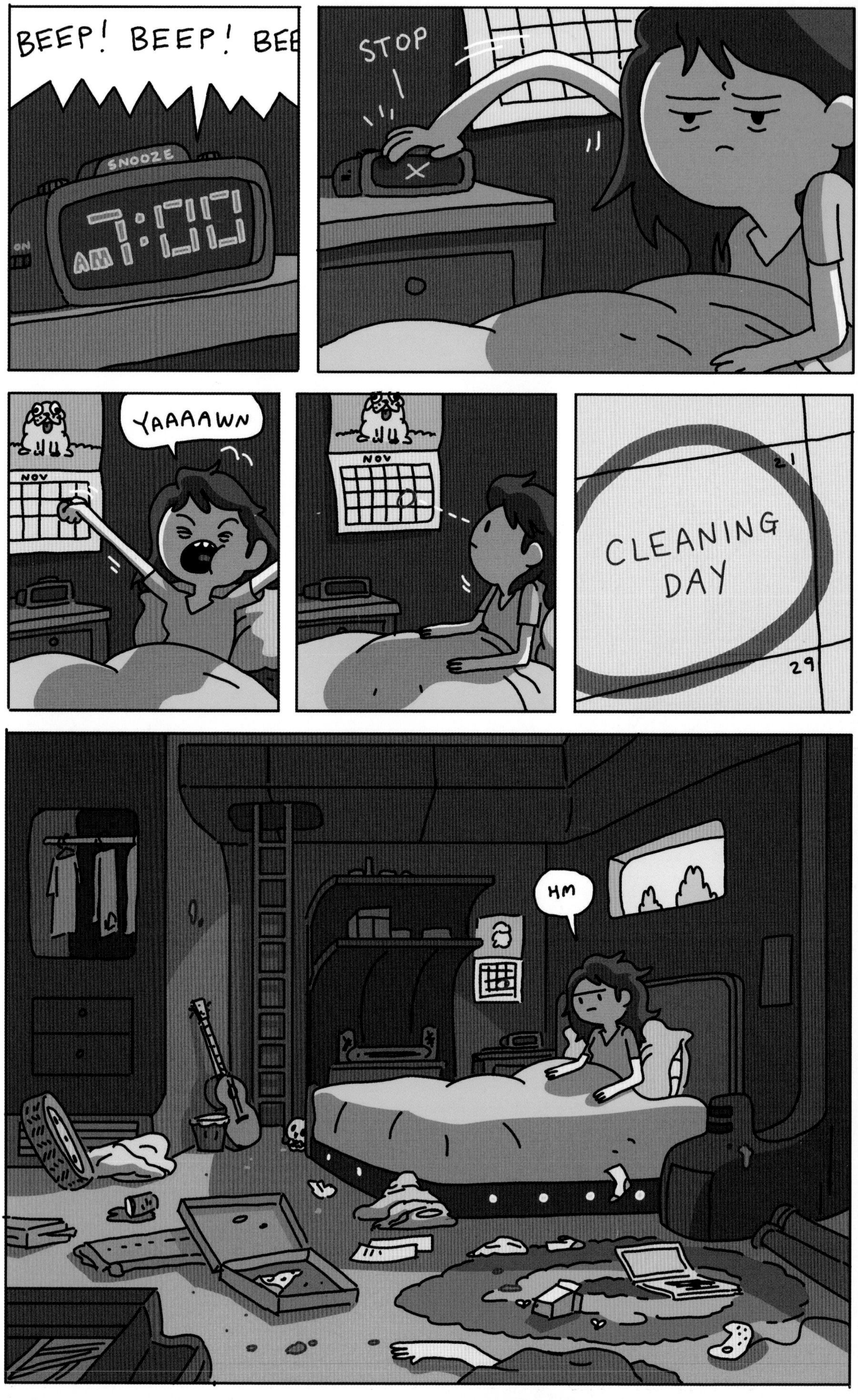
BEEP! BEEP! BEE
SNOOZE
AM 7:00
ON
STOP
YAAAAWN
NOV
NOV
21
CLEANING DAY
29
HM

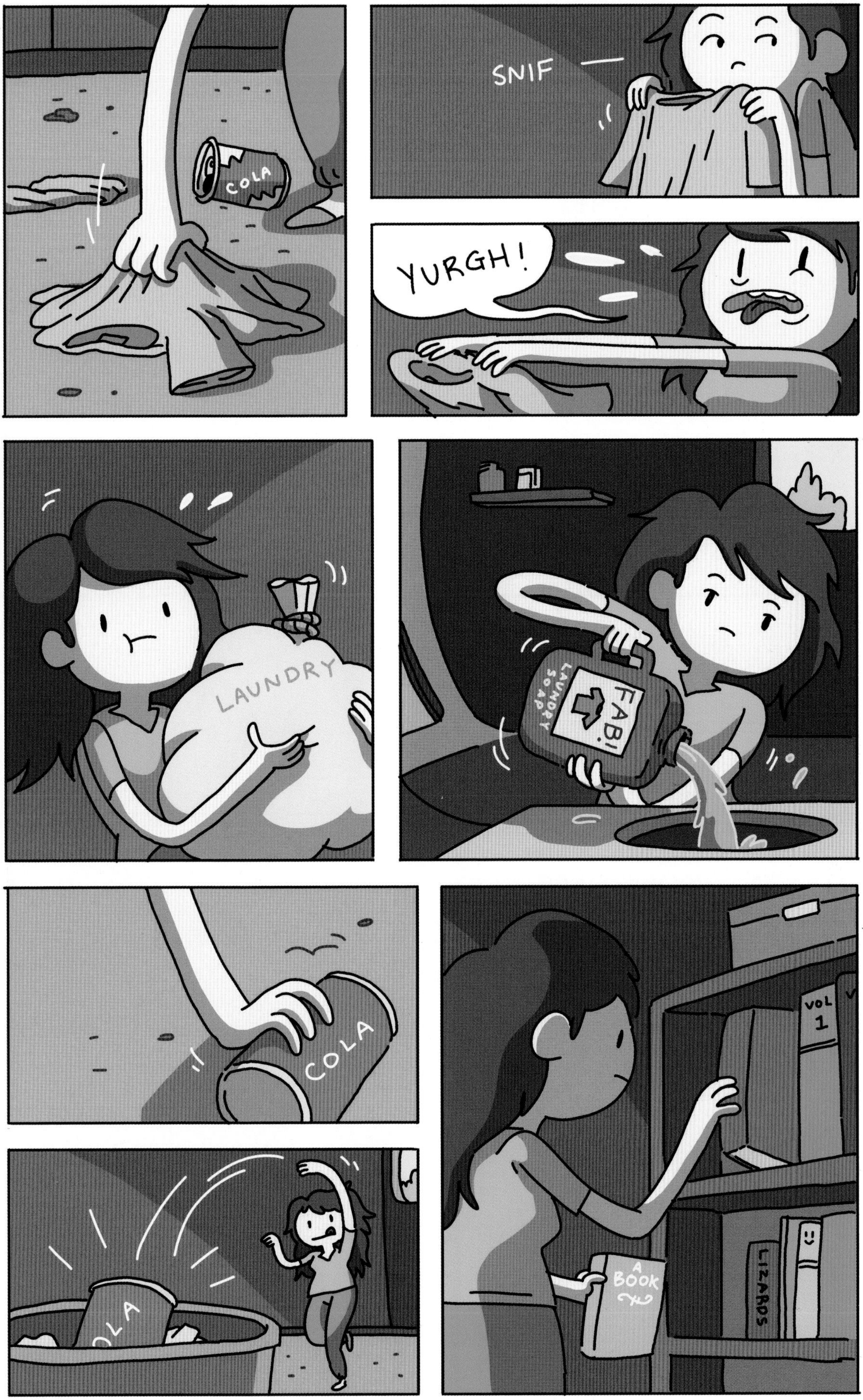
COLA
SNIF
YURGH!
LAUNDRY
FAB!
LAUNDRY SOAP
COLA
VOL 1
A BOOK
LIZARDS
OLA

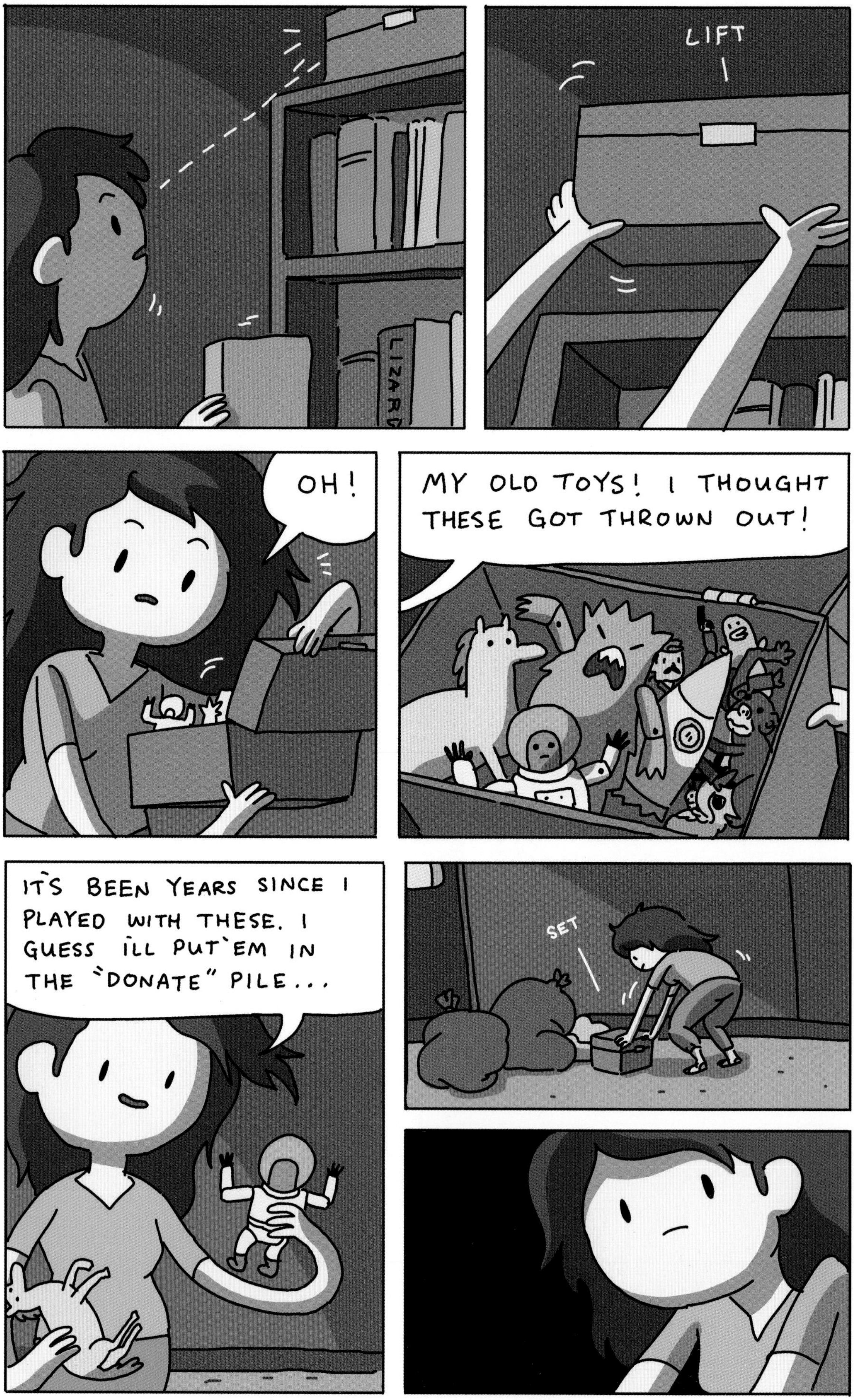
LIFT
OH!
MY OLD TOYS! I THOUGHT THESE GOT THROWN OUT!
IT'S BEEN YEARS SINCE I PLAYED WITH THESE. I GUESS I'LL PUT 'EM IN THE "DONATE" PILE...
SET

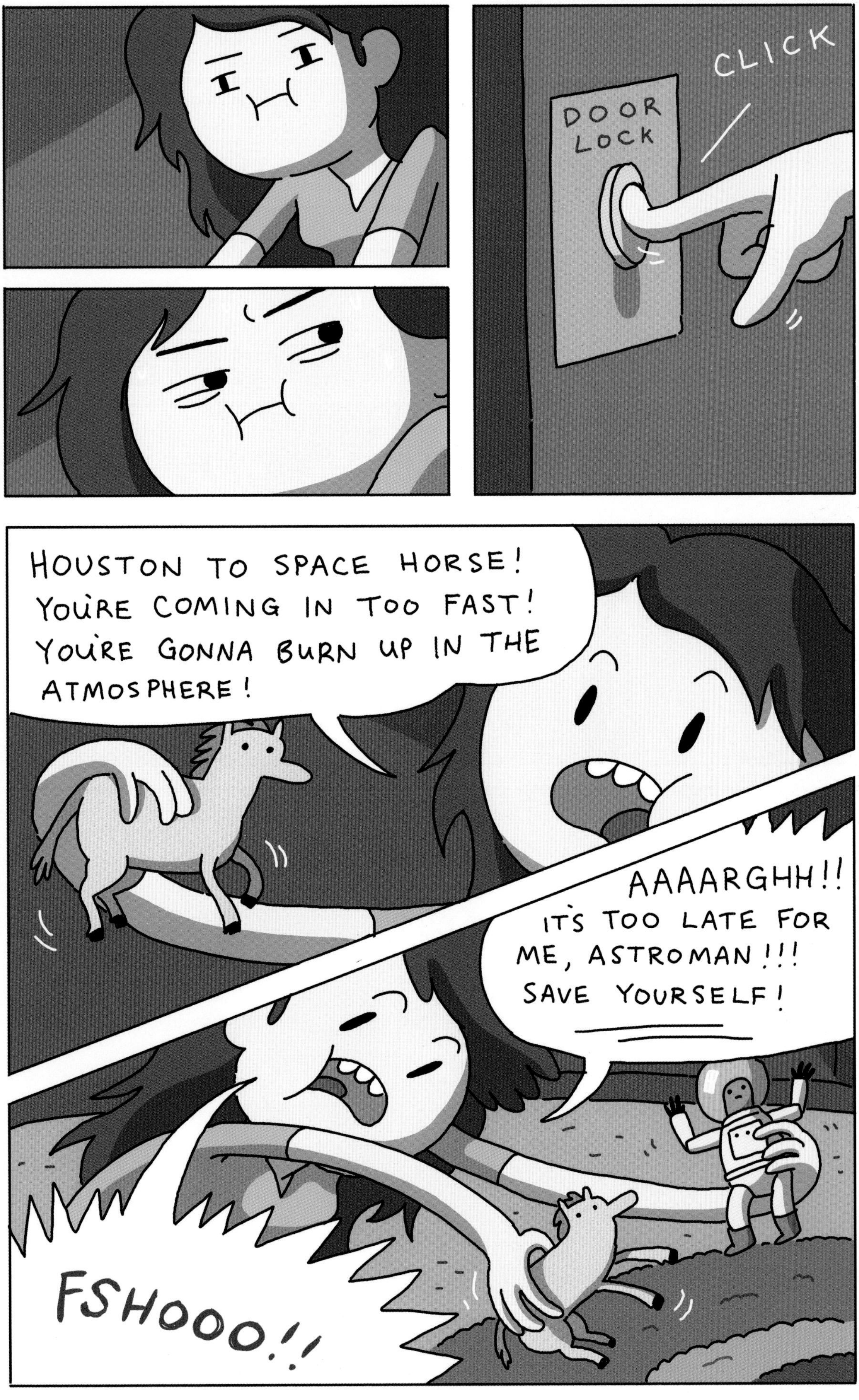
DOOR LOCK
CLICK
HOUSTON TO SPACE HORSE! YOU'RE COMING IN TOO FAST! YOU'RE GONNA BURN UP IN THE ATMOSPHERE!
AAAARGHH!! IT'S TOO LATE FOR ME, ASTROMAN!!! SAVE YOURSELF!
FSHOOO!!

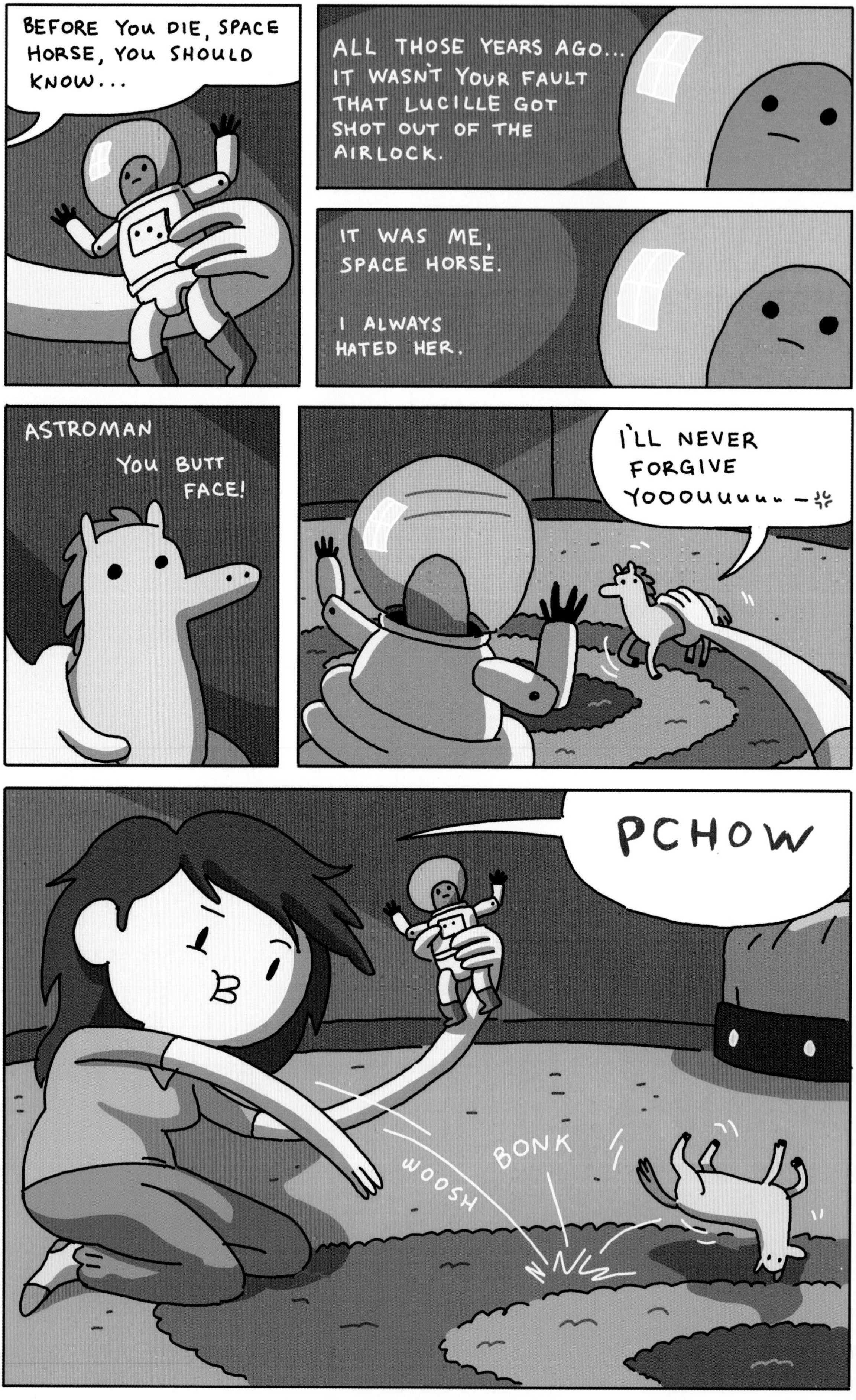
BEFORE YOU DIE, SPACE HORSE, YOU SHOULD KNOW...
ALL THOSE YEARS AGO... IT WASN'T YOUR FAULT THAT LUCILLE GOT SHOT OUT OF THE AIRLOCK.
IT WAS ME, SPACE HORSE.
I ALWAYS HATED HER.
ASTROMAN
YOU BUTT FACE!
I'LL NEVER FORGIVE YOOOUUUUU--
PCHOW
WOOSH
BONK

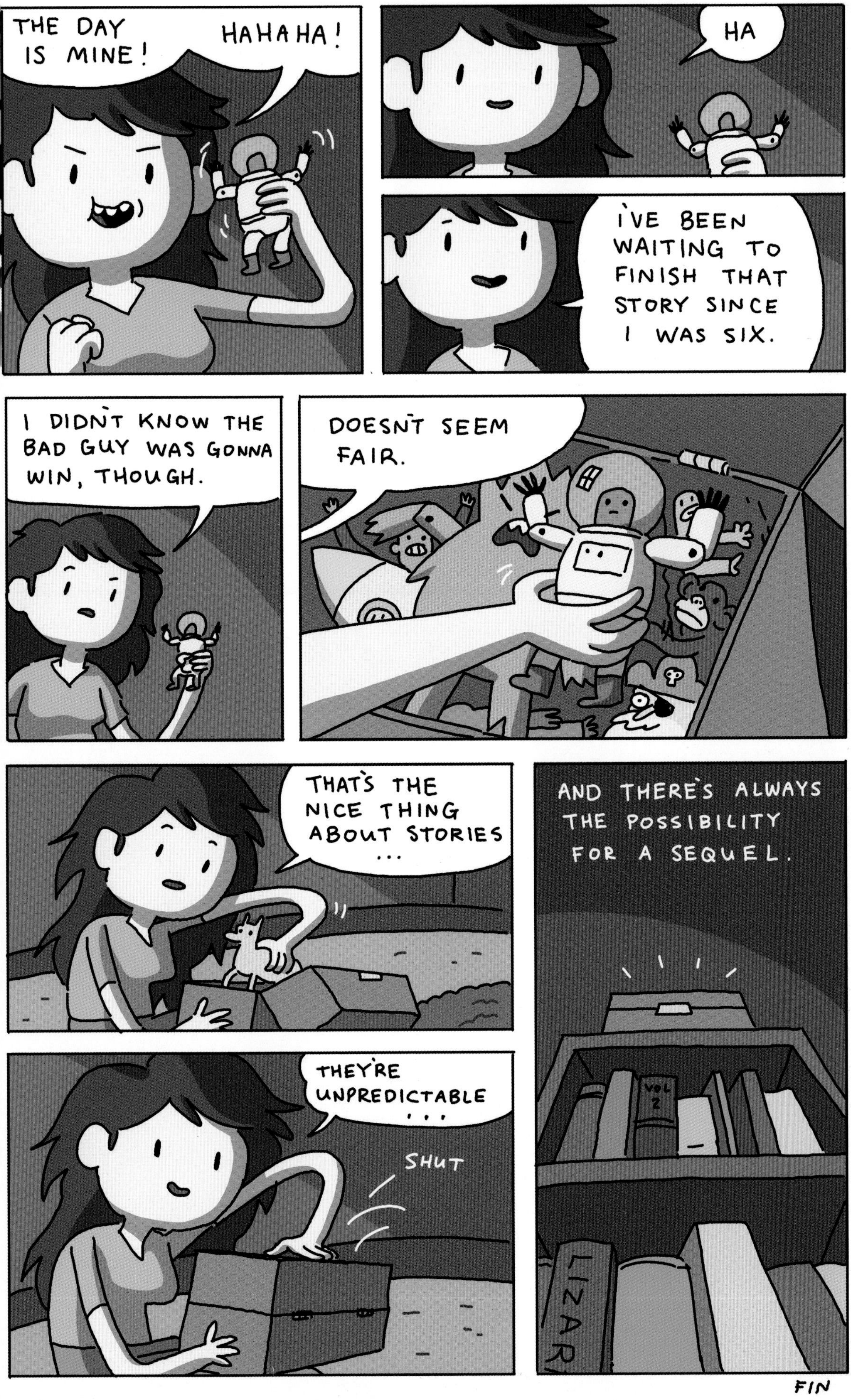
THE DAY IS MINE!
HAHAHA!
HA
I'VE BEEN WAITING TO FINISH THAT STORY SINCE I WAS SIX.
I DIDN'T KNOW THE BAD GUY WAS GONNA WIN, THOUGH.
DOESN'T SEEM FAIR.
THAT'S THE NICE THING ABOUT STORIES ...
AND THERE'S ALWAYS THE POSSIBILITY FOR A SEQUEL.
VOL 2
THEY'RE UNPREDICTABLE ...
SHUT
LINAR
FIN

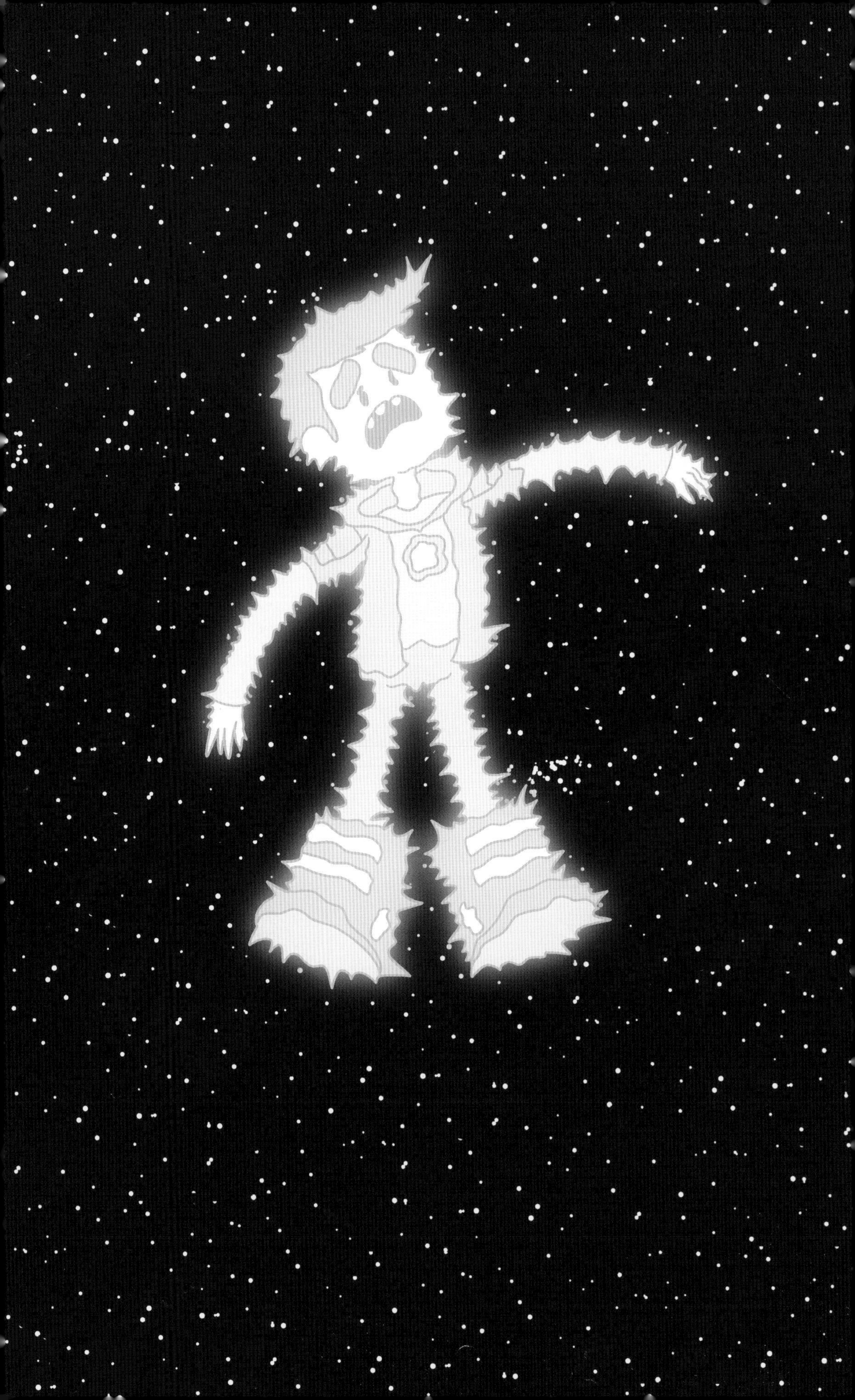

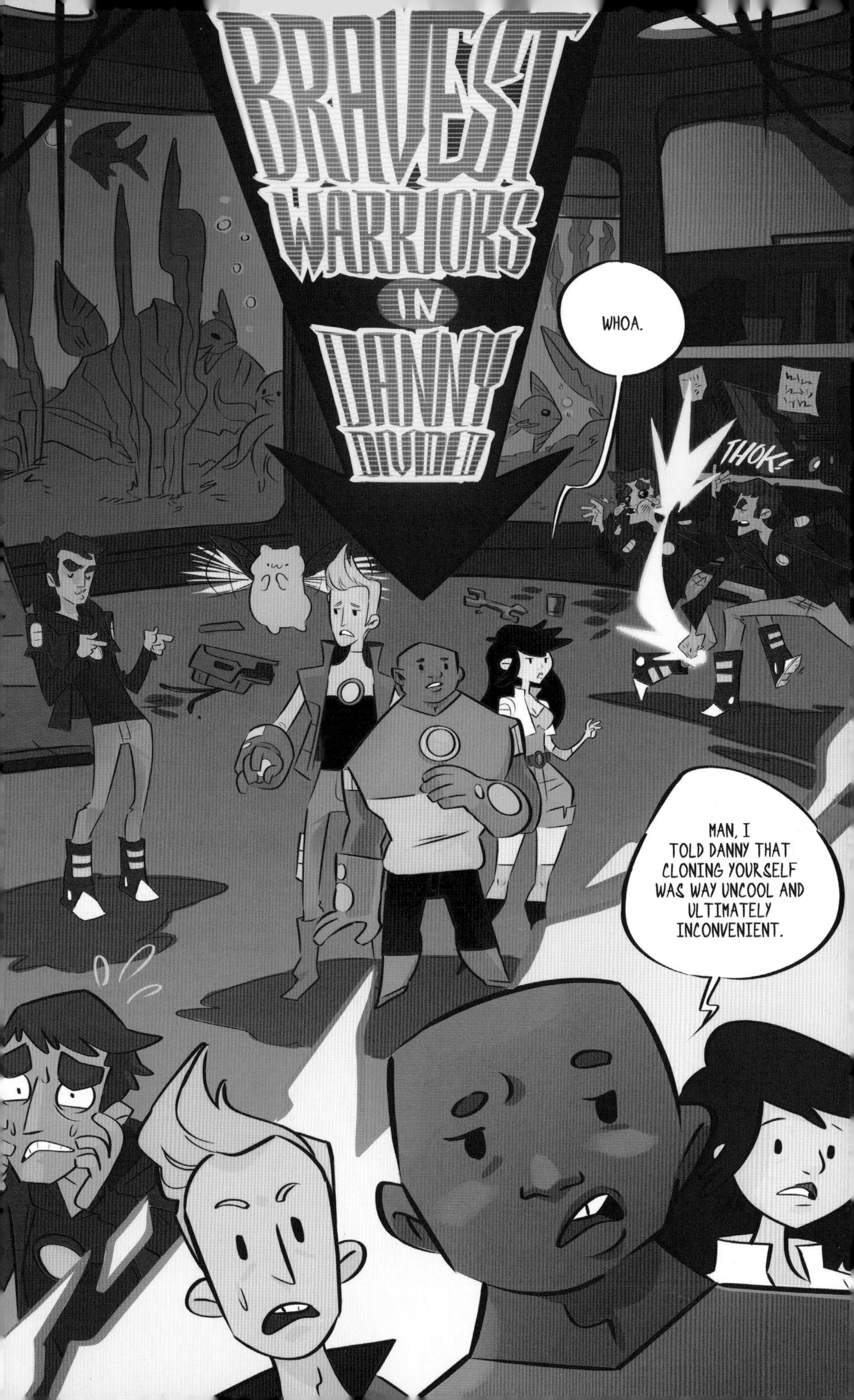
BRAVEST WARRIORS
IN
WHOA.
THOK!
MAN, I TOLD DANNY THAT CLONING YOURSELF WAS WAY UNCOOL AND ULTIMATELY INCONVENIENT.

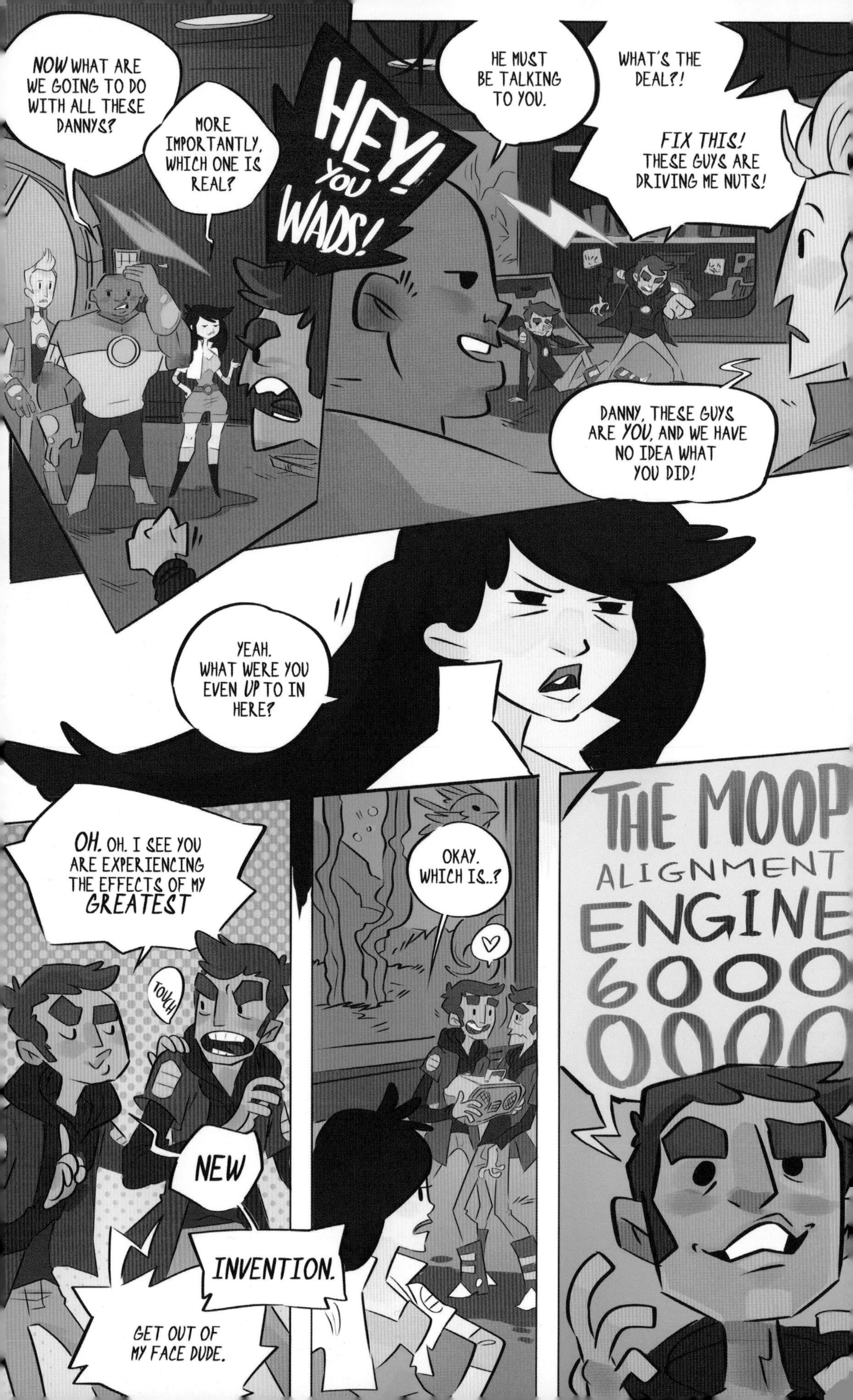
NOW WHAT ARE WE GOING TO DO WITH ALL THESE DANNYS?
MORE IMPORTANTLY, WHICH ONE IS REAL?
HEY! YOU WADS!
HE MUST BE TALKING TO YOU.
WHAT'S THE DEAL?!
FIX THIS! THESE GUYS ARE DRIVING ME NUTS!
DANNY, THESE GUYS ARE YOU, AND WE HAVE NO IDEA WHAT YOU DID!
YEAH. WHAT WERE YOU EVEN UP TO IN HERE?
OH. OH. I SEE YOU ARE EXPERIENCING THE EFFECTS OF MY GREATEST
TOUCH
NEW
INVENTION.
GET OUT OF MY FACE DUDE.
OKAY. WHICH IS..?
THE MOOP ALIGNMENT ENGINE 6000 0000

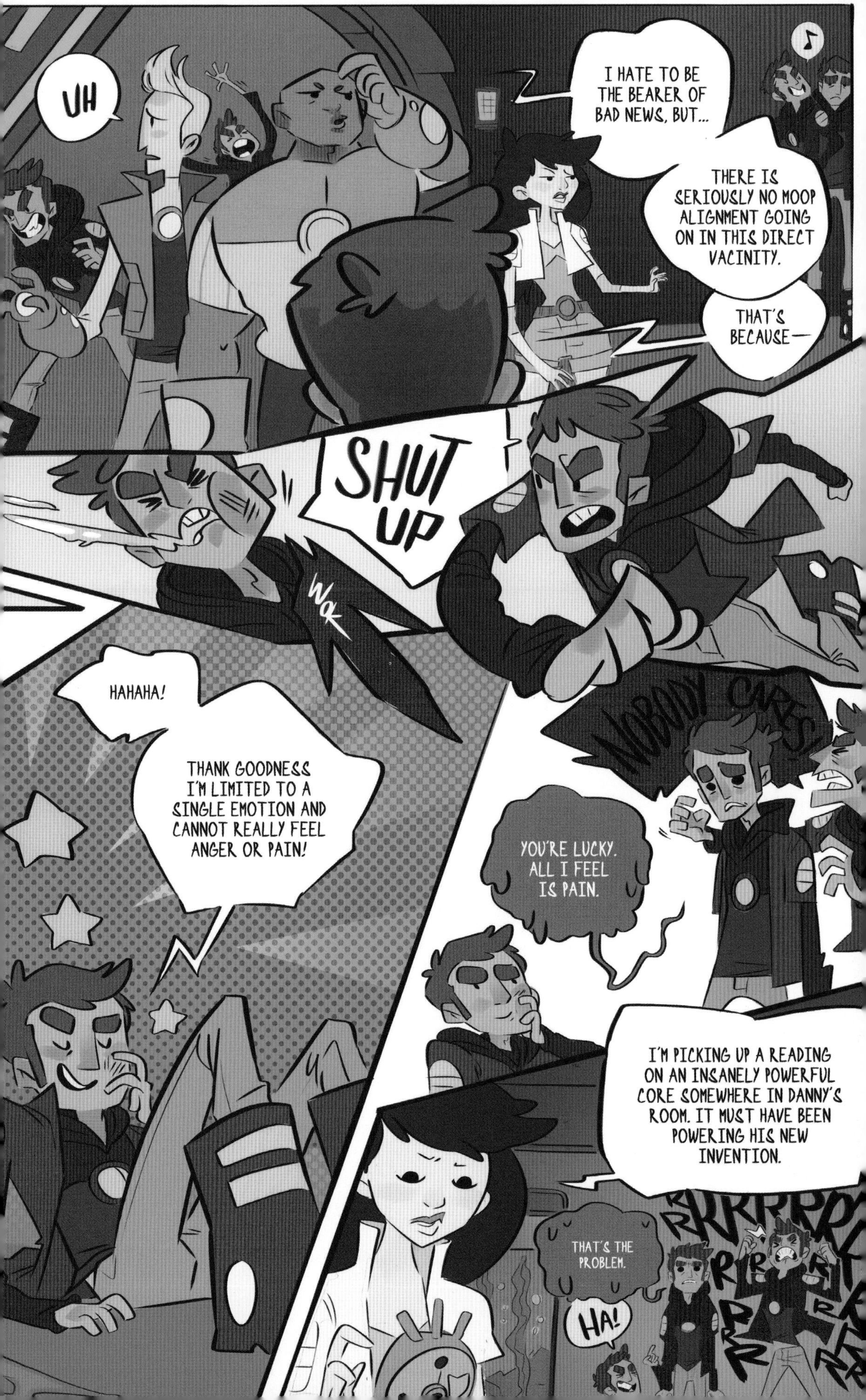
UH
I HATE TO BE THE BEARER OF BAD NEWS, BUT...
THERE IS SERIOUSLY NO MOOP ALIGNMENT GOING ON IN THIS DIRECT VACINITY.
THAT'S BECAUSE—
SHUT UP
WOK
HAHAHA!
THANK GOODNESS I'M LIMITED TO A SINGLE EMOTION AND CANNOT REALLY FEEL ANGER OR PAIN!
NOBODY CARES!
YOU'RE LUCKY. ALL I FEEL IS PAIN.
I'M PICKING UP A READING ON AN INSANELY POWERFUL CORE SOMEWHERE IN DANNY'S ROOM. IT MUST HAVE BEEN POWERING HIS NEW INVENTION.
THAT'S THE PROBLEM.
HA!

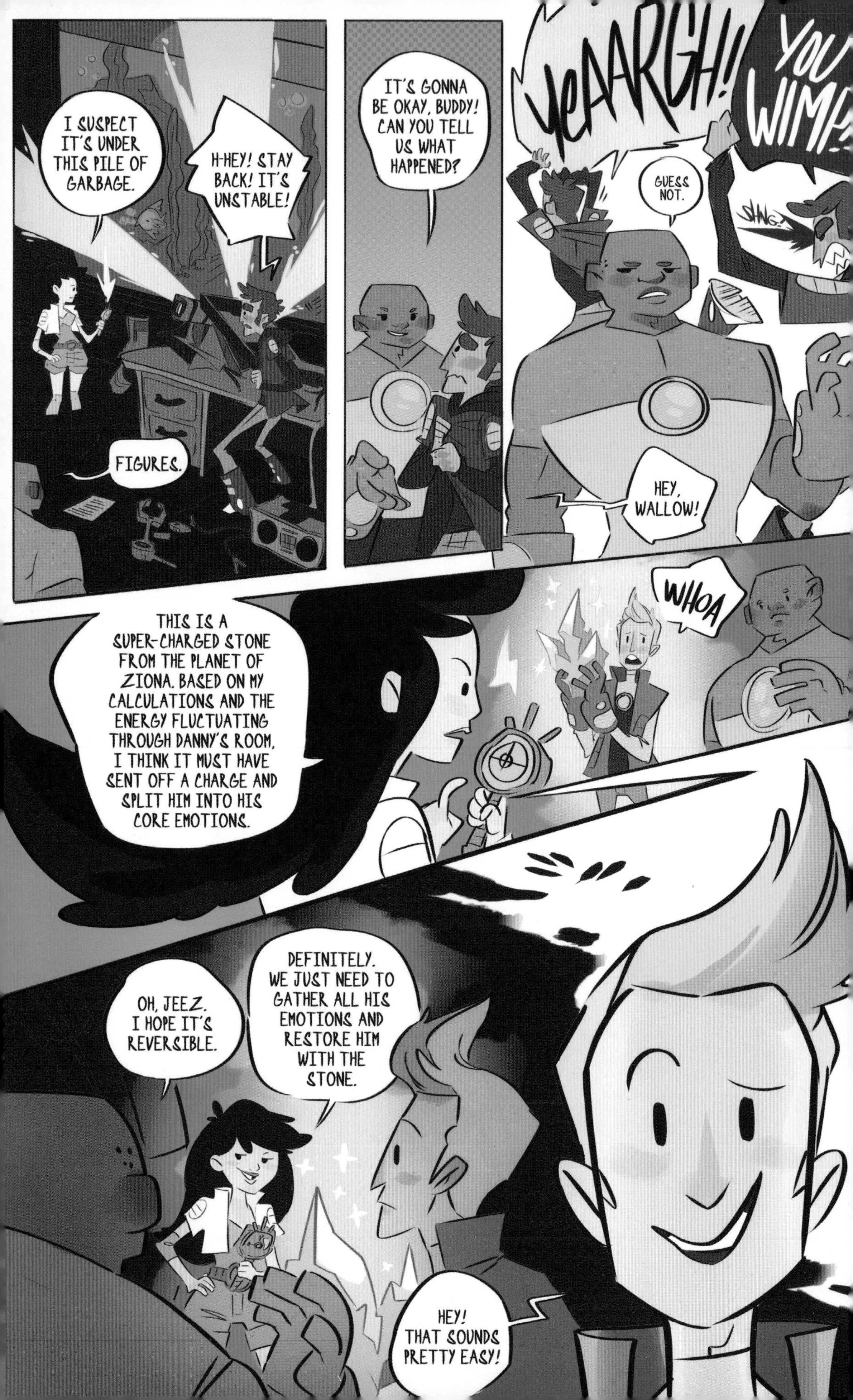
I SUSPECT IT'S UNDER THIS PILE OF GARBAGE.
H-HEY! STAY BACK! IT'S UNSTABLE!
FIGURES.
IT'S GONNA BE OKAY, BUDDY! CAN YOU TELL US WHAT HAPPENED?
YEAARGH!!
YOU WIMP
GUESS NOT.
SHING!
HEY, WALLOW!
THIS IS A SUPER-CHARGED STONE FROM THE PLANET OF ZIONA. BASED ON MY CALCULATIONS AND THE ENERGY FLUCTUATING THROUGH DANNY'S ROOM, I THINK IT MUST HAVE SENT OFF A CHARGE AND SPLIT HIM INTO HIS CORE EMOTIONS.
WHOA
OH, JEEZ. I HOPE IT'S REVERSIBLE.
DEFINITELY. WE JUST NEED TO GATHER ALL HIS EMOTIONS AND RESTORE HIM WITH THE STONE.
HEY! THAT SOUNDS PRETTY EASY!

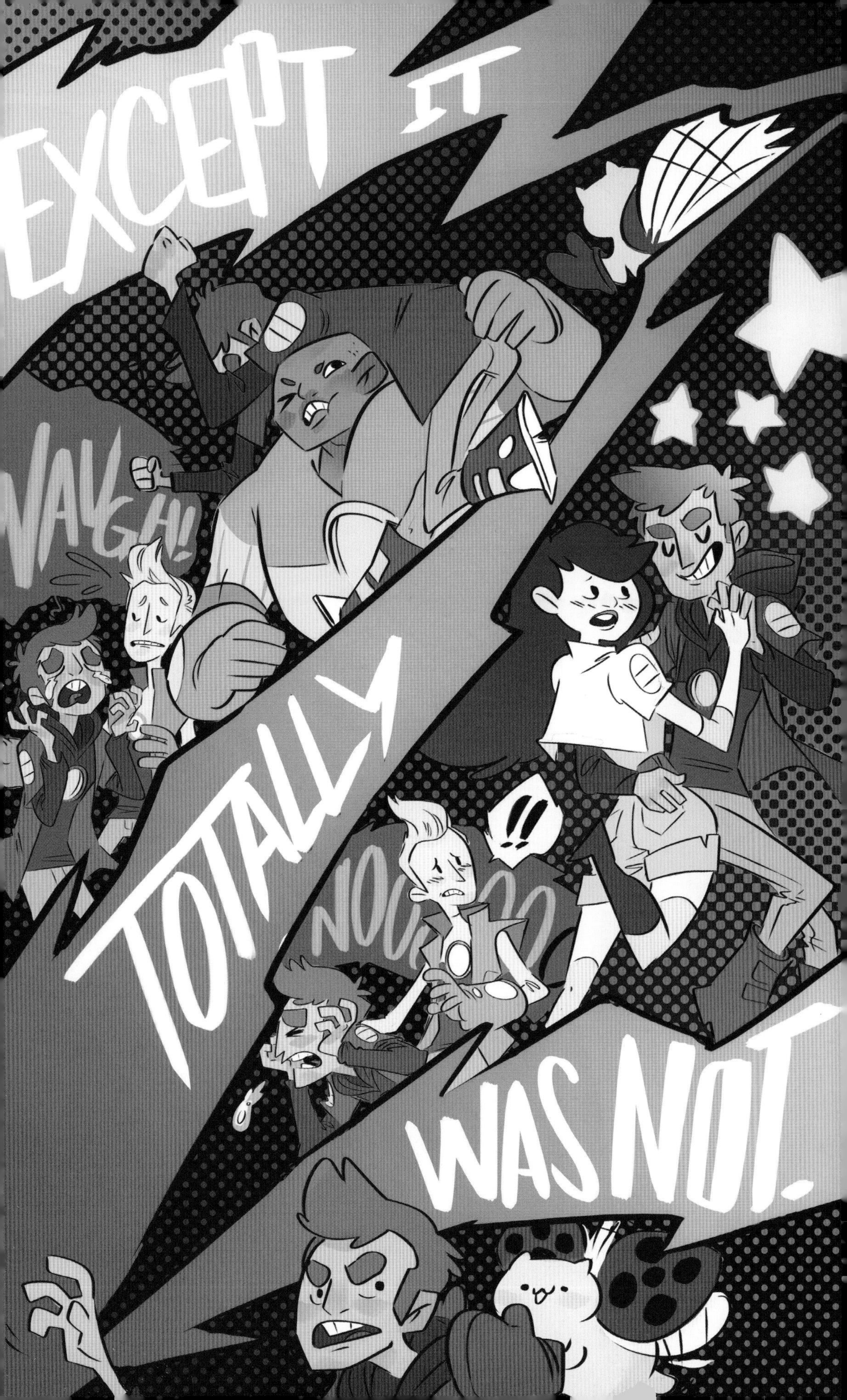
EXCEPT IT
VAUGH!
TOTALLY
WAS NOT.

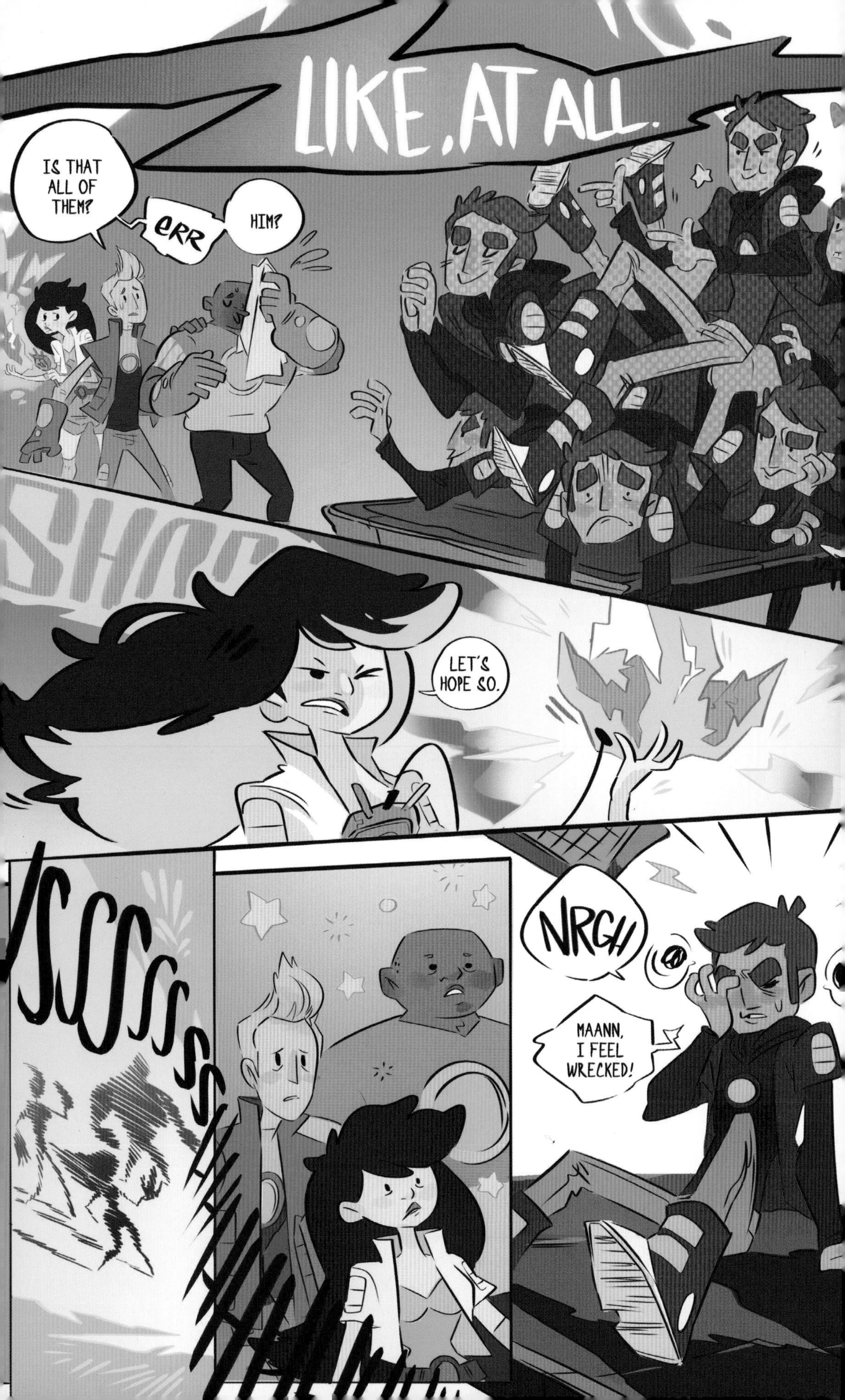
LIKE, AT ALL.
IS THAT ALL OF THEM?
ERR
HIM?
LET'S HOPE SO.
NRGH
MAANN, I FEEL WRECKED!

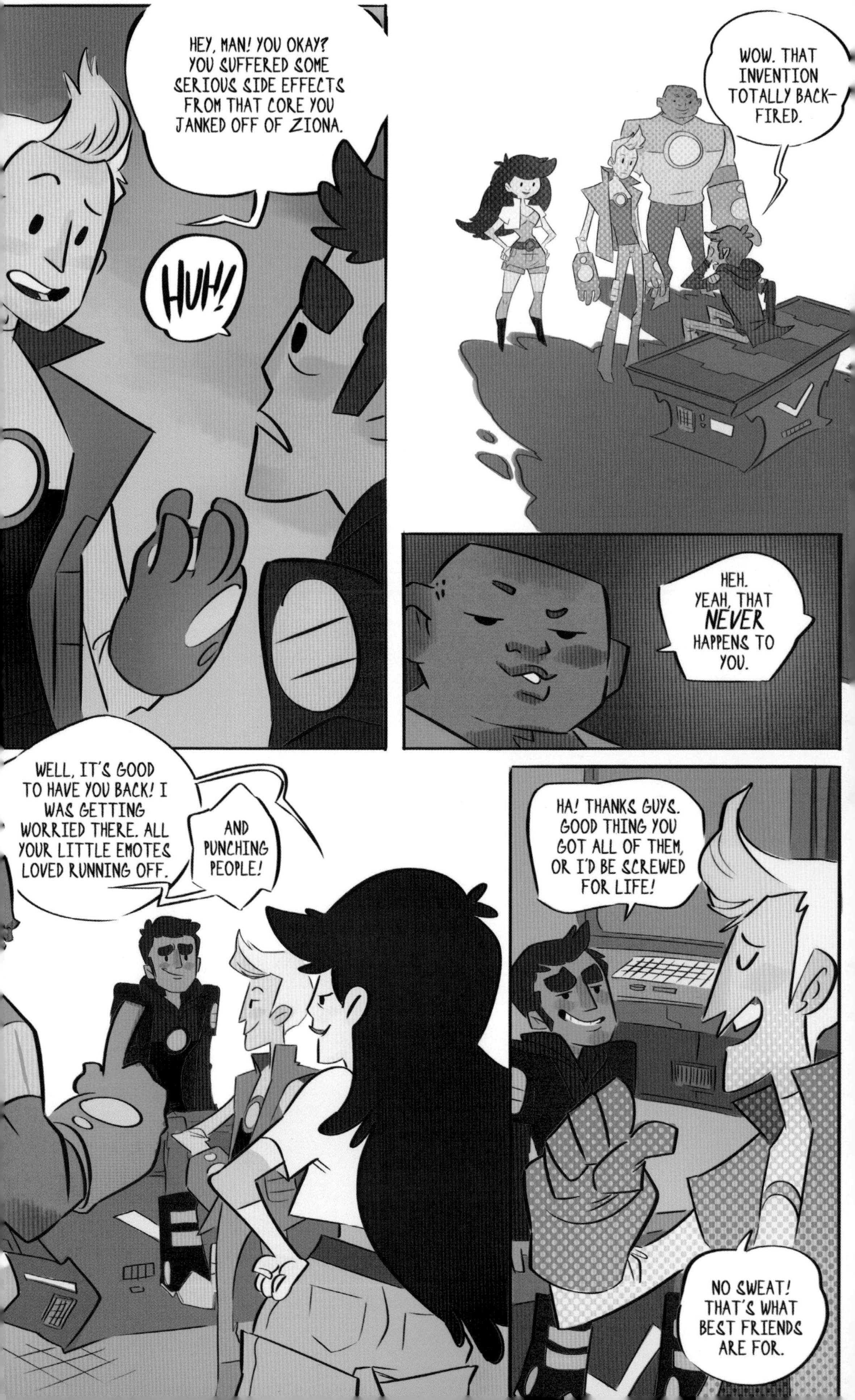
HEY, MAN! YOU OKAY? YOU SUFFERED SOME SERIOUS SIDE EFFECTS FROM THAT CORE YOU JANKED OFF OF ZIONA.
HUH!
WOW. THAT INVENTION TOTALLY BACK-FIRED.
HEH. YEAH, THAT NEVER HAPPENS TO YOU.
WELL, IT'S GOOD TO HAVE YOU BACK! I WAS GETTING WORRIED THERE. ALL YOUR LITTLE EMOTES LOVED RUNNING OFF.
AND PUNCHING PEOPLE!
HA! THANKS GUYS. GOOD THING YOU GOT ALL OF THEM, OR I'D BE SCREWED FOR LIFE!
NO SWEAT! THAT'S WHAT BEST FRIENDS ARE FOR.

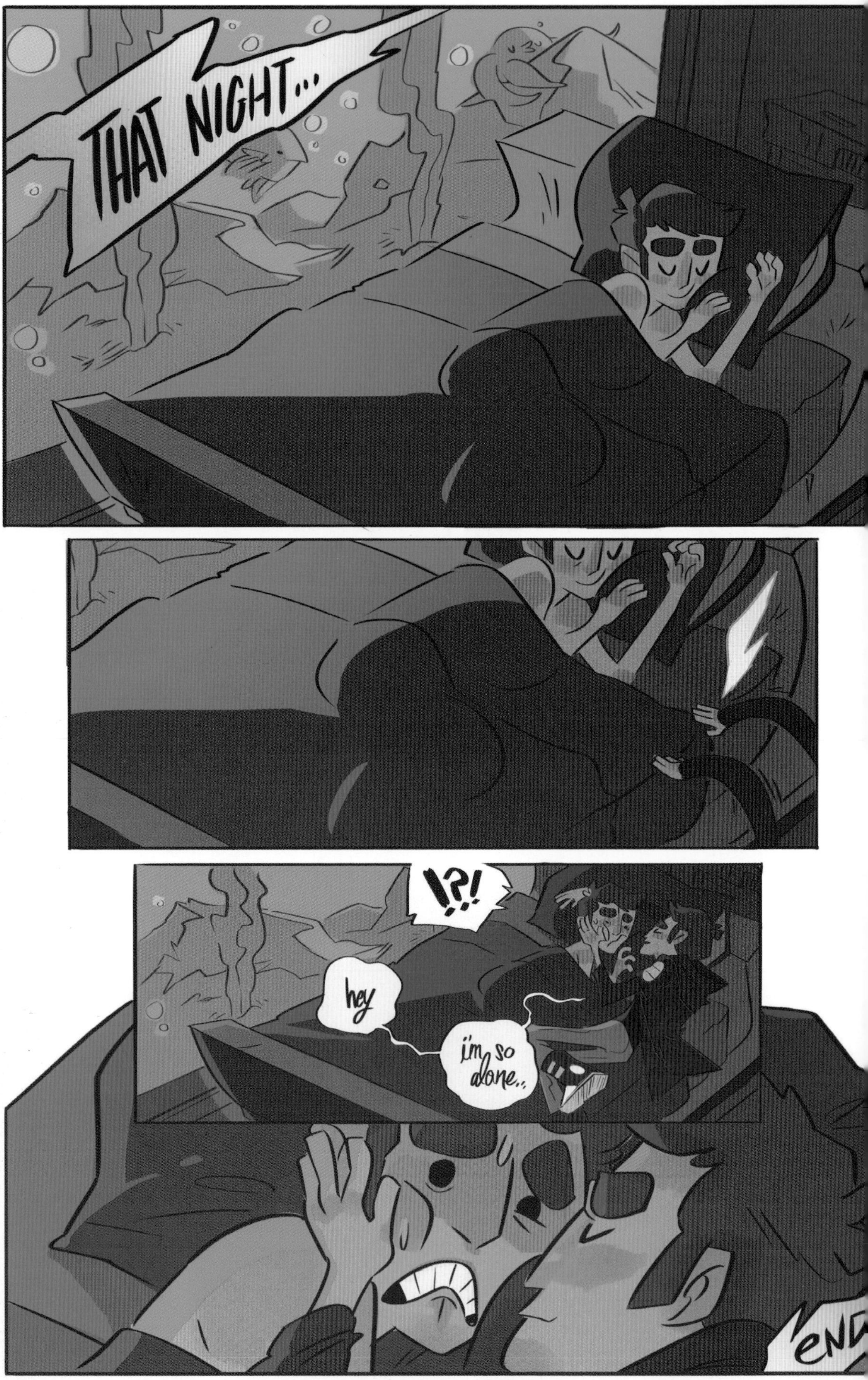
THAT NIGHT...
!?!
hey
i'm so done..
END

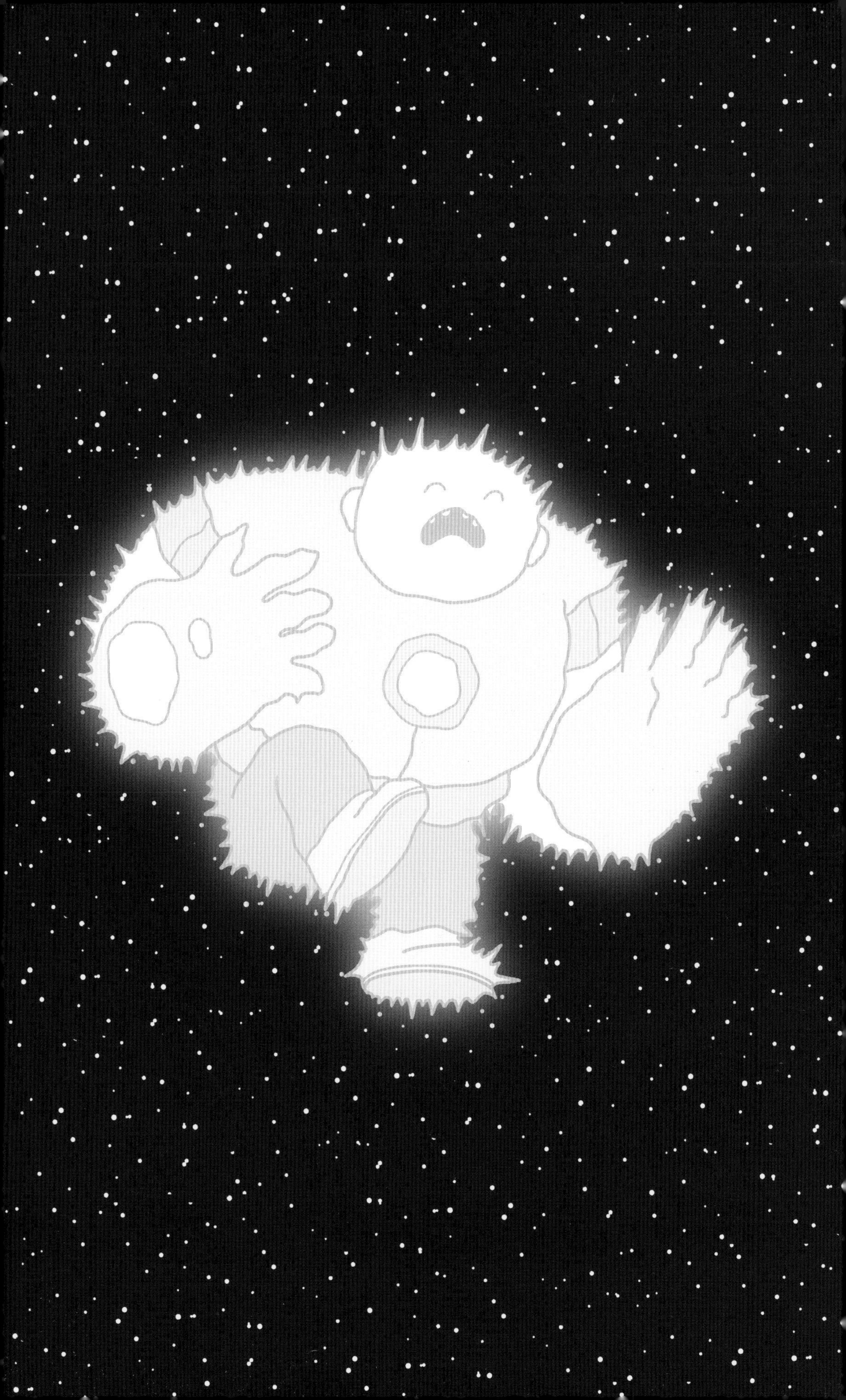

CHAPTER SIXTEEN

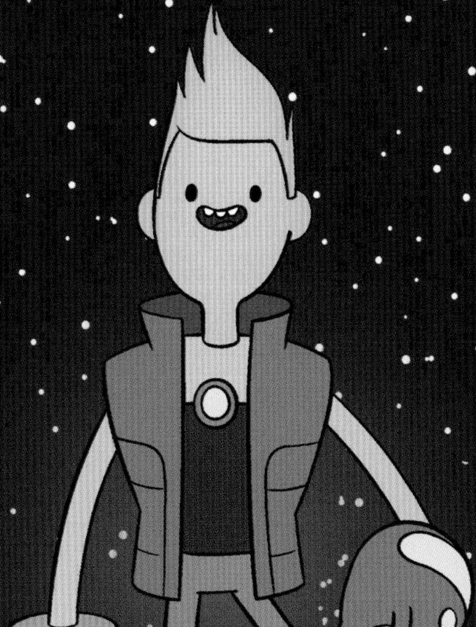

DOWN, LEFT, UP, UP,
B, A, SELECT, START

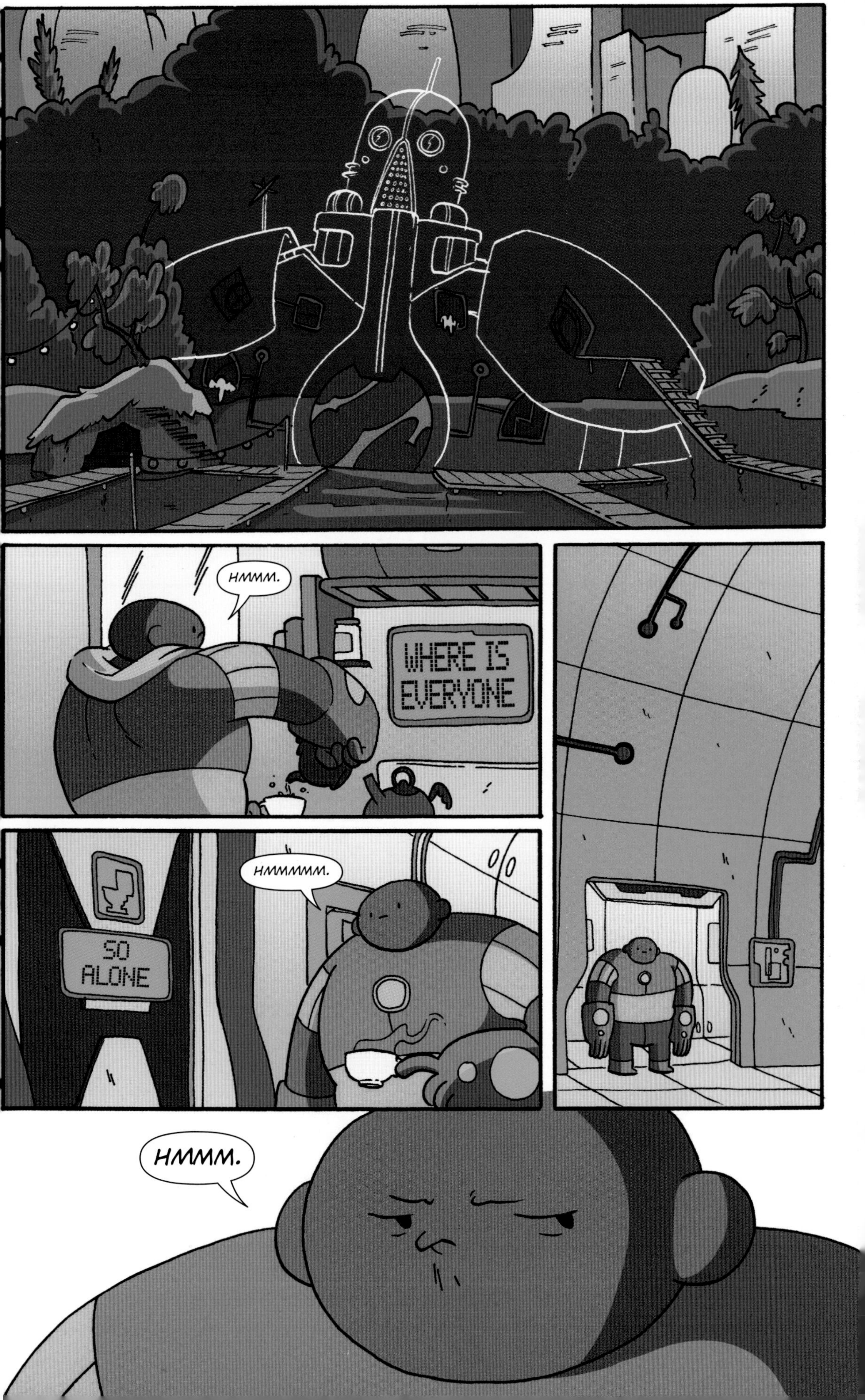
HMMM.
WHERE IS EVERYONE
SO ALONE
HMMMMM.
HMMM.

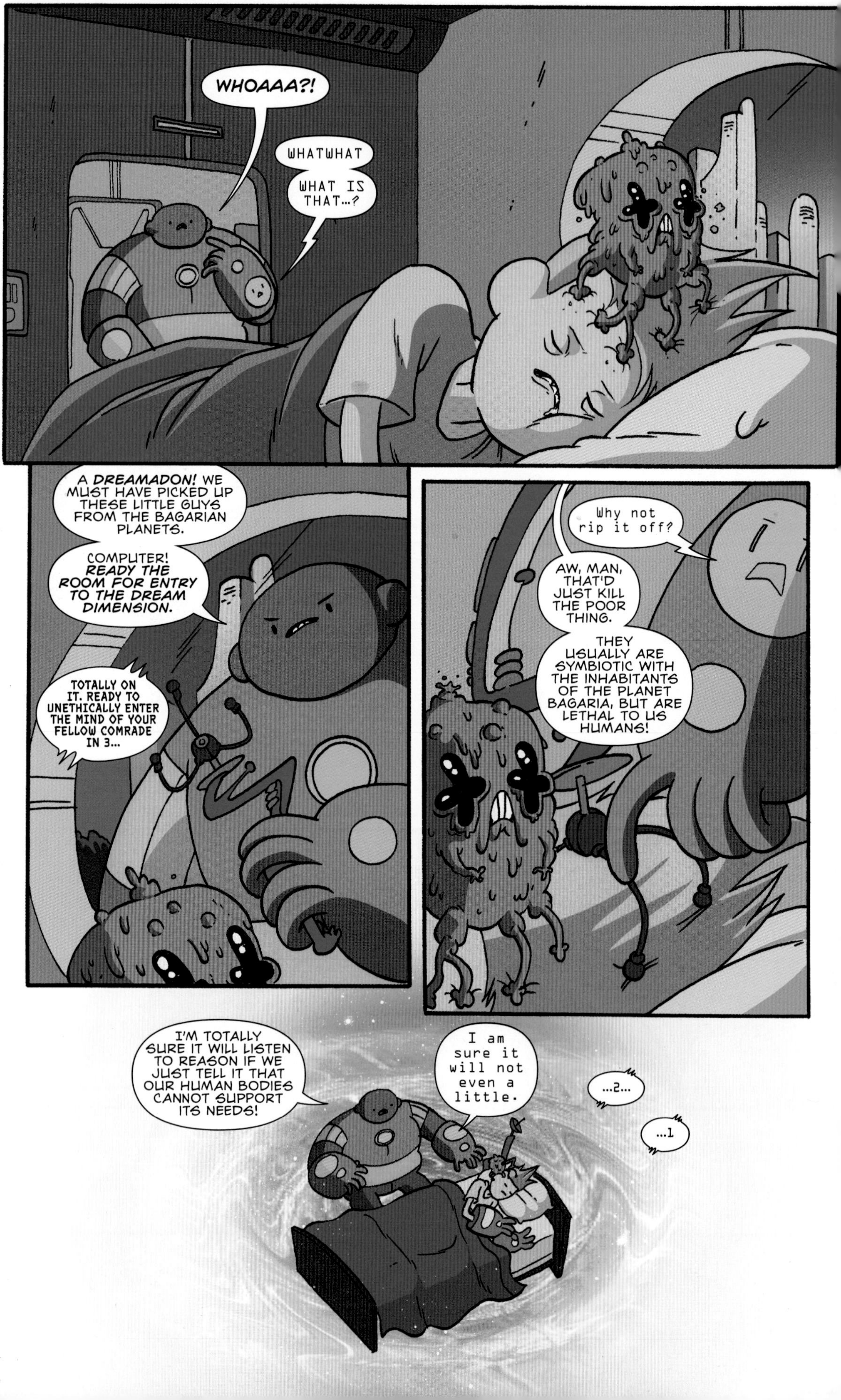
WHOAAA?!
WHATWHAT
WHAT IS THAT...?
A DREAMADON! WE MUST HAVE PICKED UP THESE LITTLE GUYS FROM THE BAGARIAN PLANETS.
COMPUTER! READY THE ROOM FOR ENTRY TO THE DREAM DIMENSION.
TOTALLY ON IT. READY TO UNETHICALLY ENTER THE MIND OF YOUR FELLOW COMRADE IN 3...
Why not rip it off?
AW, MAN, THAT'D JUST KILL THE POOR THING.
THEY USUALLY ARE SYMBIOTIC WITH THE INHABITANTS OF THE PLANET BAGARIA, BUT ARE LETHAL TO US HUMANS!
I'M TOTALLY SURE IT WILL LISTEN TO REASON IF WE JUST TELL IT THAT OUR HUMAN BODIES CANNOT SUPPORT ITS NEEDS!
I am sure it will not even a little.
...2...
...1

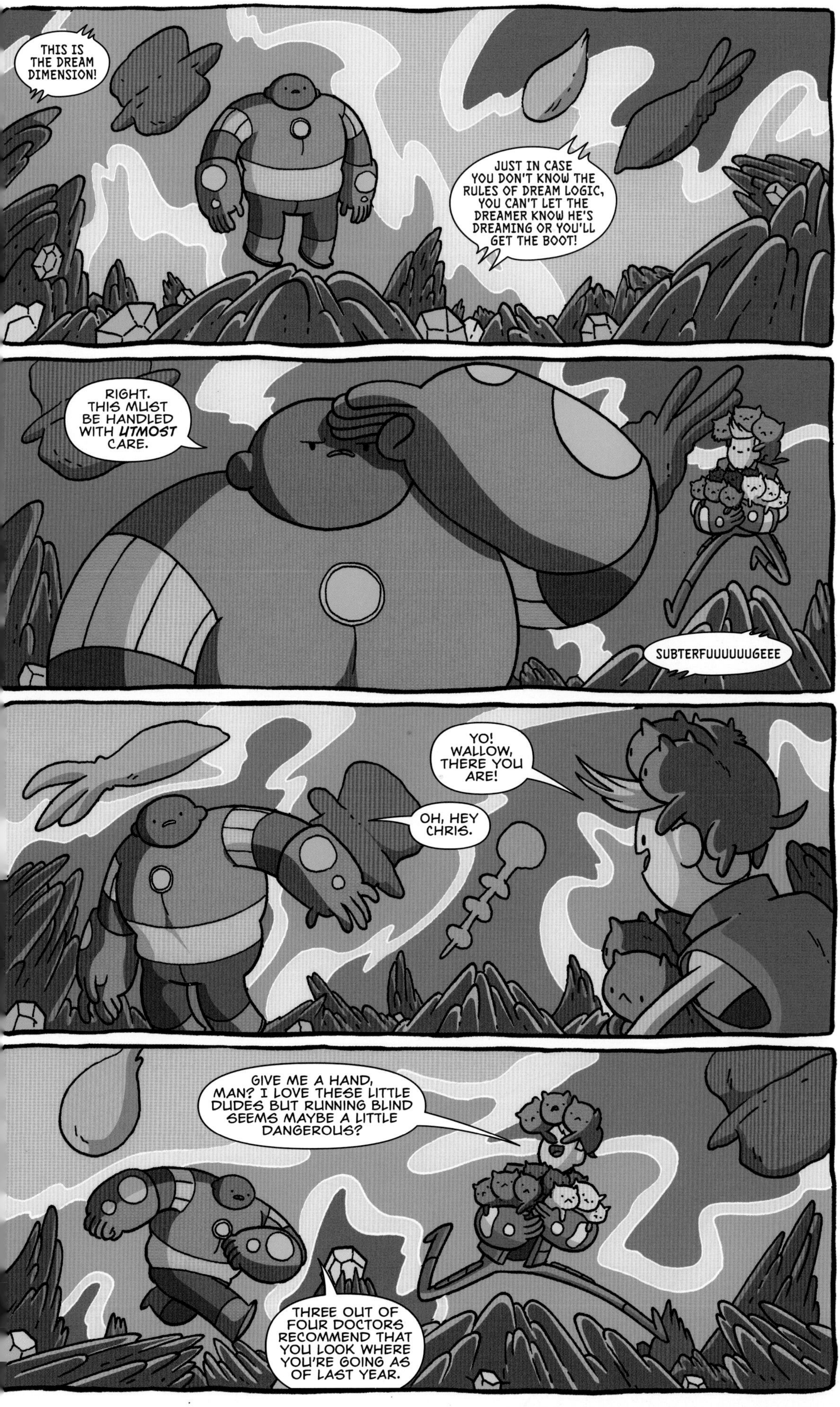
THIS IS THE DREAM DIMENSION!
JUST IN CASE YOU DON'T KNOW THE RULES OF DREAM LOGIC, YOU CAN'T LET THE DREAMER KNOW HE'S DREAMING OR YOU'LL GET THE BOOT!
RIGHT. THIS MUST BE HANDLED WITH *UTMOST* CARE.
SUBTERFUUUUUUGEEE
YO! WALLOW, THERE YOU ARE!
OH, HEY CHRIS.
GIVE ME A HAND, MAN? I LOVE THESE LITTLE DUDES BUT RUNNING BLIND SEEMS MAYBE A LITTLE DANGEROUS?
THREE OUT OF FOUR DOCTORS RECOMMEND THAT YOU LOOK WHERE YOU'RE GOING AS OF LAST YEAR.

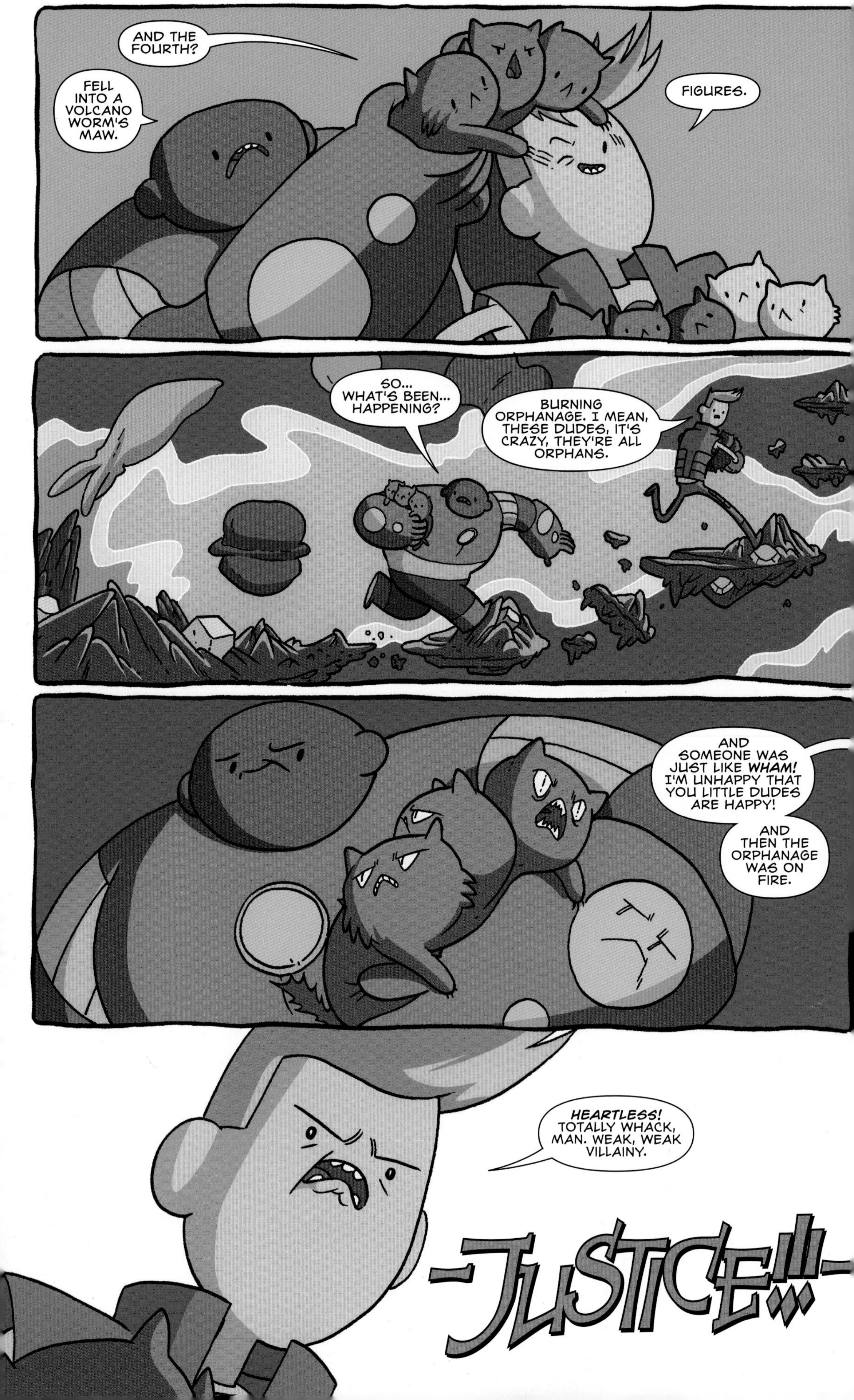
AND THE FOURTH?
FELL INTO A VOLCANO WORM'S MAW.
FIGURES.
SO... WHAT'S BEEN... HAPPENING?
BURNING ORPHANAGE. I MEAN, THESE DUDES, IT'S CRAZY, THEY'RE ALL ORPHANS.
AND SOMEONE WAS JUST LIKE *WHAM!* I'M UNHAPPY THAT YOU LITTLE DUDES ARE HAPPY!
AND THEN THE ORPHANAGE WAS ON FIRE.
HEARTLESS! TOTALLY WHACK, MAN. WEAK, WEAK VILLAINY.
-JUSTICE!!!-

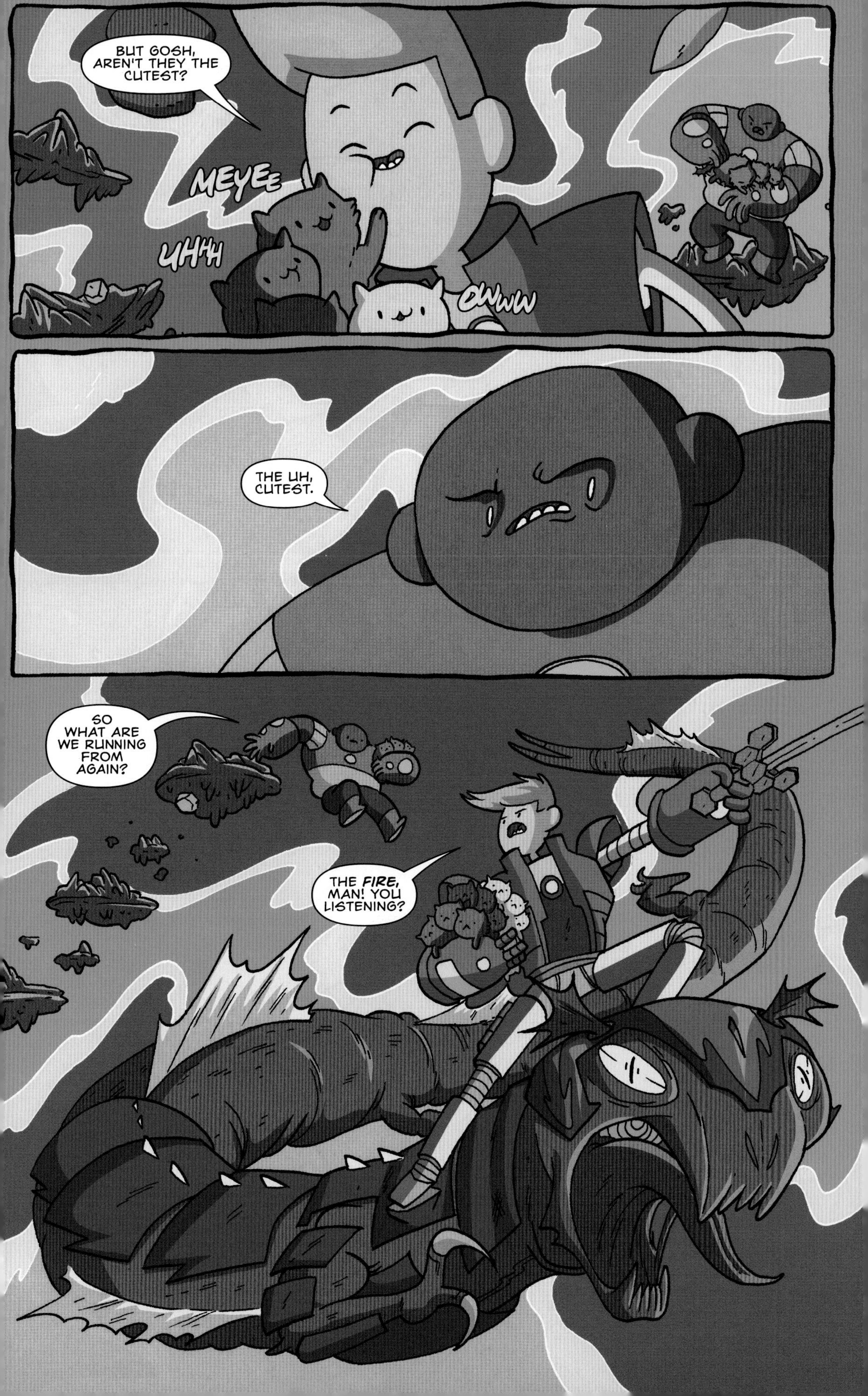
BUT GOSH, AREN'T THEY THE CUTEST?
MEYEE
UHHH
OWWW
THE UH, CUTEST.
SO WHAT ARE WE RUNNING FROM AGAIN?
THE *FIRE*, MAN! YOU LISTENING?

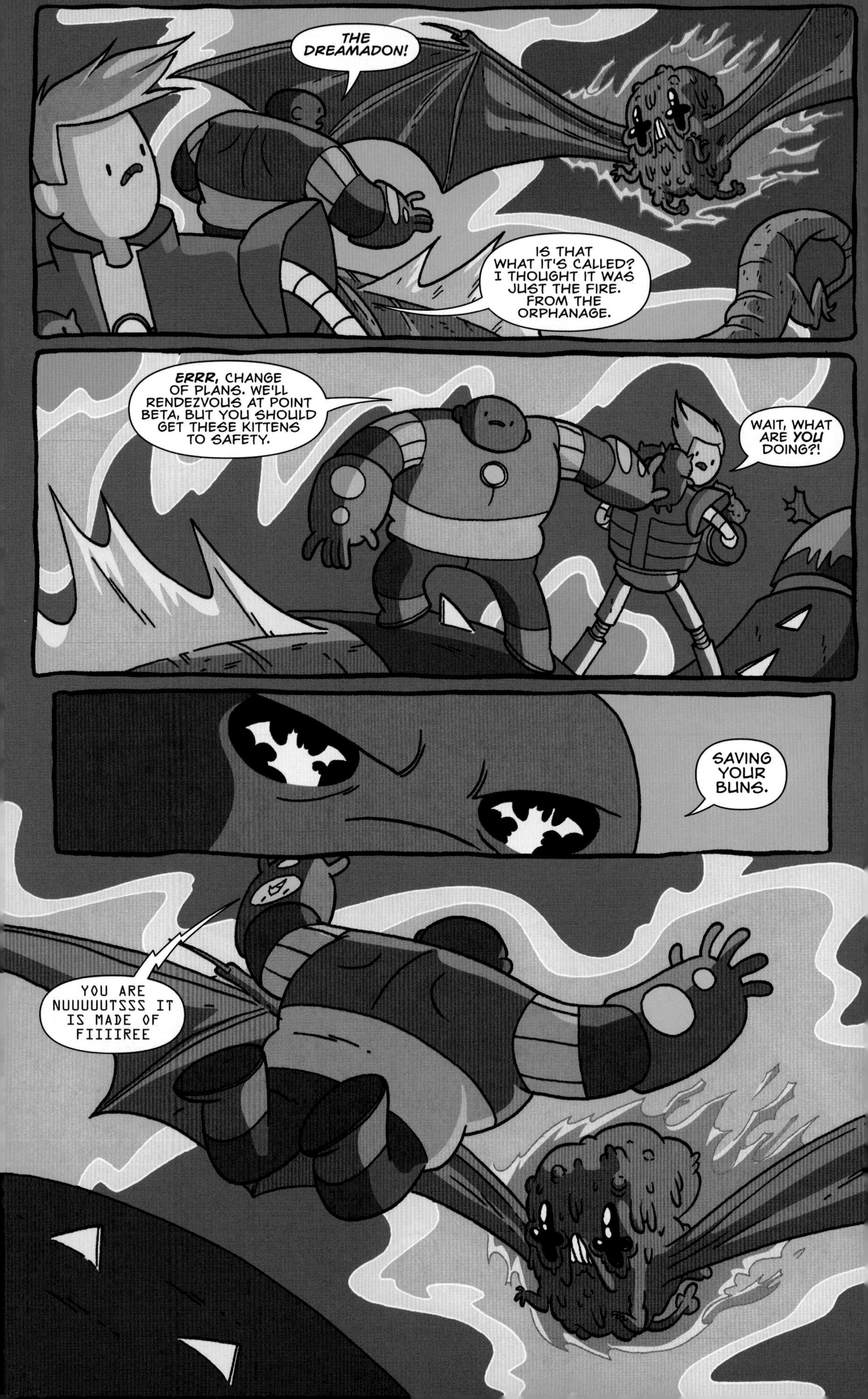
THE DREAMADON!
IS THAT WHAT IT'S CALLED? I THOUGHT IT WAS JUST THE FIRE. FROM THE ORPHANAGE.
ERRR, CHANGE OF PLANS. WE'LL RENDEZVOUS AT POINT BETA, BUT YOU SHOULD GET THESE KITTENS TO SAFETY.
WAIT, WHAT ARE YOU DOING?!
SAVING YOUR BUNS.
YOU ARE NUUUUUTSSS IT IS MADE OF FIIIIREE

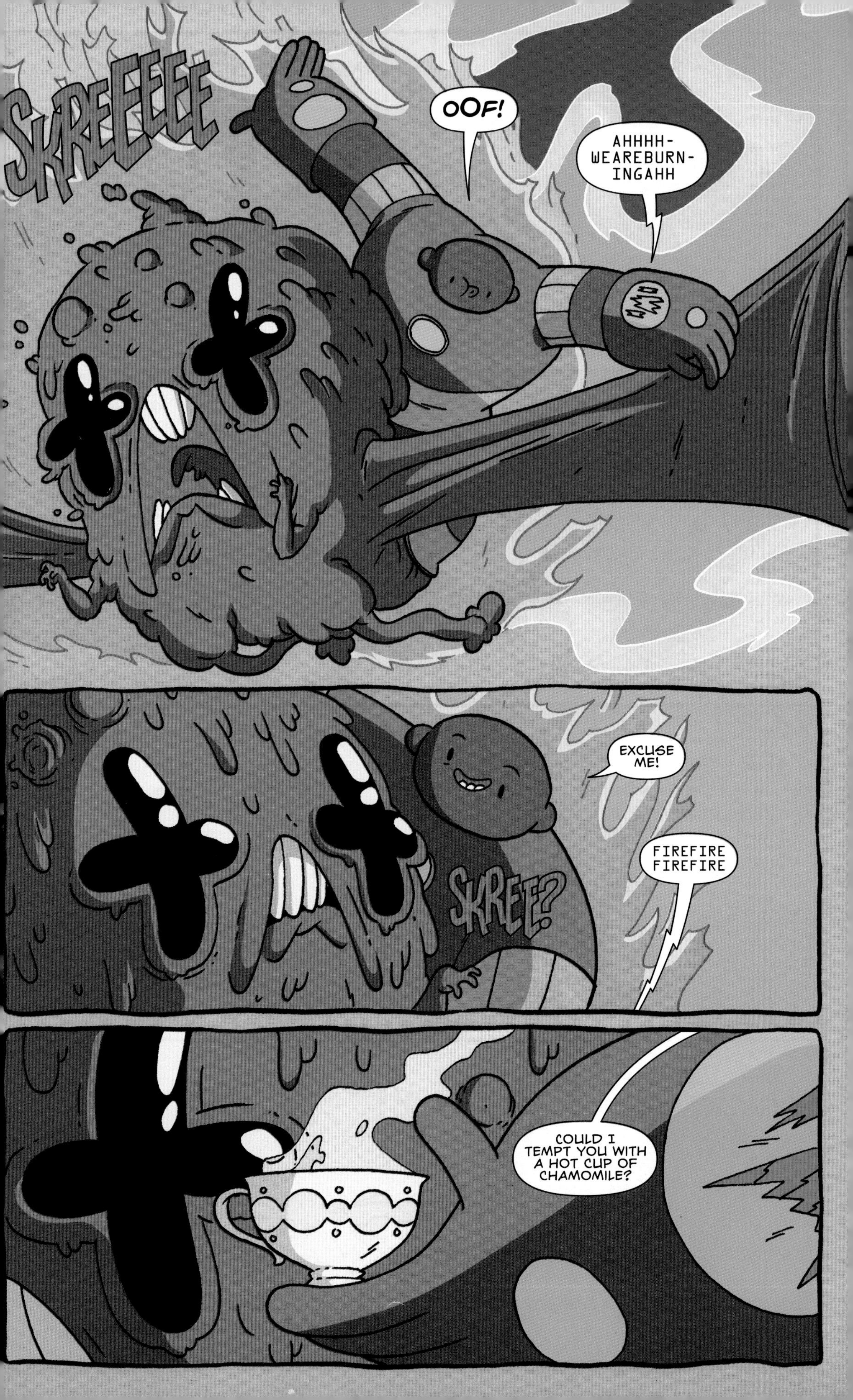
SKREEEEEE
OOF!
AHHHH-WEAREBURN-INGAHH
EXCUSE ME!
SKREE?
FIREFIRE FIREFIRE
COULD I TEMPT YOU WITH A HOT CUP OF CHAMOMILE?

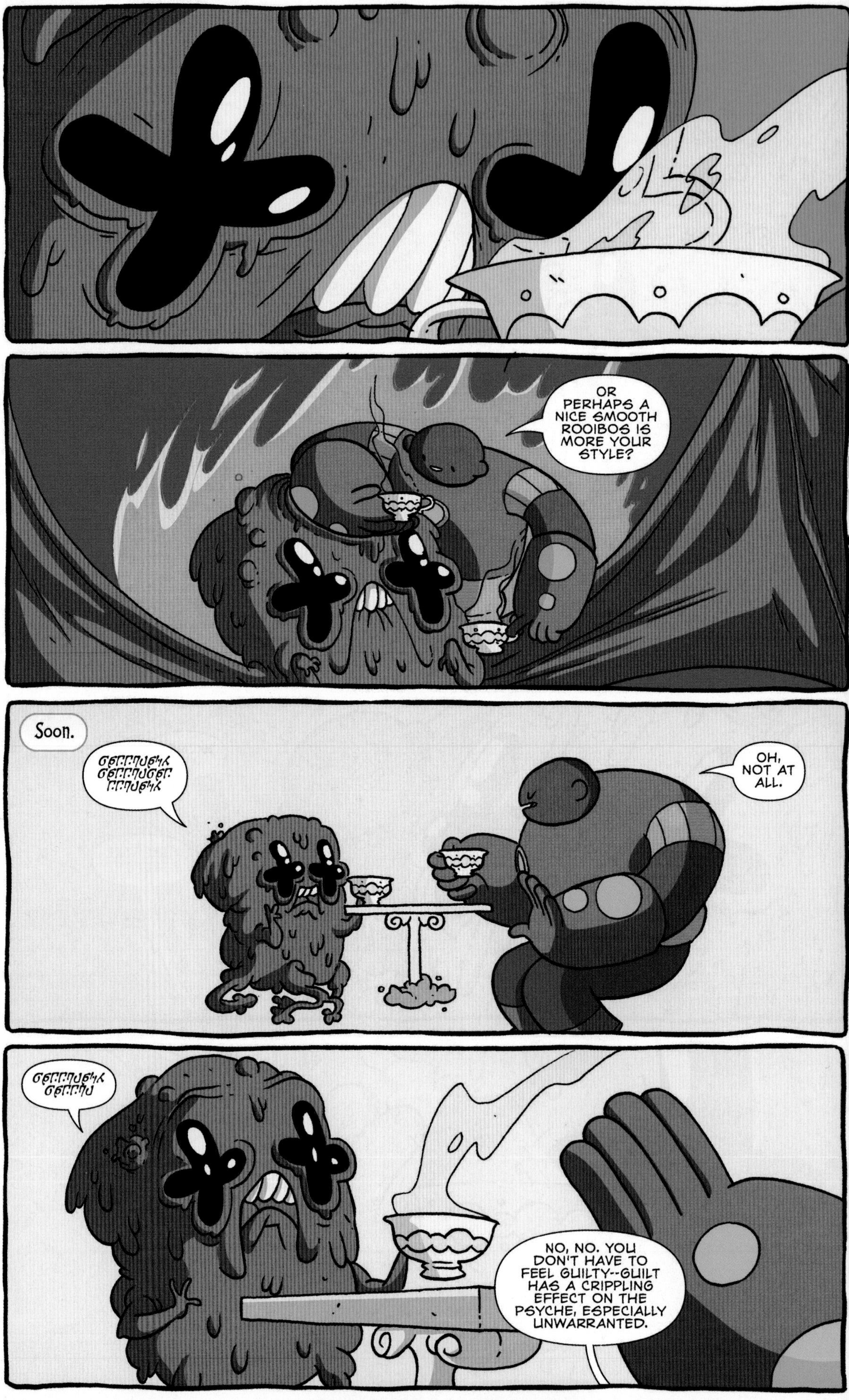
OR PERHAPS A NICE SMOOTH ROOIBOS IS MORE YOUR STYLE?
Soon.
OH, NOT AT ALL.
NO, NO. YOU DON'T HAVE TO FEEL GUILTY--GUILT HAS A CRIPPLING EFFECT ON THE PSYCHE, ESPECIALLY UNWARRANTED.

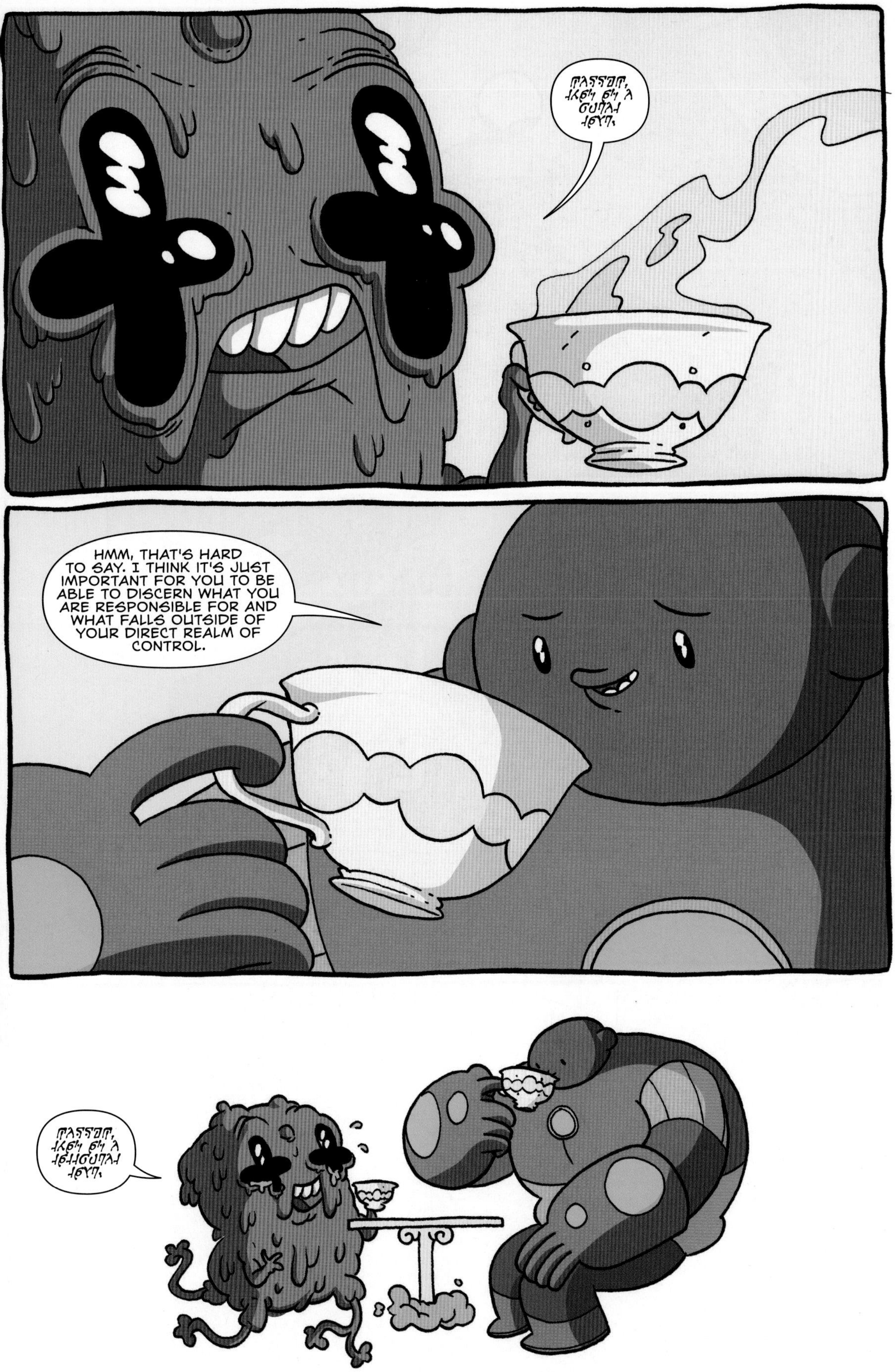
HMM, THAT'S HARD TO SAY. I THINK IT'S JUST IMPORTANT FOR YOU TO BE ABLE TO DISCERN WHAT YOU ARE RESPONSIBLE FOR AND WHAT FALLS OUTSIDE OF YOUR DIRECT REALM OF CONTROL.

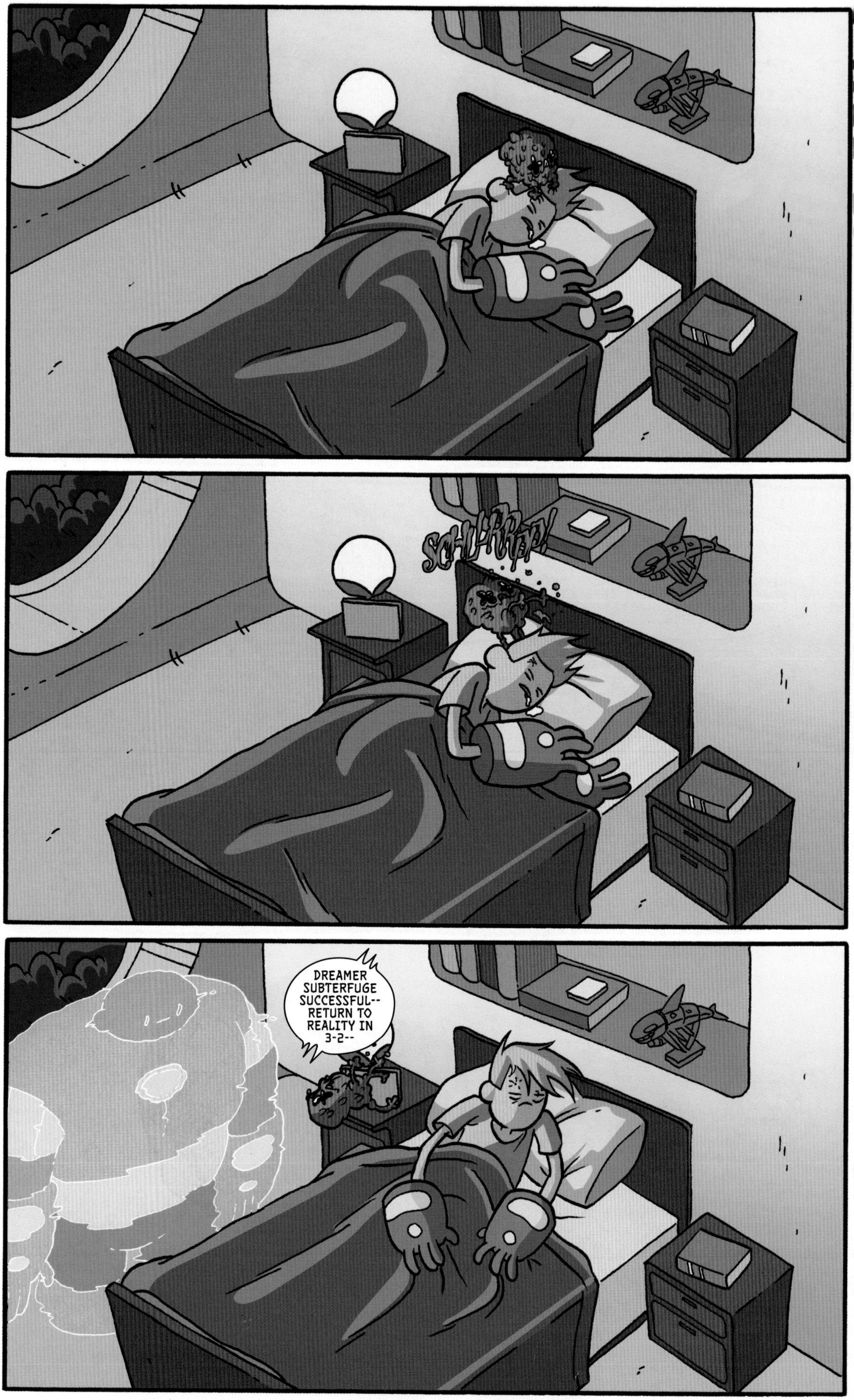
SCHLRRPP!
DREAMER SUBTERFUGE SUCCESSFUL-- RETURN TO REALITY IN 3-2--

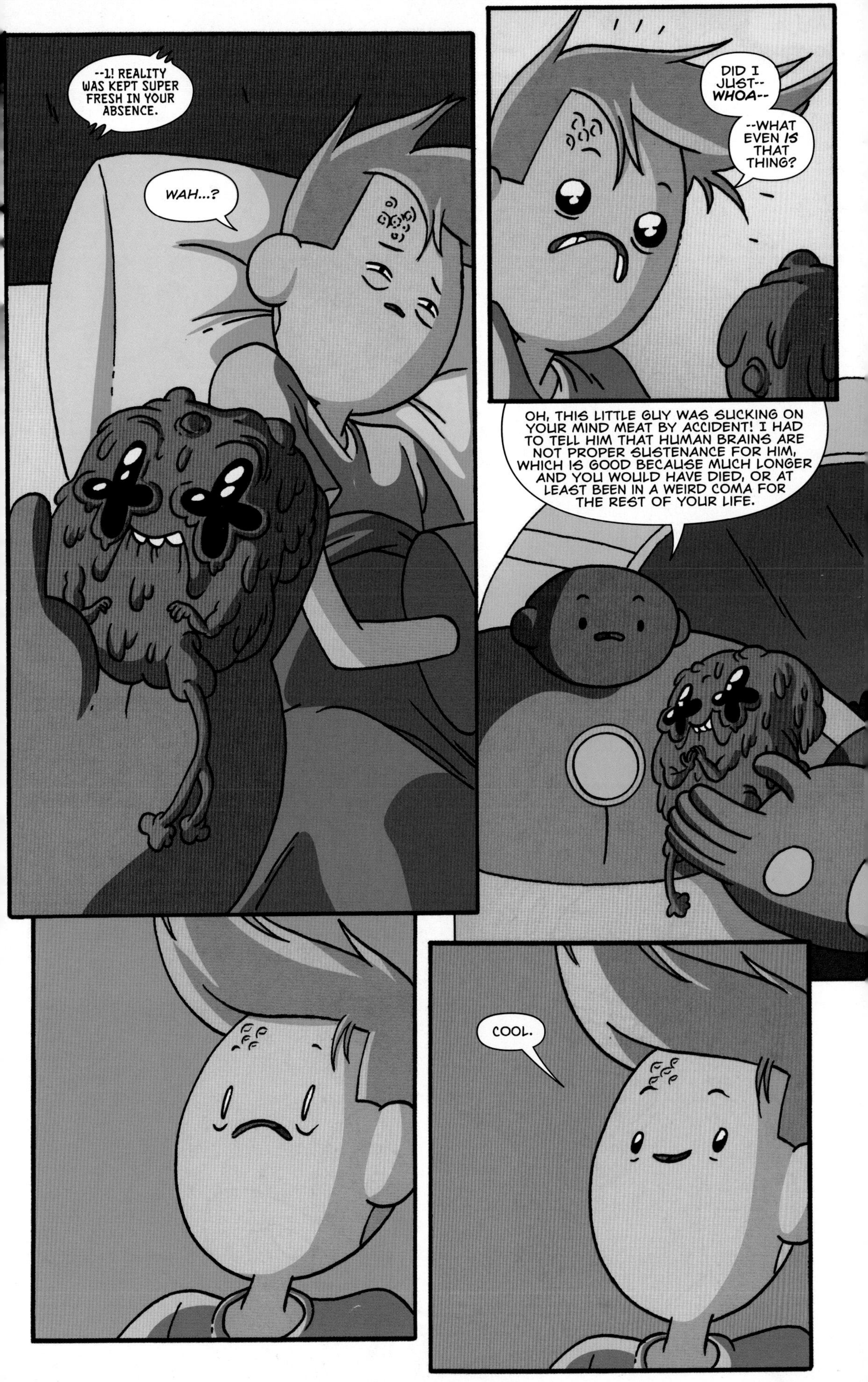

--1! REALITY WAS KEPT SUPER FRESH IN YOUR ABSENCE.
WAH...?
DID I JUST-- WHOA--
--WHAT EVEN IS THAT THING?
OH, THIS LITTLE GUY WAS SUCKING ON YOUR MIND MEAT BY ACCIDENT! I HAD TO TELL HIM THAT HUMAN BRAINS ARE NOT PROPER SUSTENANCE FOR HIM, WHICH IS GOOD BECAUSE MUCH LONGER AND YOU WOULD HAVE DIED, OR AT LEAST BEEN IN A WEIRD COMA FOR THE REST OF YOUR LIFE.
COOL.

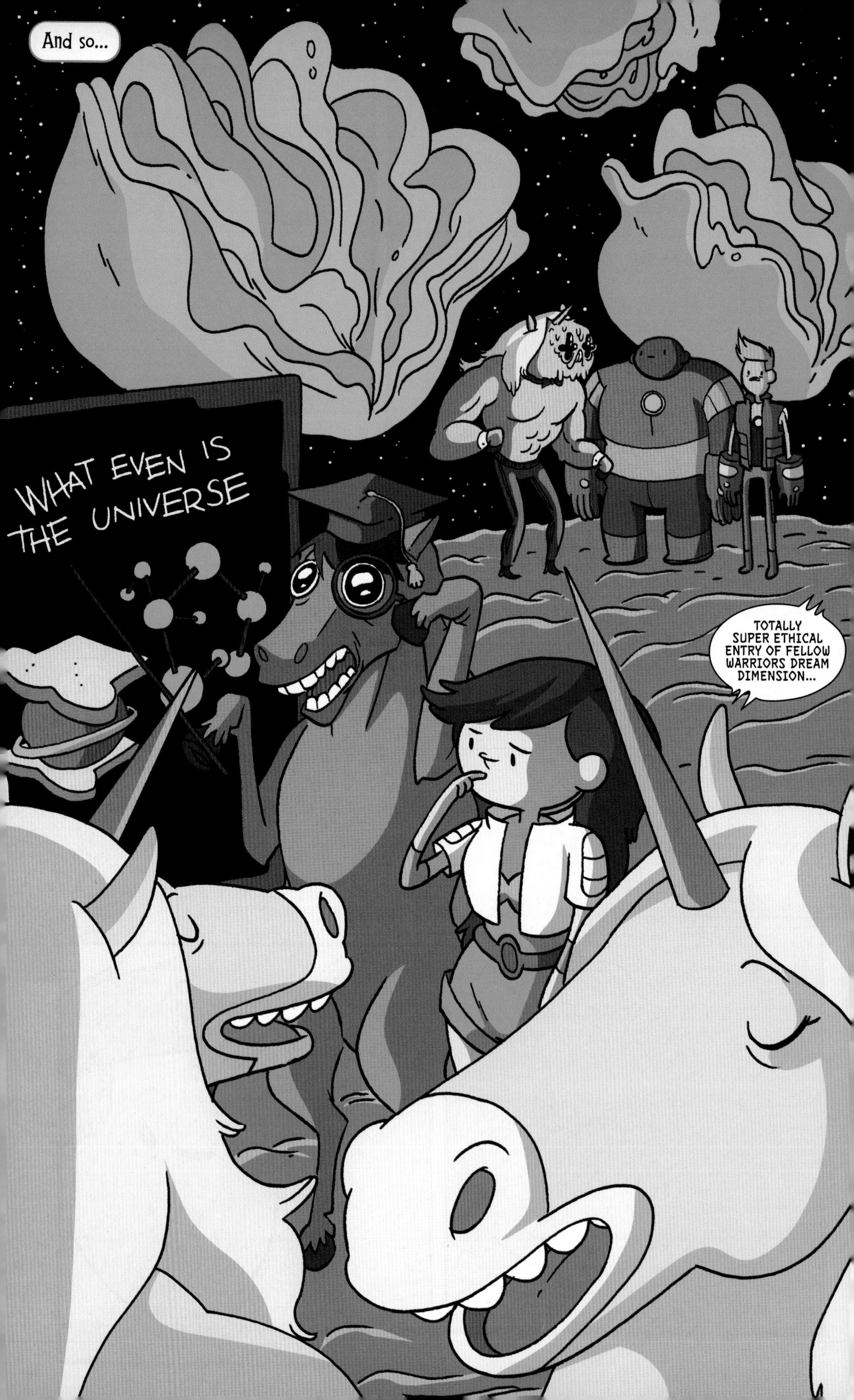
And so...
WHAT EVEN IS THE UNIVERSE
TOTALLY SUPER ETHICAL ENTRY OF FELLOW WARRIORS DREAM DIMENSION...

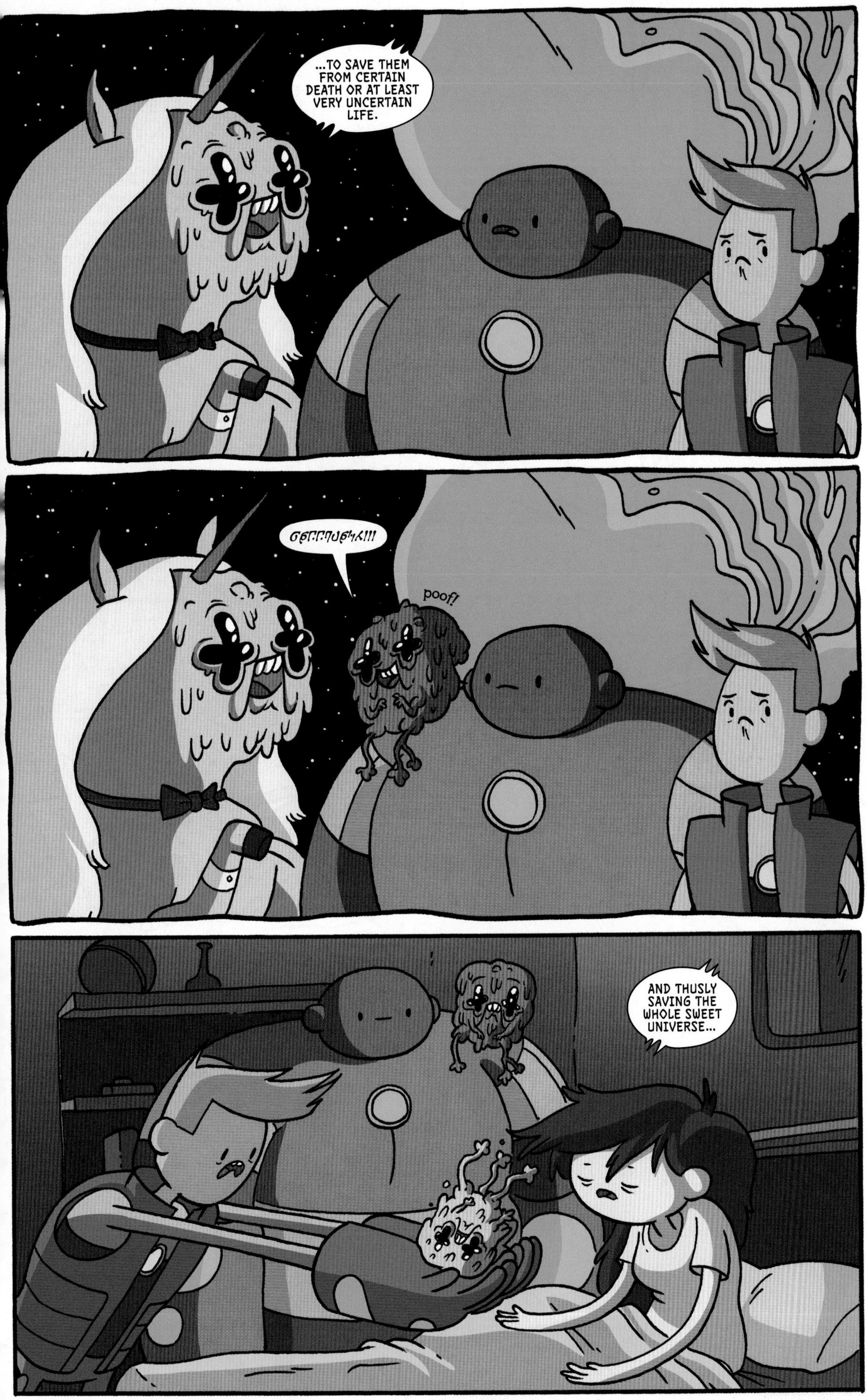
...TO SAVE THEM FROM CERTAIN DEATH OR AT LEAST VERY UNCERTAIN LIFE.
poof!
AND THUSLY SAVING THE WHOLE SWEET UNIVERSE...

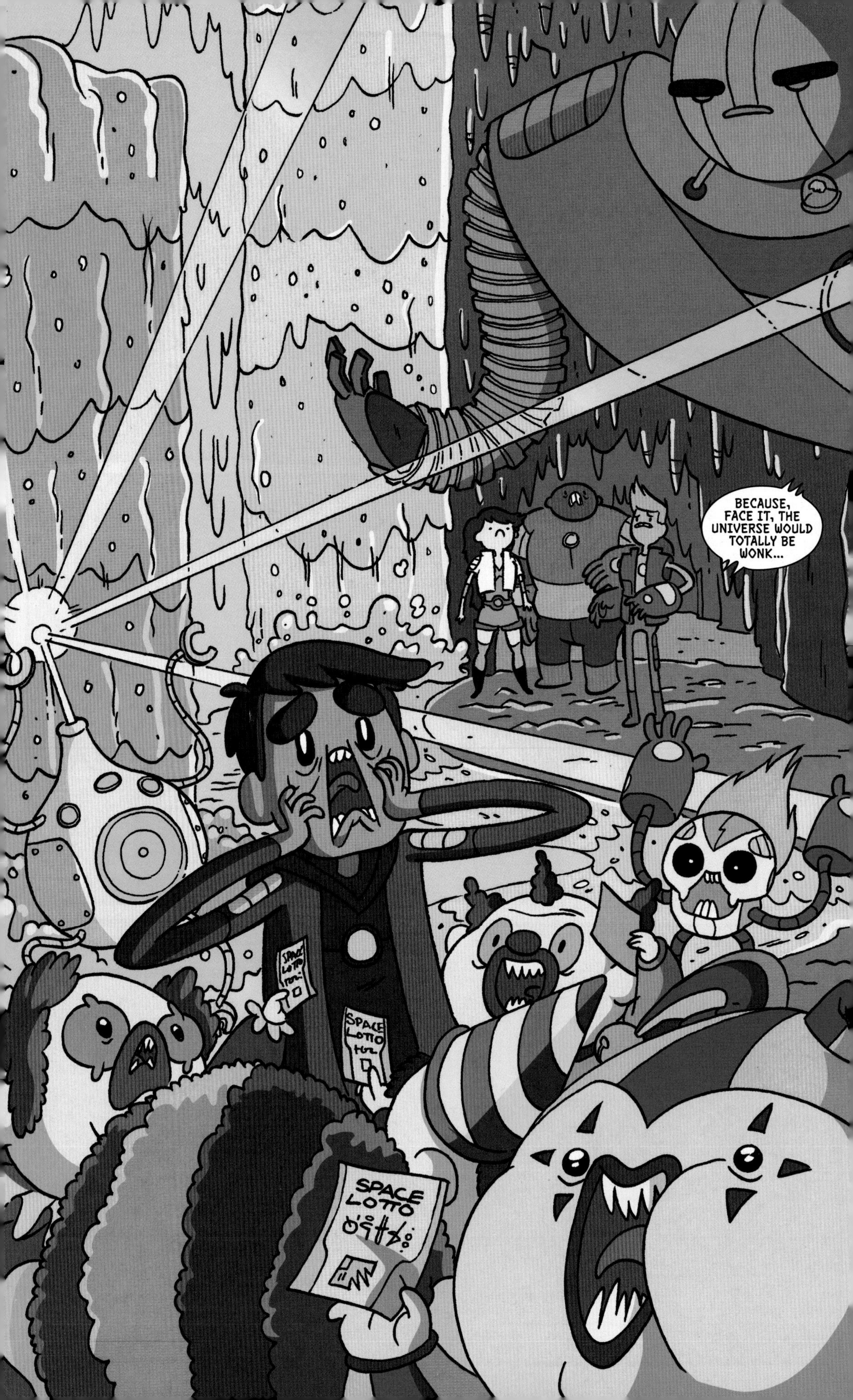
BECAUSE, FACE IT, THE UNIVERSE WOULD TOTALLY BE WONK...
SPACE LOTTO
SPACE LOTTO
SPACE LOTTO

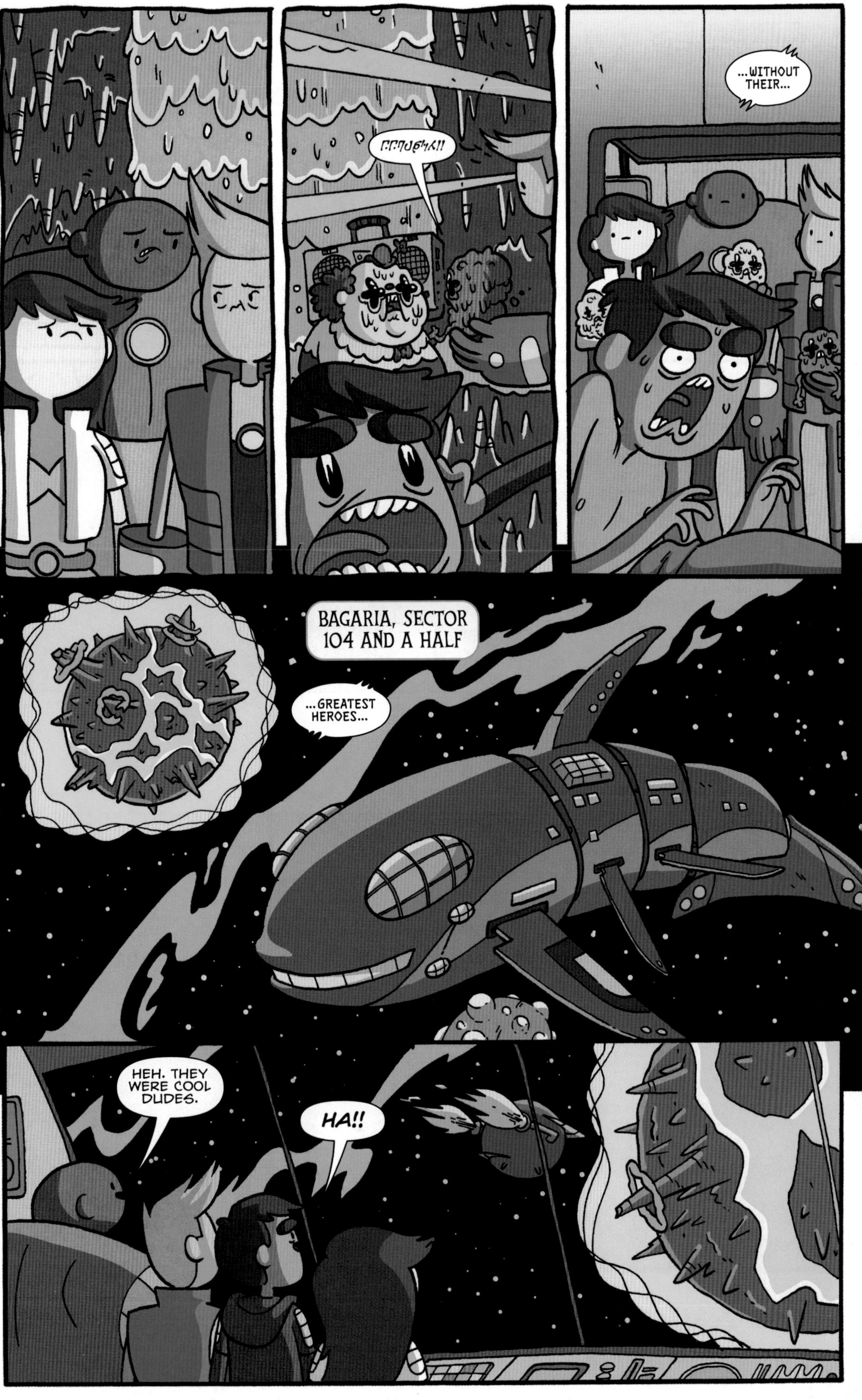
...WITHOUT THEIR...
BAGARIA, SECTOR 104 AND A HALF
...GREATEST HEROES...
HEH. THEY WERE COOL DUDES.
HA!!

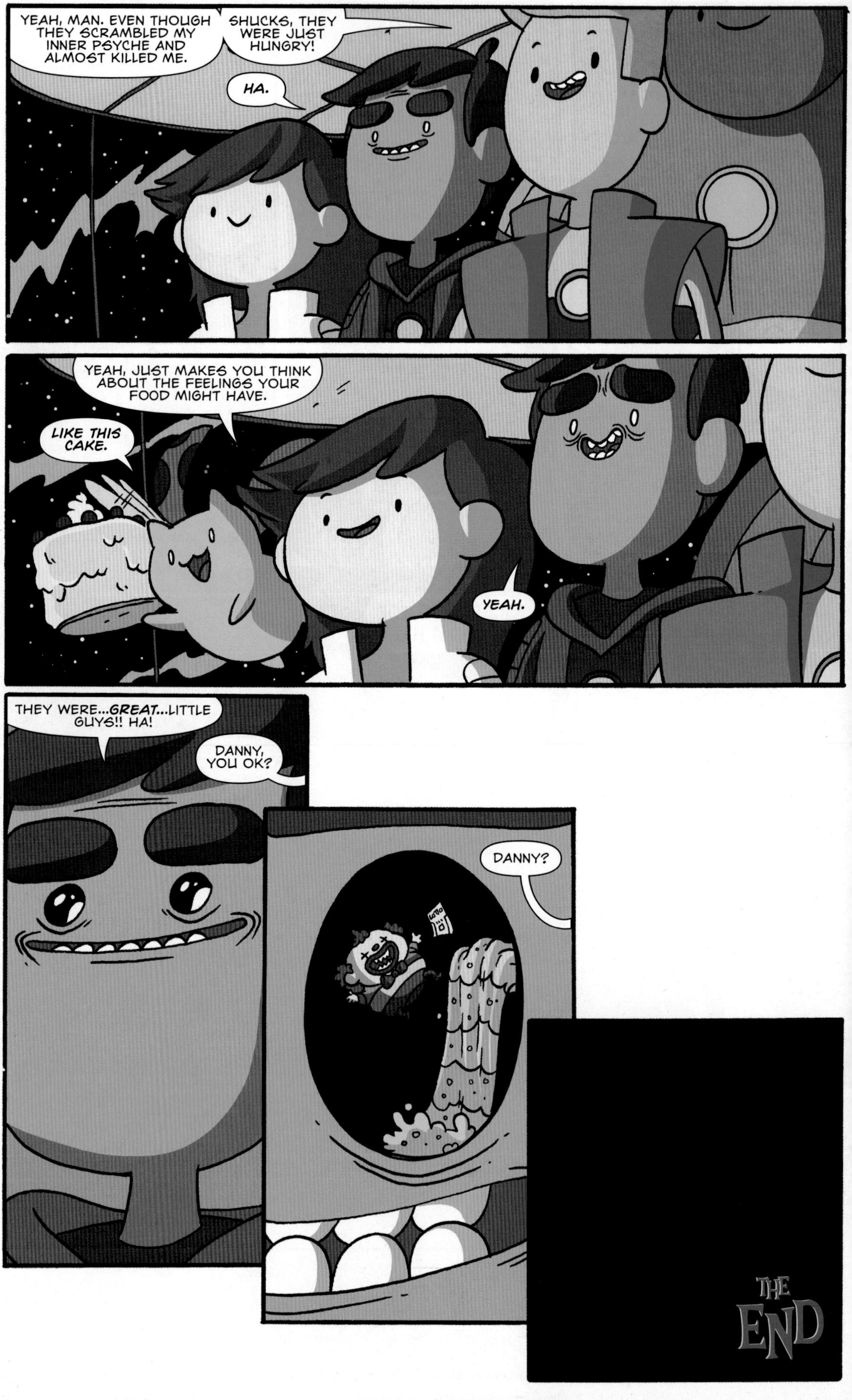
YEAH, MAN. EVEN THOUGH THEY SCRAMBLED MY INNER PSYCHE AND ALMOST KILLED ME.
SHUCKS, THEY WERE JUST HUNGRY!
HA.
YEAH, JUST MAKES YOU THINK ABOUT THE FEELINGS YOUR FOOD MIGHT HAVE.
LIKE THIS CAKE.
YEAH.
THEY WERE...GREAT...LITTLE GUYS!! HA!
DANNY, YOU OK?
DANNY?
THE END

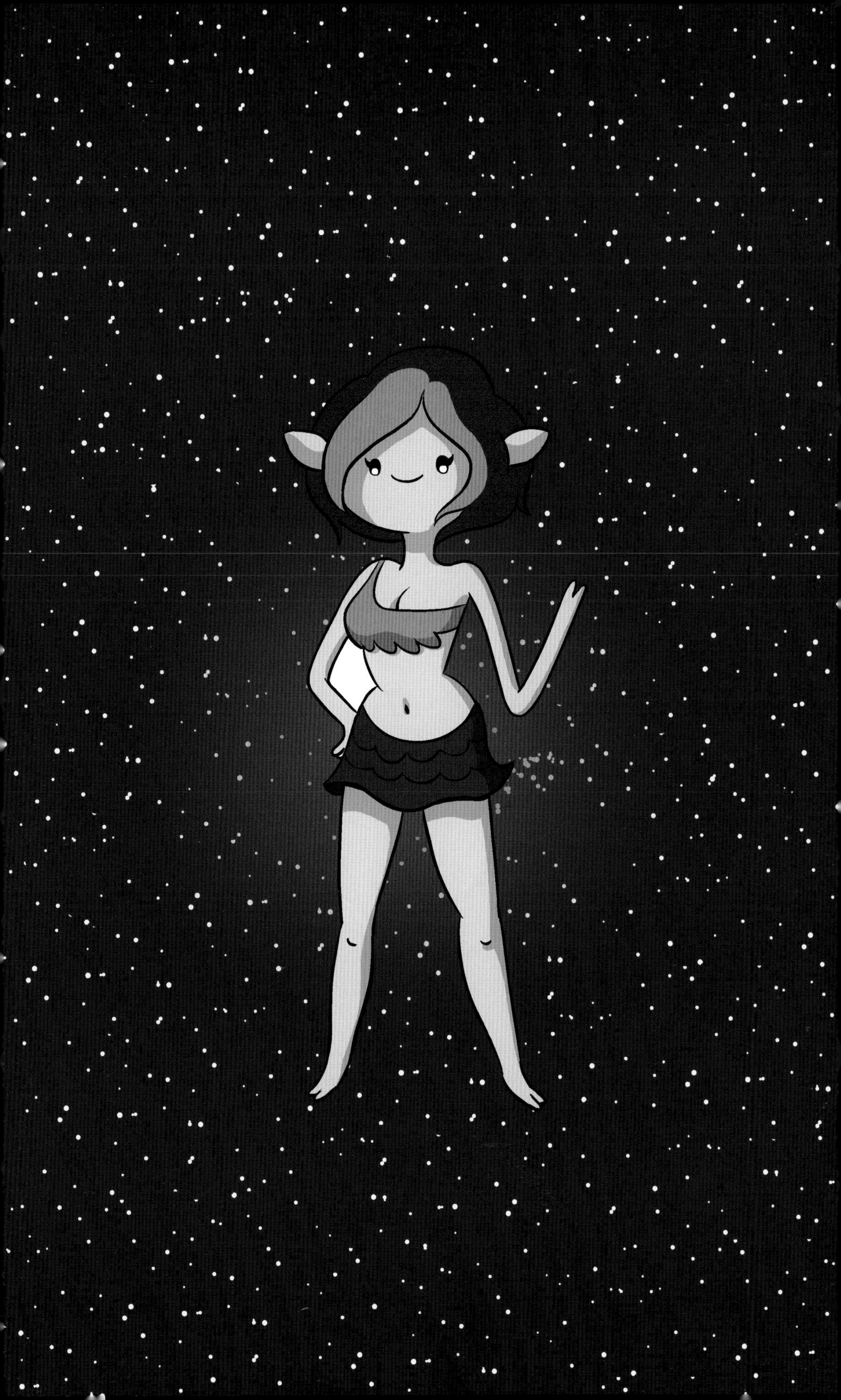

SHORT MISSIONS

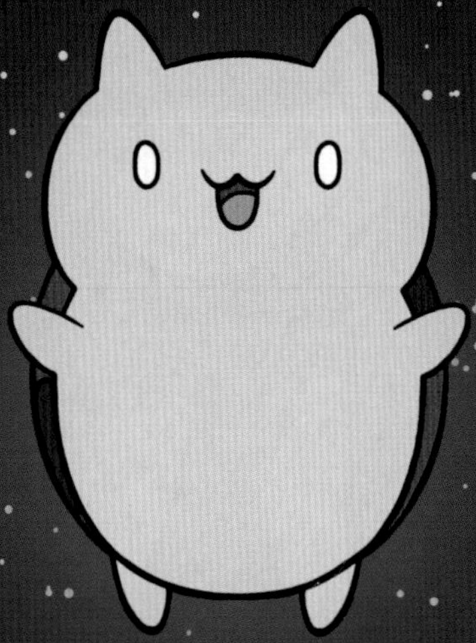

UP, UP, RIGHT, LEFT,
A, B, SELECT, START

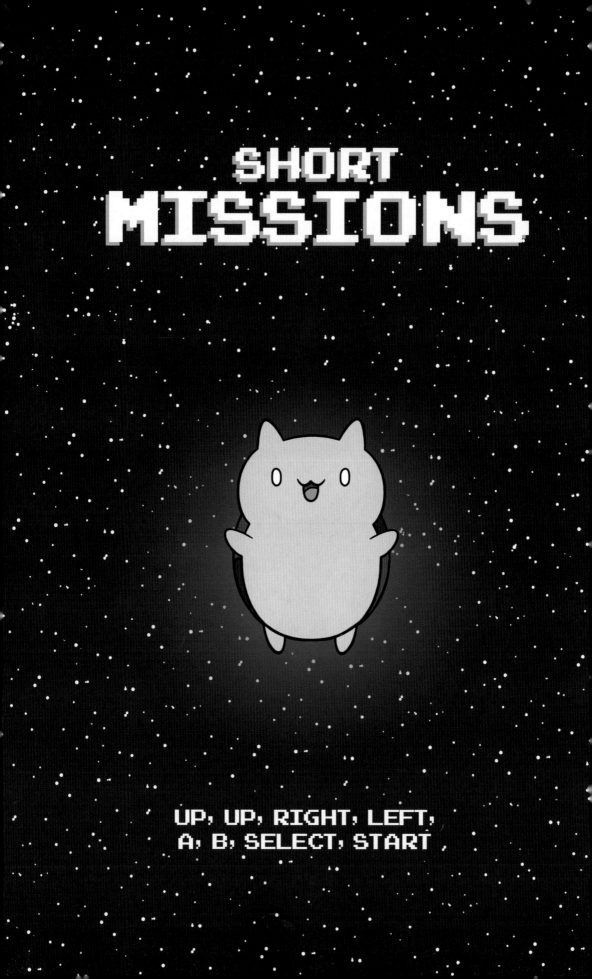

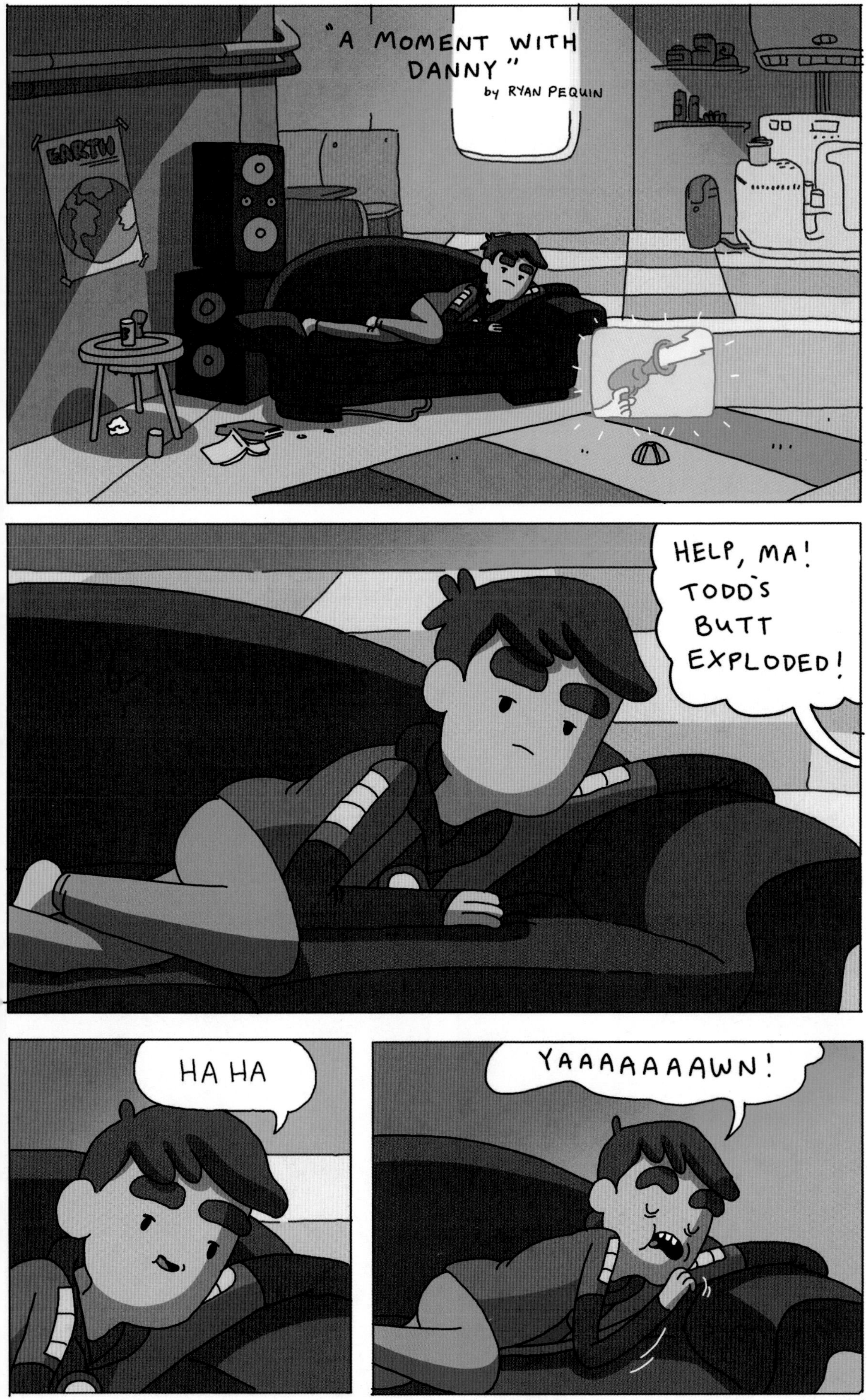
"A MOMENT WITH DANNY"
by RYAN PEQUIN
EARTH
HELP, MA! TODD'S BUTT EXPLODED!
HA HA
YAAAAAAAAWN!

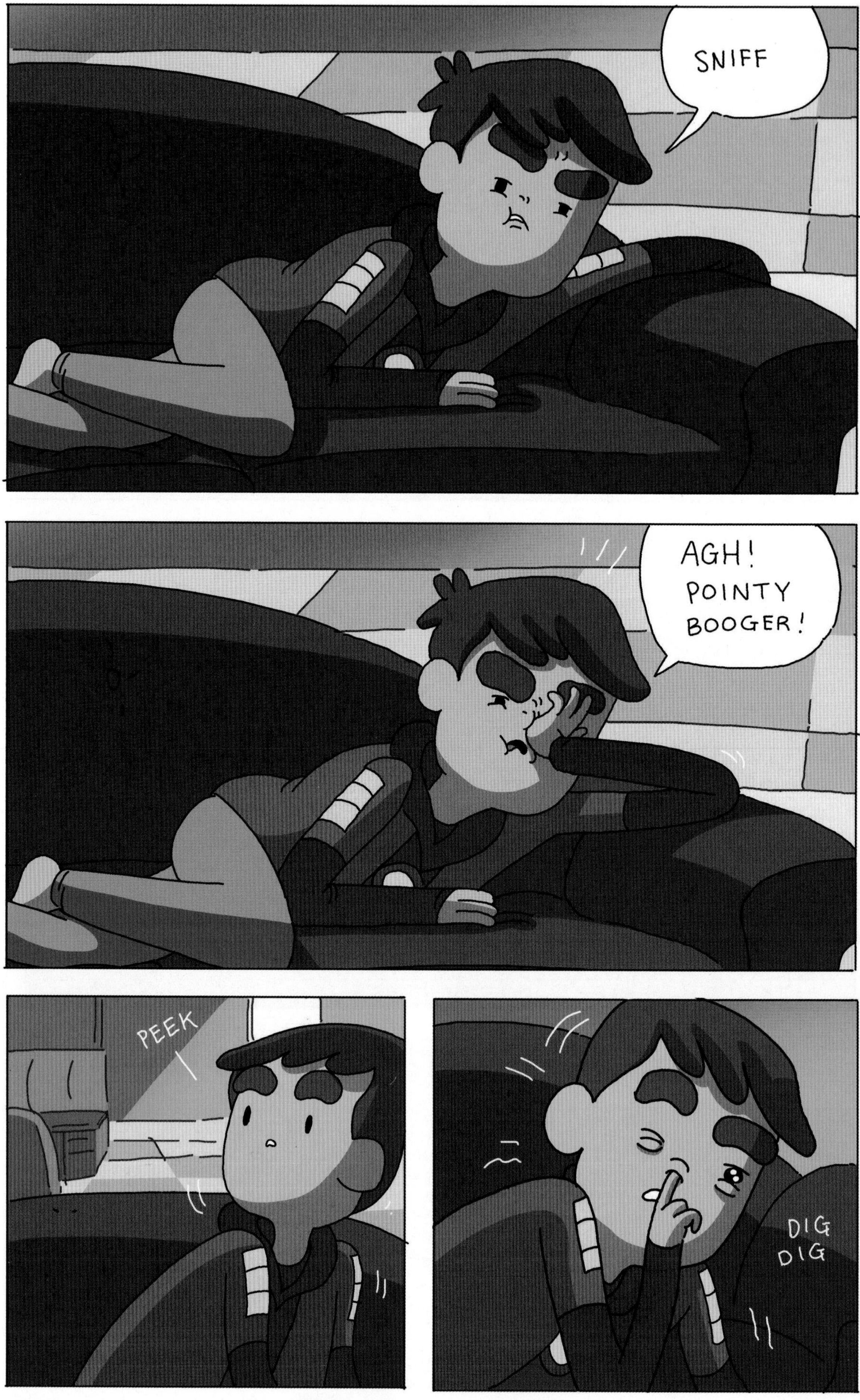
SNIFF
AGH! POINTY BOOGER!
PEEK
DIG DIG

BOOGER
REMOVAL
MANEUVER
1 :
THE FLICK

FLICK!

BOOGER
REMOVAL
MANEUVER
2 :
THE
PINCH + ROLL

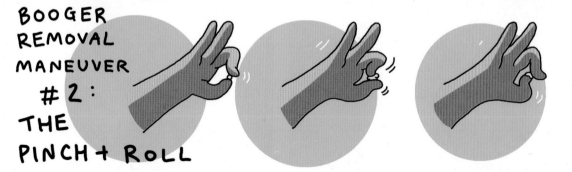

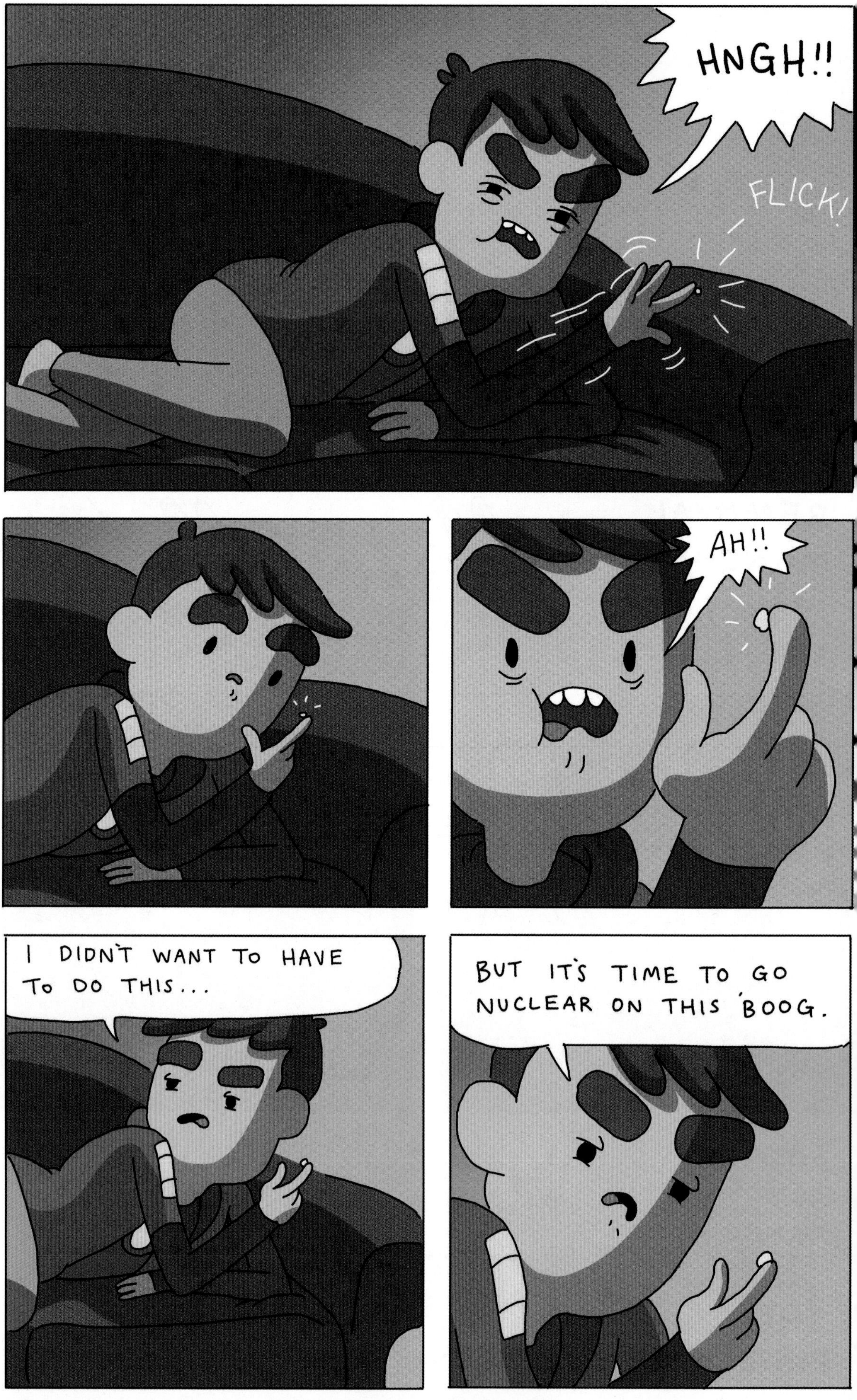
HNGH!!
FLICK!
AH!!
I DIDN'T WANT TO HAVE TO DO THIS...
BUT IT'S TIME TO GO NUCLEAR ON THIS 'BOOG.

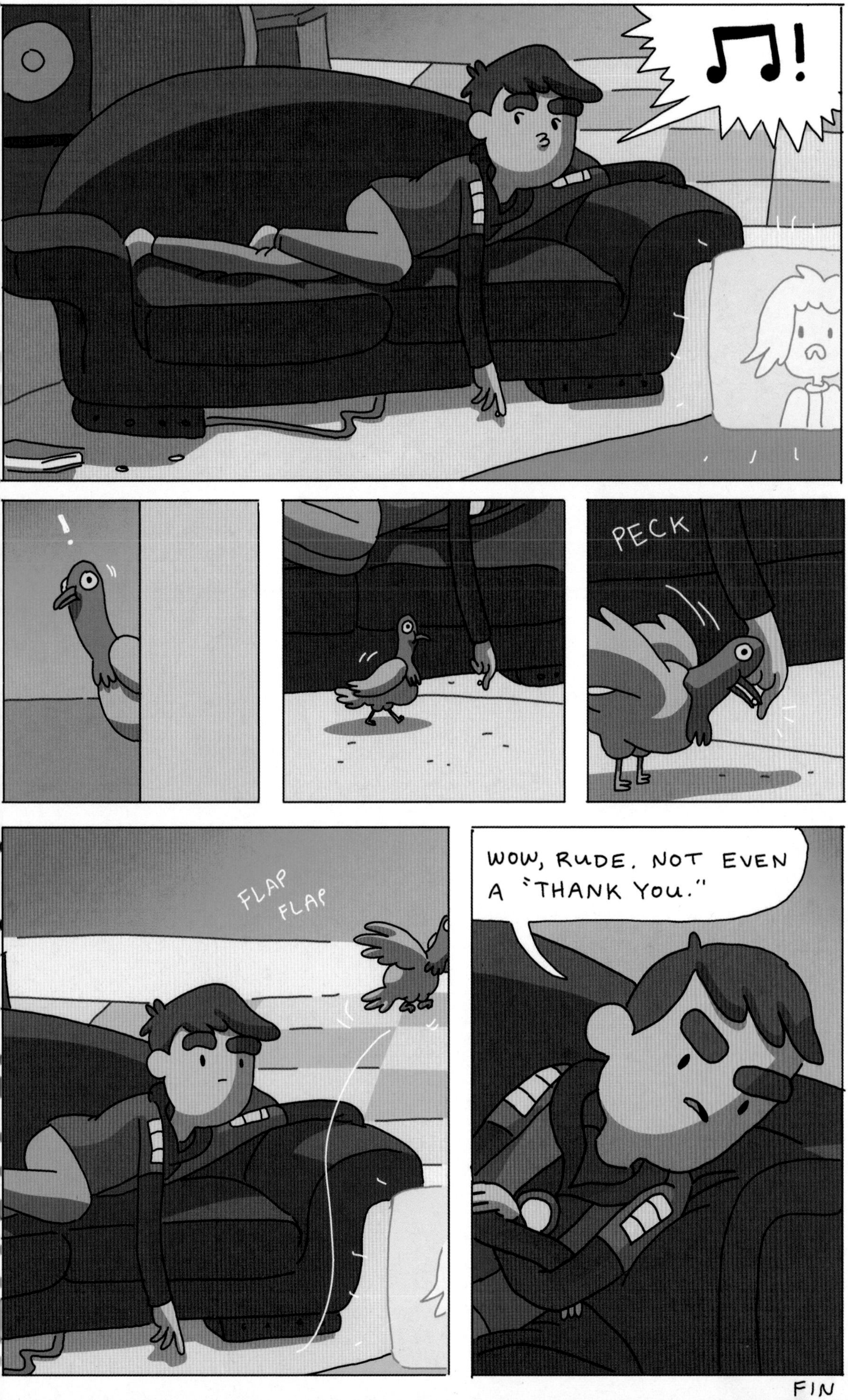
♫!
!
PECK
FLAP
FLAP
WOW, RUDE. NOT EVEN A "THANK YOU."

FIN

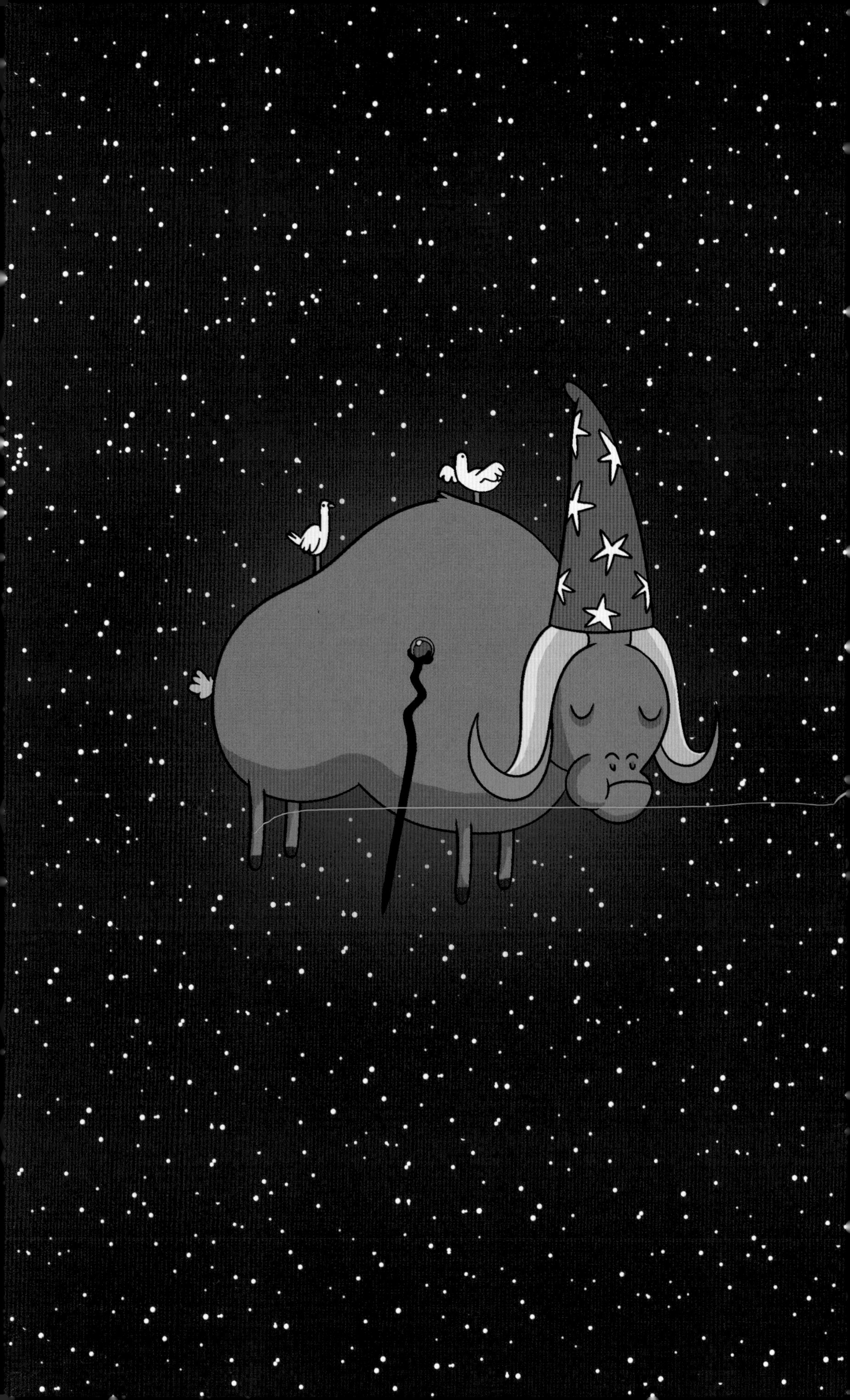

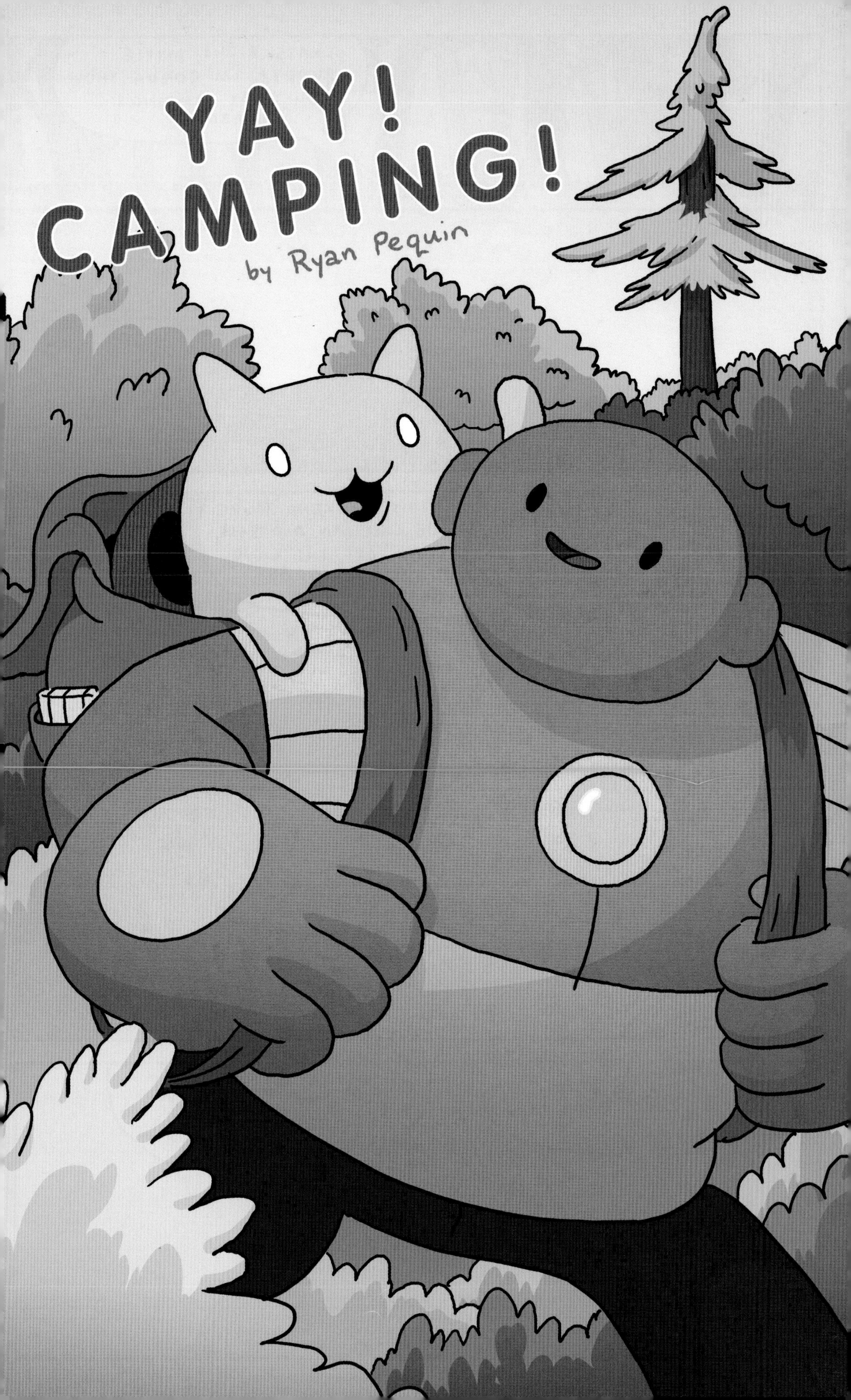
YAY!
CAMPING!
by Ryan Pequin

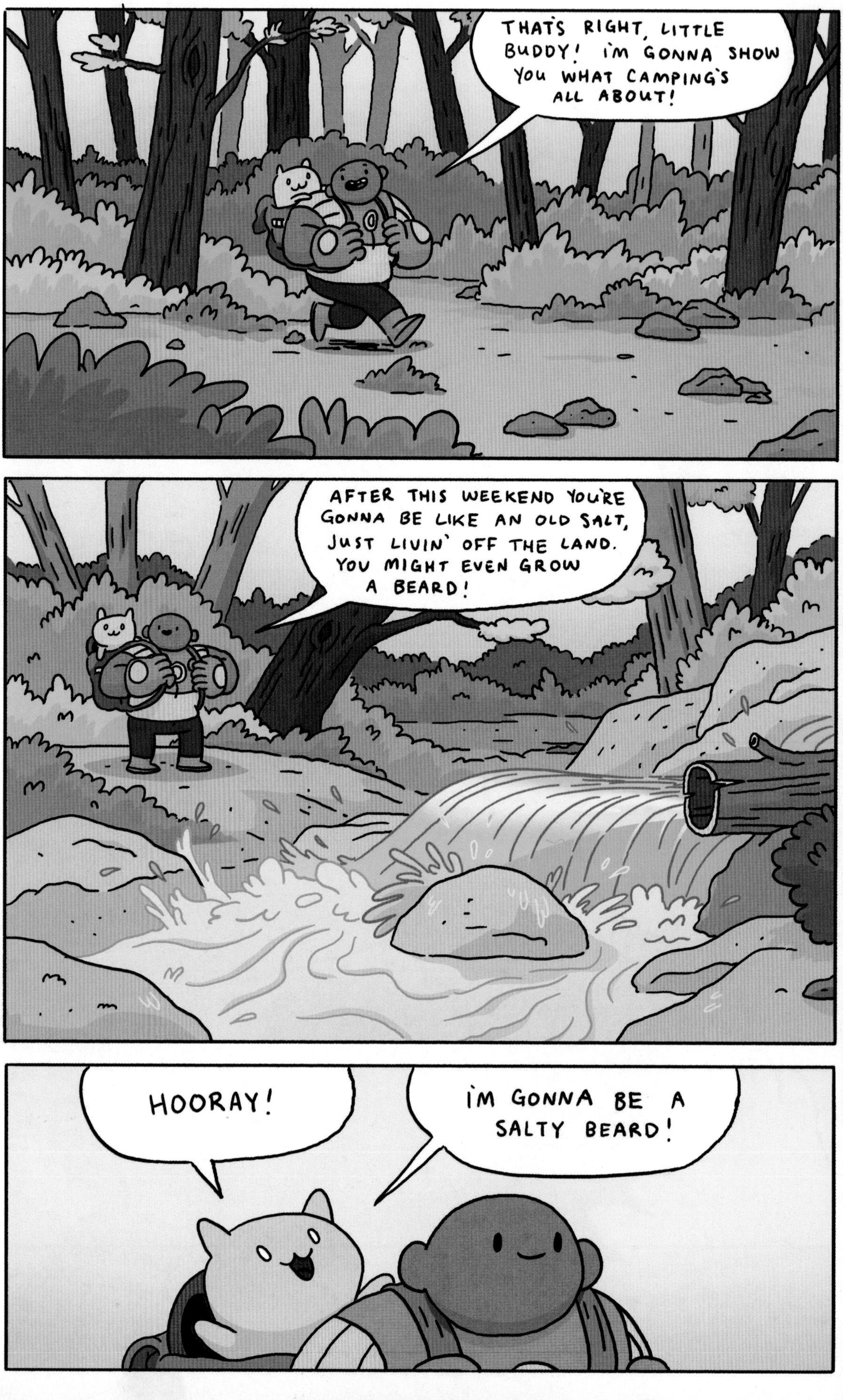
THAT'S RIGHT, LITTLE BUDDY! I'M GONNA SHOW YOU WHAT CAMPING'S ALL ABOUT!
AFTER THIS WEEKEND YOU'RE GONNA BE LIKE AN OLD SALT, JUST LIVIN' OFF THE LAND. YOU MIGHT EVEN GROW A BEARD!
HOORAY!
I'M GONNA BE A SALTY BEARD!

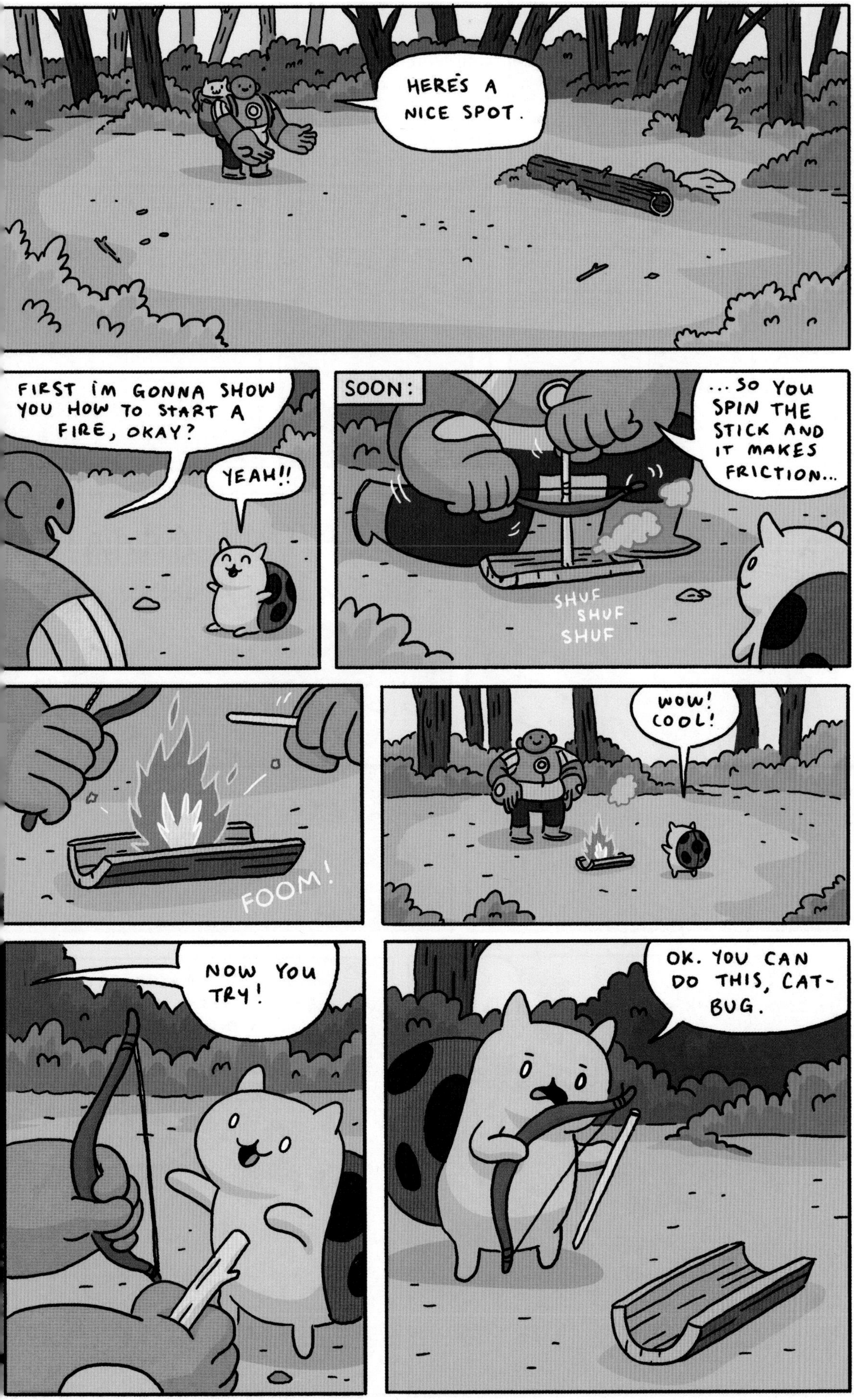
HERE'S A NICE SPOT.
FIRST I'M GONNA SHOW YOU HOW TO START A FIRE, OKAY?
YEAH!!
SOON:
...SO YOU SPIN THE STICK AND IT MAKES FRICTION...
SHUF SHUF SHUF
FOOM!
WOW! COOL!
NOW YOU TRY!
OK. YOU CAN DO THIS, CAT-BUG.

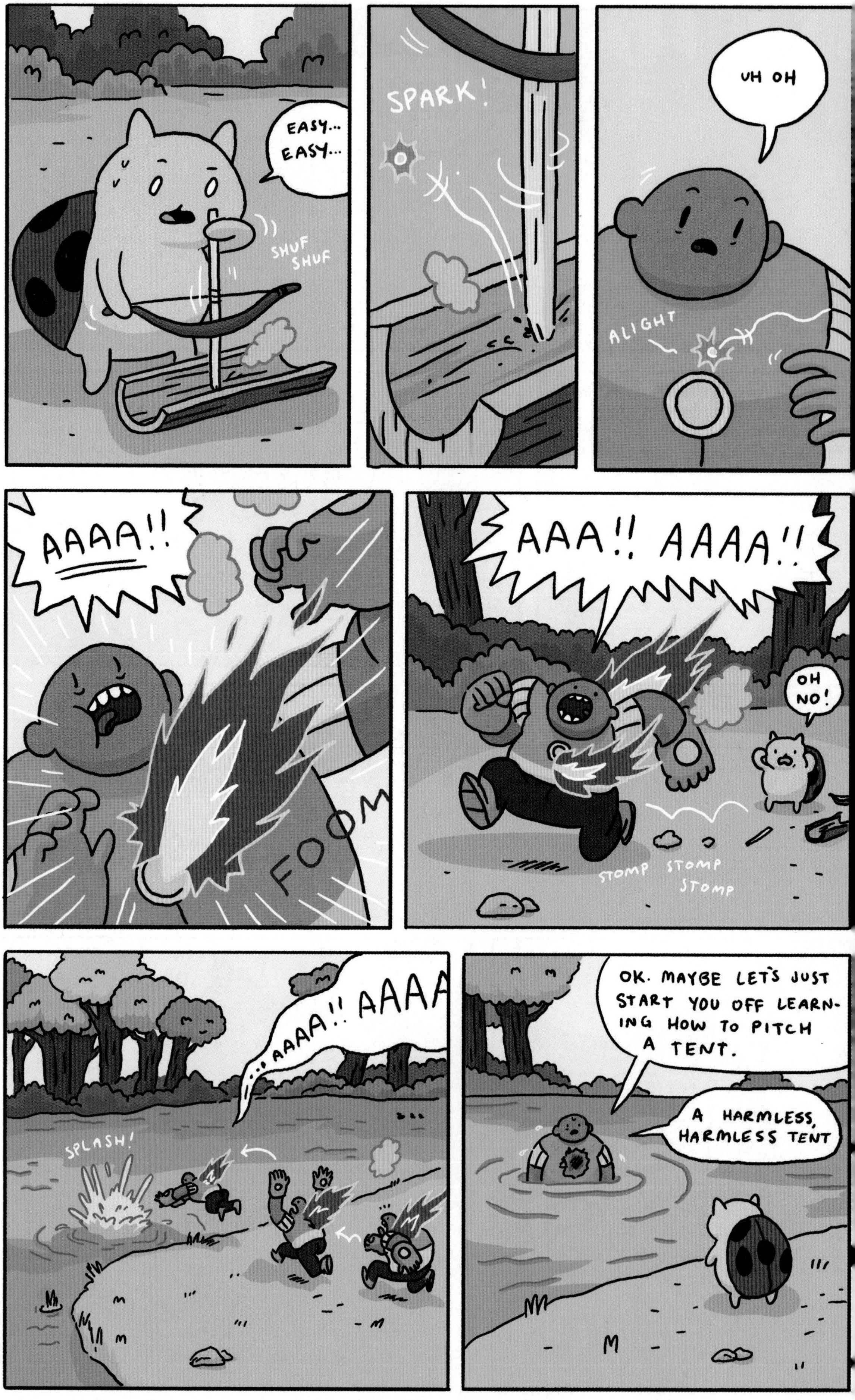
EASY...
EASY...
SHUF SHUF
SPARK!
UH OH
ALIGHT
AAAA!!
FOOM
AAA!! AAAA!!
OH NO!
STOMP STOMP STOMP
...AAAA!! AAAA
SPLASH!
OK. MAYBE LET'S JUST START YOU OFF LEARN-ING HOW TO PITCH A TENT.
A HARMLESS, HARMLESS TENT

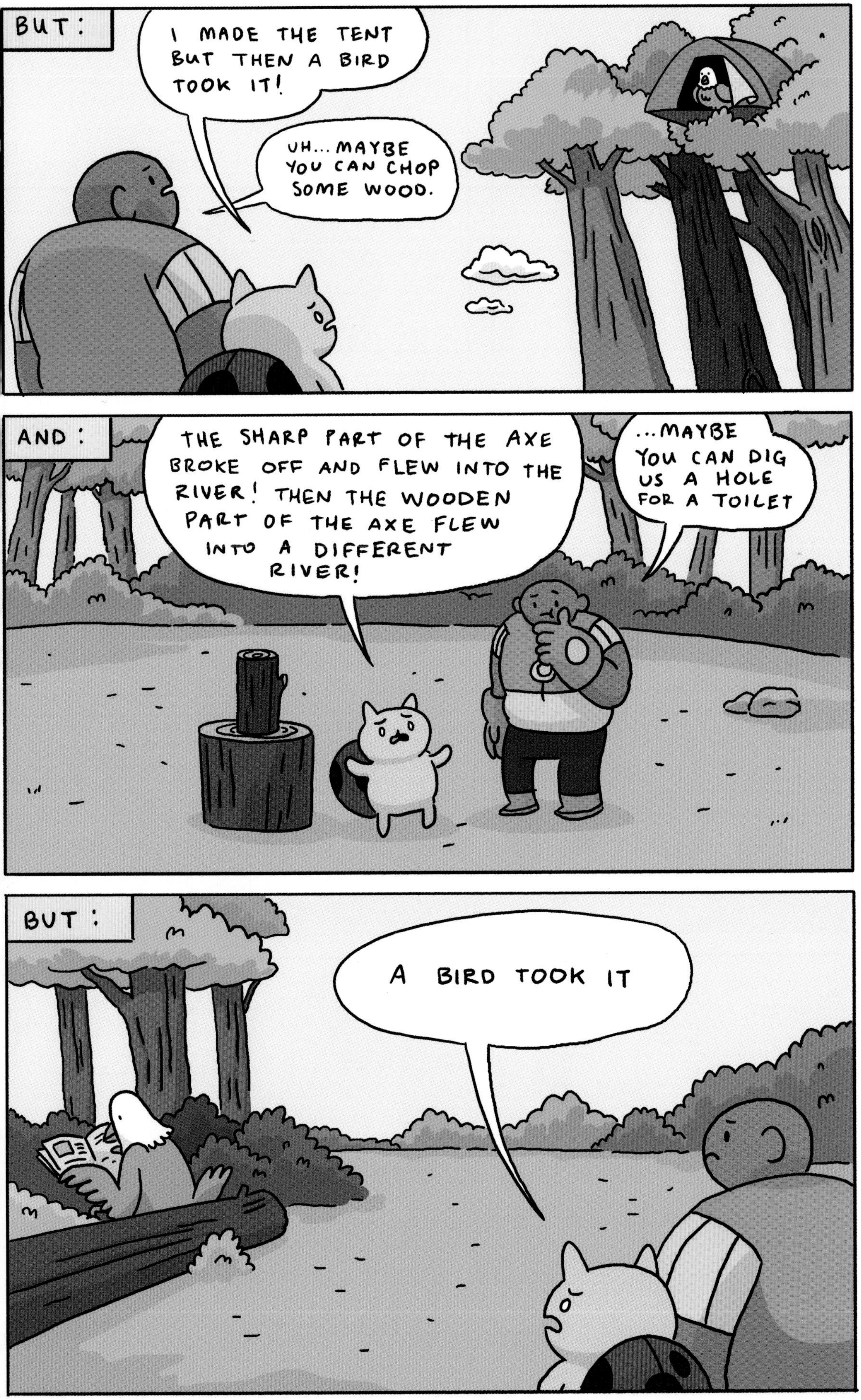
BUT:
I MADE THE TENT BUT THEN A BIRD TOOK IT!
UH... MAYBE YOU CAN CHOP SOME WOOD.
AND:
THE SHARP PART OF THE AXE BROKE OFF AND FLEW INTO THE RIVER! THEN THE WOODEN PART OF THE AXE FLEW INTO A DIFFERENT RIVER!
...MAYBE YOU CAN DIG US A HOLE FOR A TOILET
BUT:
A BIRD TOOK IT

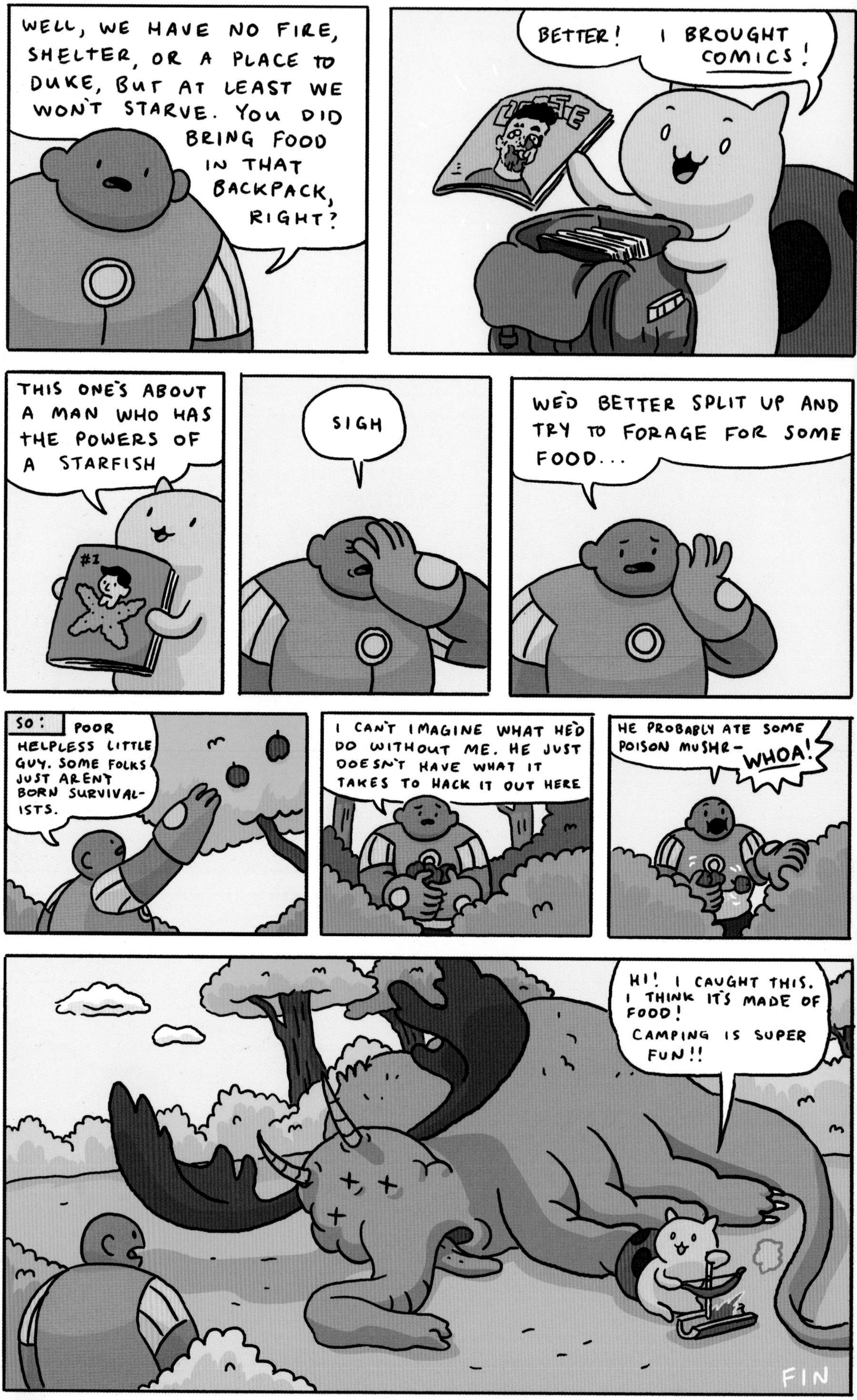
WELL, WE HAVE NO FIRE, SHELTER, OR A PLACE TO DUKE, BUT AT LEAST WE WON'T STARVE. YOU DID BRING FOOD IN THAT BACKPACK, RIGHT?
BETTER! I BROUGHT COMICS!
THIS ONE'S ABOUT A MAN WHO HAS THE POWERS OF A STARFISH
SIGH
WE'D BETTER SPLIT UP AND TRY TO FORAGE FOR SOME FOOD...
SO:
POOR HELPLESS LITTLE GUY. SOME FOLKS JUST AREN'T BORN SURVIVALISTS.
I CAN'T IMAGINE WHAT HE'D DO WITHOUT ME. HE JUST DOESN'T HAVE WHAT IT TAKES TO HACK IT OUT HERE
HE PROBABLY ATE SOME POISON MUSHR–
WHOA!
HI! I CAUGHT THIS. I THINK IT'S MADE OF FOOD!
CAMPING IS SUPER FUN!!
FIN

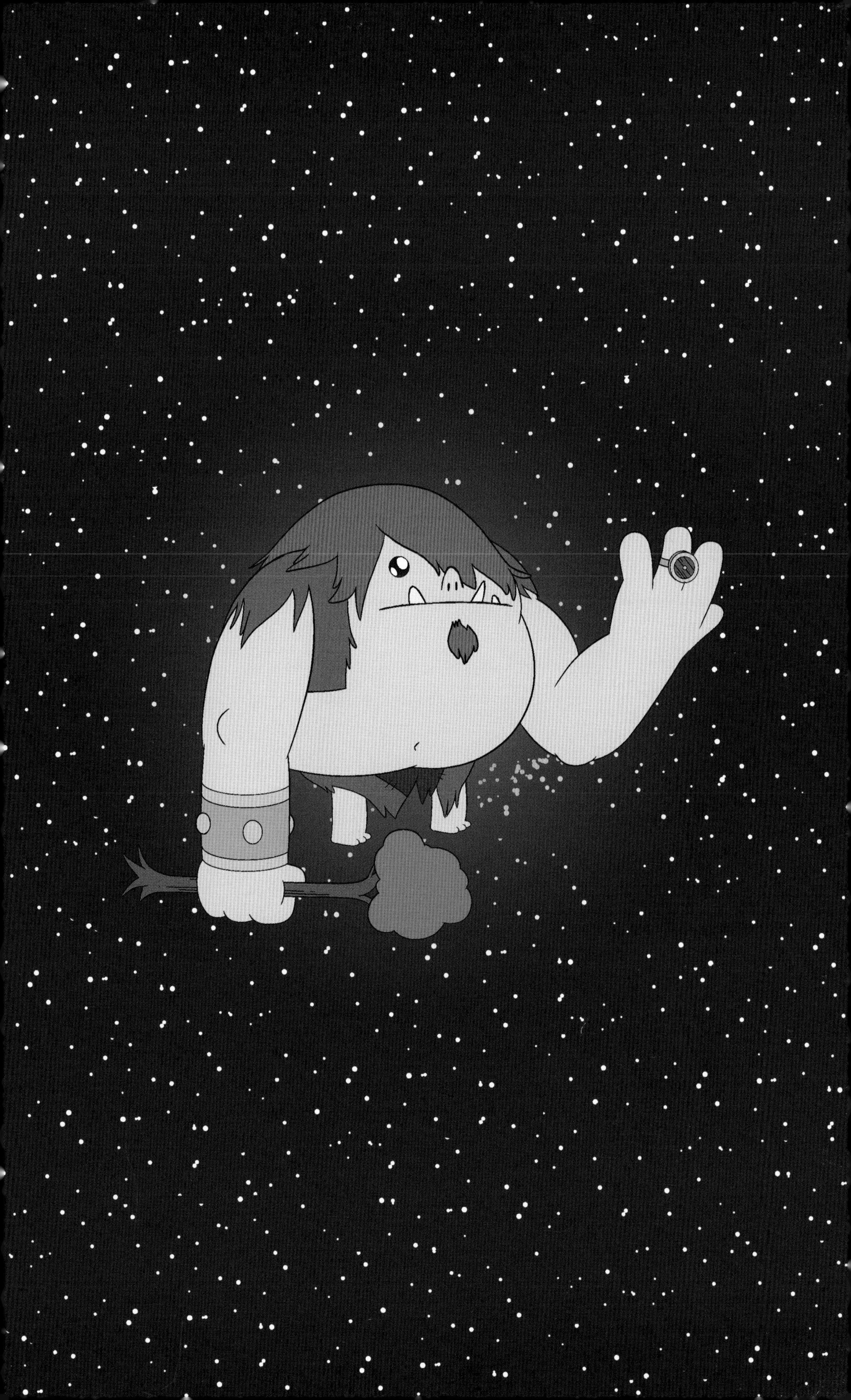

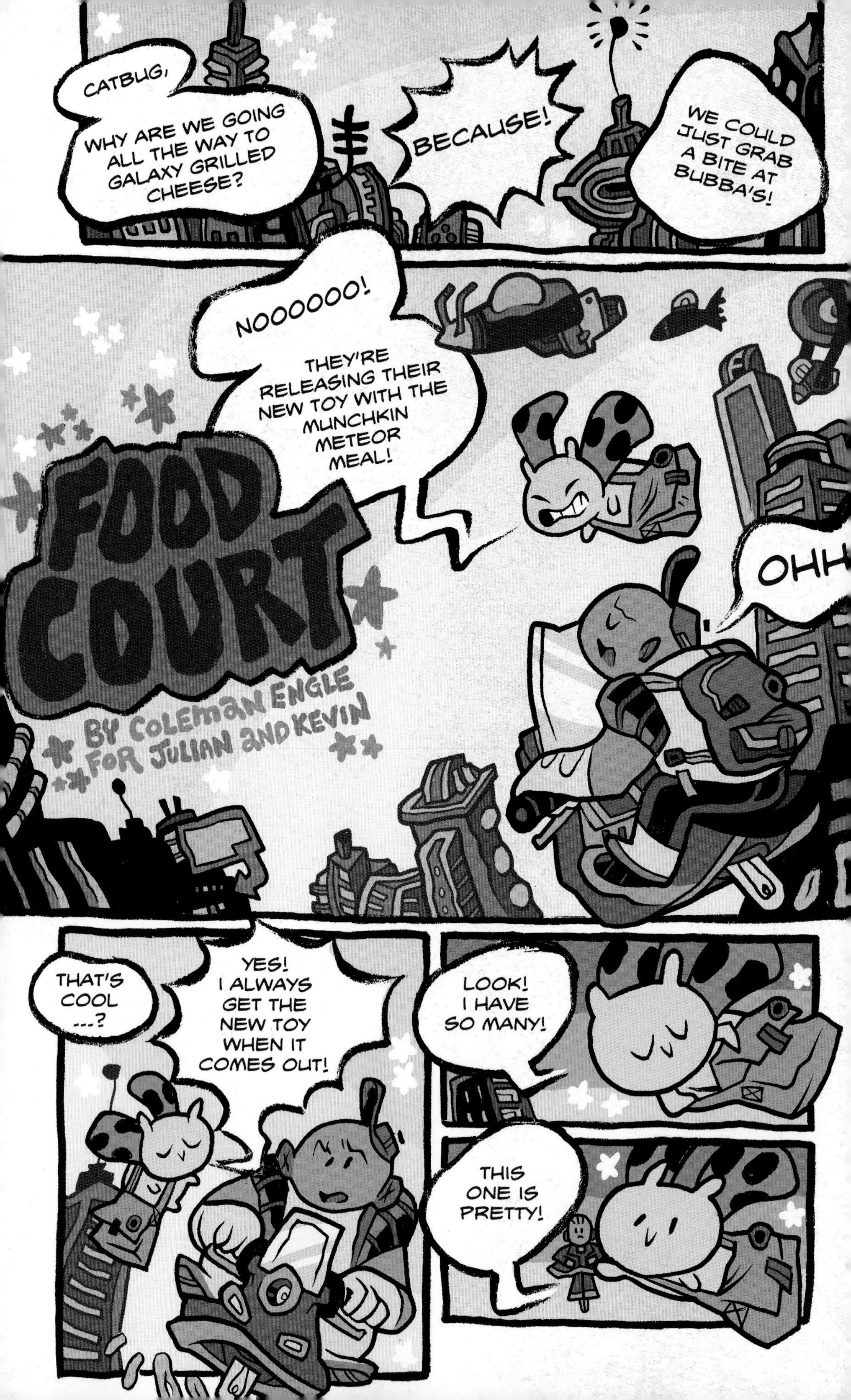
CATBUG,
WHY ARE WE GOING ALL THE WAY TO GALAXY GRILLED CHEESE?
BECAUSE!
WE COULD JUST GRAB A BITE AT BUBBA'S!
NOOOOOO!
THEY'RE RELEASING THEIR NEW TOY WITH THE MUNCHKIN METEOR MEAL!
FOOD COURT
BY COLEMAN ENGLE FOR JULIAN AND KEVIN
OHH
THAT'S COOL ...?
YES! I ALWAYS GET THE NEW TOY WHEN IT COMES OUT!
LOOK! I HAVE SO MANY!
THIS ONE IS PRETTY!

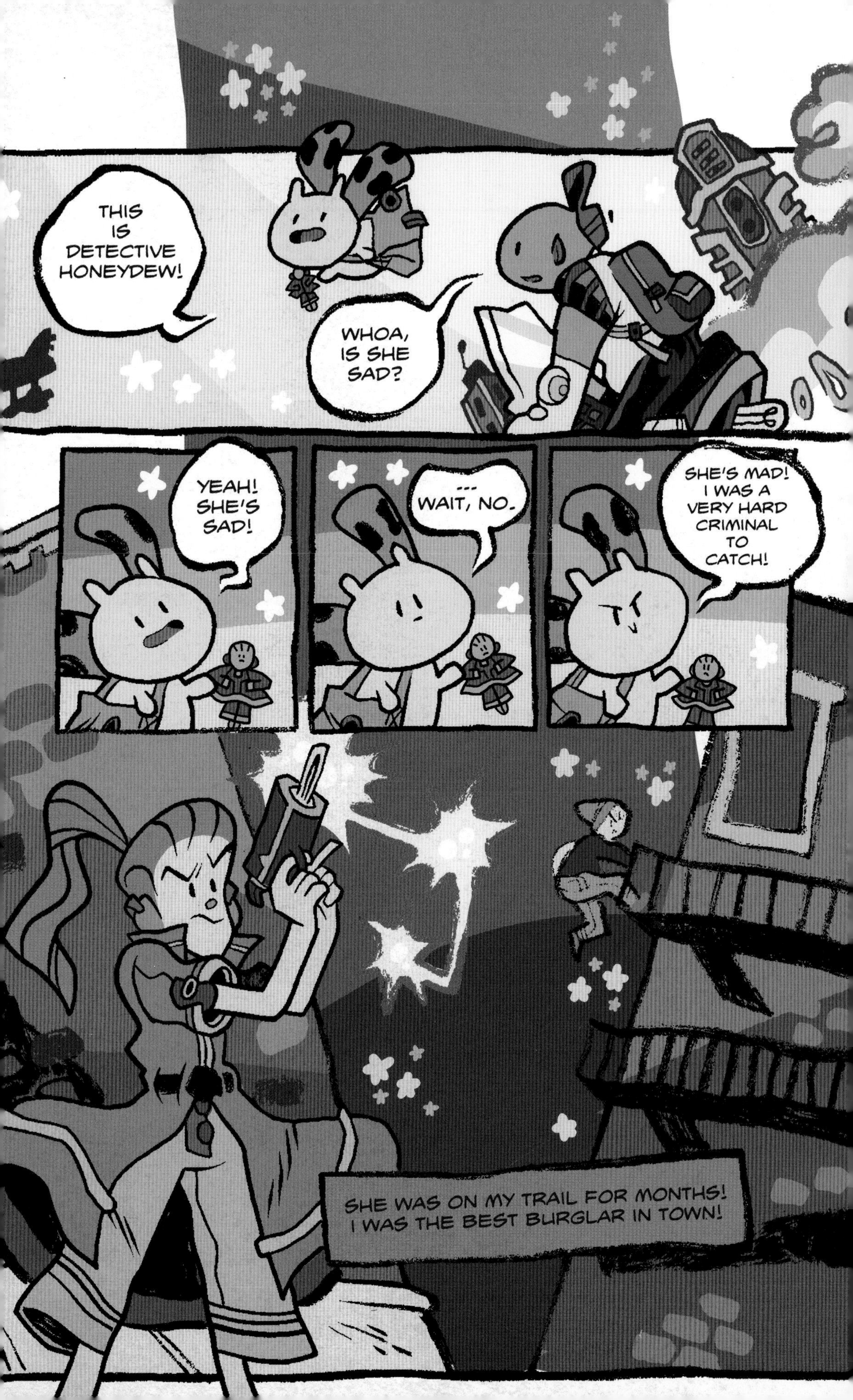
THIS IS DETECTIVE HONEYDEW!
WHOA, IS SHE SAD?
YEAH! SHE'S SAD!
... WAIT, NO.
SHE'S MAD! I WAS A VERY HARD CRIMINAL TO CATCH!
SHE WAS ON MY TRAIL FOR MONTHS! I WAS THE BEST BURGLAR IN TOWN!

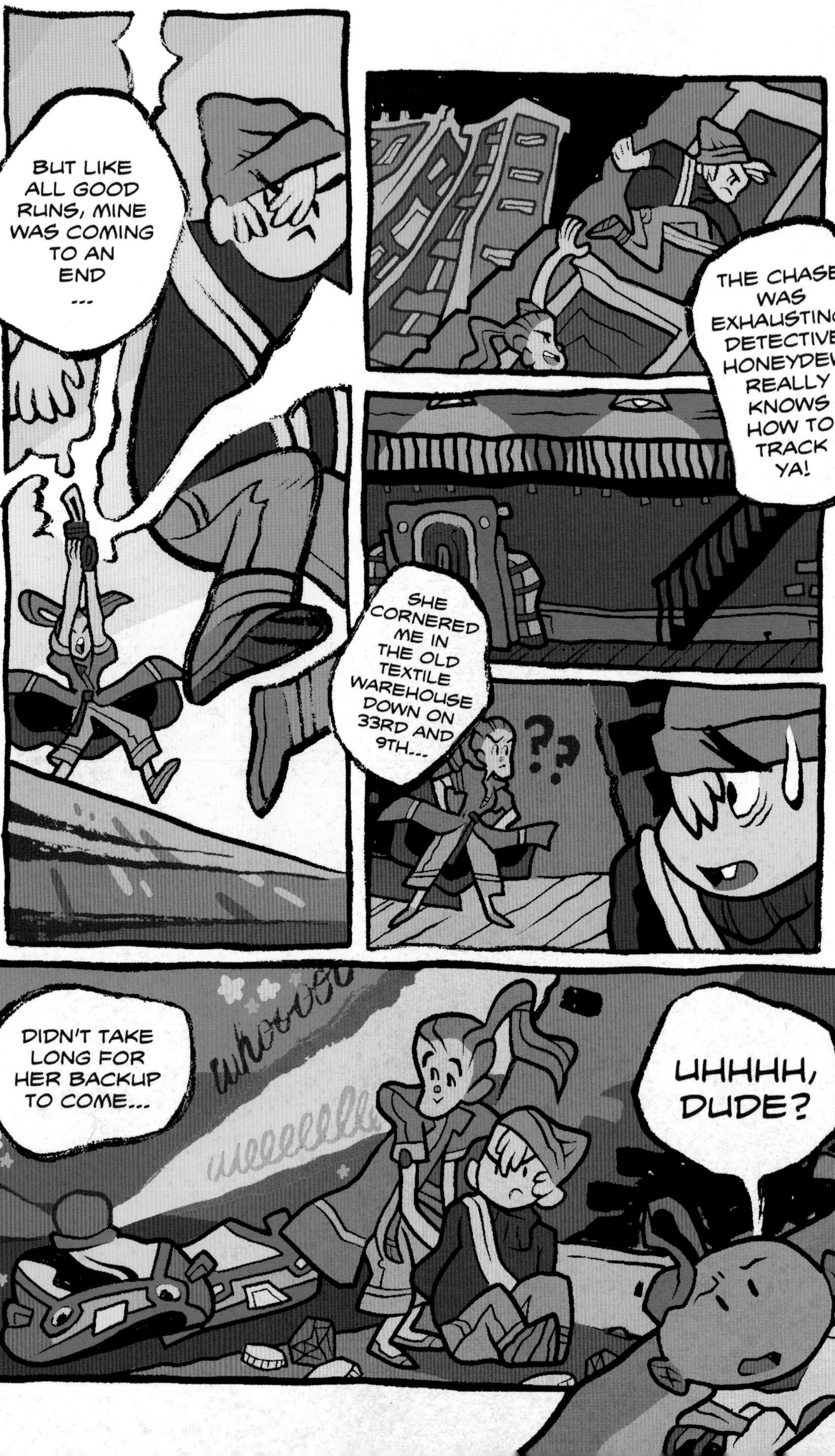
BUT LIKE ALL GOOD RUNS, MINE WAS COMING TO AN END ...
THE CHASE WAS EXHAUSTING! DETECTIVE HONEYDEW REALLY KNOWS HOW TO TRACK YA!
SHE CORNERED ME IN THE OLD TEXTILE WAREHOUSE DOWN ON 33RD AND 9TH...
??
DIDN'T TAKE LONG FOR HER BACKUP TO COME...
whooooo
weeeeeee
UHHHH, DUDE?

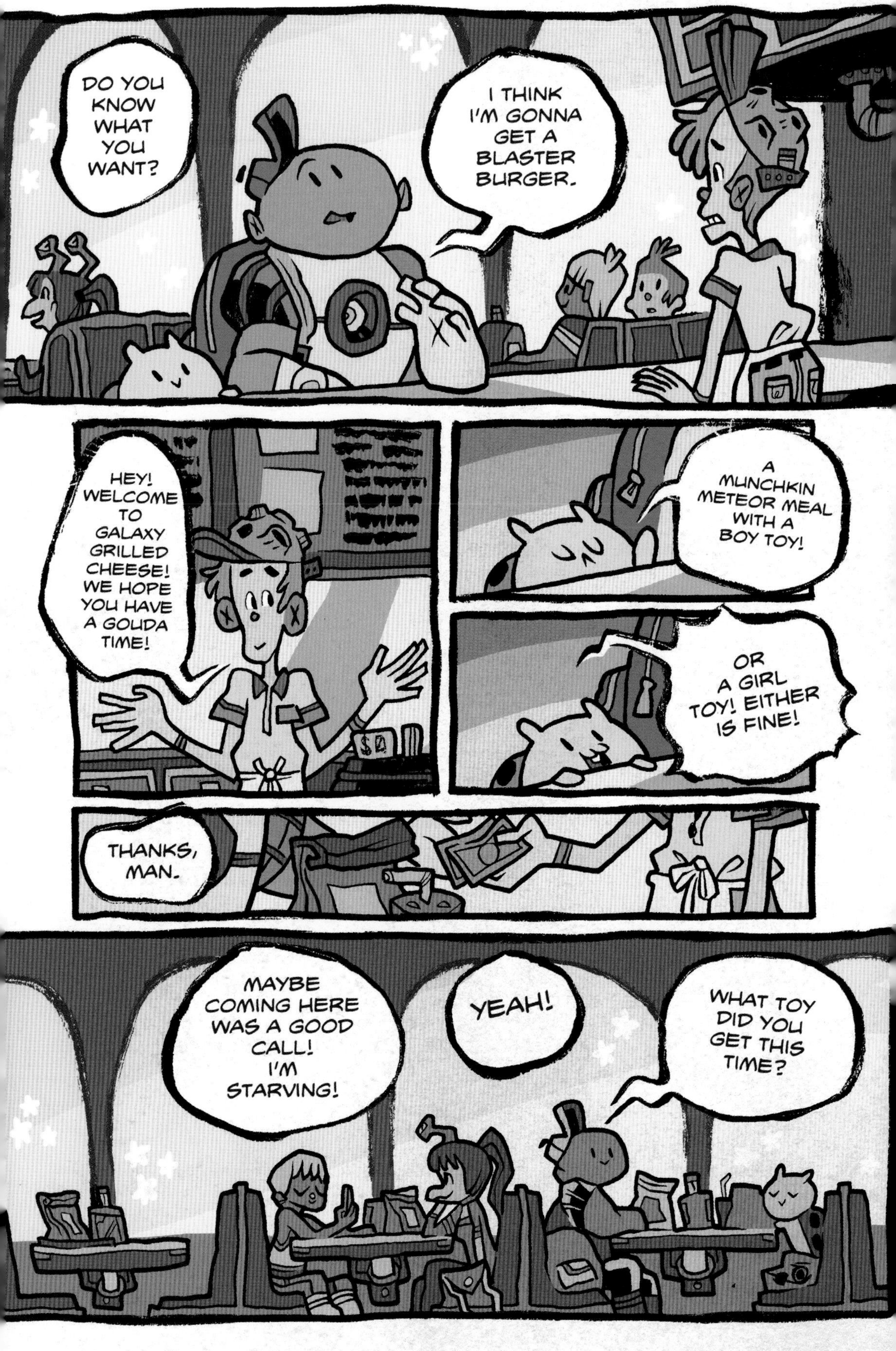
DO YOU KNOW WHAT YOU WANT?
I THINK I'M GONNA GET A BLASTER BURGER.
HEY! WELCOME TO GALAXY GRILLED CHEESE! WE HOPE YOU HAVE A GOUDA TIME!
A MUNCHKIN METEOR MEAL WITH A BOY TOY!
OR A GIRL TOY! EITHER IS FINE!
THANKS, MAN.
MAYBE COMING HERE WAS A GOOD CALL! I'M STARVING!
YEAH!
WHAT TOY DID YOU GET THIS TIME?

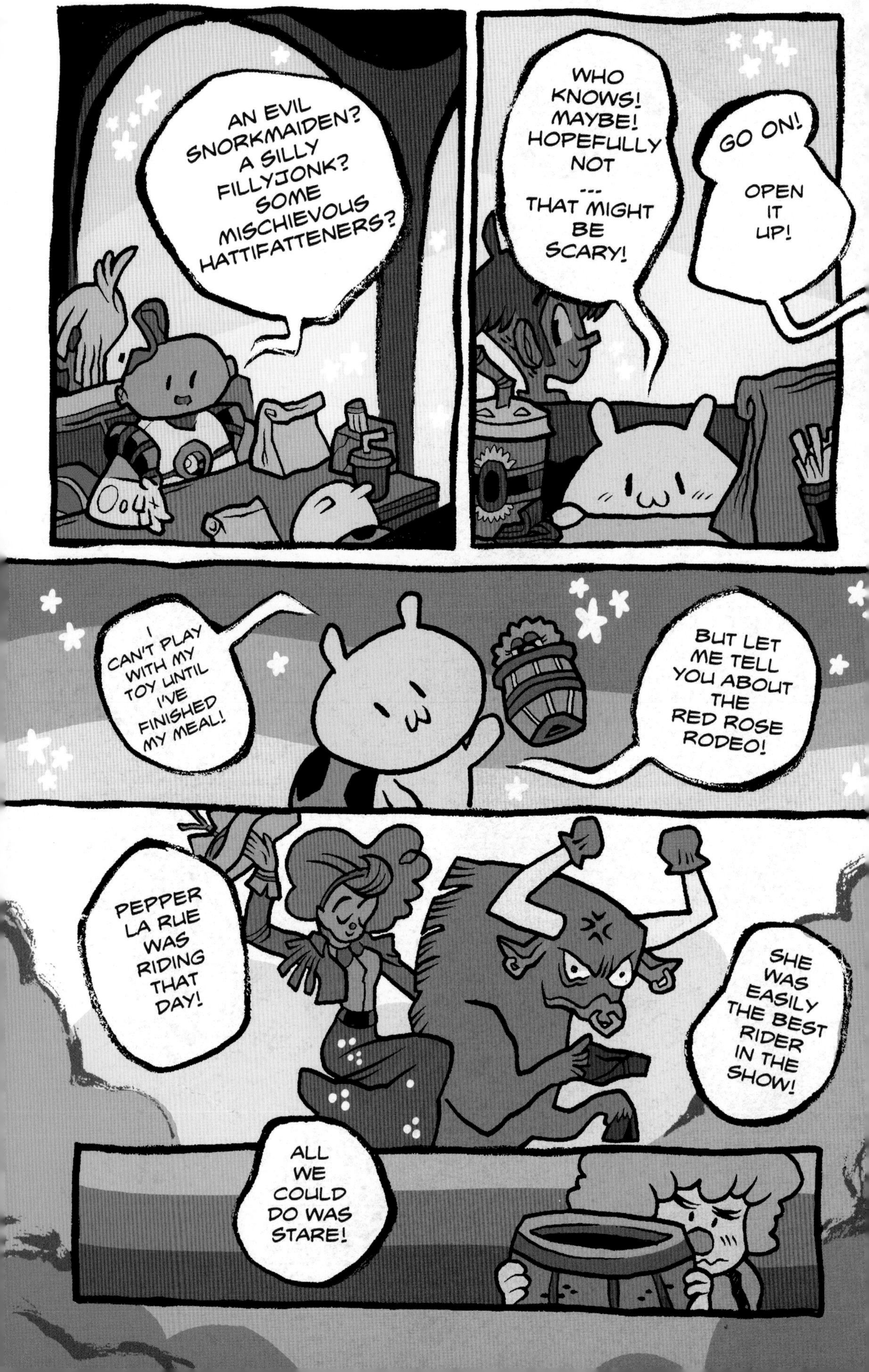
AN EVIL SNORKMAIDEN? A SILLY FILLYJONK? SOME MISCHIEVOUS HATTIFATTENERS?
WHO KNOWS! MAYBE! HOPEFULLY NOT --- THAT MIGHT BE SCARY!
GO ON! OPEN IT UP!
I CAN'T PLAY WITH MY TOY UNTIL I'VE FINISHED MY MEAL!
BUT LET ME TELL YOU ABOUT THE RED ROSE RODEO!
PEPPER LA RUE WAS RIDING THAT DAY!
SHE WAS EASILY THE BEST RIDER IN THE SHOW!
ALL WE COULD DO WAS STARE!

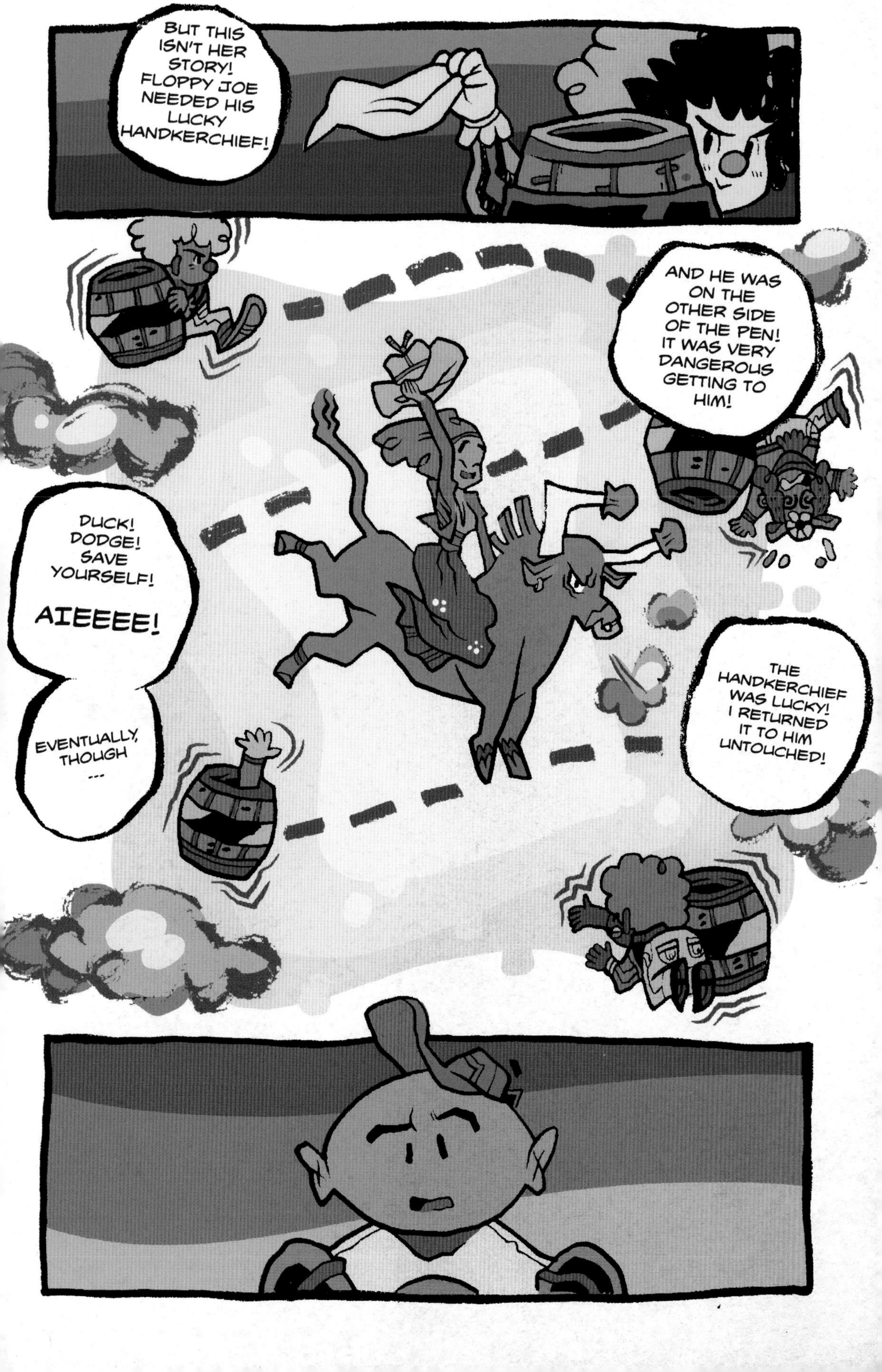
BUT THIS ISN'T HER STORY! FLOPPY JOE NEEDED HIS LUCKY HANDKERCHIEF!
AND HE WAS ON THE OTHER SIDE OF THE PEN! IT WAS VERY DANGEROUS GETTING TO HIM!
DUCK! DODGE! SAVE YOURSELF!
AIEEEE!
THE HANDKERCHIEF WAS LUCKY! I RETURNED IT TO HIM UNTOUCHED!
EVENTUALLY, THOUGH ---

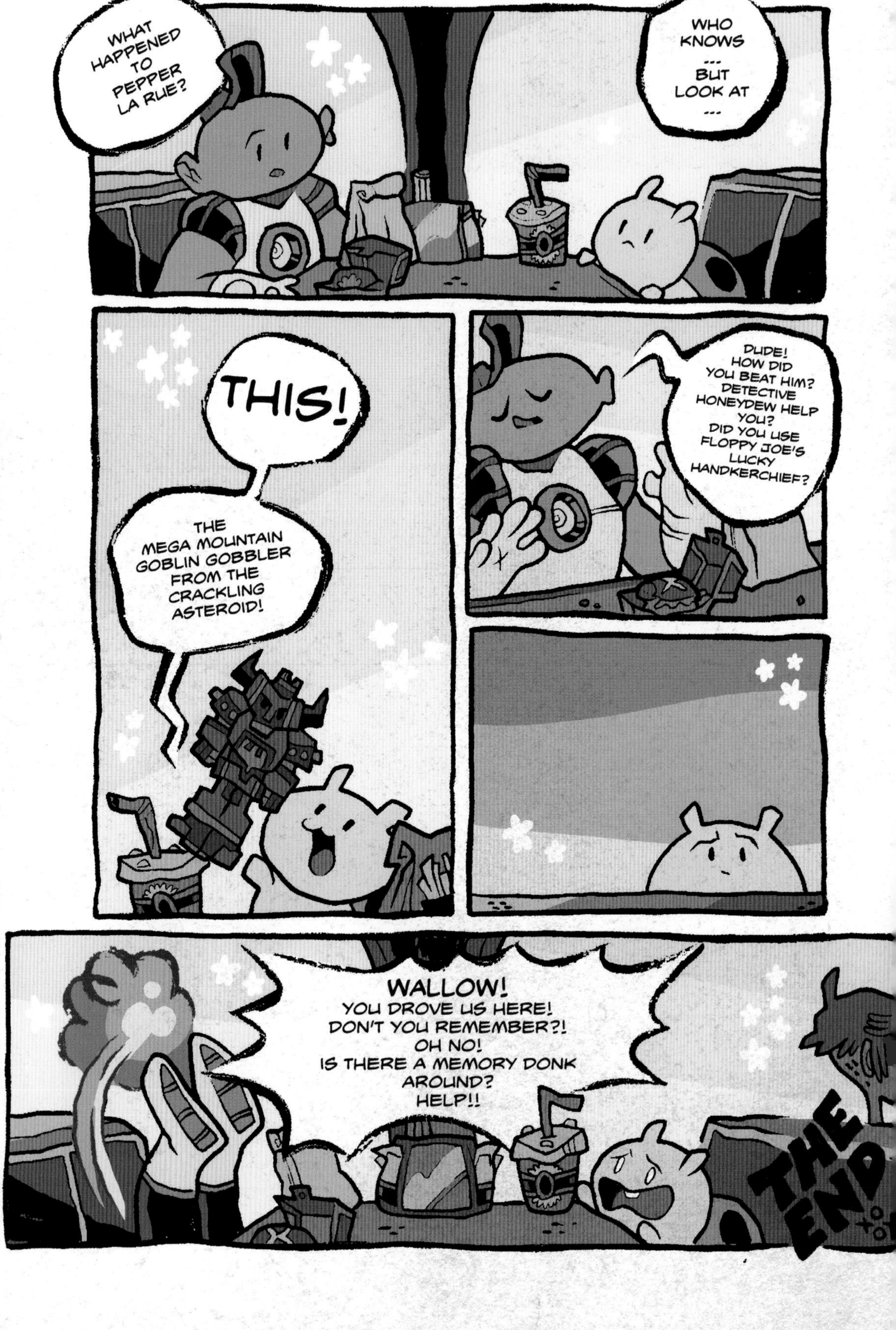
WHAT HAPPENED TO PEPPER LA RUE?
WHO KNOWS ... BUT LOOK AT ...
THIS!
THE MEGA MOUNTAIN GOBLIN GOBBLER FROM THE CRACKLING ASTEROID!
DUDE! HOW DID YOU BEAT HIM? DETECTIVE HONEYDEW HELP YOU? DID YOU USE FLOPPY JOE'S LUCKY HANDKERCHIEF?
WALLOW! YOU DROVE US HERE! DON'T YOU REMEMBER?! OH NO! IS THERE A MEMORY DONK AROUND? HELP!!
THE END

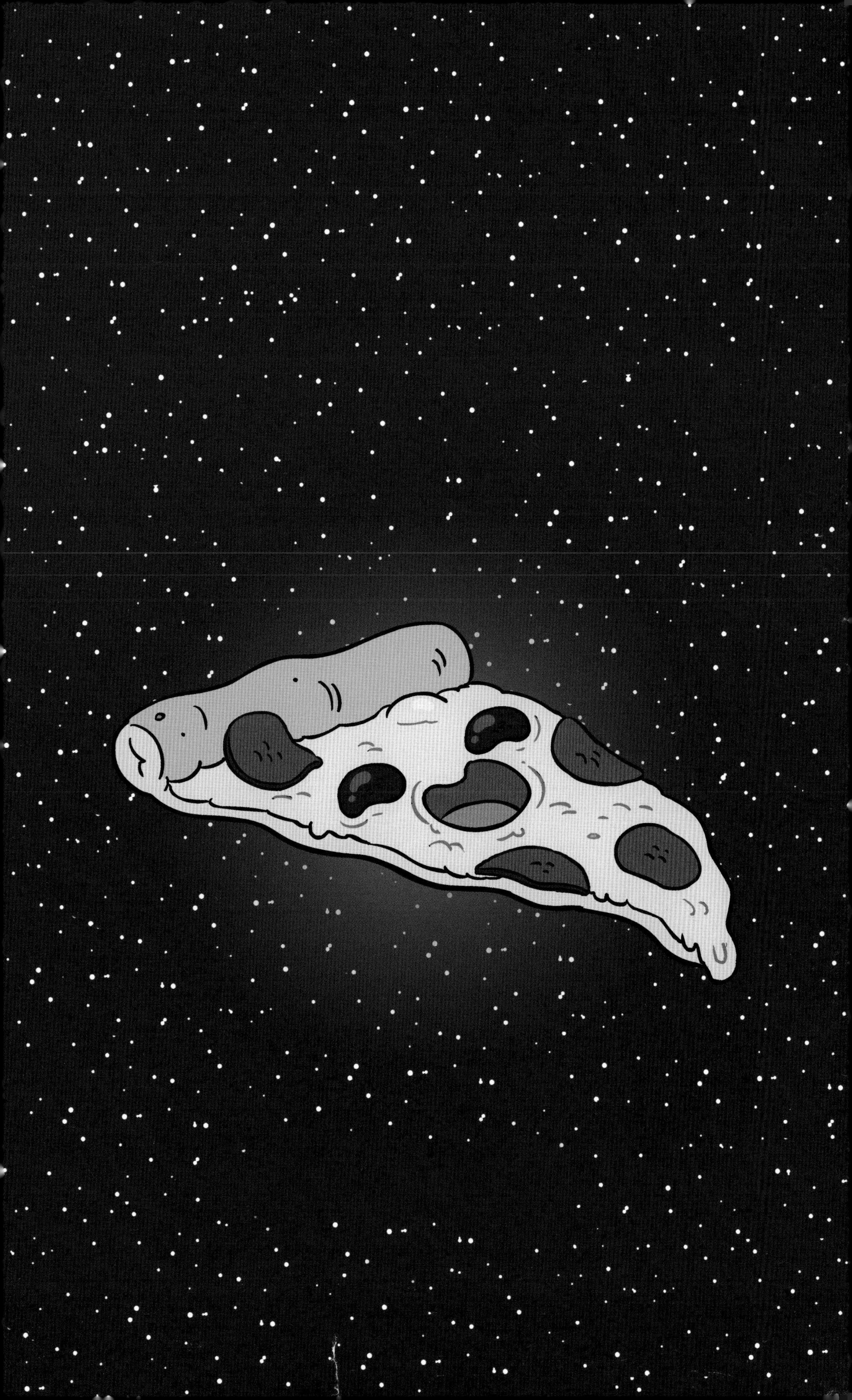

COVER GALLERY

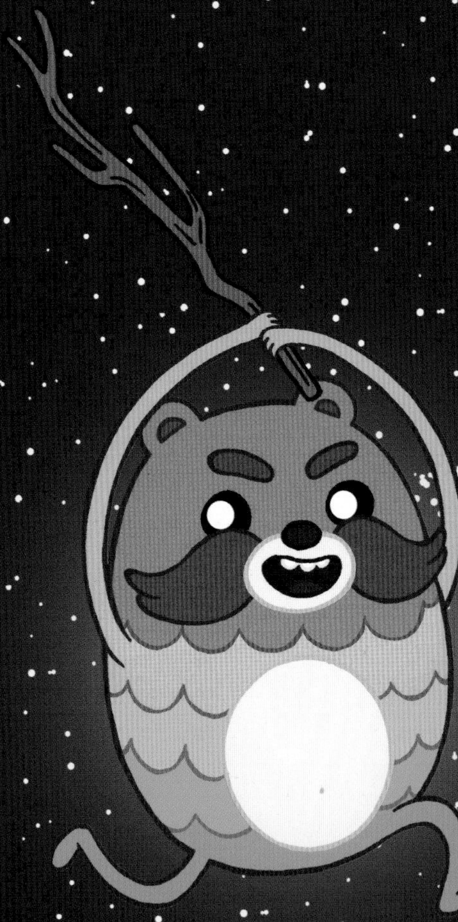

RIGHT, DOWN, DOWN, UP,
LEFT, B, A, SELECT, START

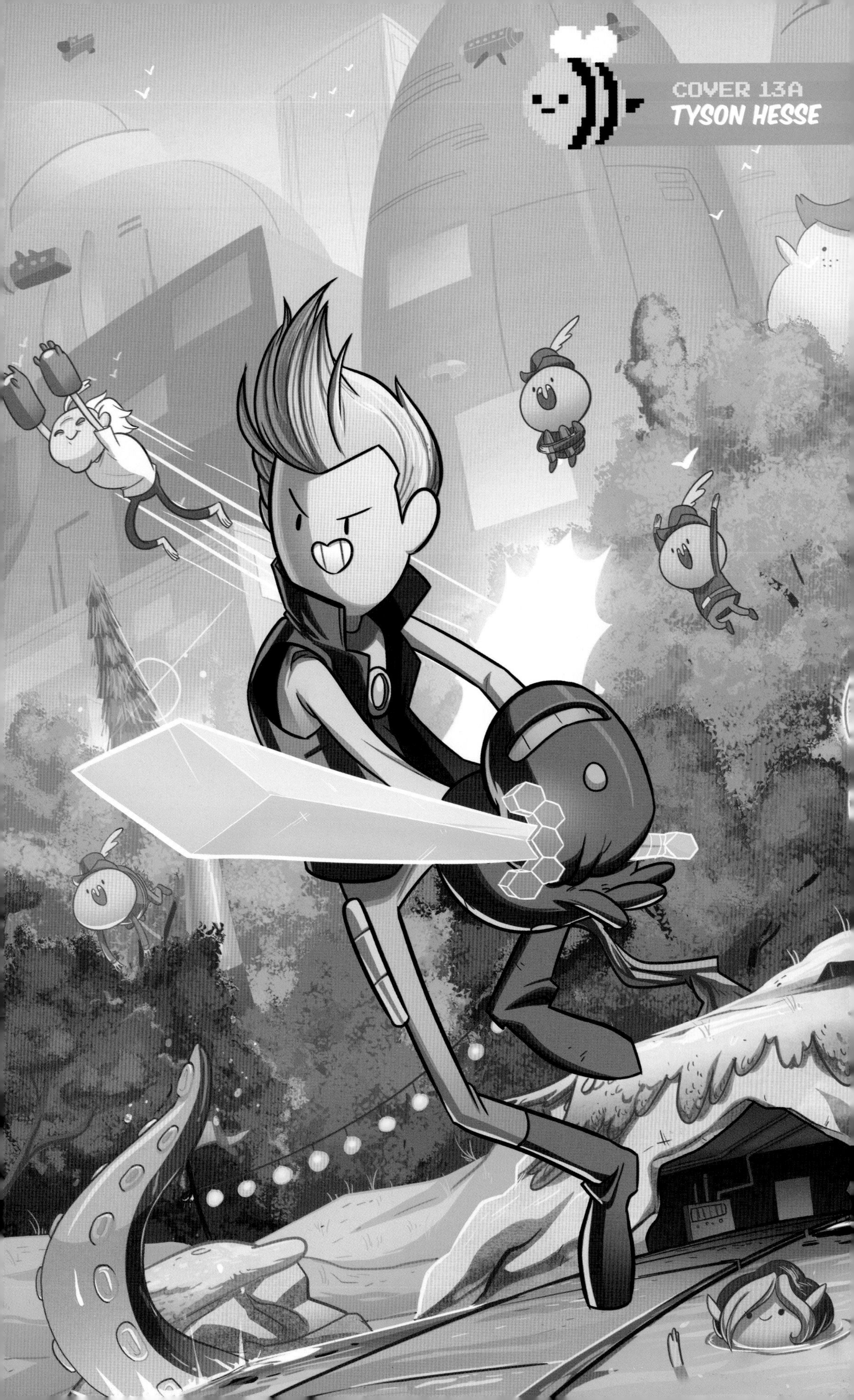
COVER 13A
TYSON HESSE

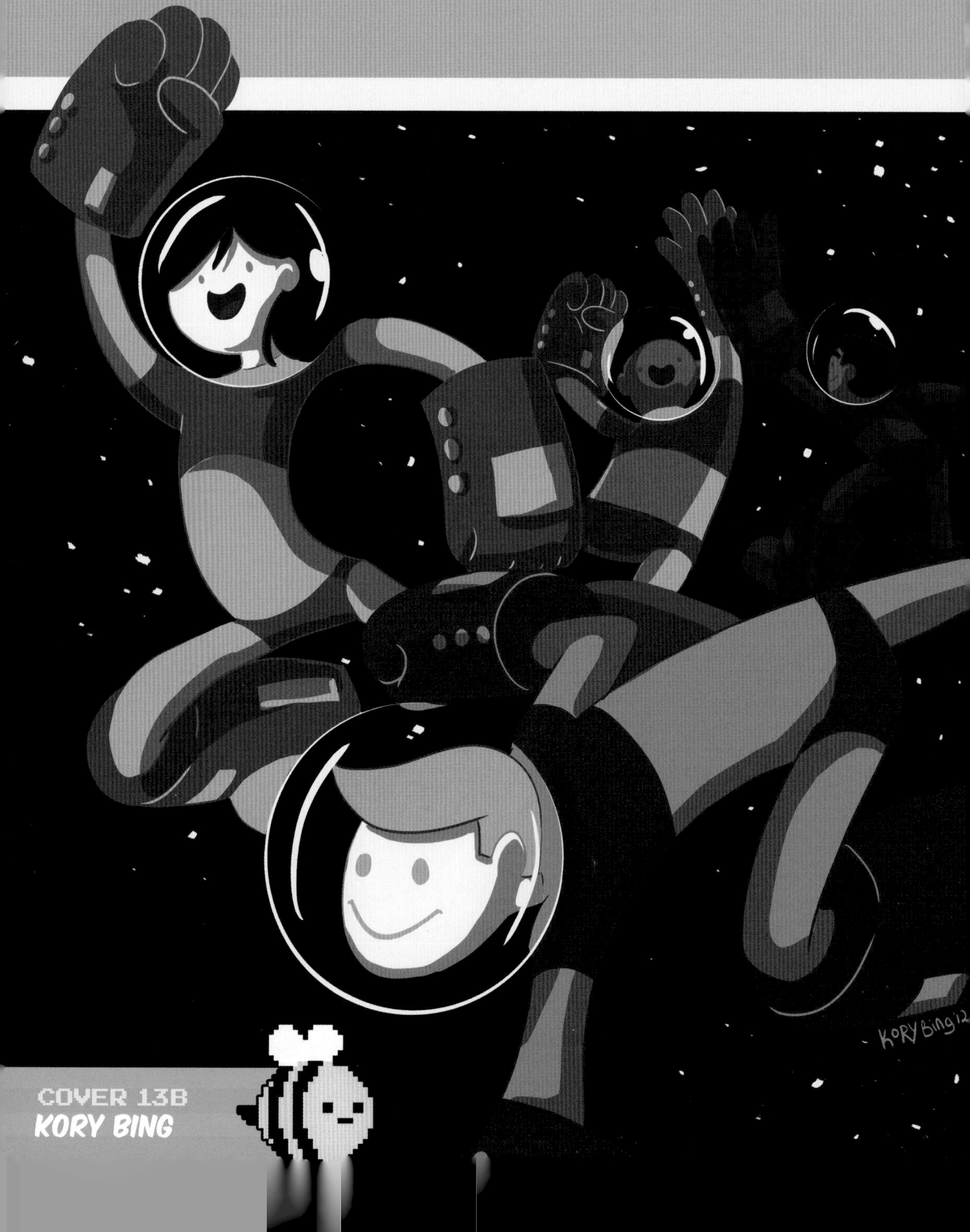
KORY BING'12

COVER 13B
KORY BING

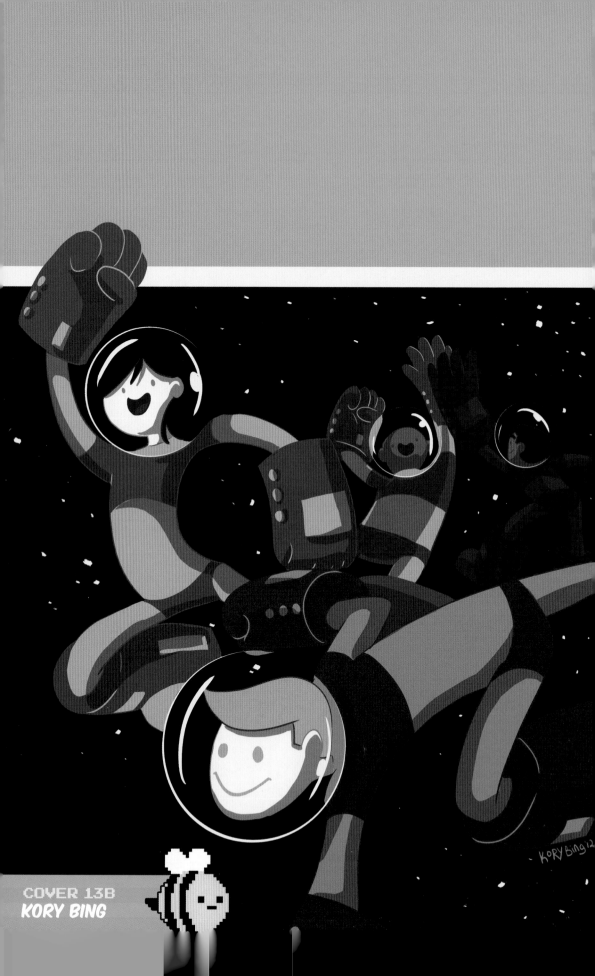

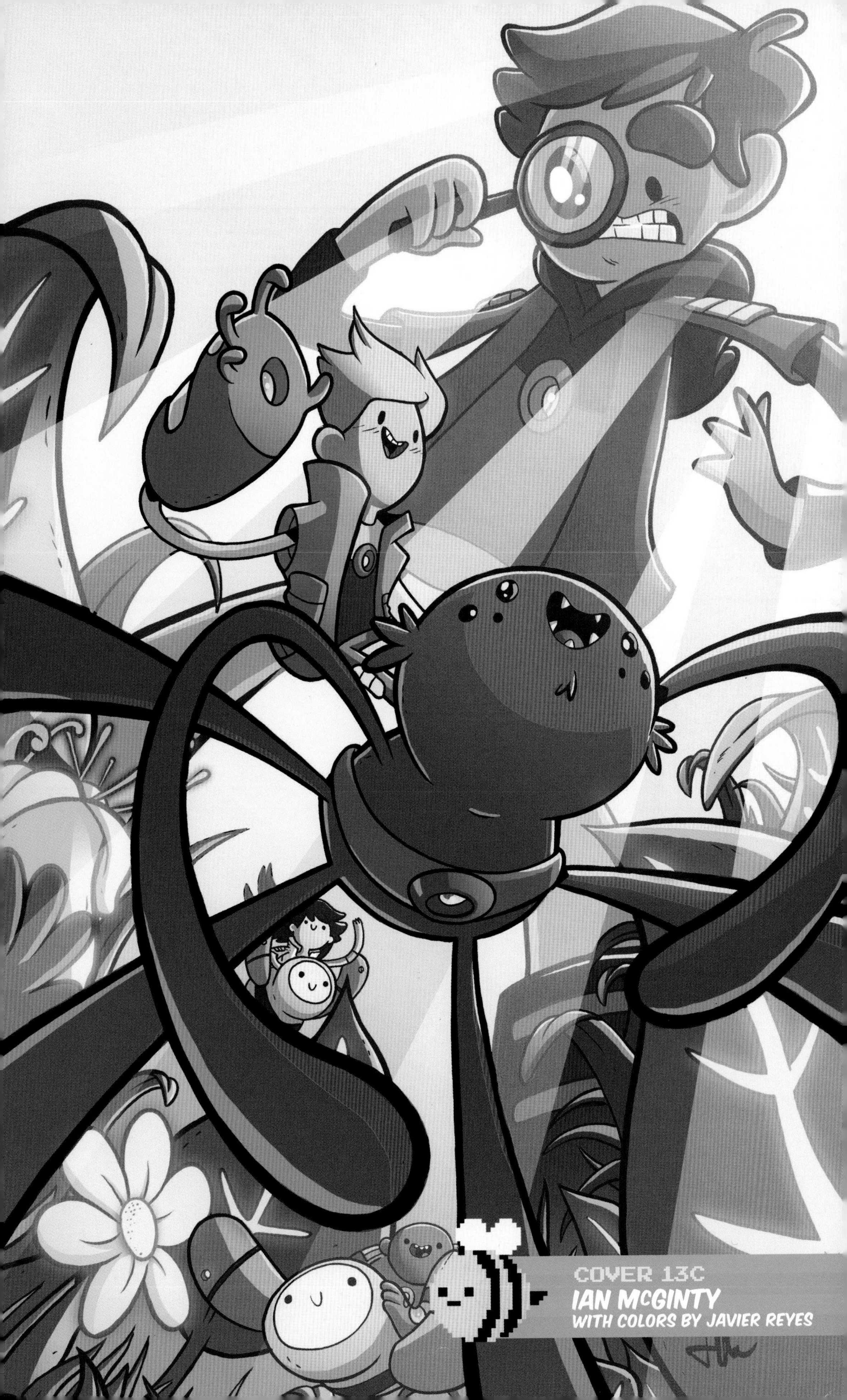
COVER 13C
IAN McGINTY
WITH COLORS BY JAVIER REYES

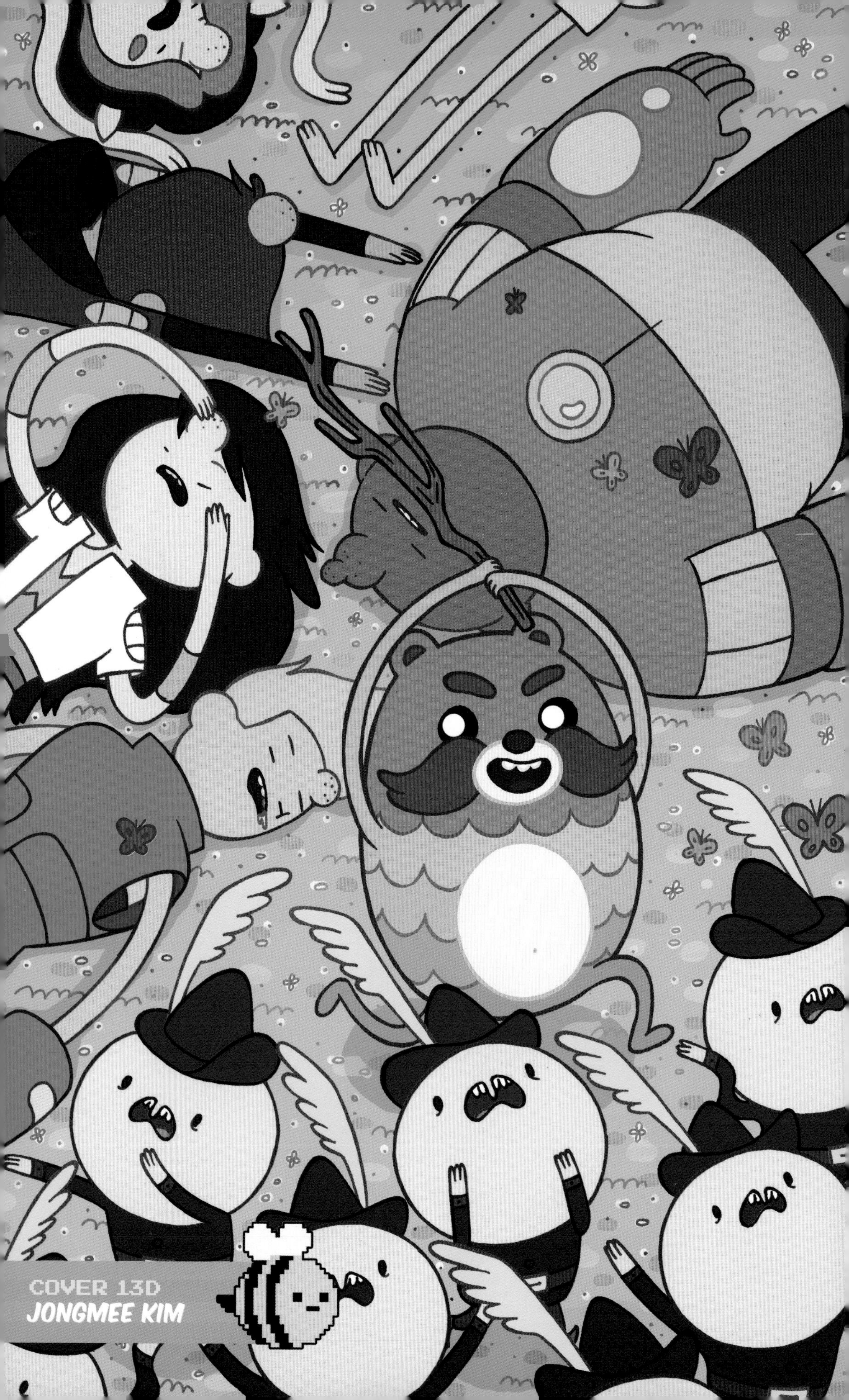

COVER 13D
JONGMEE KIM

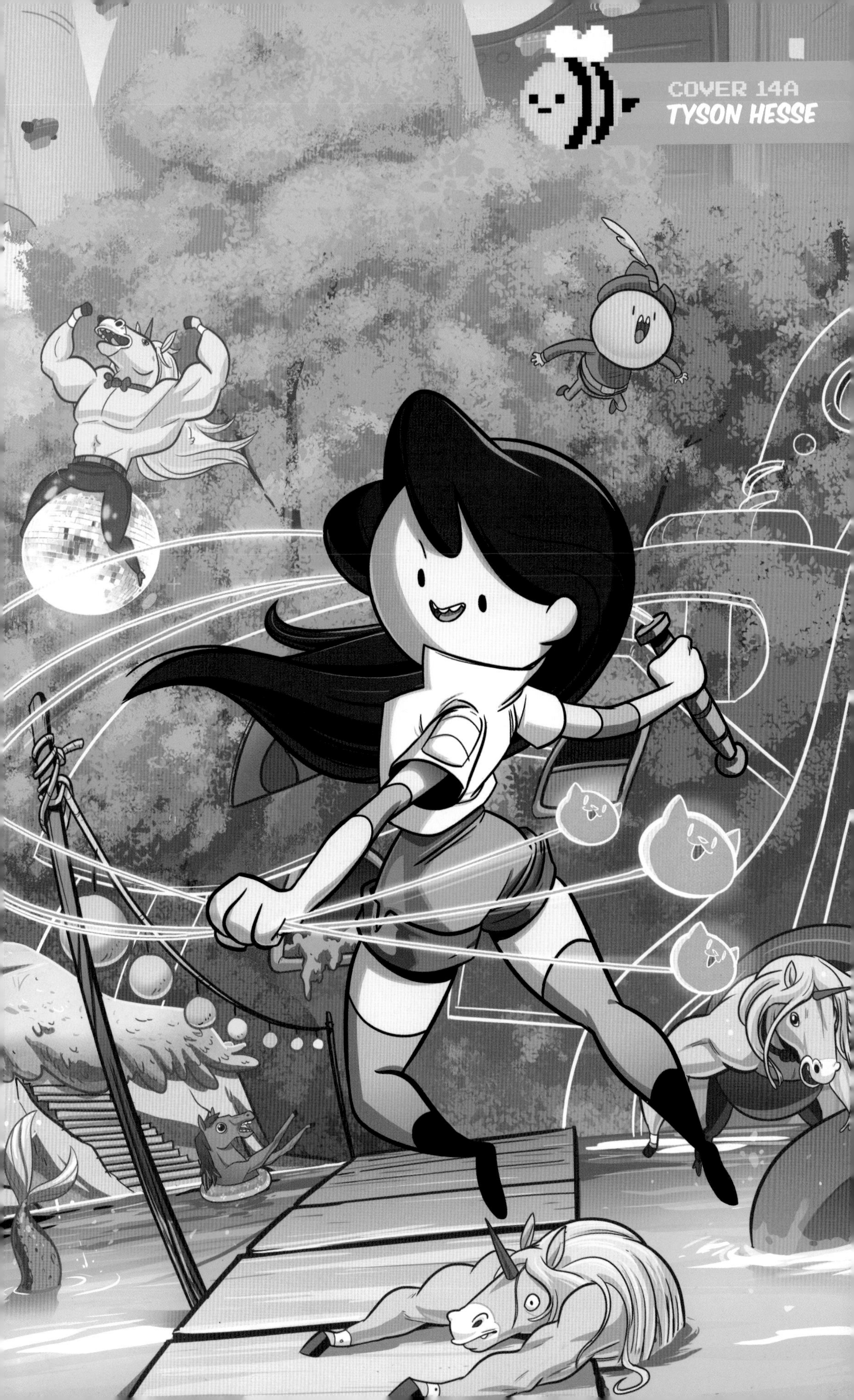
COVER 14A
TYSON HESSE

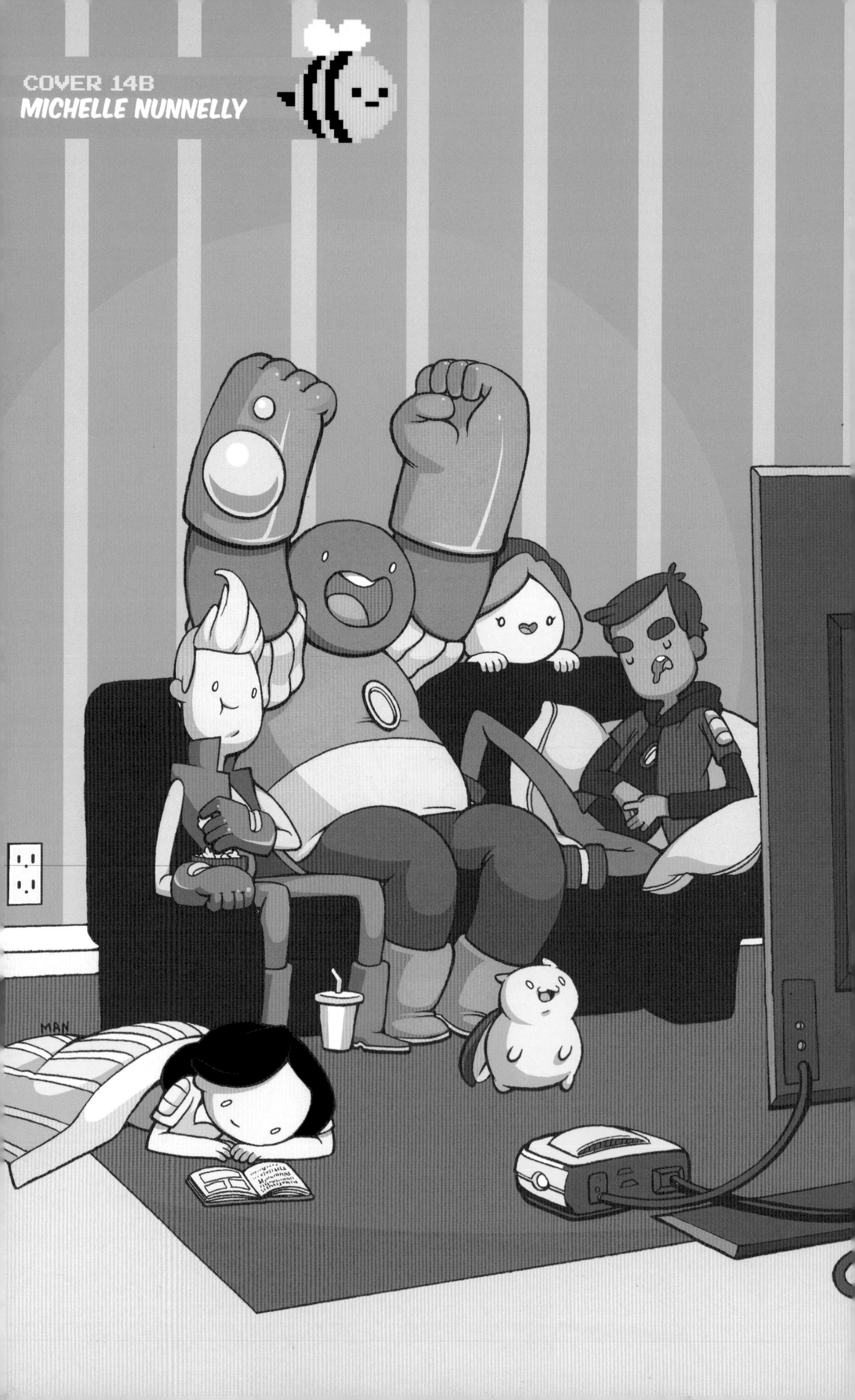
MAN

COVER 14B
MICHELLE NUNNELLY

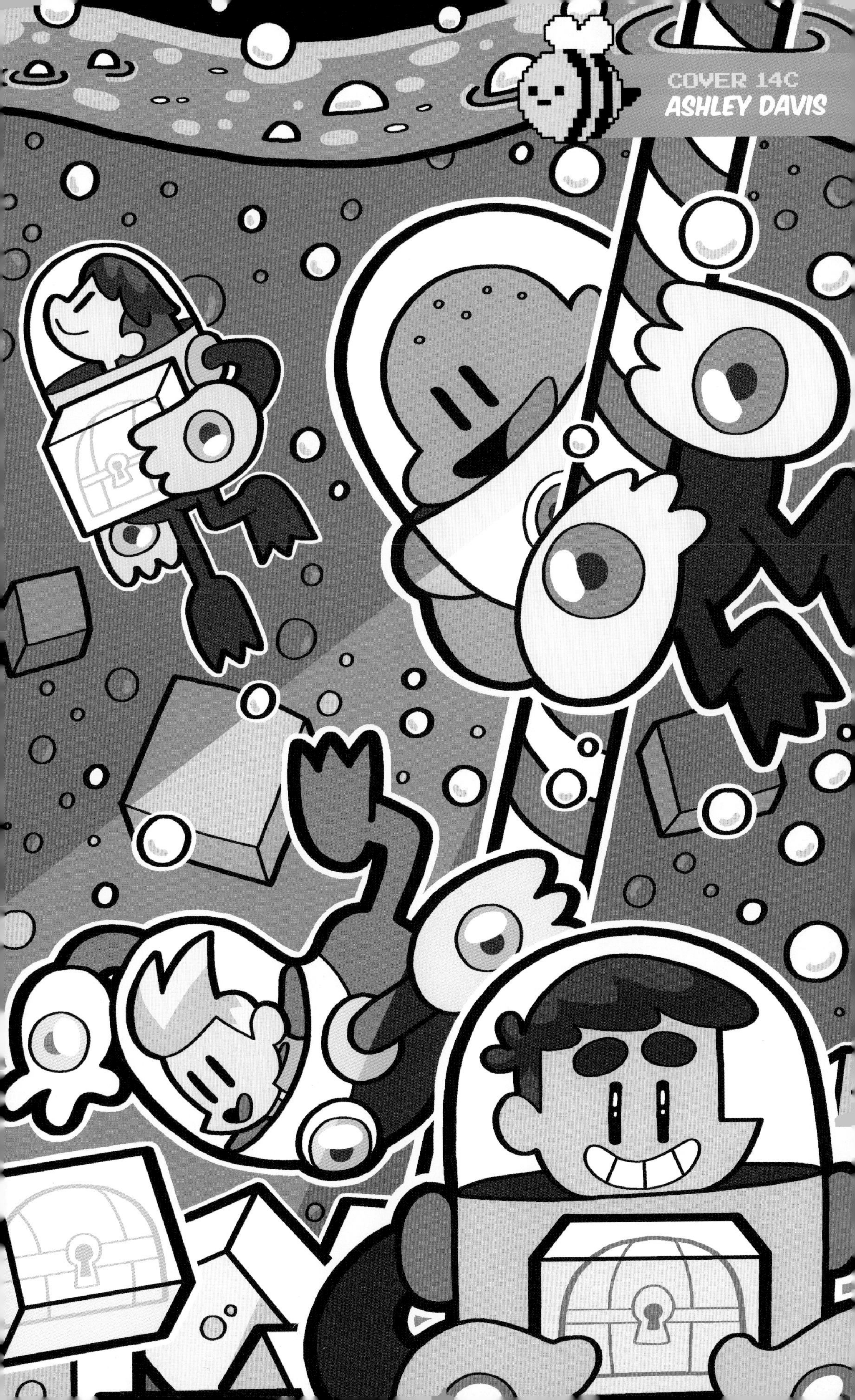
COVER 14C
ASHLEY DAVIS

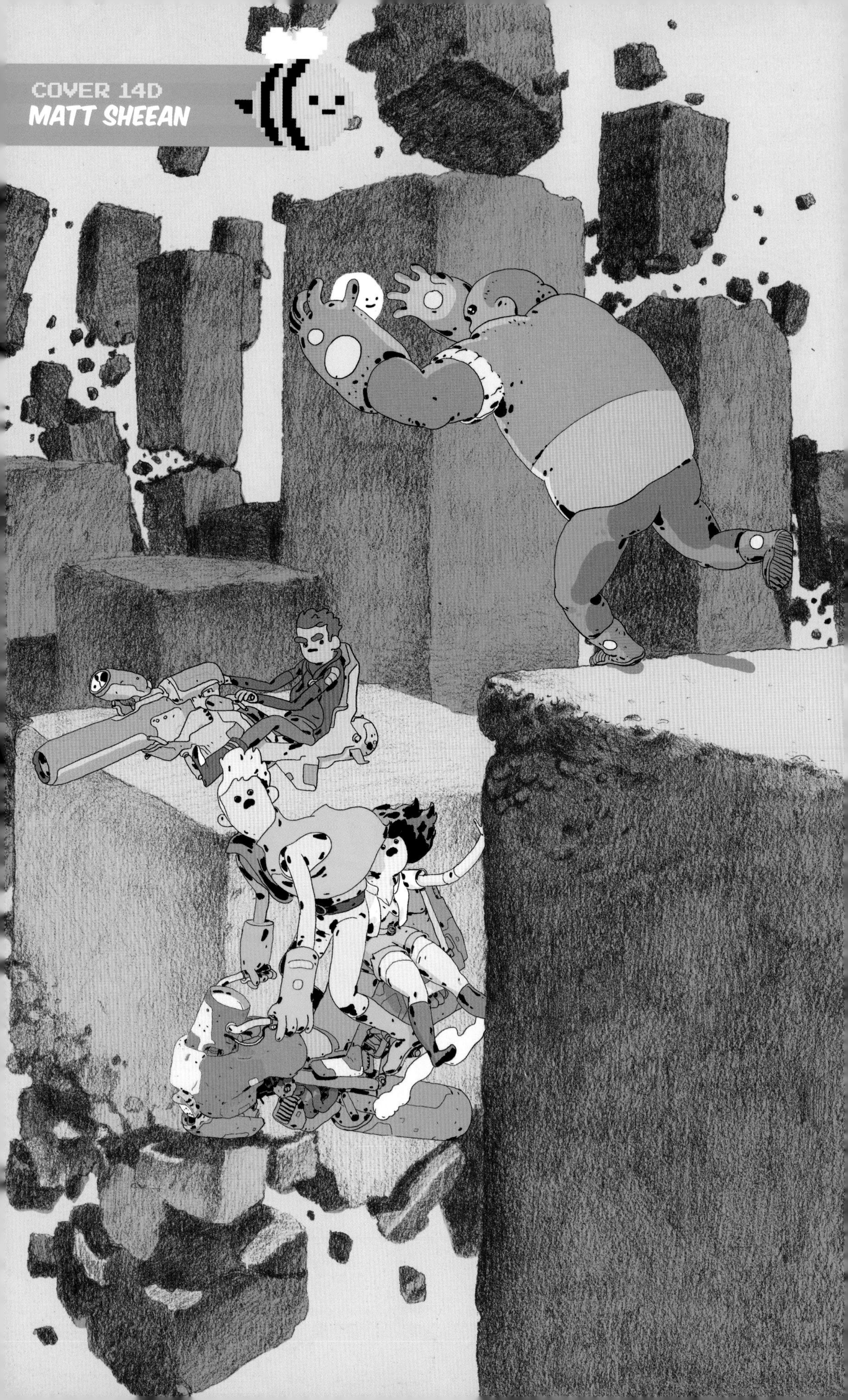
COVER 14D
MATT SHEEAN

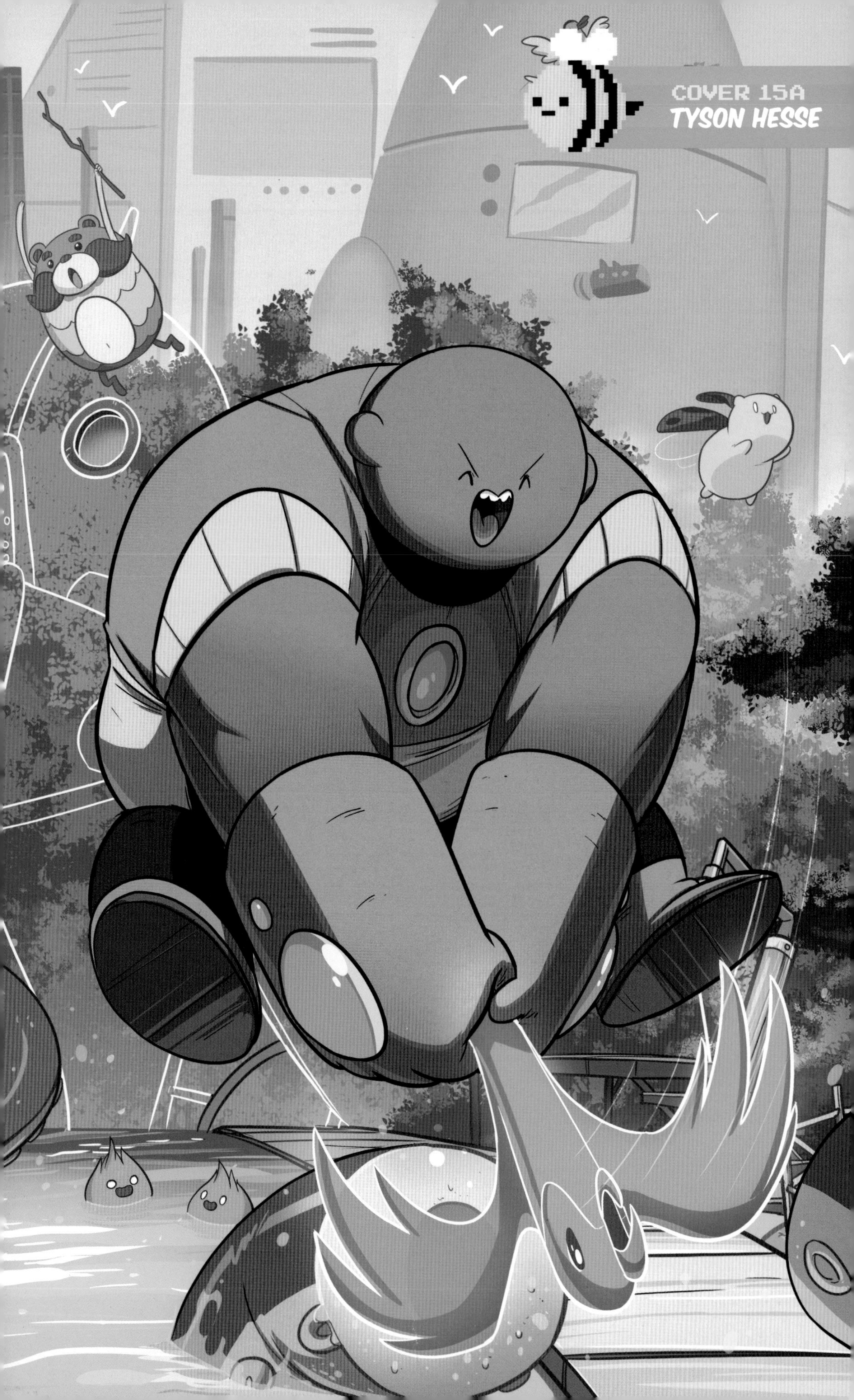
COVER 15A
TYSON HESSE

COVER 15B
KALI FONTECCHIO

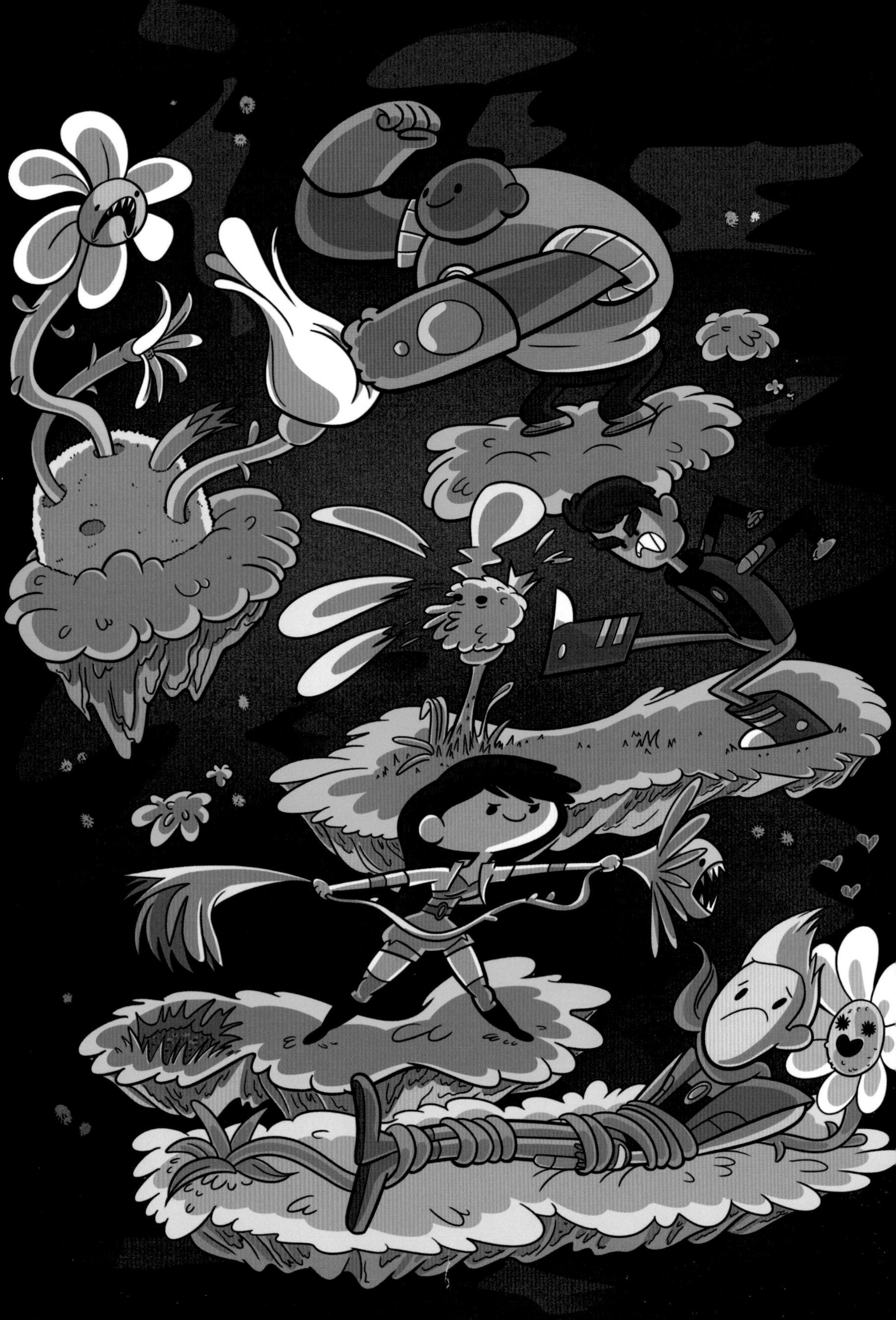

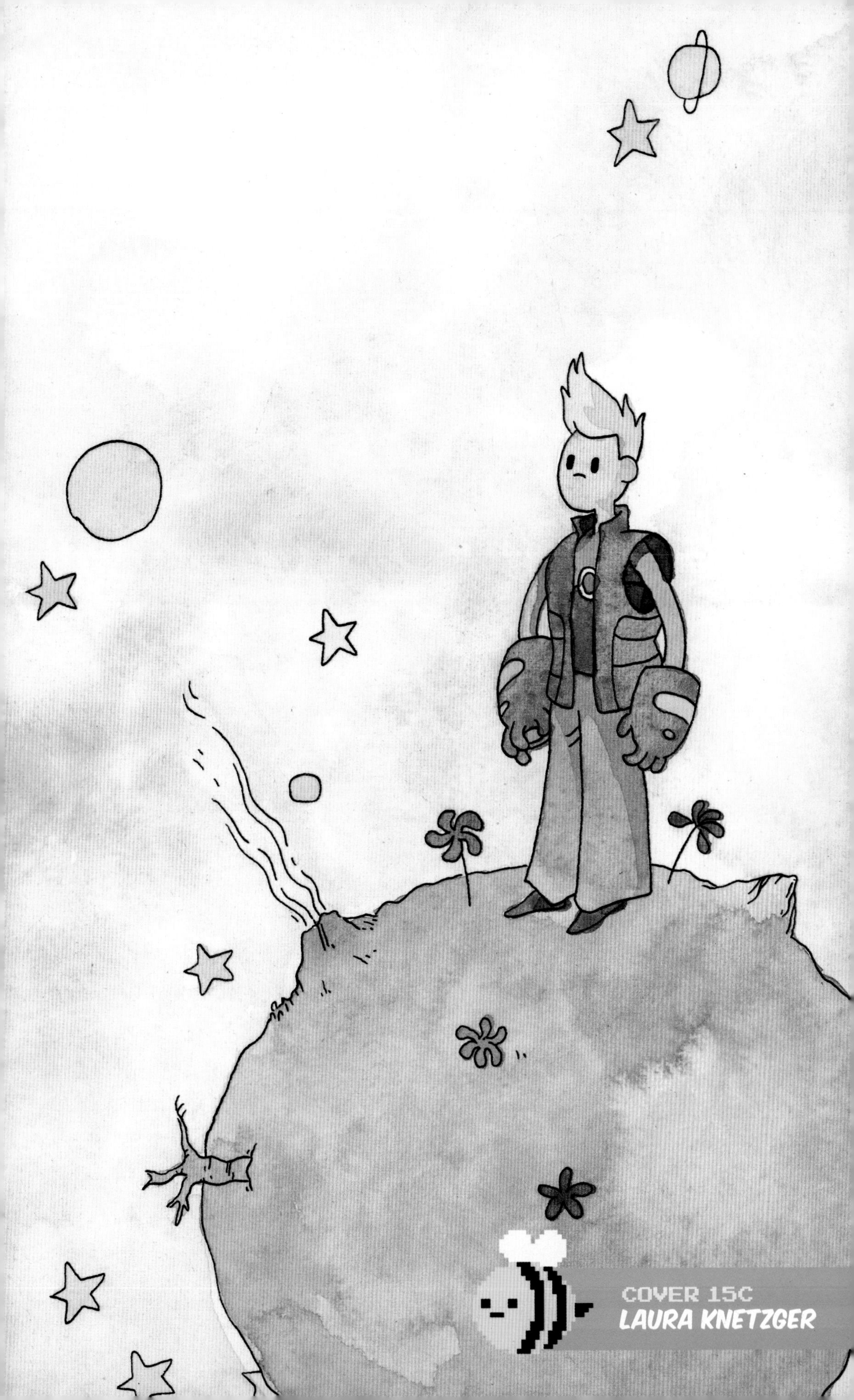
COVER 15C
LAURA KNETZGER

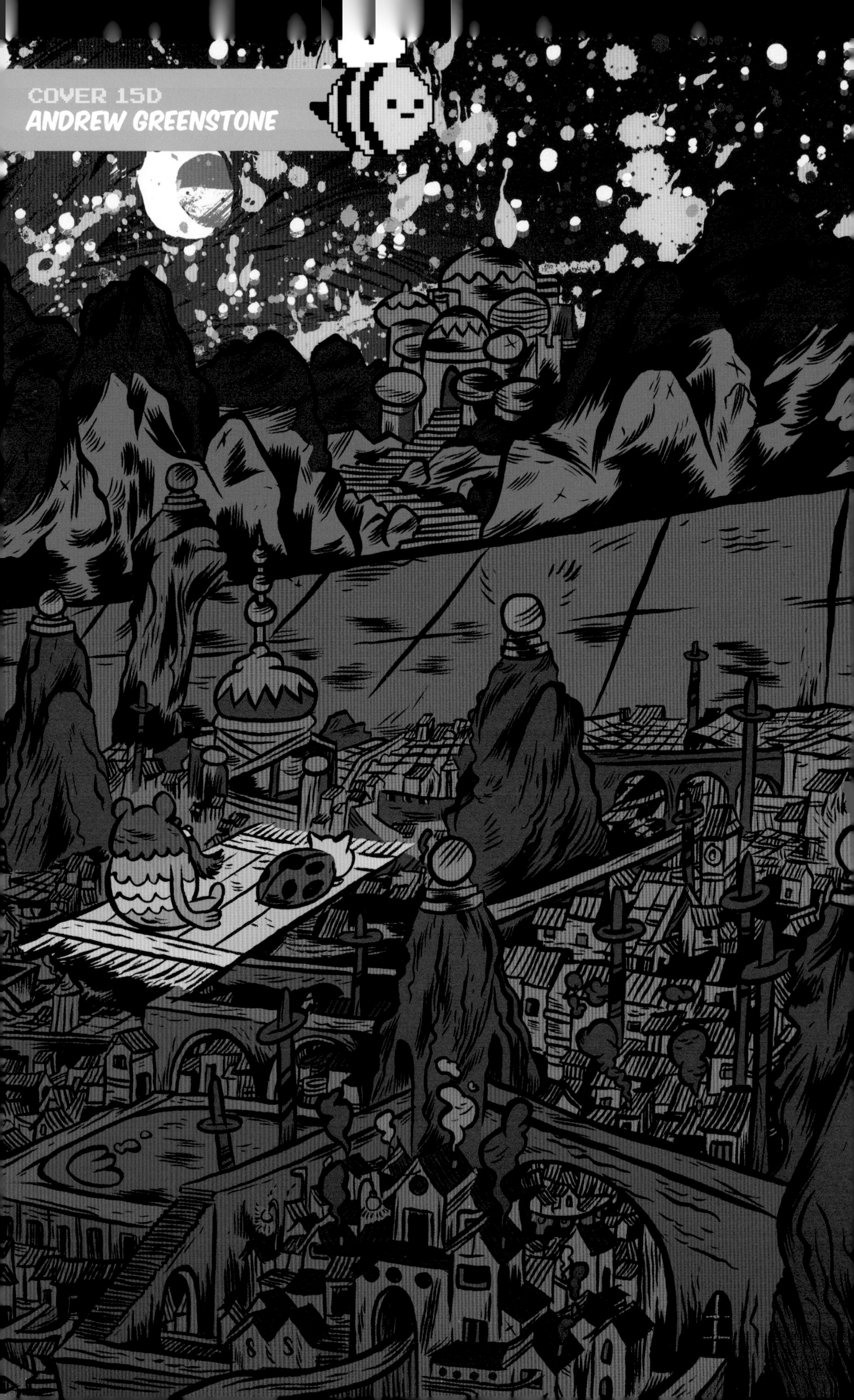

COVER 15D
ANDREW GREENSTONE

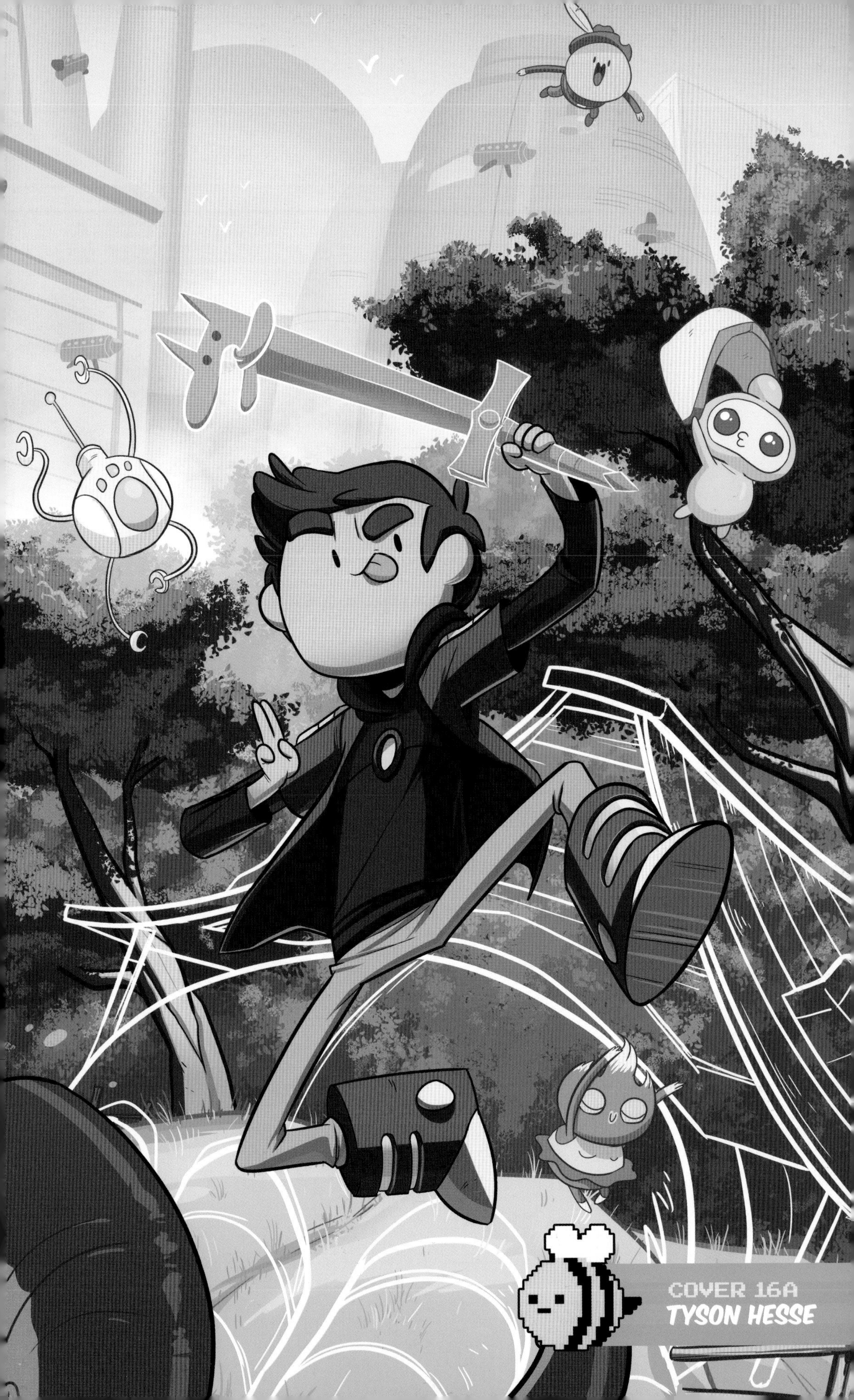
COVER 16A
TYSON HESSE

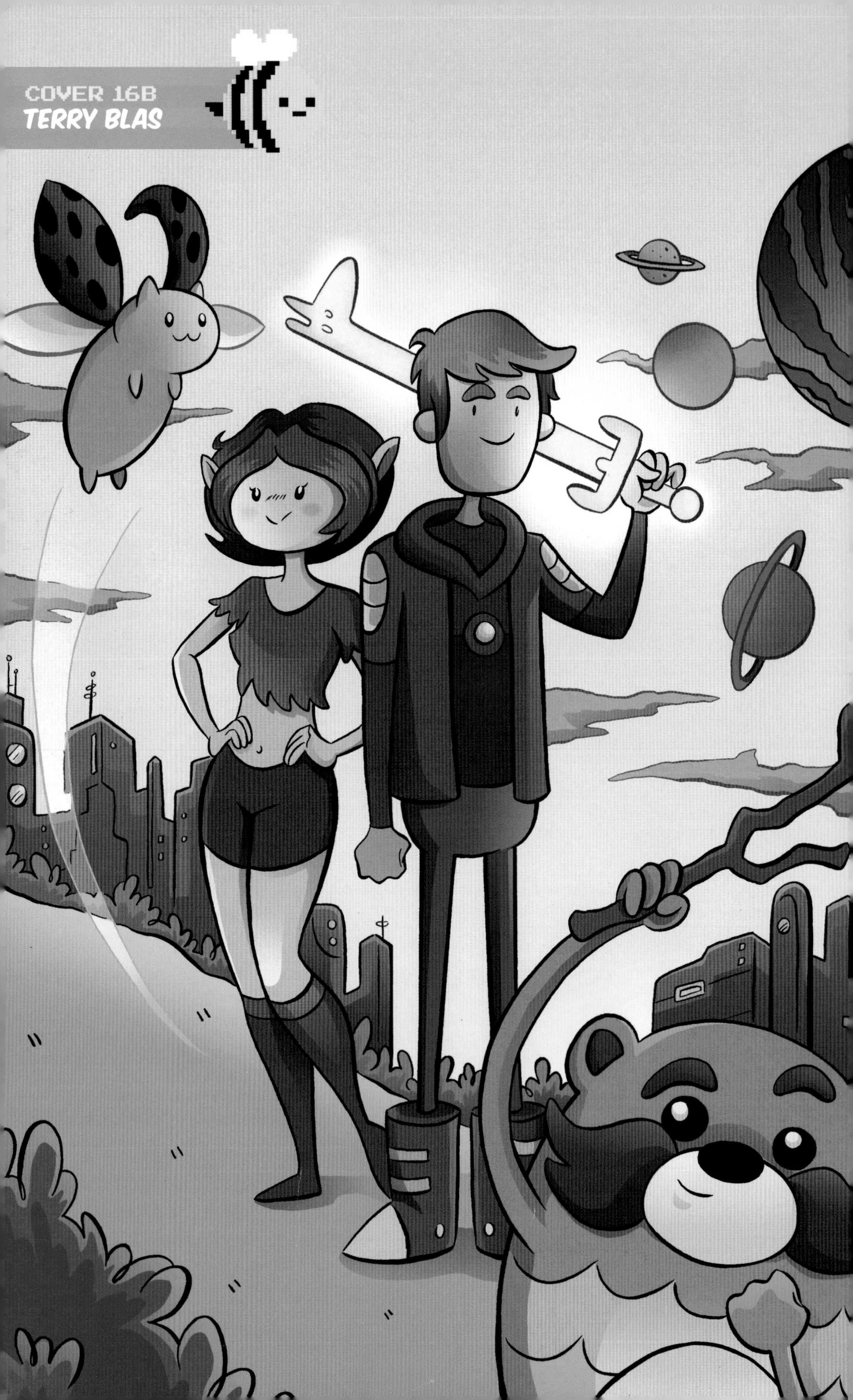
COVER 16B
TERRY BLAS

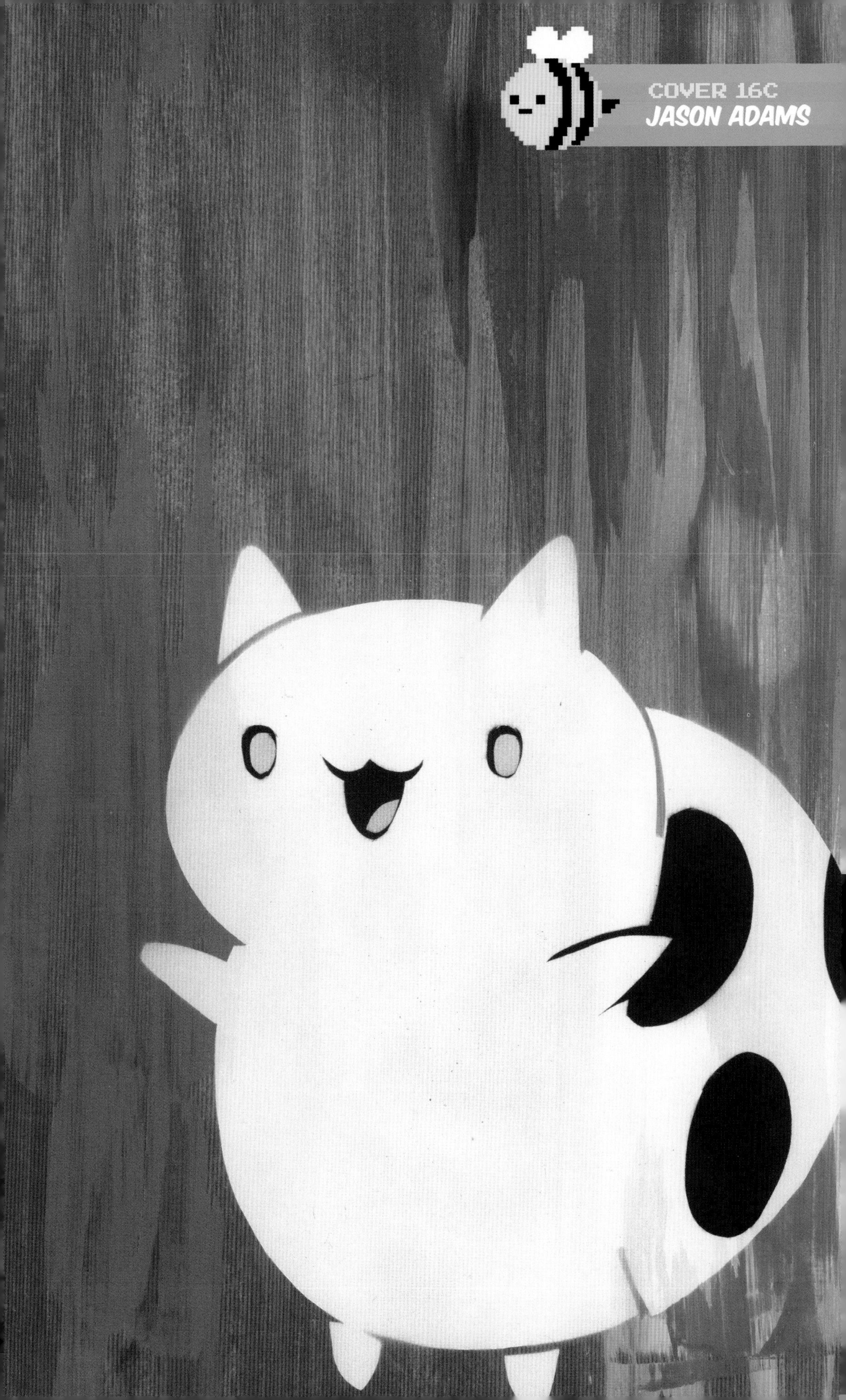
COVER 16C
JASON ADAMS

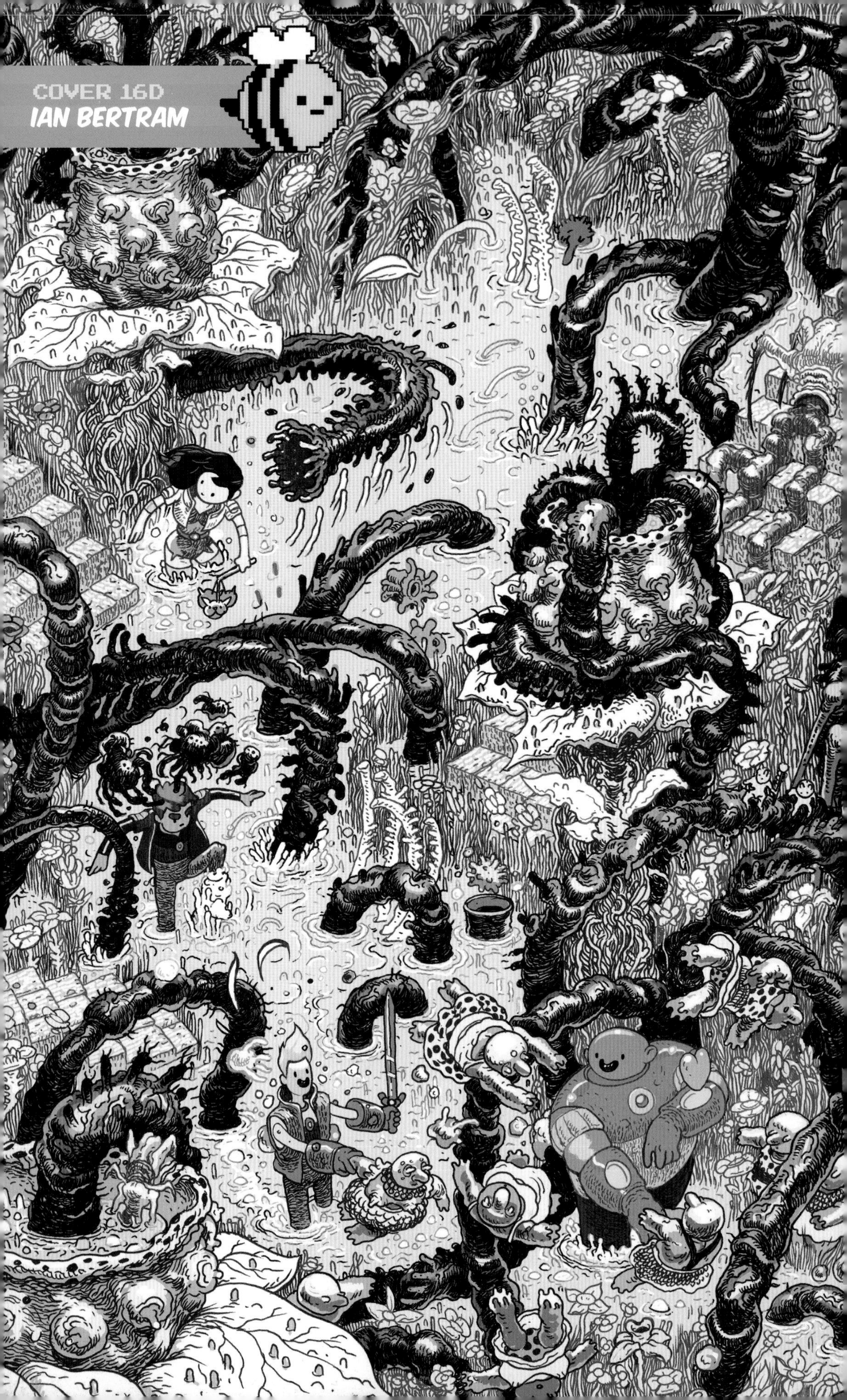

COVER 16D
IAN BERTRAM

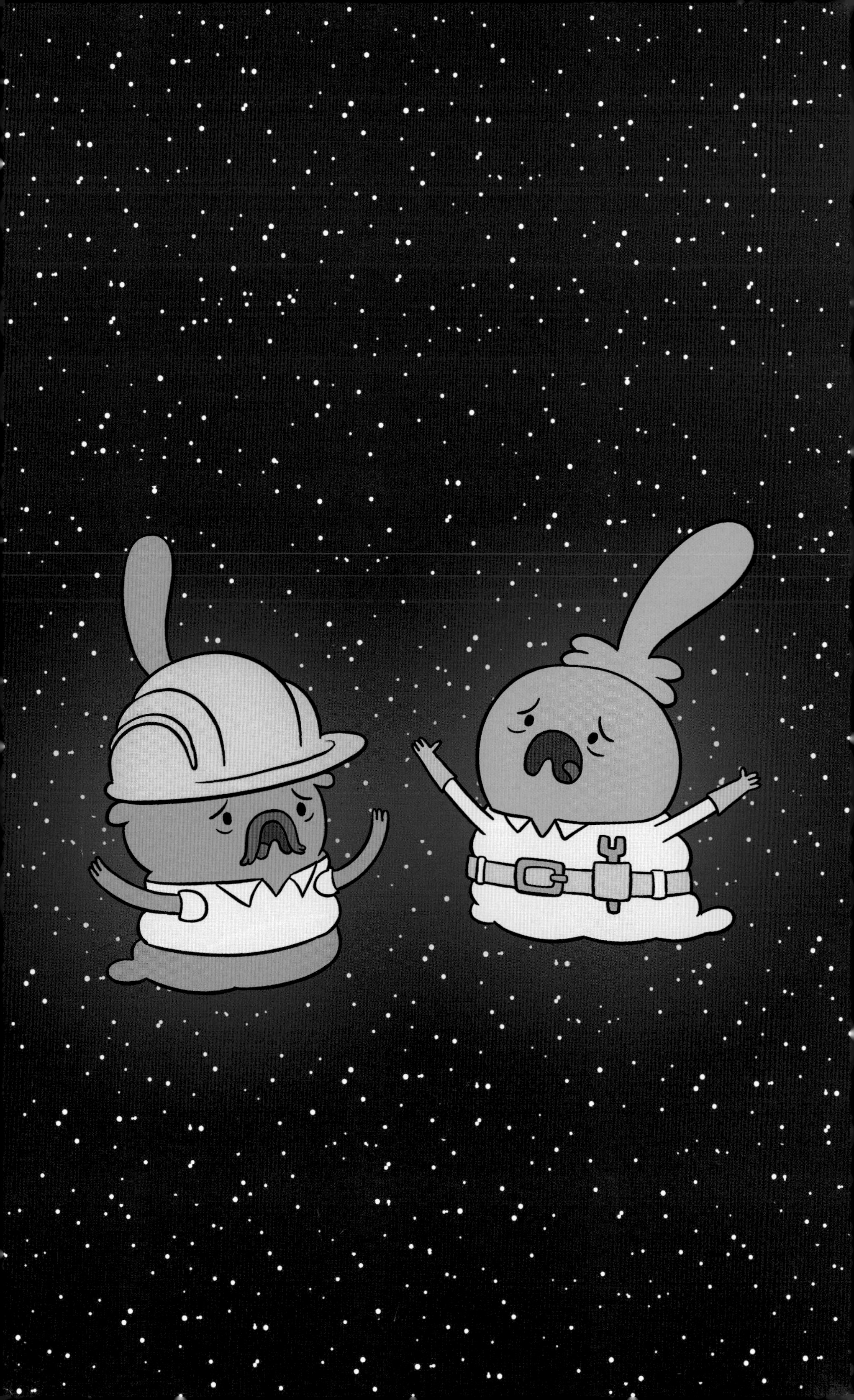

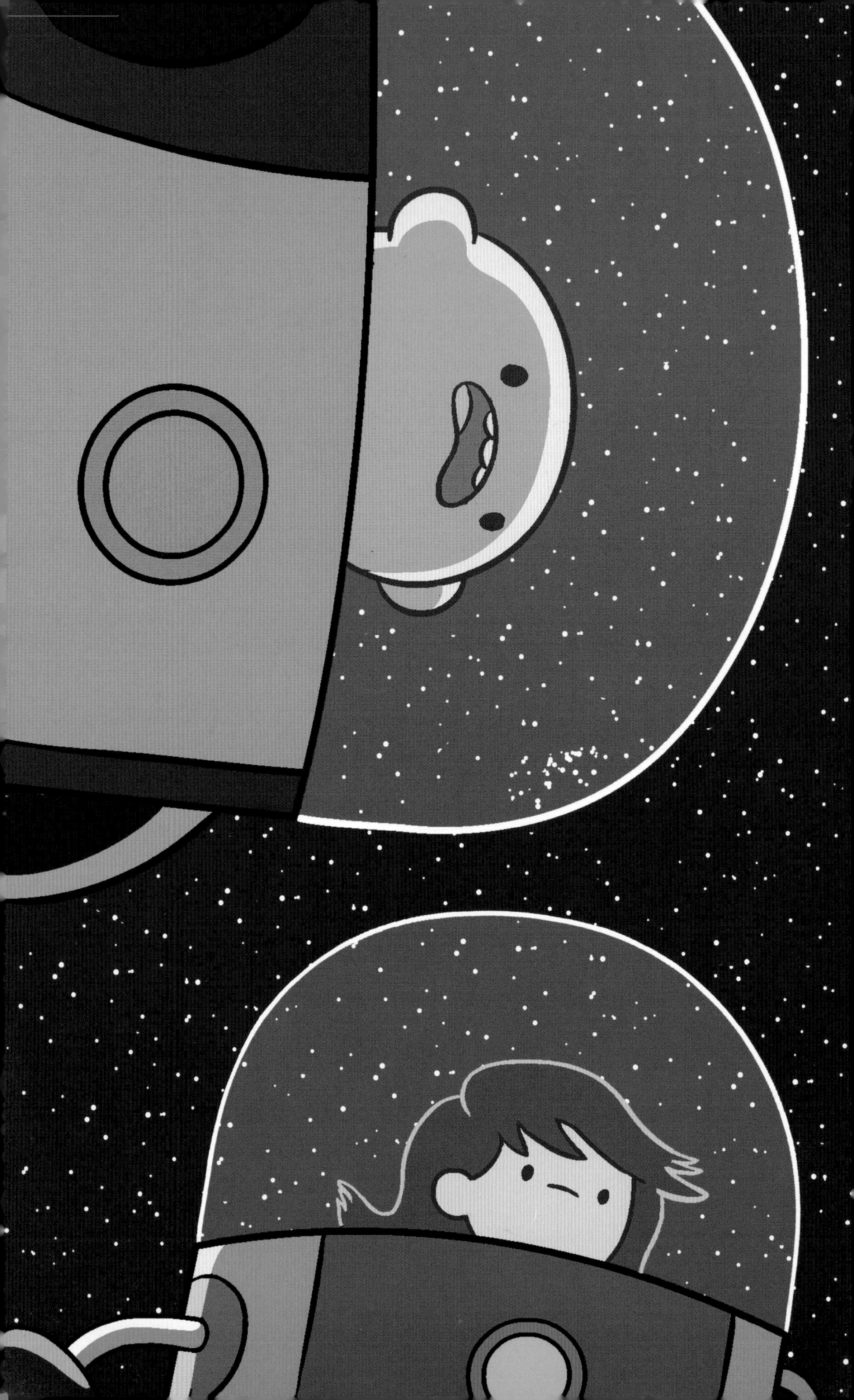

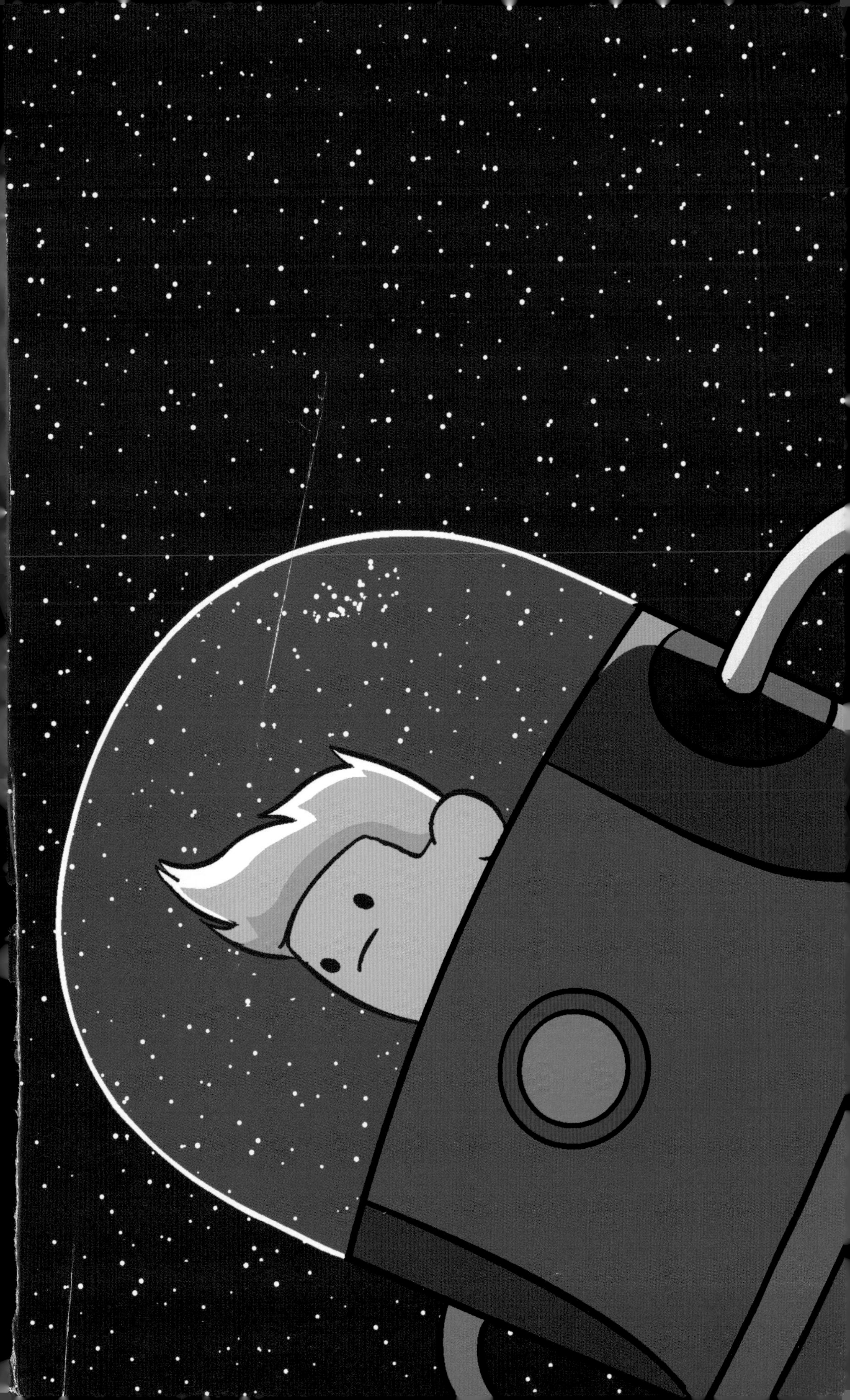

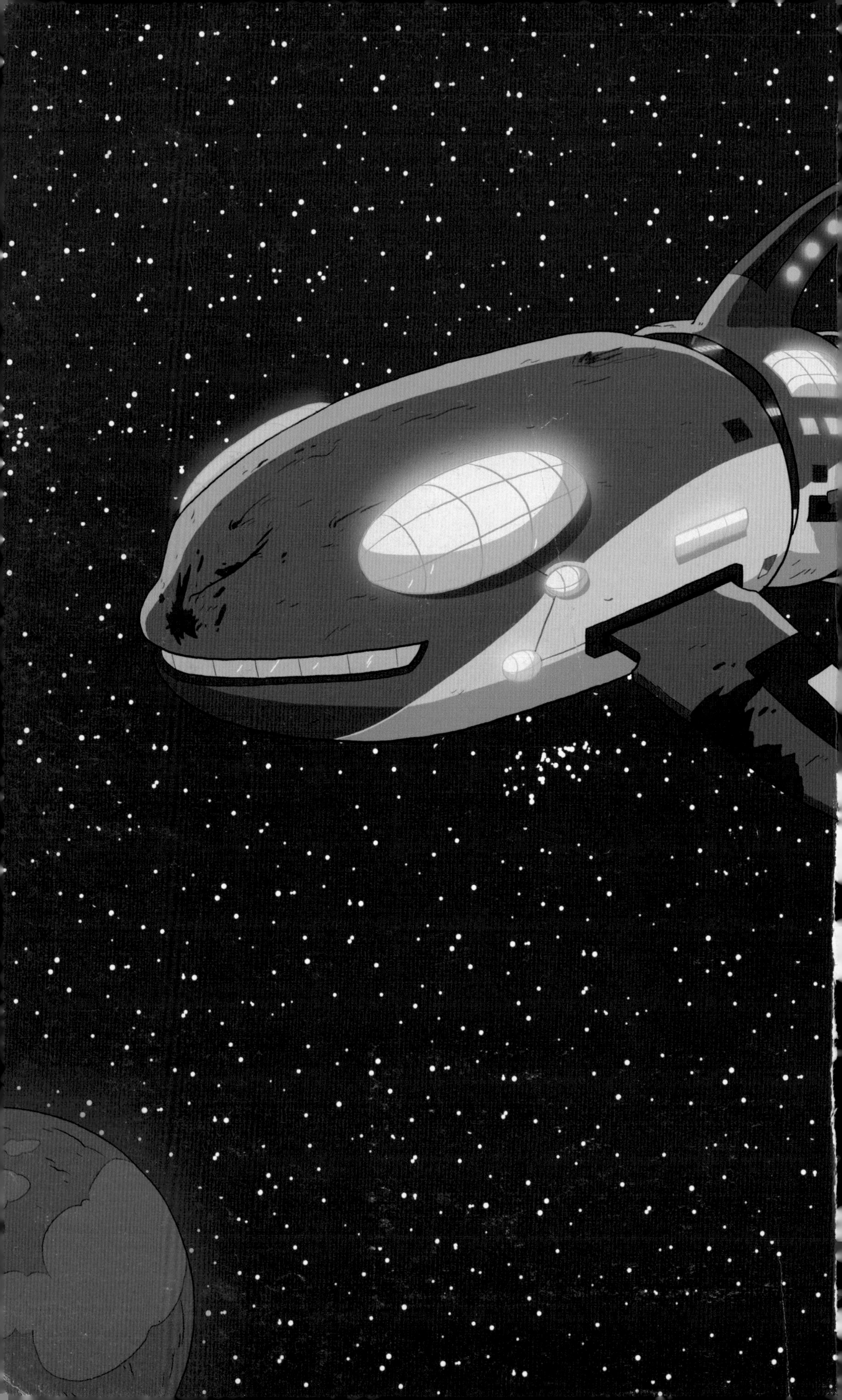